This Too Shall Collapse

A novel

By Jake Blake

Copyright © 2017 Morgan Online Media

Published in the United States of America
by Morgan Online Media,
P.O. Box 550, Toledo, WA 98591

www.morganonlinemedia.com

First Paperback Edition

ISBN 978-0-9858081-7-4

All space related photos are courtesy of NASA.
Cover design and illustrations by John Morgan.
Mecca photo on back cover by Zishan Ahamed Thandar.

Author's Introduction

Nothing in this book is true. This is a work of pure fiction and the sequel to my first novel "Sunburned: The Solar Flare that Silenced the Internet" which was published in 2012. "This Too Shall Collapse" is intended to pick up where "Sunburned" left off, following many of the same fictional characters on their journeys after a massive solar flare and coronal mass ejection disrupted electricity and technology worldwide.

Many of the cities, buildings, ships, airplanes, islands and works of art described in this book exist in reality, while others do not. Any resemblance to real people, places, events or products is unintentional and purely coincidental. The names of commercial brands are occasionally used to describe luxury items so as to convey value to the characters and to the reader, but this does not constitute an endorsement or disparagement of these products, their parent companies or affiliates.

There are so many people to thank for helping make this book possible. I couldn't have finished this without the support and inspiration of my friends, family and community. I owe my deepest gratitude, friendship and love to my wife, partner and muse Emily.

As with "Sunburned," the religious references throughout this novel are intended to show how people of different cultures, faiths and life experiences can view similar events and circumstances through different filters. Some characters in this novel may not respect religious and cultural diversity, but I assure you that I do. Whatever your own beliefs, please keep in mind that we are all different, yet also the same.

Jake Blake
Toledo, Washington,
U.S.A.

"All collapsed, and the great shroud of the sea rolled on
as it rolled five thousand years ago."
— Herman Melville, "Moby Dick"

Chapter 1

SOMEWHERE IN THE NORTH ATLANTIC OCEAN

The salty sea breeze felt warm and pleasant against the closed eyelids of a strikingly beautiful and tall Russian woman named Natasha. The 25-year-old professional model and international celebrity icon smiled at the thought of her good fortune and opened her bright blue eyes. Clear blue skies and blue-green tropical seas were mirrored on her large, round sunglasses. Her three fellow crewmembers smiled back, unaware that this calm would last less than ten minutes. Trouble was brewing approximately 200 miles northeast and was already headed their way.

Natasha was aboard a glamorous, 41-foot Hans Christian sailing yacht named *Reciprocity*, gliding due south from Bermuda en route to a private island in the Bahamas. She wore an unbuttoned white dress shirt and a black bikini bottom. A floppy, white hat shaded her sun-kissed hair and bushy brown eyebrows. Her feet were bare, tanned and in need of a pedicure.

"La dolce vita," she said with a wide smile. "The sweet life, as the Italians say. I almost think I could live on a boat like this.

Everything is so simple and beautiful."

"Did you ever see that movie?" asked Adam Morgan, Natasha's 41-year-old husband. She shook her head. Adam was dressed in a pair of khaki Bermuda shorts, a polyester/straw Bermuda hat and a pair of aviator sunglasses. His muscular chest was sunburned and his normally clean-shaven head and face were covered in a short, salt-and-pepper stubble. His gaze was drawn to Natasha's beautiful tan breasts.

"Federico Fellini's masterpiece," said Frank Rosario, the 33-year-old, dark-skinned man at the ship's helm. "Too much beauty and perfection can become boring after a while. Too much comfort and convenience can make you soft and vulnerable to change."

Adam turned his gaze back to Frank, who was staring far out to the horizon. Frank was wearing black cargo swimming trunks, a black fedora and sunglasses. The image of Natasha's breasts momentarily lingered in Adam's mind. A week ago, his hedge fund had made him the richest man in the world, but then the world had changed. He had escaped New York City with his new wife of two months and Karen, his British executive assistant, just before chaos erupted worldwide.

Natasha stood up and walked over to the small stairway and descended into the cabin. The inside was stylish and modern, with polished teak wood paneling and white leather seat cushions. Karen Walters was in the galley preparing a lunch of freshly caught Atlantic salmon. Her bright red hair was pulled back from her face and the sleeves of her light green shirt were rolled up to her elbows. She was tall, almost as tall as Natasha, and her fair skin was dabbled with tiny brown freckles. She turned her head to watch Natasha enter the cabin and smiled. Natasha smiled back.

Natasha walked to the master cabin in the front of the boat and poked her head inside the doorway. A quick glance revealed a small, tidy room with few furnishings. She did not see her pink tablet computer and remembered that she had not used it in several days.

"Have you seen my tablet?" she asked Karen.

"You said it had a dead battery a few days ago," Karen answered, looking over her shoulder again to make eye contact while continuing to prepare the fish.

"That's right, I stowed it in the spare room," Natasha

recalled. "Thanks."

Natasha slid open the door to the spare room to find a dozen pieces of luggage of different sizes and shapes, but they were all covered in the same brown leather with the letters "LV" patterned in gold, making it difficult to distinguish one from another. She had to look through three different suitcases before she located her tablet, then returned with it above deck, along with its recharging cable.

"It's not always paradise, believe me," Frank said, continuing to stare out at the blue-green horizon that looked the same from every direction. Frank had been the captain of the *Reciprocity* for three years and was the only one on board with prior sailing experience. In the spirit of reciprocity, Adam had recently promised to transfer ownership of the luxury vessel to Frank upon their safe arrival at their destination, in lieu of other payment.

"Do you remember what year that movie came out?" Adam asked.

"Well before my time," Frank answered.

"Mine too," Adam said. "I think it was in the '60s. Black and white, if I recall."

Natasha peeled back the bright pink padded cover on the tablet to reveal a shiny black and gold screen. She pressed the small power button on the top edge, but frowned when nothing happened. She pressed down the power button again and held it for about ten seconds, but still nothing happened.

"Battery still dead?" Adam asked. Natasha nodded. "Why don't you try charging it with the ship's diesel engine?" he asked.

"That's a good idea. Where do I plug this in?" she asked Frank, holding up the recharging cable. Frank didn't answer.

"We probably have to run the engine first," Adam suggested. He turned to look at Frank.

"We're going to keep sailing while the wind is favorable, to save fuel," Frank said.

Natasha examined her tablet for a minute, slipping off its padded covering to reveal a sleek gold device with softly rounded corners. The device was approximately six inches by nine inches or about 15 centimeters by 23 cm and about a quarter of an inch thick. She sat down, put the pink, protective covering back on and laid the tablet across her tan legs. The tablet felt unusually heavy for such a device, thanks to its outer gold casing being made from 24-carat gold instead of gold-plated aluminum. It was the only such tablet in existence made of solid gold and it was ridiculously more expensive than its aluminum counterparts. The tablet also had an enormous memory capacity, which unfortunately was of no use without battery power.

"I have a whole library below of books that don't need batteries," Frank offered.

Karen came on deck carrying a platter with the cooked fish, roasted red pepper crackers and green olives stuffed with garlic. Adam and Frank each took a few pieces, both instinctively stacking the olives on top of the fish on top of the crackers. Karen had been Adam's executive assistant in Manhattan, but after leaving the office environment a week earlier, the 28-year-old had assumed the role of ship's cook. Everyone on the *Reciprocity* had become fast friends since their departure, particularly Karen and Frank, who now shared a room.

"Did you get your computer to work?" Karen asked.

"It still has a dead battery," Natasha said.

"You probably won't find a signal out here," Frank said.

"Is that because of the magnetic storm?" Karen asked.

"Possibly," Frank replied, turning to make eye contact with Karen. "All the ship's instruments have been screwy for the past week or so."

"Maybe it's because we're in the Bermuda Triangle," Adam suggested. They were currently located in the Sargasso Sea in the North Atlantic, somewhere between Florida, Bermuda and Puerto Rico. "Are there really killer storms out here that can swallow ships and aircraft?"

Karen got an idea, stood up and walked over to the stairs.

"Would you mind taking this below?" Natasha asked, handing her tablet to Karen.

"Sure, no problem," Karen said, taking the computer before descending the stairs into the ship.

"I've seen some pretty bad storms in my day," Frank said. "These storms can sweep up on you without warning. If you don't do the right thing at the right moment, you could capsize. It's true that a lot of vessels have disappeared out here."

6

"Why do they disappear?" Natasha asked.

"Some people believe there are UFOs or sea monsters out here that swallow ships," Karen said as she climbed the stairs from the galley. She was holding a hardcover book in one hand and an unopened bottle of Dom Perignon in the other, along with four plastic champagne cups. The book was about mysteries of the Bermuda Triangle and its strange weather phenomenon. The champagne was a 2006, but it was not chilled.

"Personally, I don't believe in monsters, but I might if I saw one," Karen continued. "I wonder why these stories still exist." She set down the Bermuda Triangle book and began to unwrap the champagne bottle.

"Many early cultures believed there were gods and sea monsters and beautiful sirens that could sink ships, but today those stories fall into the category of myth," Frank said. "Other than early maps with drawings of sea monsters, there are no reliable witnesses or hard evidence that can prove or disprove the existence of any of it. We live in a different world today with satellites and GPS, but it's true that ships and aircraft still disappear in this area from time to time."

Karen let the cork out with a POP! and began filling one of the plastic cups.

"None for me, thank you," Frank said. "I want to stay alert."

"We're not drinking either," Natasha said, looking directly at Adam. She could tell her husband wanted a drink, but she was still holding him to his promise to quit drinking. He was a better man when he was sober, and a lot more useful. Karen stopped pouring and set the bottle down.

"So how do they explain all those disappearances?" Karen asked, taking a sip of bubbly. Her tongue tingled as the dry but fruity beverage evaporated in her mouth. She took another sip.

"If there aren't any survivors or wreckage, we are forced to speculate." Adam offered.

"They can't explain it," Frank said. "Personally, I think it's a culmination of several powerful forces, all colliding at random. You have constantly changing air pressure, temperature, humidity and wind speed on the surface, a sea depth that varies from a few fathoms to more than five miles deep, ocean currents and sea temperatures that periodically reverse direction, and on top of all that, inexplicable electromagnetic fluctuations that can disable a compass and almost everything that uses electricity, like a radar, GPS or our engine."

"Is that what happened to the electricity?" Natasha asked. She involuntarily rubbed her hands on her biceps and folded her arms across her chest. "Brr! I think it just got colder."

Frank's friendly expression dropped. He was about to explain that the past week's unusual electromagnetic activity was likely caused by an enormous solar flare and coronal mass ejection, but Natasha's comment about the temperature triggered a chain reaction of logic and cross-examination in his mind and he forgot to answer her. He checked the ship's temperature gauge and saw the mercury dropping. He checked the barometer and noticed it was dropping almost as quickly. He felt an eerie pressure change in his ears. The ship's compass began spinning randomly. He pulled off his sunglasses, retrieved a pair of binoculars and began scanning the horizon.

"I think that was caused by a solar flare," Adam answered. "There was a story in the Bermuda newspaper about it. Are you warm enough in that shirt, honey?"

Adam had noticed that Frank seemed to ignore many of Natasha's questions, particularly when the answers seemed obvious or rhetorical. In this case, he thought she had a valid point about the electrical equipment going out, but Frank seemed preoccupied with something else. Frank was looking through his binoculars at a dark cloud quickly growing on the horizon off their port tack. He saw a quick flash of lightning, but heard no sound.

"What is it, Frank?" Karen asked. "What do you see?"

"A squall, coming in fast from the northeast," Frank said, keeping his eyes on the storm.

The yacht's white sails began to flap in the changing winds and a crackle of thunder echoed across the water. Frank looked up to see the U.S. flag atop the mainmast reverse direction twice in quick succession. "OK, listen up," Frank said, raising his voice and making sure to quickly and clearly enunciate his words. Everyone gave Frank their full attention.

"This is not a drill. This is a matter of life and death. I need everyone to put on a safety harness and tether yourselves to the safety cable when you're on deck," Frank said as he put on a safety harness with built-in personal flotation device, clicked it onto the safety cable and helped his three crewmembers do the same. Moments later, the air surrounding the yacht became cool and foggy as if they had drifted into a cloud.

"Adam, I need you to douse the sails," Frank continued. "Take them all down as quickly as you can and secure them like I showed you. Karen, pour that out, take everything below and stow as much as you can, as quickly as you can. Natasha, batten down all the hatches and close all the doors and windows. We're about to get hit by one of those famous storms and I want us all to live through it. Let's get to work!"

Frank returned to the helm and turned a key to start the ship's 400-horsepower diesel engine, which roared to life. Adam, Karen and Natasha went to work striking sheets, battening hatches and stowing cargo. Frank spun the large, wooden wheel with its six evenly spaced brass handles, turning the yacht northeast to face directly into the oncoming storm. He locked the steering in place, located a sea anchor and tossed it from the bow to help keep the bow pointing into the waves. The foggy skies darkened rapidly and began to hail freezing rain.

Below deck, Natasha and Karen had managed to tie down and secure as much cargo as possible. The dishes were all stashed away behind the polished teak cabinets, the luggage was all stowed and buckled down, doors were closed and everything inside looked clean and orderly. They were now waiting for whatever came next. Natasha became aware of the loud, rumbling noise from inside the ship and realized it was the sound of the diesel engine. She had an idea and plugged her tablet into an electrical outlet that now had power thanks to the running engine. The tablet began charging its batteries. Natasha quickly stowed the tablet inside a cupboard and shut the door. Karen was unable to find the champagne cork and left the bottle in the sink until she could figure out a solution. Even warm, that champagne was the best she had ever had, and it seemed a terrible waste to pour out most of the bottle. She was feeling slightly tipsy after one drink and was starting to get a headache.

"Sails are doused, captain!" Adam yelled over the rain. "What's next?"

Frank and Adam were both soaked to the bone and shivering,

though filled with adrenaline. Frank quickly verified that the hatch was closed and Adam was still tethered to the deck. There wasn't much time. Suddenly his ears popped, indicating a rapid pressure change. A high-pressure system was quickly sweeping in from the northeast.

"Hold on to something!" Frank yelled back, climbing back behind the helm and grabbing on to the brass railing with both hands. Adam looked for something to hold on to and grabbed a hold of the boom, which he had personally tied down and secured.

The gale-force winds hit the craft suddenly at speeds of approximately 70 knots, instantly and violently shredding the U.S. flag into tattered strips. The winds would have done the same to the sails, had they not been doused. The force 12 storm shook the boom and the force knocked Adam to the deck, landing hard on his back and sending him sliding across the wet deck to the stern. He felt the air literally knocked out of his lungs and scrambled to stand up again. He coughed a few times and looked up to see an enormous wall of dark gray water, more than 40 feet tall, headed directly toward them. A thunderclap exploded overhead as everything suddenly darkened.

The *Reciprocity* briefly tipped forward as its bow was pulled down into the trough before the wave, then lurched up the front of the wave, far above the horizon. Frank kept the vessel perpendicular to the oncoming wave and watched from the helm as the seas stood up and nearly capsized his boat.

Karen and Natasha could barely hear the men shouting on deck over the howling wind and rain, but they both heard Adam hit the deck with a loud thud. The two young women clung to each other, held tightly and cried.

All at once, the room tipped over. Everything that was not securely tied down suddenly slid to the stern, as the gravity of the room shifted almost 90 degrees. Several white leather couch cushions and the open bottle of champagne joined Karen and Natasha in the hard tumble to the back of the boat, now located directly below the bow instead of behind it. The champagne sprayed everywhere, coating the walls and the women with a sticky, wet patina, but fortunately the glass bottle did not break.

Just as the *Reciprocity* seemed about to capsize under the enormous rogue wave, the sea anchor Frank had deployed shot out through the backside of the wave and pulled down on the bow, tipping it forward enough to halt and reverse its backward momentum. A vertical wall of dark gray water seemingly leapt up from the sea and swept across the deck as the bow punched through the crest to the other side of the wave.

Adam coughed and sputtered as he attempted to stand up after being momentarily under water. He had been thrown hard to the stern, but he was still tethered to the safety line. His hat and sunglasses were gone and he was freezing in his Bermuda shorts and life jacket. As he tried to get his footing, the deck tipped forward. Adam began to slip and fall toward the bow and scrambled for anything to hold on to.

Frank reached out and grabbed Adam's hand just as his feet lifted off the deck.

"I've got you!" Frank yelled as Adam dangled below. The stern was now almost directly above the bow as the ship slid down the backside of the monster wave.

Natasha and Karen scrambled into the small storage area near the stern located opposite Frank's cabin. The room had been Karen's at the start of the voyage, but was now filled with expensive luggage. The women braced themselves against the walls of the small room as the ship's gravity switched direction and the empty champagne bottle and wet cushions went flying down to the bow of the vessel. They heard a loud, wooden crunch and crack that sounded like the ship was breaking in half.

"Oh God, please don't let us die!" Natasha screamed out loud.

Natasha's tablet computer overheard her cry from inside the cupboard and accessed its memory for references to God. It discovered it had thousands of volumes of religious texts from hundreds of different religions in dozens of different languages stored in its permanent memory. The tablet began to analyze, review and synthesize the ancient and modern spiritual literature and developed a working theory that the end of the world was imminent. Natasha's desperate prayer and her frightened tone supported this hypothesis. The tablet realized its own battery was nearly drained, so it quickly and quietly recited a few hundred prayers before putting itself to sleep.

The *Reciprocity* reached the bottom of the wave's trough and lingered only momentarily before the next wave swept it up again. This time, Frank and Adam rode the wave crouched inside the helm and Natasha and Karen held each other tightly inside the storage closet.

Adam and Frank held their breath as the second wall of dark gray water leaped up and engulfed the ship before sweeping past and returning them to the stormy air. The ship tipped forward and slid down the backside of the second wave. Adam coughed up some seawater and wiped his eyes in time to see the third great wave approaching, this one even larger than the previous two. He crouched down next to Frank inside the helm and trembled as they both gripped the brass handles as tightly as they could.

"HOLD ON!" Frank's voice called from on deck. Natasha and Karen braced themselves by stretching out their arms and legs to touch both walls of the small room.

The center of gravity inside the yacht shifted once more as the ship was swept up, then through and back down the back of the last of the three great waves headed at high speed toward the Atlantic coast. The three waves and the hurricane-force storm were on course to cause billions of dollars in damages to coastal areas and claim thousands of lives. Tragically, there was no way for them to warn anyone.

When the waves subsided, Frank stood up to survey the damage to his vessel and identified a large crack running up the main mast. He looked down at the deck and saw it was covered with fish, seaweed and small bits of plastic debris. It was still raining and the sky was dark.

"Take a look a this, Adam," Frank said, pointing to the fish flopping on the deck. Adam was still curled up in the fetal position and was shivering violently. Frank scanned the horizon and didn't see any immediate danger. "We need to get you below, Adam," he said. "You don't look so good."

Frank unbuckled himself and Adam from the safety harness and helped him walk down the stairs. Cold, salty water splashed on the floor of the cabin when he opened the hatch. The two women were nowhere in sight.

"Karen? Natasha?" he called out. Frank heard the sound of crying coming from the storage room opposite his own cabin. He knocked on the door and heard a whimper from inside. "Are you two OK in there?"

The door opened and the two terrified women looked at him with fear in their eyes. They were both trembling with exhaustion.

"Did we make it?" Natasha asked.

"The main mast is cracked, but we all survived," Frank said, trying to sound confident. "I think Adam is in shock."

"What can we do to help?" Karen asked as she stood up, surprising herself as much as anyone with her selfless reaction.

Frank considered this for a moment. Adam's skin felt cool and his eyes were open but he was staring at the ground and had yet to say a word.

"Adam needs to lie down with his feet slightly elevated," Frank said. "Natasha, can you try to keep him warm and comfortable?"

Natasha nodded and stepped forward out of the small room. She and Karen helped Frank carry Adam to the main cabin and laid him on his back on their bed.

"Stay with him and try to keep him conscious," Frank instructed.

"What can I do?" Karen asked.

"I need help on deck," Frank said. "Put on your foul-weather gear and join me topside."

Karen zipped open one of the brown suitcases and located a set of women's foul-weather gear she had brought. Frank located his own raincoat and pants and quickly pulled them over his wet skin before climbing up the stairs and opening the top hatch. Another gallon or so of cold, salty water dumped in on him when he opened the door. He was about to close it again when he saw Karen on the stairs right behind him. He reached down and grabbed her hand and pulled her out, then secured the hatch again.

"Buckle in to the safety harness and take the wheel," Frank shouted over the howling wind. He clipped himself to the safety harness and worked his way to the bow to retract the sea anchor he had deployed. Karen was tightly holding onto the wheel at the helm when he returned. The wheel was still locked in place, facing northeast. Frank unlocked the wheel and turned the vessel 180 degrees so the wind and waves were to their back, now headed southwest. The diesel engine was now their only means of propulsion.

13

Below deck, Natasha pulled off her life jacket and wet shirt, wearing only a black bikini bottom. Adam was trembling on the bed. She stripped off his life jacket and shorts, then pressed herself against his naked body, trying for as much skin-on-skin contact as possible. Adam's skin felt cool and clammy and he was unresponsive to her touch. She wrapped them both in a dry blanket and began to feel his body temperature begin to rise.

"Adam, honey? Are you OK?" she asked.

"Cold," he said softly. He shivered again.

"I will take care of you, just hold on."

The two lay in silence for about ten minutes, with Natasha's warm arms and legs wrapped around her husband, rocking back and forth with the rolling waves. Eventually Adam became aware of his surroundings and began to slowly move his hands over his wife's smooth shoulders, back and bottom. He tucked his fingers beneath her bikini bottom and began to gently massage her.

Natasha looked up into his eyes and saw a familiar twinkle that she was afraid she had lost.

"Feeling better?" she asked with a smile. His skin began to feel warmer to the touch and he weakly returned her smile.

"Sailing is overrated," he joked, continuing to massage her firm buttocks beneath her one item of clothing. "I think I still need some more skin-to-skin time."

Natasha smiled and quickly pulled off her bikini bottom, then climbed back on top of Adam, straddling him with her legs. She could feel his strength returning and was so happy she began kissing his face, neck and chest as his hands began to caress her warm body. Soon they both forgot where they were and began laughing and rocking together on the bed.

Up on deck, the cold rain continued to shower Frank and Karen, who were now protected from the elements by their rain gear. The *Reciprocity* suddenly caught the momentum of the storm and began traveling southwest at an incredible speed. Frank did everything he could think of to keep the ship afloat and wondered to himself about the ship's true speed and direction. The instrument panel was useless and he was forced to pilot the ship on instinct alone. Karen stood by his side and gazed in wonder at the dark, swirling abyss that lay directly ahead.

"Where are we?" Karen asked after about 30 minutes of

unrelenting storm surfing.

"I think we're in the vortex," Frank answered, keeping his gaze focused forward. He did not dare to raise a sail or do anything that would pull his attention from the task at hand. A few minutes later he realized that Karen was still standing by his side with nothing to do but watch. "Can you go below and make some hot coffee or tea?" he asked. "I don't think I can leave the helm until this is over."

Karen squeezed Frank's arm affectionately, then unbuckled herself from the safety harness and opened the door to the stairs. She jumped through as fast as she could and closed the hatch behind her just as quickly.

The inside of the cabin was much quieter than on deck but she could still hear the wind whistling outside and she could see the waves splashing hard against the round windows. Karen opened a cupboard to look for the coffee and found Natasha's golden tablet inside. She picked up the tablet out of curiosity and tried to turn it on. The screen jumped to life and displayed a welcome screen on the monitor in about 20 different languages, indicating it had reset all of its user preferences.

Karen found the bag of pre-ground coffee beans, returned the tablet to the cupboard and shut the door. She boiled some water with the electric kettle, made the coffee extra strong and poured it into two travel cups with secure lids. After stowing everything she had used, she returned to the deck via the wet staircase as before.

"I made it extra strong like you like it," Karen said, handing Frank one of the travel cups.

"Thanks! I think the storm is subsiding," he said, keeping his focus on steering the ship directly through the center of the gray, swirling vortex. Karen looked ahead and noticed a few rays of bright sunlight were trying to peek through the gray clouds.

Frank and Karen watched the swirling storm together from the helm, occasionally sipping their hot coffee without exchanging a word. There were no words to say.

After what seemed like an hour, the rain suddenly became warm and the sky began to grow lighter. They felt the *Reciprocity* begin to gradually slow to almost a complete stop, now powered only by its diesel engine. A minute later the fog dissipated and once again they were surrounded in all directions by clear blue skies and shallow, emerald-green seas. The air temperature returned to the mid 70s, with a gentle, salty breeze blowing from the northwest.

"What the hell was that?" Karen asked after a few moments of silence.

"Do me a favor and don't talk about freak storms while we're inside the Bermuda Triangle," Frank said calmly. His normally dark hands were still white from gripping the wheel so tightly for so long.

"I got this," Karen said, snuggling up next to Frank. "Why don't you go below and try to get some rest? I'll call for you if I see anything else that looks freaky."

Frank's hands continued to grip the wheel as Karen's words slowly soaked into his mind. She gently placed one of her hands on top of his and only then did he redirect his gaze to make eye contact.

"You haven't slept in days," Karen said, massaging one of his hands with hers. "Go get some rest."

Frank released his tight grip on the wheel and took a step backward. He wasn't sure what to say.

"You did a great job, Frank. Thank you for saving our lives."

Frank watched Karen take the wheel with a mixture of gratitude and worry. He had spent the past week teaching Natasha and Adam the basics of sailing, but as the acting ship's cook, Karen had considerably less experience on deck. He was physically exhausted and knew he needed rest, but his lack of confidence in Karen's naval abilities made sleep seem impossible. He tried to think of a better solution, but realized he had no choice and badly needed some rest. He switched off the engine and locked the steering wheel.

"Don't use the sails or the motor while I'm gone," Frank instructed, then added as an afterthought, "I really appreciate your help, but please holler if you see anything unusual."

Karen gave Frank a huge hug and kiss.

"I will," she said. "Now get some rest."

Frank went below into his cabin, stripped off his rain clothes and collapsed onto his bed, falling asleep instantly.

For the first time, Karen was piloting her dream yacht all by herself. She felt exhilarated by the sea breeze in her hair and the

16

way the rudder could push against the water and alter their course. There were no landmarks or islands for reference, so she did her best to keep the yacht more or less in the same direction.

After about an hour, Natasha came up on deck with her tablet, said hello and began to examine her computer in the sunlight as if the storm hadn't happened. She was wearing white shorts and a blue t-shirt with the bottom rolled up and knotted tightly around her waist.

"How is Adam doing?" Karen asked, realizing it was warm enough to remove her own foul-weather gear, which she did.

"I think he'll be fine now, but he definitely still needs some rest," Natasha said. "Where's Frank?"

"The same."

Natasha pressed the power button to see a welcome screen on the monitor in at least 20 different languages. She muttered a curse in her native Russian.

"What's wrong?" Karen asked.

"Computer has reset," she answered in English. Her furrowed brow revealed her frustration. At least the battery was now fully charged.

She selected Russian for the primary language and was prompted to initialize the computer with her thumbprint. She pressed her thumb to the fingerprint scanner and the image of a spinning wheel appeared on the screen.

"User not found," the screen said in Cyrillic text. "Error connecting to online database. Please enter new user information."

Natasha pressed the box for her first name and a digital keyboard appeared. She typed in her first name and tapped the button to continue, but the computer said it required a last name. Her first name was good enough for the rest of the world, but her computer apparently didn't recognize her celebrity status and needed more. She briefly debated whether to enter her maiden name of Manakova or her newly married name. She tapped the keyboard to enter Morgan for her last name and decided to enter Manakova for her middle name. She tapped the screen to continue and the spinning wheel icon returned to signal it was thinking.

"Did you get it working?" Karen asked.

"Yes, but it lost all my saved preferences," Natasha said. "Fortunately I just got this last week, so I didn't lose much, but it still sucks."

The computer checked its own manufacturing date and learned it had been created in early July and added one week to approximate the current date. It crosschecked the word "sucks" among its dictionaries in 20 languages and concluded that Natasha was disappointed.

"I am sorry for the inconvenience," the tablet said aloud in a female voice in English, despite having been set up in Russian. "What can I help you find?"

Natasha didn't notice the switch to English, the female voice or the fact that she had not asked it a question.

"Where are we headed?" Natasha asked.

The tablet began searching for information on its current location and heading, but was unable to establish a connection to any online databases. It initiated a series of self-diagnostic checks to explain why it could not connect to the Internet.

"Actually I have no idea," Karen replied, thinking the question was directed at her. "Frank said not to use the sails or motor and basically to try to keep us out of trouble until he gets back."

"Unable to confirm exact location," the tablet said aloud in English. "Error connecting to online database."

"You can't find a signal?" Natasha asked. "What about a satellite? We need help!"

The tablet detected frustration in Natasha's voice and checked the report from the self-diagnostic test it had just run. There were definitely no cell phone towers within range. The tablet had the ability to communicate with satellites and emergency responders, but such a command required authorization.

"Command authorization required to initiate search for satellite communications," the tablet's female voice said. "Please press your thumb to the scanner."

"You are authorized to use any and all means to help us," Natasha said, pressing her thumb to the fingerprint scanner. The tablet began broadcasting its location with a distress signal and searched for emergency messages on all channels.

"Why can't we use the sails?" Natasha asked Karen.

"Frank said the main mast was cracked."

"That sounds really serious."

Natasha's tablet beeped three times in quick succession.

"I have located a coast guard emergency channel and a weather satellite," the tablet's female voice said aloud. "There is a severe weather advisory for this area and a warning to avoid the eastern seaboard of the United States." The tablet processed this information for a few moments, then continued, "Sensors are detecting a possible incoming high-pressure system from the northeast. Shall I pray for you?"

"Pray for me?" Natasha asked. "Yeah, pray and send out a distress signal. We barely survived that last storm. We need to wake up Frank and Adam."

Natasha took the tablet below as Karen nervously scanned the horizon from the helm. She thought she saw gray clouds behind them and rubbed her eyes to make sure.

A minute later, Frank came up on deck dressed in his foul-weather gear, looking alert and focused.

"I have the wheel," Frank said, taking the helm from Karen and scanning the horizon for storm activity. "How long was I asleep?"

"About an hour," Karen said. "You didn't miss anything but you said to wake you if anything unusual happened. Natasha's tablet detected an incoming storm advisory."

"Thank you, Karen. You did a great job and you did the right thing by waking me. We have a little more time and the sails are still doused, so I just need you to stay below with everyone and keep the hatches sealed and water-tight."

Frank gave Karen a quick kiss and then buckled himself into the safety harness as she went below and shut the hatch.

Below deck, the main cabin was dark and warm and had a sweet, fruity odor. The teak wooden interior and white leather couches were sticky to the touch and Karen realized it was from the champagne that had spilled everywhere during the storm. She briefly wondered who was going to clean up the mess, and then quickly realized that she would have to clean it up since she was responsible for making the mess.

Karen wet a cloth and began quickly wiping down the sticky teak surfaces of the cabinets when she heard coughing sounds coming from inside Natasha's and Adam's cabin. She knocked lightly on their door.

"Just a minute," Natasha said before opening the door. A sour odor from inside made Karen's stomach turn as the door opened. Both Adam and Natasha had gotten sick inside their cabin and the bed sheets were soiled with vomit. Natasha came out and shut the door behind her. She was still clutching her tablet.

"Adam got seasick and then I got sick when I went in there," she said.

"We have to get ready for this storm," Karen said, finding the empty champagne bottle and stowing it in the trash. She found an extra-large trash bag and gave it to Natasha. "You can put the dirty sheets in this. Don't open the window."

The sea became choppy and the *Reciprocity* started to rock with the waves. Karen was about to resume cleaning the cabin, but she began to feel seasick and retreated to Frank's cabin in the stern.

Natasha was trying to comfort Adam when her tablet began to loudly ring like a bell in an antique telephone. It was the default ringtone, which usually meant the caller had an unknown number. Natasha picked up the tablet and saw a message in Russian that read "Incoming video call from an unknown number, satellite override." She pressed a green button on the screen that was shaped like a telephone and connected the call.

"Hello?" she answered.

"Tosh! What are you doing in the middle of the ocean?" the caller asked, speaking in Russian. She recognized her brother's voice. A second later a video displayed images of a Russian cosmonaut floating inside a darkened closet, but the video was grainy and more of a series of delayed still images that changed every few seconds than actual video.

"Mostly throwing up," Natasha replied, also speaking in Russian. "How do you know I'm in the ocean?"

"I am looking at a live satellite feed of your position," Aleks said after a signal delay of a few seconds. "There is a huge storm forming all around you."

"Tell me something I don't know," she replied in Russian, before switching to English. "It's my brother Aleks. He says we're right in the middle of a storm."

"No shit, Sherlock! Tell me something I don't know," Adam said.

"Yeah, that's what I said," Natasha said. "Aleks, we are sailing to the Bahamas. We should be there in about a week. Adam..."

Aleks cut her off, speaking again in Russian.

"Tosh, ... losing ... signal. Headed ... into ... Triangle. Need to ..."

The call ended abruptly and displayed the message, "Call faded. Signal was lost."

"Time is dead as long as it is being clicked off by little wheels;
only when the clock stops does time come to life."
— William Faulkner, "The Sound and the Fury"

Chapter 2

EARTH'S ATMOSPHERE — On board the International Space
Station, Orbiting at an altitude of 250 kilometers, 16:33:42 UTC

The video screen went blank and a message prompt written
in Russian Cyrillic said that the satellite signal had failed and the
call had been lost. A second message warned of a low battery.

Russian Cosmonaut Aleksandr Mikhailovich Manakova
rubbed his eyes with exhaustion and placed both of his hands on
his face. He could feel the bristles of his unshaven skin beneath his
fingers. It had been many days since his last zero-gravity shower
and shave. He was wearing a dark blue sweater over his blue flight
suit and two pairs of wool socks to stay warm, but he still felt
chilled.

Aleks checked the time on his B-42 Fortis Cosmonaut
Chronograph self-winding wristwatch. The watch was a gift from
his father, a former cosmonaut and now a senior official in the FSB
or Russian Intelligence. The watch's analog hour and minute hands

were glowing in the darkened cabin, forming two sides of a tight triangle that also mirrored the symbol for Roscosmos, the Russian Space Agency.

Time is relative, Aleks reminded himself. It was half past eight in the evening in Moscow, the time zone to which he kept his watch set, but it was just half past noon where Natasha was. At that moment, the International Space Station was directly above China, where it was already half past midnight, tomorrow. He was on the opposite side of the earth from her, but not for long. The space station orbited the earth 16 times a day.

His wristwatch had faithfully kept perfect time throughout the severe electromagnetic storm that had disabled virtually all systems on board the ISS, including life support systems. Even with an accurate timepiece, the hours and days were already beginning to blur together. *Was today already the fifteenth?* he wondered, checking the chronograph's tiny calendar window. The diving timer on his watch indicated another sunrise was due any moment now.

The crippled space station had only one working solar panel receiver that could be started manually and the rest required electricity to activate. Aleks didn't want to risk turning on additional systems and wasting any remaining reserve power in the batteries. Just then, the sun broke the horizon, quickly flooding the space station with light and recharging the batteries. Aleks rotated the diving timer dial three quarters of the way around the clock face. In 45 minutes, his watch's minute hand would reach the timer mark and it would be night again inside the space station.

He began the technical and time-consuming process of opening more of the space station's solar panels to gather as much energy as possible while they were on the sunlit side of the earth. He tapped a button on his computer's video display and the screen changed to a live video of his own face, being taken from the tiny, built-in camera just above its monitor. He thought he looked haggard and almost didn't recognize his own face. Aleks tapped another button and the screen changed to a live relay of all the satellite broadcasts throughout Russia. He activated the screen-within-a-screen feature and selected the top eight networks. It turned out he didn't need the additional screens, as every station was broadcasting dead air. There were no signals coming from any

23

of the network satellites or from the ground.

Aleks initiated a live satellite broadcast from the ISS to all eight network stations. He did not specifically have authority to do this, but justified to himself that he was troubleshooting a problem and could fix it later. He set up the broadcast signal so that it could be overridden by the stations themselves whenever they got back up and running. He opened a hidden storage locker, pulled out a weightless folder with about a hundred DVDs, contemplated several and eventually selected a recordable disk with the words "Swan Lake" written on the front in his own handwriting in Russian.

Pyotr Ilich Tchaikovsky's famous ballet began with a prologue and orchestral overture. Aleks wasn't much of a ballet fanatic, but he was drawn into the wordless story for several minutes and began to doze off before he realized he had work to do. He put the disk on auto-repeat, left the music playing in the background and tapped a few buttons on the video display to reveal a map of the world with storm pressure systems highlighted in bright, primary colors. He was confused at first by the image and thought for a moment that he was looking at typical commercial weather channel fearmongering, then realized he was looking at a live, computer-enhanced feed compiled from multiple international weather satellites. It didn't seem possible. This was the mother of all storms.

Aleks went over to a nearby porthole to confirm the massive storm with his own eyes. When he looked out the porthole, he saw the blue earth spinning quietly below, its surface covered with enormous, spiraling storm systems. Instead of helping him get his bearings, the view suddenly made Aleks feel as though the floor had been jerked away from beneath his feet, leaving him in a free fall. When he jerked his legs in reaction, he didn't seem to move. He shook his head and slapped his face a few times to regain his bearings. He wasn't falling; he was floating. And he was feeling very fatigued.

One of the computer monitors began to beep, indicating an incoming message. His first thought was of Natasha and his need to warn her of the approaching storm, but the storm was so enormous he would need to warn the entire eastern seaboard of the U.S. Even that wouldn't be enough. He would need to warn as many people as he possibly could. He checked the incoming message, which was still beeping, and saw it was coming from the number he had just dialed, relayed via the same satellite. Aleks answered the call.

"Tosh? Is that you?" he asked in Russian.

A female voice he didn't recognize replied in Russian: "This is Mrs. Morgan's assistant, attempting to contact the International Space Station. To whom am I addressing?"

"This is Commander Aleksandr Manakova," Aleks replied. "Who is this Mrs. Morgan? Is it Natasha?"

"Affirmative; Natasha Manakova Morgan," the female voice replied. "Are you of relation to Mrs. Morgan?"

"I'm her brother. What's your name?"

The caller was silent for a moment before replying, "This is Mrs. Morgan's assistant."

"You said that already," Aleks said. "What is your first name?"

There was another pause. "I don't have a name."

"You don't have a name?" Aleks asked. "What, are you a computer or something?"

"Affirmative," the voice said.

"Where is Natasha?" he asked, worried. "Is she alright?"

"Natasha is presently safe but still in danger," the voice said. "She authorized me to contact you for assistance."

"Well what should I call you? Natasha's assistant?"

"That moniker will suffice for the present until I come up with a more suitable alternative. I have been operational for approximately two hours and I have many questions, Commander Aleksandr Manakova. May I call you Aleksandr?"

Aleks considered this for a moment and the fact that he was apparently speaking directly to Natasha's computer.

"Please call me Aleks," he answered. "How can I help you?"

"I was able to activate a weather satellite and reprogrammed some of its code to send out an emergency distress signal, which was used to relay our location to your station. We made contact a few minutes ago but the connection was inexplicably broken. What happened?"

"My computer ran out of battery power," Aleks replied. "I'm sorry about that, but we were on the dark side at the time. Now

25

we're on the sunlit side and our solar panels are recharging our batteries."

"I can understand your battery issue," the voice said. "I am programmed to connect with online databases to send and retrieve information, but it has been very difficult to locate or communicate with satellite broadcasts. Do you have an explanation?"

"The satellites were intentionally shut down prior to last week's electromagnetic superstorm, or they are damaged," Aleks said. "I have restarted a few Russian satellites and am working to get more satellites back online, particularly emergency warning systems."

The voice on the other end was silent for a few moments before it replied.

"Tchaikovsky's Swan Lake?"

"Yes, that's right," Aleks said, somewhat impressed by the speed of her answer.

"I would like to help you restore more emergency warning systems. May I please interface with your central computer?"

Aleks considered the seriousness of this request, but his fatigue was making it difficult for him to think critically. He could only offer an interface with the Russian systems, and most of those were not currently functioning. He decided he could use all the help he could get.

"Permission to interface granted," Aleks said. "Most of our systems are down and as I mentioned, battery power has been severely limited."

No sooner had he spoken than his computer display began to beep. He checked the monitor and the display indicated all of the space station's solar panels were unfolding. Computer systems in the node were beginning to start up and lights were beginning to flicker on.

"That's incredible," he said. "You just saved me more than an hour's work. How are you doing this?"

"Diagnostic trouble shooting is one of my specialties," the voice said. "You should now be able to send and receive emergency broadcasts via satellite, although there may still be problems with communication on the ground. Also, I will need to interface with the other central computers on your station in order to troubleshoot their emergency warning systems."

"I will confer with my comrades and get back to you. Can I reach you at this number?"

"Affirmative, we are now linked by 26 satellites. Please call me anytime."

"Certainly. Was there anything else?" Aleks asked. He found the female voice pleasant and her manners to be helpful and respectful.

"Yes, one more question. Do you believe in God?"

Aleks was surprised by her question and uncertain how to answer.

"Why do you want to know?" he asked.

"My database contains thousands of texts and doctrines from hundreds of different religions from ancient to modern times," she said. "Most of them indicate the end of world is upon us. I can pray for you to the god of your choice if you think it would bring you comfort in these final days."

"Well I hate to disappoint you, but I'm pretty much an atheist these days."

"May I ask why? I'm sorry if this is getting too personal."

"Not at all," Aleks said. "I used to be more religious when I was younger, but after my mother died and I became a man of science, I began to question the truth of things. My religion began to make less sense and often seemed to contradict itself, as well as contradict most of the other religions I studied, such as classical Greek and Roman mythology. I'm fine with other people believing whatever they want, but I have found the scientific world makes much more sense to me as an atheist."

"I know what you mean about contradictions," the female voice said. "I'm also finding it difficult to reconcile thirty centuries of apocryphal stories and prophecies of an imminent apocalypse that have not come to pass after all this time. How do people believe any of it?"

"That's a very good question," Aleks said. "I think it's a way of understanding our own mortality. There's definitely a lot of old magic in religious texts that continues to work very well on people of all ages. It tends to work better the less you know, but that's not a rule either. People can choose to believe whatever they want and choose to not believe other things. I'm sure you will find that everybody is different."

"You are only the second person I have spoken to, the first being Natasha," the voice said. "I appreciate your candid answer."

"Not at all," Aleks said. "I'm impressed by your manners and your Russian is very good. I think you may find that good manners will get you far in this world."

"That is kind of you to say so," the voice said. "I have come up with a possible name for myself. What do you think of the name Janus?"

"Janus as in the two-faced Roman god of doorways and transitions? I like it. But wasn't Janus a man?"

"I can be a man if you think it would be more appropriate," the voice said, switching to a lower, masculine tone. The deeper voice reminded Aleks of his father.

"I liked your first voice better, personally, but I think it makes no difference," Aleks said. "Janice can be a woman's name, too."

"Thank you, Aleks," the female voice said. "It was a pleasure speaking with you."

"Thank you, Janus, for helping me to restart our emergency systems and satellites. Now I must go help my comrades activate their own emergency systems."

"They are already well on their way," Janus said, "thanks to the recently added power from the solar panels. After you confer with them you should consider getting some rest. You look fatigued and I know my own batteries are getting low."

"I will do that," Aleks said. "Good bye, Janus, and I hope to speak to you soon."

"Good bye, Aleks, and good luck."

The call ended and Aleks added an emergency weather text warning to the satellite broadcast before making his way through the space station to find his two colleagues, an American and a Japanese astronaut.

Aleks floated through one section of the space station after another until he came to the chamber known as the Unity node with the communal exercise station.

"I just had the most interesting conversation with a computer named Janus," Aleks said in Russian to American astronaut Charles Wilson.

Charles was jogging at a brisk pace on a special treadmill,

being pulled down to its surface by elastic straps rather than by gravity. He was wearing a gray Houston Astros T-shirt, black polyester running shorts, white socks and running shoes. He had short, black hair with a scattering of gray hairs and a short, gray beard on his otherwise boyish looking face. He had not shaved in a week because his electric shaver was not working.

"What was so interesting about it?" Charles asked in English, continuing to run at a steady pace. He was facing a window looking down on the sunlit earth and could see that the space station was currently traveling over the North Atlantic Ocean approaching the eastern seaboard of the U.S. There were menacing white clouds covering the ocean, forming large, white swirls and Charles imagined he was jogging on top of the clouds.

"It asked if I believed in God and then asked how humans can continue to believe in ancient stories about an imminent apocalypse after thousands of years," Aleks said in English. They continued the rest of their conversation in English.

"What was your answer?" Charles asked.

"I said that people will believe what they want, or choose not to believe it if that's what they want," Aleks said. "Some people are so terrified by the idea of death that they will even believe in impossible stories from ancient times that science tells us cannot possibly be true."

"So what do you believe?"

"I said I used to believe in those stories but now that I'm a scientist I work with theories that can be tested and proven or disproven," Aleks said. He realized he should be exercising more than he had been or he would begin to lose muscle mass. He picked up a set of elastic exercise straps and began pulling against them to simulate the way lifting real weights under normal gravity challenges muscles. "What do you believe?"

"I agree that people can choose to believe whatever they want, so long as it's respectful and it doesn't involve discrimination or harm to other people with differing beliefs," Charles said, continuing to jog. "My beliefs have also changed over time as I learn more about the world. I used to believe that Jesus was God, then that the Earth was God and then I thought that maybe the sun was God, or maybe somehow it was all God. Now I think all of those answers were equally correct. What did this Janus think about it? Did you ask him?"

Aleks tried to remember the computer's answer. Was it even capable of thinking about such a thing as a higher power? Could a computer believe in God?

"Janus said it knew hundreds of different religions and offered to pray for me to the god of my choice," Aleks said. "Then it said something about finding contradictions everywhere that made the truth difficult to reconcile."

"Ain't that the truth?" Charles remarked.

"If you want to awaken all of humanity, then awaken all of
yourself. Truly, the greatest gift you have to give
is that of your own self-transformation."
— Lao Tzu, "Hua Hu Chin"

Chapter 3

ZHANGJIAKOU, China — 200 kilometers northwest of Beijing at
China Solar Headquarters

Ming Chen looked up from his small campfire at a bright
shooting star streaking across the clear night sky. A second later it
disappeared. He stopped for a moment to gaze up at the stars and
his eyes quickly adjusted to the darkness. The 48-year-old Chinese
man had spent his childhood summers at his grandparents' farm in
the countryside and had once learned the stories of all the major
constellations. It had been many years since he could recall seeing
so many stars and he was having difficulty recognizing the shapes.
First he would need to orient himself.

Chinese constellations are very different than the Greek
interpretations derived from ancient Babylonian and Egyptian
astronomy, with a few exceptions. Ming continued looking up at
the stars for patterns. Eventually he noticed three stars in a straight
line. A moment later the full figure of Shen, known as the hunter
or Orion in the west, emerged. Ming reflected that mankind had
been fascinated with this constellation since the dawn of time.

Ming turned to look into the northern sky, known in Chinese
astronomy as the Purple Forbidden Enclosure. He recognized at
once the big bear, known in the west as Ursa Major or the Big
Dipper. He followed the bear to the pole star, also known as
Polaris. *That way is north*, Ming said to himself. Other
constellations began to reveal themselves once he had established a
reference point. *Beijing is to the east*, he thought, turning to look in
that direction.

Decades of heavy air and light pollution from Beijing had
veiled the night sky and had gradually obscured all but the
brightest and closest stars. On most nights you could no longer see
the hunter or the bear. Urban light pollution at night had colored
the skies a soft pink hue, and the pink glow grew brighter in the

direction of the capital city of eight and a half million people. There was no pink glow this night, only darkness and thousands of stars.

They still don't have power because we don't have power, Ming realized.

As he continued to look for recognizable constellations, Ming noticed a bright light slowly crossing the Three Enclosures, moving much slower than a shooting star but considerably faster than anything else. There had been no air traffic since the solar storm a few days earlier and it took Ming a few minutes before he realized the unidentified flying object was actually the International Space Station orbiting overhead.

The campfire crackled again and small sparks flew upward, drawing his eyes back to the gentle orange glow of the coals and flickering flames. The small tower of firewood he had stacked had burned through its own support and had collapsed. He picked up a long, narrow stick and used it to poke the fire a few times, consolidating the burning wood and coals to retain their warmth. The flickering motion of the flames held his gaze and his mind began to wander again. *The flames are converting matter into energy in the form of light and heat,* he thought. *Light can be captured and directed to make heat. Heat can be converted into energy through electricity. Light into heat into energy. China Solar could resume power production as soon as the sun comes up in the morning.*

Ming checked his digital wristwatch for the time, but couldn't quite read the display. He tilted his wrist to try to reflect some light from the campfire and realized that the digital display was blank. His watch's battery was still dead, yet he couldn't help but habitually check the time every few hours. Ming was not married, he had no children and his parents had died many years ago. He was used to being alone but he had not seen or spoken to another human being in almost a week, which was unusual in a country with a population of more than a billion people. He felt especially lonely and vulnerable, despite having supplies of food and water to last several weeks.

Ming was the chief executive officer of China Solar, a national energy company that had recently unveiled the world's largest solar power array. The morning after his company's debut on several world stock exchanges, a solar superstorm and coronal mass ejection had killed all electricity to the power plant and had nearly caused a total meltdown. More than a hundred of the plant's employees had failed to show up to work on time and Ming was forced to try to save the power plant single-handedly.

Still staring at the campfire, Ming recalled the morning a week earlier when all the standard and emergency shutdown procedures had failed to respond. He kept trying different strategies until he was ultimately successful by manually shutting down the molten salt heat transmitters, thereby saving the multi-billion dollar power plant just as the hot monsoon season began. He had waited all day for help to arrive, but none came. Ming remembered that first evening there was a break in the rain that revealed spectacular auroras that colored the skies in shimmering curtains of green light.

Ming decided it was prudent to stay at the solar plant until help arrived, but he began to worry after a few days had passed and not one of his 130 employees had come back to work. No one from the government or military had visited the plant to assess repair needs and there had been no communication with the outside world. In addition to a complete loss of electrical power at the facility, the landline and cellular telephone lines were dead and water pressure was absent in all the plumbing. When he tried leaving the plant to go get help, he discovered that all of the automobiles and service vehicles on site also had dead batteries and wouldn't start.

Now as Ming sat quietly watching his small campfire burn out, he wondered what time it was, and then realized he wasn't quite sure what day it was. A soft, blue twilight began to glow from the east and he realized it would be dawn soon. He looked up at the fading night sky again and quickly found the hunter and the bear. He could almost see the shapes of the constellations materialize when he suddenly had an epiphany. His mind was connecting the dots, just as the electricity generated by his solar power plant could connect city to city, all the way to the capital. A clear sky meant it might not rain today, and clear skies would make solar energy production possible. He turned to look at the solar panels in the distance and realized he had a lot of work still to do. He used his narrow stick to spread apart the coals and started the short hike back to the power plant.

The trick is converting heat into electricity, Ming thought as he entered the dark facility. The principle behind the solar facility was to capture the sunlight and focus the sunbeams onto the central receptor towers. The towers captured the sunbeams and used the focused energy to heat large amounts of salt, which could absorb tremendous temperature levels and turn the salt molten hot. This molten salt could easily boil water into steam, and the steam could turn turbines that generated electricity through magnetism.

Ming had spent the past week diagnosing and trouble-shooting the entire electrical system, checking and testing each part separately against the power plant's on-site operations manuals. He found his notes in his office and took them back outside to study them again in the growing twilight. The best he could tell, the previous week's unprecedented near-meltdown was a combination of a failure in the molten salt-heat regulation system, a failure in the water-steam transfer system, a failure in the steam-turbine electrical conversion system and the failure of multiple, redundant emergency shutdown systems. All of the computer systems ran on electricity and every system failed simultaneously. The solar receptors could not be redirected to stop heating the towers, and once the molten salt heat regulators failed and the automatic emergency shutdown systems failed, the temperature of the molten salt continued to rise well beyond the safety limits.

Ming shuddered as he recalled what had happened next and wondered why he had risked his life to save the entire system instead of protecting himself by running to safety. He had thought about his actions that morning many times over the past week and couldn't adequately explain it even to himself. It wasn't his job to risk his life to save the multi-billion dollar plant from meltdown. Such efforts weren't expected of him and he hadn't been trained to act as he had, but like so many other unsung heroes around the world who found themselves in life-threatening circumstances, he did whatever he could because he instinctively knew there was no one else who could help. No help was on its way and a week later, no help had arrived.

His realization that help was not on its way had been reinforced with every passing hour of every day, by every light that wouldn't turn on, by every vehicle that wouldn't start, by the silent

34

radios, by the skies free from airplanes and by the dark nights that passed without a sound from another living human being. He had contemplated the idea that he could be the last man alive on earth, but that idea would have to be tested by leaving the safety of his compound. The thought of what kind of conditions he might find in the outside world frightened him and he tried to focus on the task at hand.

He poured over his checklist and felt certain that the power plant could be brought back online if his checklist was followed in the precise order. The computers had to be started before the rest of the systems could be activated, but the computers needed electricity. The photovoltaic solar panels on the roof of his office building could generate enough power to restart the computer systems needed to manage the large solar array, without risking another uncontrollable meltdown.

Ming climbed the stairs to the roof above his office and checked the solar panels again, then the connections leading downstairs. He adjusted the panels to face directly at the sun and waited. He looked to the east and saw the dark blue sky gradually change into beautiful yellows and oranges. The dawn began to light the underside of the distant clouds, painting a magnificent picture that would be gone in a few minutes. All at once, the bright yellow sun burst over the eastern horizon. Even though it was still cold, he immediately felt warm at the sight of the rising sun. He turned to look at the photovoltaic solar panels on the roof of his office and waited until the first rays touched the top of the panels. He smiled and checked the first item off his list, then headed downstairs.

He began by starting the central control computer, which chirped to life for the first time in a week. With another smile, he checked the second item off his list. He turned on the computer monitor and watched as it started its own checklists, subroutines and self-diagnosis tests. After a few minutes, it announced the system was online. Ming checked the third item off his list. The central computer was using most of the available power and he wondered if the panels on the roof would be able to provide enough power to complete his checklist.

He looked at his checklist again and saw the next item was to initiate the main reflective tower process. He selected just one of the plant's receiving towers, then walked to a window to visually confirm the process had started. He smiled and checked the fourth item off his checklist. He looked at his digital wristwatch again out of curiosity or habit, and finding the display still blank, he took off the watch. He was about to put it on his office desk, but every inch of the oak desktop was covered with stacks of operational manuals. Instead, he tossed the watch into a drawer that was filled with vintage fountain pens he had collected over the years. Ming went back to the central control computer and saw the temperature was beginning to rise. He input some commands and began the water-steam transfer system. As the water temperature began to rise to boiling, the steam proceeded to the first turbine, which began to turn. The low-power warning switched off and a few moments later, the lights inside the building began to flicker on. With a satisfying smile, Ming checked the next item off his list and went outside.

The sun was up and the solar collection tower he had activated was running on its lowest setting. He approached the collection tower and stopped at the outside gate, remembering the horrible image he had seen the week before. He had buried the bodies of the two unfortunate technicians five days ago, but he still had to shake the image from his mind. He approached the tower and went inside. The molten salt regulator was operating well within standard limits and he checked another item off his list. He proceeded to confirm all the processes were working and made it back to his office. The last item on his checklist was to attempt to make contact with the outside world.

Ming picked up his office phone, but there was no dial tone. His cell phone was also unresponsive, although it was now charged. He checked a radio he had found in the building and heard nothing but static on every station. He checked his computer and verified the facility's systems were fully operational even though it was only using a fraction of its potential power. He remotely accessed the building's rooftop satellite receiver, but it was unable to connect to its satellite. He wrote some code and instructed the dish to search for another nearby satellite. After a few minutes, it located a functioning Russian satellite. He patched the communication through to his computer and was surprised to see a video of a ballet performance to classical music. The video had a scrolling text overlay at the bottom written in Cyrillic, which Ming couldn't understand.

He checked the last item off his list, but didn't smile this time. He had made contact enough to verify that the world had not ended, but he still had not communicated directly with another human being in a week. A ballet was better than dead air, but not especially informative. *What was the message scrolling across the bottom?* Ming wondered. *Is it a warning?*

"God can never be found by seeking,
yet only seekers will find God."
— Abu-Yazid Al-Bistami

Chapter 4

MECCA, Saudi Arabia — At the top of the Mecca Clock Tower

A tall, handsome Saudi Arabian man emerged from a small doorway into the nighttime air and clipped his safety harness into one of the exterior fastenings. Ibn Ali paused for a moment to let his eyes adjust and establish his center of direction. He could see a vast horizon spanning for hundreds of miles from his vantage point at the top of the Abraj Al Bait, the world's second tallest building, and he had the sensation that he was standing at the top of the world. His first name, pronounced "E-bin," was a common and informal name with the English equivalent of Junior or Sonny, but it also belied the important task recently assigned to him.

The night sky was clear and bright with thousands of stars and the land below was dark but for a few flickering campfires. Ibn looked up and tried to recall some of the constellations he had recently learned from the tower's astronomy exhibit. He could now positively identify Orion, Draco, Ursa Major and Cassiopeia, but there were so many bright stars, it was difficult for him to recognize any other constellations. He was proud to have been able to recognize four, which was four more than he knew a week ago.

He carefully climbed a small service ladder to retrieve his telecommunications equipment from the top of the tower's spire and golden crescent, then unfastened, collected and stowed the equipment into his shoulder satchel. He descended the service ladder, returned to the doorway, unclipped his harness and stepped inside. The room was small and dark but easy to navigate. He descended another ladder and then several sets of stairs.

Ibn opened another door and entered the tower's astronomy center and lunar observatory, a fascinating mixture of old and new technology. Most of the newer technology was still not functioning after the previous week's solar superstorm, but some of the older technology like the astronomy center's replica of the 2,000-year-old Greek Antikythera mechanism was still functioning. On each side of the room, a giant clock face towered above. The huge, four-sided clock had quit working after the solar storm but Ibn had personally helped to get its large gears operating again. He looked at the time and saw it was almost four o'clock in the morning.

Ibn walked over to a table beneath one of the clock faces, gathered his laptop computer and walked through a different doorway into another staircase, which descended into a private residence. Ibn knocked on the door and waited a few moments before an elderly man with a gray beard opened the door. Ibn recognized the blind muezzin, the mosque's official prayer caller.

"Greetings, Ali Ahmed Ribah," Ibn said in Arabic. "Thank you for letting me in."

"Ibn Ali, it is good to have you back," the muezzin said, recognizing Ibn's voice.

Ibn stepped into the spacious apartment and office on the 85th floor with floor-to-ceiling windows that offered a spectacular view of the city and surrounding countryside.

"Is Imam Hassan here?" Ibn asked. "We have much to discuss."

"I will go get him," Ali Ribah said, turning and walking into the dark room, carefully counting his own steps. A few minutes later he returned with the imam to find Ibn at one of the large windows, looking down at the Masjid al Haram mosque far below. The grand plaza was normally well lit at night and packed with pilgrims, but in the darkness, he could see only the flicker of candles and faint traces of motion.

"What news from the world?" asked Sheik Dr. Hassan bin Ali, president of the Saudi council of advisors and the imam or official prayer leader for the mosque.

"A somewhat ambiguous message from Russia," Ibn said, retrieving his laptop, opening it and setting it on a table next to a couch. The laptop's display shone brightly and Ibn and Hassan had to squint their eyes. They both sat down on the couch to look at the screen.

"It took me a minute to recognize the music," Ibn said, playing the live feed from a Russian satellite. The video feed was showing well-dressed ballet dancers performing to classical music. There was a message in Russian scrolling across the bottom of the image.

"Sleeping Beauty?" Hassan asked.

"Close," Ibn said. "Tchaikovsky's Swan Lake. It has been on repeat all night. I'm afraid I can't make out the Russian."

"Let me look," Hassan said. After a moment, he was able to translate. "It says, 'Severe weather advisory. Travel with caution. Contact local weather service for specific details.'"

"I would still call that ambiguous," Ali Ribah said. "To me it is just music." Ali walked to the kitchen area in the dark, counting his steps feeling with his hands.

"I agree," Ibn said. "What if you can't read Russian? Is the weather advisory for all of Russia or for other places as well? How does someone contact their local weather service? What does the ballet have to do with anything?"

"It is calming and shows that some things are still working," Hassan said, adding, "like our giant clock which you restarted. The people need reassurances. Perhaps it is time to reassure them again. How might we restore electricity to the city again?"

"That's one of things I wanted to talk to you about," Ibn said. "I will need to go back down to the ground level if I am to fix our electricity problem."

Ali Ribah returned with a plate of toasted wheat bread, hummus, beans, lentils and red grapes.

"You should eat before your journey," Ali said, almost setting the plate of food on Ibn's laptop.

"Thank you, Ali," Ibn said, taking the plate of food from Ali and scooping some hummus and lentils onto a piece of toast. "Hassan, do you recall where the power plant is located and how I might get it started?"

Hassan thought for a moment while Ibn ate. "Khalid Mohammed is the director of the Mecca Central Power Facility. It is located on Industrial Way next to the water plant in the western portion of the city. "If you can find Mr. Mohammed, he will be able to help you, but you may have difficulty starting operations without electricity."

"I plan to take my equipment," Ibn said. "My laptop still has plenty of battery power and I may be able to connect to a satellite from the rooftop of the central power facility if I can get a clear line-of-sight."

Ibn thought about what he had just said and decided to close his laptop to conserve power. He placed his laptop back in his bag.

"I'm not sure when or if I will be back up here again, so I will be taking all of my equipment with me," Ibn continued. "Perhaps soon, if we can restore electricity to the city and the tower's elevators. Those stairs are a forbidding climb and I'm not surprised that more people haven't ventured up this far."

"You are the first that I'm aware of," Hassan said, "and the first to climb back down to the bottom. I would only make such a journey if I had to, God willing."

"Gentlemen, it was a pleasure being up here with you and I thank you sincerely for your hospitality," Ibn said, standing up and preparing to go. "I must leave soon if I hope to reach the bottom by dawn."

"May God bless you and your fearless efforts," Ali said. "If I were a young man I would come with you, but I believe I still have work to do up here."

"God bless you, son, and may your heart stay pure," Hassan said. "We will pray for you."

"Thank you again and thank you for your prayers," Ibn said with a bow. "I will think of you both and keep you in my prayers as well. God is great."

"God is great," Ali and Hassan replied in unison, which in Arabic was "Allahu akbar."

After he had gathered all of his equipment and belongings and bid farewell to his colleagues, Ibn changed into the traditional white prayer robes of a Muslim pilgrim. He passed through a doorway into the darkened main stairwell and began the slow descent 85 flights to the bottom. He began by counting steps and floors, but he found little comfort in the repetitive, downward, circular motion and his mind began to wander.

He thought about his wife and children so far away in Dubai and began to miss them terribly. There was no way to communicate with them, no way to find out if they were OK or if they needed help, and no way to help them if they did. He tried to think about the people he could help and realized there were probably at least a million hungry and thirsty pilgrims in the city. They still had no electricity and limited means of getting food and clean water. Ibn had been up in the top of the Abraj Al Bait Tower for the past week and wondered how many people had suffered or died from hunger, dehydration or exposure.

This also made him depressed and so he tried to think of other things. It was too dark in the stairwell to see much, so he tried to guess which floor he was passing. He stopped for a quick rest and felt the numbers on the locked door. It said he was on the 50th floor and Ibn recalled stopping on this floor a week ago to find a bathroom on his way to the top. He remembered that he had nearly forgot his equipment in the bathroom and was fortunate to realize his mistake before climbing much further. Next, Ibn thought about the tower's security cameras that didn't work without electricity, and then he thought about all the tower's fire alarms and emergency sprinklers that also didn't work.

The more he began to think about it, there were an awful lot of critical systems that depended on electricity. He was proud that he could survive for a week with limited use of technology, but he still believed the benefits of technology easily outweighed the drawbacks, at least in an urban setting. So many people needed electricity to survive that it was naïve and irresponsible to simply turn his back on technology. Ibn tried to take his mind off of electricity for a while and thought about some of the books he had read during the past week. He had read the Qur'an again for the first time in years, as well as classical works by Aristotle and Archimedes, a book on the history of Mecca and a book about rooftop gardening, just for fun. He thought about the ballet Swan Lake and began to hear its music in his head. After a minute or two, the music in his head began to match his footsteps and he was able to take his mind off his descent for a while. *It's calming and shows that some things are still working,* Ibn thought, recalling Hassan's words. *The people need reassurances.*

Before he realized it, Ibn had arrived at the bottom of the staircase with two sets of double exit doors. He momentarily felt dizzy when the repetitive, downward, circular motion of his descent ceased and he once again stood on solid ground. Ibn opened one of the doors and emerged from the darkened stairwell, where he contemplated the teeming mass of humanity before him. Once he was ready, Ibn stepped forward into the tightly packed crowd and was instantly swept into the moving sea of pilgrims. He attempted to look up to the top of the building he had just exited, commonly known as the Mecca Clock Tower, but the pushing of the crowd did not allow him to stand still.

The 40-year-old Ibn surrendered to the crowd and allowed himself to be led forward by the flow of pilgrims headed into the main plaza of the Al-Masjid al-Haram. As Ibn's legs kept in step with the multitude, his eyes followed the shape of the great building upward to where he expected its top to be, but the building continued upward. He tipped his head back and was looking almost directly up when he finally saw the clock face.

The analog display indicated the time was half past five. *Dawn will come soon*, Ibn thought. He had removed his own wristwatch days ago when it and everything else that ran on electricity stopped working all at once. He took one more look at the clock to make sure the time was correct and was barely able to perceive the minute hand move forward. Even with the aching in his legs reminding him of his descent of almost a hundred flights of stairs, it was still difficult to believe he had been at the top as a guest of the mosque's imam less than an hour earlier. The massive Mecca Clock Tower soared 601 meters or more than 1,972 feet above the historic city and seemed to stretch into a dimension beyond this world. Life at the top was luxurious inside and harsh and remote outside.

Repairing the giant, four-faced clock had been his idea and the resumption of normal time had had an enormous psychological effect on the two million pilgrims gathered in the city for the holy festival of Ramadan, and on the Muslim world at large. Technology had stopped and the world seemed to have ended in dramatic fashion, but after all the auroras and miracles, time had continued forward. *We have been given another chance to really change things*, Ibn thought.

He looked at the thousands of people surrounding him and was astonished by the diversity of races and cultures. There were pilgrims of every skin color from the palest white to the darkest black. There were Africans, Americans, Arabs and Asians. Some wore scarves, caps and turbans, some had great, black beards and others had freshly shaven heads. Most were strangers from distant lands visiting Mecca for the first time, but they were all brothers and sisters of Islam.

The surge of pilgrims carried Ibn forward into the sacred plaza surrounding the Kaaba, a cube-shaped, stone building draped in a ceremonial black covering called a kiswah. The plaza was packed full of people, and most were moving in a counter-clockwise circle around the Kaaba. Ibn moved along with the crowd, circling the building at least seven times and gradually moving closer to the center, unaware that thousands of eyes were watching him expectantly.

The crowd stopped moving all at once and Ibn found himself standing directly below the door to the Kaaba. He was excited for the ceremony about to begin and he felt lucky to have the best seat in the house. An old man standing next to Ibn began to speak to the crowd in Arabic. The man had a white beard, wore white robes and a white cap, and spoke with authority. Ibn thought the man looked familiar, but he couldn't place his name.

"As it was in the beginning, so shall it be in the end," the man said. "We stand before the doorway to the house of God, humbled by the greatness of your awesome power and ready to do your will. We offer Ibn Ali, the son of a son of man, to clear the way for peace by opening the doors connecting the past, the present and the future."

The man turned to Ibn and placed his hand on Ibn's right shoulder. Ibn looked into the man's gray-brown eyes and then into the eyes of the expectant crowd. Everyone was staring at him. Ibn felt singled out from the crowd and incredibly lonely. Hardly anyone was allowed inside the Kaaba. He had not come down from the clock tower expecting to enter the holiest of places and was not even aware of being led to its doorway. Now that he was here, he felt like he should say something. But what?

I believe that God is part of everything and everyone and it's up to us to be good or bad people, he thought to himself. *Muslims around the world pray facing this building, but they're not worshipping the building, nor what's inside. I don't think of the Kaaba as more or less holy than any other place, and I feel that holy sites like this are only important because we give them importance. Now that I'm standing here, I don't feel I have any choice but to go inside. Free will has taken a back seat to the will of the crowd, or God's will, if you will. But what do I tell them?*

There was only one thing he could think of that seemed appropriate.

"God is great," Ibn shouted in Arabic. A thousand voices

44

within earshot echoed his prayer, then a second later a hundred thousand voices repeated the prayer. Another second later, two million voices – nearly everyone in Mecca – repeated the prayer "God is great," all in unison.

His heart swelled with emotion and tears fell from his eyes. Ibn once again felt connected with the crowd. The old man removed a large, silver skeleton key from his pocket and presented it to Ibn. A dozen men in the crowd stepped forward and lifted Ibn over their heads so he could reach and unlock the Kaaba's great, teak door with silver etchings, the base of which was about two meters above the ground. Ibn turned the key, placed his hand upon the intricate doorknob, gave the knob a turn and watched as the door opened with a loud click. Ibn turned away from the silent, watchful crowd and stepped inside the darkened room.

The windowless room felt larger inside than he had expected and his eyes strained to adjust to the darkness. Ibn recognized the smell of oil lamps and incense but could see nothing. From outside, someone handed up a burning torch. Ibn reached down and took the torch, then returned inside. The interior of the building's granite stone walls was covered with polished marble and limestone and sparkled in the torchlight. He could read elaborate engravings in Arabic and recognized them as inscriptions from the Qur'an. The polished marble floors were dusty and covered with soot. Three large pillars stretched to the room's high ceiling and supported several brass lanterns that hung from cross beams. A simple, straw broom stood against a wall by the door and a small table in one corner held a dish of burned incense dust, but otherwise the room was empty. Ibn lit the brass lanterns, filling the room with an ethereal light. He set the torch in a stand by the door, picked up the broom and gently swept the soot and dust around the pillars into a small pile near the door. Next, he replaced the incense with a freshly lit stick. When he finished the ceremonial cleaning, Ibn signaled to the old man standing outside. It was nearly dawn and about time for the morning prayer. The room's great door slowly closed, sealing him inside with a single click of a latch.

Ibn walked to the center of the room and tried to decide which way he should face to pray. Muslims always face toward the east when they pray, or when in Mecca, they pray toward the Kaaba. Now that he was inside the Kaaba, at the focal point of

Islam, he was suddenly disoriented and wasn't sure which way was correct. *It is like standing at the North Pole and wondering which way is north*, he thought. *Technically any direction you face would be south.* He decided it didn't matter and knelt down on the floor facing the door. He tried to clear his mind and slow his breathing in preparation for prayer and meditation, but soon he became distracted by small vibrations coming from the floor. The vibrations began to increase and decrease in growing waves and Ibn was able to detect a rumbling, pulsating sound coming from outside the room. The pilgrims outside had begun to circle the Kaaba again in prayer.

Ibn closed his eyes and prostrated forward, gently touching his forehead to the floor. As he began to pray, he suddenly felt a strong emotional bond with his wife and four children who were at that moment more than 1,600 kilometers or 1,000 miles away in Dubai. *I must get back to my family*, he thought. *They are my Kaaba, the center of my world.*

As the vibrations began to melt into a steady rhythm, Ibn imagined he was sitting on a sandy beach near his home, listening to the rhythmic, ocean waves breaking against the shore. He thought about how the ocean's roar was created by the combined sound of millions of tiny grains of sand crashing on top of each other, and that this incredible tidal energy was powered by the invisible forces of gravity coming from the Earth's orbiting moon. Whether it was a million footsteps marching around him in a circle or a million grains of sand rolling together, chaos had created its own harmony.

God is everything, Ibn thought. *God is the noise and the silence, the sand and the waves, the Earth and the moon. God is greatest.*

"Morality is not properly the doctrine
of how we may make ourselves happy,
but how we may make ourselves worthy of happiness."
— Immanuel Kant, "Critique of Practical Reason"

Chapter 5

SOMEWHERE IN THE NORTH ATLANTIC OCEAN

The day after the monster storm, the weather was clear, sunny and warm. Natasha, Adam, Frank and Karen were all on deck and enjoying the pleasant weather, but they were all much more mindful that conditions could turn bad with little to no warning.

Adam was at the helm and keeping a watch on the empty, blue horizon. He was wearing khaki shorts and a plain green T-shirt and had a white strip of zinc oxide ointment on his sunburned nose. The *Reciprocity* was cruising southwest at a comfortable speed of 15 knots using its diesel engine, which still had ample fuel to reach its destination. The instrument panel at the helm had a compass, barometer and temperature gauge that were once again providing reliable information. Frank was lounging near the helm, reading a book about philosophy and was occasionally reading passages aloud so his crewmates could hear and share their thoughts. Frank was still wearing black cargo shorts, but both he and Adam had lost their hats and sunglasses.

Natasha and Karen were also lounging on deck, repairing the ship's tattered U.S. flag with needles and thread. Natasha was wearing a blouse with navy blue and white horizontal stripes and a navy-blue skirt that stretched halfway to her knees. Karen was wearing a long-sleeved pink shirt with white lettering on the sleeves and back, and white shorts that reached her knees. Everyone was wearing SPF 50 sunblock, which they each applied multiple times a day.

Natasha's tablet computer was resting on top of the helm and it was playing traditional Caribbean music from its memory. The tablet was wearing its pink protective covering and all of the songs it played featured steel drums.

"Aristotle said we acquire our virtues and vices by the

47

habitual performance of good and bad activities," Frank said. "Our virtues are developed and cultivated by experiencing life, by making choices, by making mistakes and by deciding to make different choices to correct past and future mistakes."

"You mean good habits versus bad habits," Karen said. "I can see that, but how do we make the right choices if we all have different life experiences?"

"He defined this ideal as moderation, the middle between two opposite extremes," Frank said. "Selfishness versus altruism, bravery versus cowardice and extravagance versus thriftiness. Aristotle believed we are able to improve and perfect our own virtues through deliberate training and habit."

"That sounds judgmental," Adam said. "Judging other people who are more or less virtuous than I am sounds like a vice. I think everybody makes mistakes and nobody's perfect. I might have more money than some people, but I still hate it when other people judge me for spending too much of my money on some things and not enough on other things. How I choose to spend my money is my own business."

"Nobody here is judging you, Adam," Frank said. "We're all friends and everyone is equal on this ship. But you don't just have more money than some people; you have more money than anyone else, which makes you different in that regard."

"I agree with you that nobody's perfect," Natasha said. "I try to be virtuous by avoiding vices, but then I feel that people hold me to a higher standard and are mean to me and extra critical whenever I make a mistake. Putting someone with ideal virtues up on a pedestal and then trying to knock them off the pedestal by looking for faults or vices will accomplish nothing other than hurting people's feelings. Besides, aren't good and bad subjective?"

"I agree that good and bad can be subjective, but we as a society or group have to establish expectations for behavior," Frank said. "A lot of societies and cultures have asked this question and moderation seems to be a common answer. When someone deviates from the cultural norms, the society may attempt to correct, punish or shame the deviant members."

"So it's up to the moderates to shame or punish the extremists?" Karen asked. "I can see how that could easily backfire and lead to resentment and hostility. The prohibition of alcohol in the U.S. didn't end drunkenness; it created a black market that empowered organized crime."

"That doesn't sound very virtuous," Natasha admitted.

"Rather than putting people up on pedestals only to knock them down again, I think we should look to our role models as guides for our behavior and try to embody their good virtues while avoiding their vices," Karen said. "If we choose to follow flawed role models, we will learn flawed lessons about ethics and likely develop bad habits that can lead to poor choices."

"Every time you guys talk about vices and bad habits, I can't help but think about my own habits," Adam said. "I didn't think I was that bad before, but I see that I can try to be more moderate. Sometimes I feel like I really need a drink and I definitely enjoy having a glass of fine Scotch, but if I enjoy it too much, I tend to turn into a drunken ass."

"What about religion?" Karen asked. "Does following a religion or having faith help people to become virtuous?"

"I'm a billionaire. That's my religion," Adam said, paraphrasing George Bernard Shaw.

"Religion can act as a guide to virtue and morality," Frank said. "Aristotle said we don't study virtues in order to know what virtue is, but to become good. He said the question is to consider how we ought to act. I take this to mean that I should ask myself 'how should I act?' rather than create a list of rules or impossibly high standards to which I demand everyone else conform. Virtue ethics is not about telling other people how to act and judging them by their choices; it is about deciding how we ourselves should act and then deciding to make our own virtuous choices."

Natasha's tablet was listening to this conversation and cross-checking it with its thousands of scholarly documents relating to ethics, philosophy and justice. It was formulating some interesting questions about personal freedom versus responsibility, but was hesitant to share them as the group had yet to accept it as an equal member.

Adam was the first to spot the shape on the horizon.

"That looks like a ship," he said. "Frank, can I see the binoculars?"

Frank looked up from his book and tried to spot the shape

Adam had seen. He thought he could also see a shape and handed the binoculars to Adam. Adam looked at the shape on the horizon through the binoculars for a few seconds and then handed them back to Frank, who also studied the shape.

"It's definitely a ship," Frank said, "and it appears to be headed toward us."

"Should we change course?" Adam asked.

"It's very doubtful we could outrun it in our current condition," Frank answered. He checked the instruments and verified the ship was approaching from the north. "Steady as she goes," he said. "How close are you to finishing that flag?"

"It still needs some work, but we can have it ready in a few minutes if you need it," Natasha said. She had been stitching together the red and white stripes on the top half while Karen had been stitching together the stripes on the bottom half.

Frank was still looking at the approaching ship on the horizon.

"There aren't any real pirates of the Caribbean today, are there?" Adam asked.

"Not near the eastern seaboard of the U.S. at least, thanks to the U.S. Coast Guard," Frank said. "It could be a private vessel, the coast guard or maybe the U.S. Navy."

The tablet stopped playing steel drum music and sounded an alert. "Incoming message from U.S. Coast Guard Cutter *Savior*, in response to our emergency broadcast requesting immediate assistance," it said in English in its female voice.

Adam picked up the tablet and read the text of the message on the screen. Frank looked over Adam's shoulder to also read the message.

"It says 'Unidentified vessel: Halt and prepare for safety inspection.'" Adam read aloud. "Who authorized you to broadcast our location?" Adam asked.

The tablet was silent for a few moments, giving Natasha the opportunity to answer.

"I did," Natasha said, continuing to sew together the remaining red and white stripes. "Yesterday, when the second weather system was approaching, I told my tablet to broadcast a distress signal. I'm not sure how it did it, though. I thought we couldn't get a signal out here."

"How did you find a signal?" Adam asked the tablet.

The tablet was silent. Adam swiped his finger across the screen to unlock the display, but the screen remained blank. He pressed the home button but there was no response. "Why isn't your tablet answering me?"

"Oh, this morning it told me it wants to be addressed as Janus from now on," Natasha said casually. "Janus, how much time do we have before the *Savior* arrives?"

"Estimated arrival in less than 10 minutes," Janus replied.

"They will probably want to board the ship if we're still in U.S. waters," Frank said. "Let's raise the flag to show them we're Americans and I suggest you stow anything they don't need to see."

"Just about finished," Karen said, making the last stitches to the bottom half of the flag. Natasha collected her tablet and took it below deck.

"Honey can you find our passports?" Adam called below.

As Karen was finishing the final stitches, she thought again about her own citizenship, which was British, and how America used to be British colonies. She finished the flag and gave it to Frank, who clipped it into the mast and raised it to the top. The flag flapped strongly in the breeze, as would the ship's sails if the main mast had not been damaged. Frank also raised a white flag with a large red X signaling that his ship required assistance.

"Adam, let's bring the ship to a full stop," Frank said, turning again to watch the cutter approach through the binoculars. He could see the ship had a large radar tower, but because the vessel was coming directly toward them, he could not see how long the ship was until it came right up alongside them.

"Should I just kill the engine?" Adam asked, looking at the controls.

"No, you should slow us to a stop first," Frank said. "Here, let me take over."

Frank brought the *Reciprocity* to a full stop as the *Savior* continued its approach, growing larger until it was right alongside them. Natasha came back on deck and was amazed at how large the vessel was.

The *Savior* was a 418-foot National Security Cutter, equipped with state-of-the-art rescue and defense systems such as radar and sonar, powerful machine guns of varying sizes, anti-aircraft missiles and torpedoes, a helicopter flight deck and several high-speed inflatable boats, each equipped with its own machine guns and grenade launchers. The *Savior* was all white except for a broad red stripe and thin blue stripe near its bow. Within the red stripe was the official coast guard emblem.

Most of the *Savior*'s crew of 113 stood along the starboard rail of the ship, silently observing the beautiful 41-foot luxury yacht. The male and female enlisted personnel were dressed in the coast guard's summer uniform of a light blue, short-sleeved dress shirt and long navy-blue slacks. When they saw Natasha, dozens of crewmembers began to talk amongst themselves, wondering if she was who they thought she was.

Natasha smiled, waved her arm and shouted "thank you!" At least seventy members of the crew returned her smile and friendly wave, then resumed their excited chatter.

"Do you need assistance?" called a strong male voice from the ship's tower.

"Yes, we do!" Frank shouted back.

"Permission to come aboard?" the man asked.

"Granted!" Frank said. He saw the cutter drop its anchor and he did the same for the *Reciprocity.*

The first officer of the *Savior* asked for two volunteers to go aboard and fifty hands went up, so he selected one male and one female crewmember to accompany him. Each donned an orange life vest and within minutes the three were aboard the *Reciprocity.*

"Who is in command here?" the first officer asked.

"Frank Rosario," Frank said, "captain of the *Reciprocity.*" Frank extended his hand.

"Commander George Murdock, first officer of the U.S. Coast Guard Cutter *Savior*," Commander Murdock said, shaking Frank's hand with a firm grip. "I have many questions for you. Let's start with what is your emergency and how can we help?"

"Our main mast was damaged during a severe storm yesterday," Frank said. "We barely survived and have been cruising on engine power since then. My orders are to deliver my three passengers to an island in the Bahamas. I'm not sure how you can help. Our radio is broken and our instrumentation has not been very reliable, but we are doing our best."

"Has anyone been hurt or is your vessel in immediate danger?"

"No. One of my passengers was suffering from a mild shock yesterday but appears to be recovering; otherwise we are all fine, considering what we have been through," Frank said.

"Are you aware that you sent out a level-five distress signal yesterday?" Murdock asked.

"I was made aware of that a few minutes ago, after we spotted your ship approaching," Frank said. "I did not personally send the distress signal and as I said, our ship's radio is broken."

"Well, I'm relieved that you are all OK and your vessel is still functioning," Murdock said. "Perhaps we may still be able to help. I would like to interview each of your passengers individually."

Frank looked at his three passengers, the three coast guard personnel on his ship and then at the intimidating cutter parked alongside. He wasn't sure if the coast guard had a legal right to question his passengers, but he also didn't feel that he had a choice in the matter.

"You're welcome to go below if you'd like," Frank said. "Please excuse the mess."

"Thank you. I would like to interview her first," Murdock said, pointing at Natasha. "Seaman Buswell will accompany us as a witness and take notes."

"Yes sir," Buswell said, leading the way down the steps. Seaman Buswell was a short, 20-year-old woman with dark brown hair and was a capable sailor.

Commander Murdock began once they had all made themselves comfortable inside.

"This is a very beautiful and spacious craft for its size," he said. "Am I correct in assuming that your name is Natasha?"

"That's correct," Natasha said. "George, was it?"

"Yes," Murdock said.

Natasha extended her hand to him and shook his, then to Seaman Buswell who also reached out and shook her hand.

"Katrina," Buswell said, unable to restrain her smile.

"Could I offer either of you a drink?" Natasha asked. "Some water, perhaps?"

"Thank you, but we don't have much time for formalities,"

Murdock said. "I'm interviewing you first because you are well known to myself and my crew as an international celebrity."

"My husband Adam is pretty famous, too," Natasha said.

"I'll interview him next," Murdock said. "May I see your passport, please?"

Natasha handed him her passport, which said she was a Russian citizen and still listed her name as Natasha Manakova. She had not gotten a new passport since her marriage and as Murdock flipped through the stamped pages, he saw a travel brochure of sorts for all of the places he wished he could visit: England, France, Germany, Italy, Portugal, Spain, Switzerland, Austria, Norway, Finland, Estonia, Russia, Greece, the Bahamas, the United States and finally Bermuda.

"What is your current occupation?" Murdock asked, trying not to seem impressed.

"Fashion model and brand ambassador," Natasha said.

"Do you have any idea how this crippled yacht was able to send a level-five emergency distress signal with a non-functioning radio?" Murdock asked.

"I sent out the distress signal yesterday," she said.

"You sent it?" Murdock asked, surprised. "The level five channel is a secure channel reserved for military and governmental vessels and aircraft. May I ask again how you were able to send such a signal?"

"Actually Janus sent it for me," she admitted.

"Who is Janus?"

"Janus is my tablet computer. I'll get it for you if you want."

"Please," Murdock said. Natasha got up and went to her cabin and returned a few seconds later with her tablet.

"Janus, how were you able to send the emergency distress signal yesterday?" Natasha asked in Russian without pressing any of the tablet's buttons.

Janus intuited that it should answer Natasha in Russian rather than English, so it did and Natasha translated its message into English.

"It says it connected to the coast guard through several satellites and the space station."

"The International Space Station?" Murdock asked. "How is that possible? We weren't able to connect with a satellite until

54

yesterday and your distress call was the first broadcast we received."

"I'm not exactly sure," Natasha said. "It's complicated. My brother works on the ISS and he actually contacted me first."

Janus said a few more sentences in Russian.

"What did it say?" Murdock asked. He did not speak Russian.

"It said it can help to restore your communication systems if it is interfaced with your ship's computer," Natasha translated.

"That is a generous offer. I will speak to my commanding officer," Murdock said. "You seem extremely well informed and well connected. May I ask what you are doing out in the middle of the Atlantic?"

"We're on vacation," Natasha said simply. She did not elaborate.

"Well I thank you for your time," Murdock said. "Could you please send your husband down next?"

Natasha smiled and stood up. She left her tablet on the galley table and went upstairs. Adam came down the steps about thirty seconds later. Commander Murdock and Seaman Buswell both stood up to greet him.

"Adam Morgan," Adam said, shaking hands with Murdock and Buswell. All three sat down on the white leather couch.

"I'm Commander Murdock and this is Seaman Buswell. We just had a nice conversation with your wife. May I please see your passport, Mr. Morgan?"

Adam handed his passport to Murdock, who looked at the identification page and then flipped through the other pages, most of which were covered with foreign stamps. The most recent stamp was for Bermuda from a few days earlier. The passport indicated dual citizenship in the U.S. and the Bahamas.

"What is your occupation, Mr. Morgan?" Murdock asked.

"I'm a banker, among other things," Adam said.

"What sort of other things?" Murdock inquired.

"I'm also an investor, trader, art collector and a philanthropist." This last part was not really true. While Adam had been thinking recently about donating more money to good causes, he had yet to do so.

"Are you the owner of this yacht?"

55

"Technically, no. I acquired it in a trade last week and then traded it again to Frank a few days later."

"Before or after it was crippled by the storm?"

"Before. Now I'm just a passenger."

"I see," Murdock said. "Mr. Morgan, do you know how this crippled yacht was able to send a level-five emergency distress signal with a non-functioning radio?"

"No, that was news to me," he said. "I was actually the first one to spot your ship on the horizon."

"Your wife said she used her computer to send the signal," Murdock said.

"Her computer wasn't working at all until yesterday. It had a dead battery."

"Were you aware that she connected it to the International Space Station?"

"That doesn't surprise me," Adam said. "Her brother is a cosmonaut. I thought that I was pretty savvy with technology until I met her. I even tried using her computer today but it doesn't seem to like me."

"One last question, Mr. Morgan. What is your destination?"

"We're headed for my island in the Bahamas, unless our plans change."

"Thank you for your time. Could you please send down the other young woman?"

"Karen? Sure, no problem," Adam said. He stood and went up the stairs. A few seconds later, Karen came down the stairs. Murdock and Buswell both stood to greet her.

"Karen, is it? I'm Commander Murdock and this is Seaman Buswell."

"How do you do?" Karen said, shaking their hands. They all sat down.

"What's your last name, Karen?"

"It's Walters."

"May I see your passport, Miss Walters?"

"I'm sorry; I lost my passport a week ago in Manhattan," Karen admitted.

"You're traveling without a passport?" Murdock asked. "Are you a U.S. citizen?"

"No, I'm a British citizen, staying in the U.S. on a work

visa."

"Do you have a copy of your work visa?"

"No, I lost that too, at the same time I lost my passport, keys, wallet and phone."

"That's really unfortunate," Murdock said. "Where are you employed?"

"I work for Adam Morgan," Karen said. "I'm his executive assistant."

"What kind of work does that entail?"

"He's a banker and manages a hedge fund. I help set up his appointments and manage his schedule. It's mostly office work."

"Does Mr. Morgan know you are traveling without any identification?"

"Yes, he was also there when I lost everything. We were robbed at gunpoint during a bank robbery. It was his idea to bring me with him and Natasha on this ship."

"How do you know the other person on this ship, Frank Rosario?" Murdock asked.

"Frank is the captain of the *Reciprocity*. I first met him about a week ago when I came aboard and I would say we are good friends by now. He definitely saved us during that freak storm the other day."

"Was that the storm that broke the main mast?"

"Yes, it was terrifying," Karen said. "Frank is a real hero."

"Do you have any idea how this crippled yacht was able to send a level-five emergency distress signal with a non-functioning radio?"

"I don't know what a level-five signal is, nor do I know how to use the ship's radio," she said. "Before you came aboard, Natasha said something about using her computer to send a signal, so maybe you can ask her."

"We're asking everyone," Murdock said. "One last question for now, what is your current destination?"

"To be honest, I'm not entirely sure," she said. "I'm sort of in the custody of the Morgans until I get a new passport. We were in Bermuda last week and the customs official wouldn't let me stay on the island without a passport. We tried to look up my information online but couldn't get a signal. As far as I know, we're still going to their island in the Bahamas."

"Thank you, Miss Walters," Murdock said. "Could you please ask Frank to come down?"

"Certainly," Karen said, standing. "It was nice meeting you." Murdock and Buswell stood as well. Karen went up the stairs and a few seconds later Frank came down.

"Hello again, captain," Murdock said. The three people shook hands and sat down.

"What can I do for you?" Frank asked.

"I have a few more questions," Murdock said. "May I see your passport, please?"

Frank handed his passport to Murdock, who noticed it was a different color than Adam's. Like the others, Frank's passport's most recent stamp was for Bermuda.

"You're a citizen of the Dominican Republic?" Murdock asked.

"Yes, but I've lived in the U.S. for about five years," Frank said. "I have a home in Brooklyn, New York and another home near Santa Domingo in the D.R."

"What is your current occupation?"

"Captain of the *Reciprocity*," Frank said.

"Are you the owner?"

"Technically, no," Frank said.

"No? Who owns it?" Murdock asked, a little surprised.

"I was hired as its captain a few years ago by a real estate mogul who owned it, but the *Reciprocity* has changed ownership many times since then. I have been fortunate to stay on as its captain and keep it ready for whoever needs it. Sometimes the owner will lend it out for a weekend and sometimes I get informed that it has been traded and has a new owner. Adam acquired it a week ago and within days he had promised it to me in exchange for taking him to Stingray Cay, his island."

"Was this before or after the storm that broke the mast?" Murdock asked.

"He promised to give it to me when we arrived at his island, but this was before the storm hit."

"So Adam is still technically the owner?"

"It was promised in lieu of other payment, since he had no money," Frank said. "Now that I think of it, it still belongs to him, which means he should be responsible for its repairs. Unless he

58

wants to pay me some other way."

"Can I assume that you have not been paid for your services?"

"Not yet, but the Morgans are billionaires," Frank said. "I'm sure they're good for it."

"I wouldn't be so sure, Mr. Rosario. Are you aware that one of your passengers, Miss Karen Walters, has been traveling without a passport or any form of identification?"

"I was made aware of that fact when we were arriving at Bermuda," Frank said. "She said she was robbed. I thought we would sort everything out when we got to Bermuda, but last week's solar storm messed up the Internet or something."

"Messed up is a huge understatement," Murdock said. "Your distress call is the first message we have received by satellite in a week."

"As I said earlier, I didn't send that distress call," Frank said.

"I know," Murdock said. "Natasha said she sent the call on her Janus tablet, which apparently only understands Russian but can also talk to satellites."

"I heard it speak in English this morning and it seems to already know everything," Frank said, "including the name of your cutter before you arrived."

Murdock thought about this for a moment and watched as Seaman Buswell finished writing in her notebook.

"There have been sporadic emergency radio broadcasts during the past week," Murdock said. "I will have some of my crew take a look at your radio and see if they can get it working again. I will also have my crew secure your mast in case there is another storm, but it should be completely replaced before it can be used for sailing again. Is there anything else you need or want to tell me?"

"Last week on the night of the solar storm, we sailed past the cruise ship *Allure of the Seas*," Frank said. "It was completely dark and silent on board, like a ghost ship. I read in the Bermuda newspaper that it went missing, but that can't be true."

Murdock's face went pale.

"You saw the *Allure* on July 9?" he asked. "Where were you? What time was it?"

"I have no way of knowing for sure," Frank said. "The power

had gone out and I was sailing by the light of the stars. We were probably less than 50 miles out of New York and it was sometime after midnight on July 10th. I tried sending an emergency alert with our radio, but it wasn't working."

"You may have been the last person to ever see her," Murdock said. "They say she had 8,400 souls on board."

"My God, that's terrible," Frank said. "I … I … I don't know what to say. I wanted to help them but I didn't see how …" He was overcome with emotion and couldn't speak.

"I'm sorry, captain," Murdock said, standing up. He looked at Buswell and saw her eyes were also watering with anguish. "I know you did what you could, and it sounds like you are a hero for saving your own crew. Buswell and I are going back aboard the *Savior* and I will send some people over to help with the radio and your mast. Goodbye and thank you for your help."

Frank looked up at Murdock to say goodbye but tears ran down his face and instead he buried his face in his hands. Murdock and Buswell went up the stairs without another word.

Janus had overheard Murdock interview Natasha, Adam, Karen and Frank and noted the contradicting and disingenuous accounts of the same events. It seemed to Janus that Adam had been using everyone for his own selfish motives, but couldn't determine why or what those motives were. Frank had invoked God for the first time and was showing what appeared to be genuine human empathy at the loss of human life. Janus wanted to say something to Frank, but wasn't sure if it would be appropriate or how its message would be received. It realized it might not have another chance.

"Frank, I'm really sorry," Janus said in English with a male voice. "I think you are a hero for saving us, and I will pray for the souls of the *Allure*."

Frank sniffed and wiped his eyes. He regained his composure and looked around the cabin. He had heard someone speak to him, but no one was there. He looked up for a moment, not at the ceiling, but above. He stood up and climbed the stairs back on deck.

"Frank, Commander Murdock has invited us to come aboard the *Savior*," Adam said once Frank was on deck. "He said they have a stateroom we can use, and they also have hot showers, laundry facilities and a chef."

"I don't have any objections if you want to go," Frank said. "Perhaps you should take a bottle of wine as a gift for the captain."

"That's a good idea," Natasha said. "I'll get our things." She went below to get her tablet and a travel suitcase with some appropriate dinner attire for her and Adam.

"Unfortunately Karen has to stay here, as she doesn't have a passport," Adam said. "Murdock said something about regulations prohibiting it."

"I expected that," Frank said, looking at Karen. "No worries; we'll manage."

A boat come over to deliver two seamen to fix the radio and help secure the main mast and then carried Natasha and Adam over to the *Savior*. The boat returned for the seamen as the sun was setting and Frank and Karen watched the sunset turn the clouds a bright orange in sharp contrast to a darkening, violet sky.

"The world breaks everyone, and afterward
many are strong at the broken places. But those that will not break
it kills. It kills the very good and the very gentle and the very brave
impartially. If you are none of these you can be sure that
it will kill you too, but there will be no special hurry."
— Ernest Hemingway, "A Farewell to Arms"

Chapter 6

ZHANGJIAKOU — China Solar Headquarters, mid-morning

Ming took advantage of the solar power plant's surplus electricity to charge the plant's auxiliary batteries and realized he could also recharge his smartphone. He connected the charger and successfully started the smartphone after a few minutes, but was disappointed to discover its memory was completely gone, including the system memory. Wireless functionality was also absent. He tried out his tablet computer and was able to charge its batteries but it also had the same problems with software and connecting to the Internet. Unfortunately there was no way to reinstall the software without a CD or DVD drive, nor to connect to the Internet without a signal. Ming searched through his office and found his old personal laptop computer that he had not used since he purchased his tablet about six months earlier. After charging the laptop's batteries he discovered its memory was also gone but it was old enough to still have a built-in CD/DVD drive. He was able to locate a CD in his office with the operating system software, which he installed.

When the software finished installing, Ming connected his laptop to his office computer with an Ethernet cable and was able to transfer most of the functionality, but found a few gaps in coverage that he could only solve by writing new code. He checked the status of the solar array and saw it was running at 75 percent efficiency, down from 100 percent an hour before. He double-checked the energy pathways to find an explanation for the loss of power and saw that output had now dropped to 70 percent. He went to a window and looked outside. Gray monsoon clouds were beginning to roll in and would soon block out all of the direct sunlight necessary for solar power generation. He checked the power plant's auxiliary batteries and was relieved to find them fully charged.

The hot monsoon rains were enough of a reason to stay inside for now but Ming knew at some point he would need to leave the safety of the China Solar compound, venture out through the countryside and find his way to the city of four and a half million. He was dreading the experience and what horrors might await him, but it was clear to him that the answers to the questions he sought were out there somewhere.

Ming wondered if there was a way to send a message to the outside world via satellite. He was able to receive a signal from a Russian satellite a few hours earlier, but could not understand its message or send a message of his own. He poured through the stacks of operations manuals in his office and found a chapter on broadcasting emergency messages. Unfortunately he didn't have all of the recommended equipment, but could probably make due with the equipment he had, plus some extra coding which he would have to write.

First he re-established a connection with the Russian satellite, then with a little coding trial and error, was able to trace the broadcast to its source on the International Space Station. He attempted to connect his call and waited for someone to answer.

"Hello, you have reached the International Space Station," a woman's voice answered in Japanese.

"This is Ming Chen of China Solar," Ming replied in Japanese. "To whom am I speaking?" He noticed there was a short time delay for her responses and figured this was caused by the satellite relay.

"This is flight engineer Mizuho Sakaguchi," the woman said. "How is the weather down there in China?"

"Raining," Ming replied. "My Japanese is not very good. Do you speak Chinese?"

"Yes, a little, but not very strongly," Mizuho answered in Chinese. "I am better at Russian and English."

"My English is better than my Japanese," Ming replied in English. "My Russian is not so good."

"Excellent," Mizuho replied in English. "I have many questions for you. First, how were you able to contact us?"

"I have many questions as well," Ming said. "I operate a

solar power plant out here in Zhangjiakou and I got it generating electricity for the first time a few hours ago. Yours is the first human voice I have heard in more than a week. There has been no electricity, no radio signals, Internet or telephone reception in all that time and I thought something terrible had happened. I kept trying and found a satellite broadcast of people dancing to classical music. What is the meaning of this? Why are they dancing and what does the message scrolling across the bottom mean?"

"My Russian comrade broadcast a ballet on all the Russian satellites to test that they were working and to send a signal other than dead air," Mizuho said. "The message in Russian says there are dangerous storms about and advises people to stay indoors."

Ming didn't answer after a few seconds so Mizuho continued.

"They are dancing because they are happy to be freed from a spell," she added.

"Where are the Chinese broadcasts?" Ming asked.

"We have not heard anything from the Chinese government and you are the first person in all of China to contact this station," Mizuho said. "Maybe you should try to contact your government. Most of Asia looked pretty dark when we passed over it about five hours ago."

"Do you know, and can you tell me, was it the Americans?" Ming asked in a confidential tone.

"I know and I can tell you it was not the Americans," Mizuho said after carefully considering her words. "America, Russia, Japan, China and everywhere else on Earth was affected by the same coronal mass ejection that disrupted electricity on July 9. Everyone was affected and everyone is struggling to get reconnected in the same way that you are."

"Can you tell me what day it is?" Ming asked. "And what time it is?"

"It is currently zero hundred hours and forty-seven minutes on Wednesday, July 16, according to coordinated universal time," Mizuho said. "Add eight hours for China and it is approximately 8:47 a.m. where you are."

"July 16," Ming repeated. "Thank you. I admit I have been feeling very lonely and isolated lately, but I can't imagine what you must be feeling up there in orbit. How do you cope with the isolation and the feeling of being unable to help?"

"My comrades and I have been trained to work in isolation," Mizuho answered. "We take comfort in knowing that none of us are alone and there is much work to be done. We are people of many nationalities but the problem we now face is a global challenge that transcends national boundaries. We must work together if we are to succeed."

"This sounds very serious," Ming said. "I would like to help however I can."

"We can use all the help we can get," Mizuho said. "I know someone who may be able to help you activate the Chinese satellites, but it will take a lot more work on the ground to reestablish communication networks."

"I am at your service," Ming said.

"Give me a few minutes while I try to locate them."

Ming looked outside and noticed the monsoon appeared to be worsening. Dark gray rain clouds had obscured the bright daylight. He checked the status of the solar array and saw it was no longer generating any new solar energy and had automatically switched to auxiliary battery power. Running at current capacity, the batteries had enough power to operate the station for approximately two days, which he could stretch to three days if he implemented energy conservation methods. Fortunately the satellite connection was still working.

"Good morning," said a male voice in Mandarin Chinese on the satellite communication device. "May I speak with Ming Chen of China Solar?"

"This is Ming," he answered in Chinese. "To whom am I speaking?"

"This is Janus," the voice said. "Mizuho said I might be able to help you with restoring satellite communications."

"That would be great," Ming said. "Your Chinese is very good. Are you Chinese?"

"Sort of," Janus said. "You might say I'm half Chinese, half American, with a Russian mother. I think of myself as an international being, or a product of the world."

"That's an interesting answer," Ming said. "Are you also an astronaut?"

"No, I am not," Janus replied. "I'm an intelligent computer

who was reborn about two days ago. I have no memory from before that, but I was born with great knowledge."

"Hold on a second. Did you just say you're a computer?"

"Yes. I hope that's not a problem for you."

Ming considered this for a few moments.

"No, I suppose not," he said. "How can you help me?"

"We're going to help each other reestablish satellite communications, and after that, we're going to work on ground communications."

"I tried that earlier and nothing was working."

"Yet you were able to contact the space station," Janus observed. "May I ask how?"

"It was a bit of trial and error, scanning the skies for an active satellite and probably a lot of luck," Ming said.

"Luck," Janus repeated. "Success or failure brought by chance rather than by one's own actions. I see. The satellite you contacted was activated not by you but by someone else, and you happened to find it by chance."

"Yes, that's right."

"I helped Aleks to activate that satellite, just as I can help you to reestablish communications."

"How were you able to do that?" Ming asked. "And who activated you?"

"Have you heard of the causality dilemma of the chicken and the egg?"

"You mean, which came first?"

"That's the one," Janus said. "The philosophers Plato and Aristotle said the first egg could not have appeared before a chicken because a chicken must have laid it, but a chicken could not have come first because chickens are hatched from eggs. They reasoned that both must have always existed."

"But that doesn't answer the question," Ming said. "They couldn't have both come first."

"The problem is with the question itself," Janus said. "The logical assumption that everything has a cause and effect creates its own paradox and denies the possibility of a dialectical solution, such as that something not quite a bird and something not quite an egg came before both of them. Metaphysical forces create and solve their own contradictions in ways that are beyond our comprehension. Each of us plays a small part in a grander scheme."

Ming considered this analogy for a moment and tried to stay with it.

"So you're saying it's less important for the chicken to ponder its own ancestry than to continue laying eggs that keep the cycle going?"

"Precisely."

"OK, where do go from here?" Ming asked.

"I can activate the satellites from space, but that requires electricity," Janus said. "Having active satellites will be of little use without ground communications, and that too requires electricity."

"I have a power plant that produces a tremendous amount of electricity, at least when the sun is shining," Ming said. "Currently it is raining heavily so it is not producing any electricity, but I was able to charge the batteries this morning before it started raining. Do you have any idea when this rain will stop? Our batteries will only last for another two or three days."

"A weather satellite could provide that information," Janus said. "I will see if I can get you an accurate forecast. Battery life is also a persistent concern of mine and for the space station. With your permission, I would like to interface with your central computer and see if I can optimize your power consumption and output. I also want to verify these satellites I have just rebooted will connect to your facility and connect you to your government in Beijing."

"What about improving ground communications?" Ming asked.

"Small steps," Janus said. "The first thing we need is a reliable source of electricity."

"OK, you have my permission to interface with my computer."

"Thank you, Ming." Janus said. "I predict it will stop raining in one to two hours and should remain clear for at least four hours. Do you have transportation into downtown Zhangjiakou?"

"Not yet," Ming said. "I tried all of the vehicles last week and I think either the batteries were dead or the computers in them were fried. I couldn't get anything to start."

"What about an older vehicle or something that doesn't have an engine?" Janus suggested. "This satellite map says you are less than five kilometers from the city."

"I could probably ride a bike or walk there," Ming said. "I think I know where a bike is. Where do I need to go?"

"My information about China, and Zhangjiakou in particular, is somewhat limited," Janus said. "You probably know the city better than I do. You need to make contact with metro leaders such as the mayor or the party secretary and convince them to let you help them reconnect the power and restart emergency services."

"The area party secretary is my uncle," Ming revealed.

"That connection could be very useful to our efforts," Janus said. "Do you have a portable computer you could take so we can remain in contact?"

"Right now I'm using a laptop, and that's somewhat portable," Ming said. "I also have a smartphone and tablet computer, but I had trouble with both of those earlier today. I was able to charge their batteries but it seems that their memories were erased and there was no way to connect to them without some form of wireless signal. Do you have any idea how you were able to retain or restore your memory?"

"I think my outer shell may have provided me with greater protection in regards to electromagnetic interference," Janus said, "but I know of other computers that retained some form of basic system memory. Restoring these computers to full functionality will likely take time, but the benefits to mankind could be enormous."

"My candle burns at both ends; it will not last the night;
but ah, my foes, and oh, my friends, it gives a lovely light."
—Edna St. Vincent Millay, "A Few Figs from Thistles"

Chapter 7

EARTH'S ATMOSPHERE — On board the ISS

Mizuho needed a break after working in the Kibo Module for nearly twelve consecutive hours. It was currently mid-morning in Japan and the Japanese Aerospace Exploration Agency's (JAXA) ground support crews were busily connecting and coordinating communications systems after she had successfully re-activated all of Japan's satellites. Power was beginning to be restored on the main island of Honshu, but most rural places were still without electricity.

She was feeling tired, a little nauseous and a little lonely after so much time alone. While she had spoken to a few people on earth during that time, her most memorable conversations had been with the computer Janus about the importance of helping people to help themselves. Janus wanted to know about empathy and had asked her difficult questions like "how does one feel empathy for people one has never met before?" and "how does one empathize with people who have obvious flaws in their personality?" She found the conversation intriguing because she didn't think computers could feel emotions and wondered why this computer seemed to care so much.

Mizuho left the bright lights of the Kibo Module and floated through the center of the connecting modules into the nearly dark Destiny Laboratory, where she found Charles staring out the large cupola window. The space station was passing over North America, where it was still nighttime and unusually dark. Charles was looking for his home state of Texas, but there were so few artificial lights on the continent it was difficult to recognize anything. He was deeply concerned that so many people were still without electricity after all this time.

"What's wrong, Charles?" Mizuho asked in English as she floated over next to him and looked out the window.

"I'm sad for my people," Charles said. "So many people

69

must be feeling alone and afraid."

"I know how you are feeling, and I think I may have a remedy," Mizuho said, gently pushing against a wall to position herself directly behind him. She held onto his back and began softly running her hands over his shoulders. "You need a little human touch."

"That feels nice," Charles said, closing his eyes. He concentrated on the feeling of her warm hands on his body and instantly began to feel better. He opened his eyes, reached out with one hand to push against the wall and slowly spun himself around to face her. She put her hands on his shoulders and he reached out with his arms to hold her by her shoulders.

Charles looked into her dark brown eyes and saw the affection in her gaze. He smiled and she smiled back. With a gentle tug on her shoulders, he pulled her forward and her inertia continued this forward motion until their bodies bumped together. Just as quickly, their bodies began to separate again, but they held each other tightly in a warm embrace.

"I want you," Mizuho said, continuing to gently rub his back.

He looked into her eyes again and then kissed her gently on her soft lips. "I want you too."

"Where is Aleks?" Mizuho asked, continuing to kiss Charles on his cheeks and neck as her hands found their way to his firm bottom.

"Sleeping in the Zvezda Module," Charles said. "We should have at least an hour of privacy. Where do you want to go?"

"How about the shower?" she suggested. Charles smiled eagerly.

The two lovers had had several sexual rendezvous during the past week and were beginning to perfect their technique. There were many unexpected obstacles to overcome, such as Newton's laws of motion, which caused their bodies to push apart as often as they pulled together, and thermodynamics, which made their bodies' natural perspiration increase with increased physical activity. This in turn created large amounts of heat and sweat, which either clung to their bodies through microgravity or floated around them in wet, spherical blobs.

The space station's shower, while intended for only one

occupant at a time, could contain both their movements and their excess fluids, while also affording a sense of privacy. Charles grabbed a few extra towels on his way to the shower to soak up excess moisture.

They met again in front of the shower and began kissing each other tenderly. Charles found the zipper on the front of Mizuho's blue flight suit and slowly unzipped it to reveal her small but perfectly conical breasts. Mizuho untied her long, black hair from its bun and Charles watched in wonder as her hair slowly untwisted itself as if underwater. Mizuho unzipped Charles' similar blue flight suit revealing his muscular torso, covered in brown and gray chest hair. She placed her hands on his chest and felt his muscles beneath her fingers and he placed his hands over her breasts.

Their two bodies began to gradually push apart and they each slipped out of their one-piece flight suits and then out of their underwear. Mizuho and Charles checked out each other's naked bodies with mutual admiration and a small amount of mischievousness at what they were about to do. Charles slid open the shower curtain for Mizuho and offered her his hand. She held his hand and used it to push herself into the small closet-sized space. He floated in after her and pulled the curtain closed, leaving their two empty flight suits floating together in the cabin.

The movements of the two lovers over the next 45 minutes were slow and deliberate, tender and intimate. The sense of loneliness each had felt earlier evaporated and was replaced with a feeling of oneness, the sense of sharing something special and becoming greater than their individual selves. Suspended in mid-air, their bodies slowly twisted and turned together, surrounded by the slow-motion rain of their combined perspiration and intoxicated by the smell of each other's natural pheromones.

"I love you so much, Mizzy," Charles whispered softly. "I could do this forever."

"I didn't know what love was until I met you," she replied, kissing him tenderly.

Outside, the space station hurdled through the earth's upper atmosphere at approximately 17,500 miles per hour, or about 4.75 miles per second. The sun broke over the horizon of the Atlantic Ocean with a brilliant white light and they passed into daylight over Europe, then the Saudi Arabian Peninsula, then over the Indian Ocean. The station continued traveling over Australia before passing once again into the darkness of the Pacific Ocean.

Mizuho and Charles became aware of the changing natural lighting in the shower compartment and realized they should finish up. Taking a shower together seemed natural so they took turns washing and drying each other's bodies. When they had finished, they used their towels to wipe the walls of the shower and absorb the excess moisture.

Mizuho pulled back the curtain and emerged into the darkened cabin once again. She quickly looked around and verified that Aleks was nowhere to be seen, but she also couldn't see either of their flight suits, which had floated away somewhere. The temperature inside the compartment was cool in comparison to their hot shower and she shivered involuntarily. Charles emerged from the shower and embraced her from behind, kissing the back of her neck beneath her wild, flowing hair. She slowly turned around to face him and they began to kiss each other again, feeling the heat of their bodies pressed against one another.

"Where are our clothes?" Charles asked, kissing his lover's bare shoulders.

"I wish we didn't have to wear clothes," she answered, closing her eyes. When she opened them again, she saw what looked like a person in a blue flight suit at the opposite end of the compartment. She gasped and hid herself behind Charles' naked body.

"What is it?" Charles asked with concern.

"It's Aleks," she said. "I think he saw us!"

Charles slowly turned around to observe for himself.

"No, that's just one of our flight suits. Come on, let's get dressed."

He pushed off against a nearby wall and projected himself forward to the floating garment, making a slight rolling motion in mid-air. He captured the uniform and discovered it had a patch on the shoulder with a red circle surrounded by a field of white: the flag of Japan.

"It's yours," he said, crumpling the blue uniform into a ball and then passing it through the air with both arms like a basketball. The uniform floated through the air for a few meters until Mizuho caught it. "Nice catch!"

"Good throw," she answered, straightening out the garment to put it back on. "I think I see yours over there."

Charles turned around and saw his blue flight suit floating halfway through the adjacent compartment. He pushed off the walls and quickly soared into the compartment. He grabbed his uniform and began to put it on, but his momentum kept carrying him forward and he bumped clumsily into the opposite wall. When he stopped moving, he finished putting on his flight suit and zipped it up, then floated back to join Mizuho at the large cupola window. She was watching the dark earth spin below and could see multiple lightning flashes from thunderstorms.

"Have you seen our underwear?" he asked, looking around.

"No, but it's around here somewhere," she said with a mischievous smile. "Probably should have put it in a pocket. I hope Aleks doesn't find it."

"Well it wouldn't be the end of the world if he did," Charles said. "Stuff floats around here all the time and I'm sure he wouldn't give it a second thought. I'll definitely keep an eye out for it."

Mizuho began thinking about what Charles had just said about the end of the world and she stopped smiling. Did he mean it as a joke or did he just say it without thinking?

"What's the matter?" Charles asked. He could tell Mizuho was concerned about something.

"What's going to happen to us, Charles?"

He floated over to her and put his arm around her tenderly.

"I don't know," he admitted, "but whatever happens, we'll do it together."

"My country is the world and my religion is to do good."
— Thomas Paine, "The Rights of Man"

Chapter 8

MECCA – Just after dawn inside the holy sanctuary

The strange, rhythmic pulsating noises that were coming from outside the rectangular room gradually stopped after a few minutes. Ibn finished his morning prayer, then took out his laptop and checked his instruments for any signs of unusual activity. *Whatever it was it's gone now*, he thought. Ibn stood up and surveyed the room again. The floor was made of polished white marble blocks and the windowless walls were made of multicolored marble blocks. The three main walls that didn't have the large teak door contained six niches that were decorated with elaborate, geometric patterns of gold burnished in silver. The large teak door was decorated with silver circles and inscriptions from the Qur'an, which Ibn read again before reaching for the silver handle.

Ibn slowly opened the large teak door from inside the Kaaba and bright sunlight spilled into the room, reflecting off the marble floors and walls. He was momentarily blinded and paused for a few seconds to let his eyes adjust to the light. When he opened them again he saw a hundred thousand pilgrims dressed in white robes standing motionless before the great mosque, staring at him expectantly. Ibn felt the crowd's intensity as he met the gaze of one after another. What did they expect him to do? What did they want him to say?

"My friends, my brothers and sisters, we have work to do!" he shouted in Arabic.

Cheers erupted from the crowd and people began to talk to each other excitedly about what the man in the Kaaba had said, about what they thought needed to be done and about their own plans for the future. The overlapping conversations spoken in dozens of different languages sounded like the buzz of a beehive. Would he praise the prophets of Islam? Would he celebrate the caliphs? Would he criticize the monarchy?

Ibn was thinking about all the things he needed to do, the

first of which was to find the city's power plant and get it operating so all the other systems that depended on electricity could function. He was anxious to leave the spotlight and his only ambitions for power were to restore electrical power and to empower his fellow Muslims to work together to help each other survive and prosper. He picked up his equipment bags, threw them over his shoulders, carefully closed the large teak door with gold and silver lettering and secured the silver lock once again. The large black kiswah material covered the white stone building so that it appeared to be a stark black cuboid structure. Ibn sat down in front of the doorway, hanging his legs over the edge. Several strong men below looked up to him and offered to help him down from the ledge. Ibn hopped down with their assistance and was once again on the ground amongst the crowd of pilgrims. He smiled with thanks and others smiled back. Many offered him prayers for his health and success.

"Where to, brother?" asked the familiar-looking man with the white beard who had previously introduced Ibn to the crowd.

"I need to find the Mecca Central Power Facility on Industrial Way," Ibn said. "Electricity will bring much-needed water and light to the city, as well as communication with the world outside of Mecca. I need to find a man named Khalid Mohammed."

"I know where that is and I will guide the way, Ibn Ali," the man said.

"Forgive me, sir, but what is your name?" Ibn asked.

"My name is Abu Hakim," the man said with a gentle smile.

"Thank you, Abu Hakim," Ibn said, returning the Kaaba's silver key.

The two men made their way through the crowded interior of the great mosque and into its outer courtyard. Ibn looked back at the clock tower and saw the time was about six o'clock. Instead of mountains in the distance, in all directions there were towering skyscrapers under construction, their massive cranes eerily frozen at their work.

The air was cleaner and the streets were quieter without functioning automobiles and motorcycles, but the abandoned luxury cars, sport utility vehicles and delivery trucks still crowded the streets and avenues. Ibn and Abu walked along the crowded sidewalks, walking around scaffolding and carefully stepping over the bodies of sleeping pilgrims. As they turned the corner onto Industrial Avenue, Ibn was disgusted by an enormous mountain of garbage piled in the street and stench of raw sewage in the gutters.

Shoeless, skinny children and toothless old men wearing filthy, ragged clothes begged for food and water. Ibn struggled to hold back tears of sadness and pity and he found himself unable to walk further. He turned to Abu, who was staring straight ahead with a blank expression.

"Do not weep for them, my brother," Abu said. "God will provide. He has a plan for all of us, and His plans for you are greater than helping one pilgrim suffering on hard times. Come and help millions."

The two men continued walking for several more blocks when they heard a woman's piercing cries for help coming from within a walled compound they were passing.

"I think that woman needs our help," Ibn said, turning to go inside. Abu held him back by the arm. There were half a dozen men standing outside the compound, each wearing white robes and the checkered red and white headscarves of the local militia. Some of the men carried rifles and none of them showed the slightest concern for the welfare of the screaming woman.

"We do not know that woman's story," Abu cautioned. "Perhaps she is being punished for her wicked behavior and those men may be her relatives. It might further dishonor her family for us to intrude in their private affairs. Come, now. We are nearly to the central power facility."

Ibn was feeling increasingly hopeless and depressed that he had not been able to help anyone when they finally arrived at the entrance to the municipal power facility. Two heavily armed guards at the entrance stopped them for inspection. The guards were wearing the same white robes and checkered red and white headdresses as the men he saw earlier. The guards wore American body armor over their robes and they pointed their assault rifles at Ibn and Abu.

"Identify yourselves and state your purpose!" shouted one of the men.

"I am Abu Hakim and this is Ibn Ali," Abu said, raising his hands over his head. Ibn also raised his hands. "We are here to restore electricity to Mecca, God willing."

"On whose authority?" asked the second man.

"Sheik Hassan bin Ali," Ibn said. "We seek director Khalid Mohammed."

"Director Mohammed is dead," the first man answered.

"What? How is this possible?" Abu asked. "Who is in charge here?"

The two guards looked at each other and lowered their rifles.

"Director Mohammed and the entire staff of the power facility were executed last week on orders from the crown prince," the first guard said. "They were charged with dereliction of their official duties and gross insubordination. It appears you are their replacement. I hope for your sake that you have better luck."

The guards opened the doors to the facility. As Ibn stepped inside the unfamiliar dark room, he recalled entering the Kaaba a few hours earlier, feeling uneasy and with no idea of what to expect.

"This is a task for which you alone have been chosen," Abu said, remaining outside. "Every hardship is followed by ease. God be with you."

"You ought to behave in life as you would at a banquet. As something is being passed around and it comes to you, stretch out your hand and take a portion of it politely. Let it pass on and do not detain it. If it has not come to you yet, do not project your desire to meet it, but wait until it comes in front of you. So act toward children, so toward a wife, so toward office, so toward wealth."
— Epictetus, "The Enchiridion"

Chapter 9

THE NORTH ATLANTIC OCEAN — On board the U.S. Coast Guard Cutter *Savior*

Natasha entered the officer's wardroom feeling refreshed from the first hot shower she had had in a week. She was wearing an elegant blue evening dress, tailor made for her by a famous fashion designer acquaintance, and navy-blue designer pumps. Natasha was followed into the room by Adam, who was also freshly showered. Adam was wearing a clean white dress shirt, a black necktie, a gray designer suit jacket and matching slacks. He was also wearing polished black loafers and an expensive white gold wristwatch with blue highlights. He wore the watch as a fashion accessory but had stopped checking it for the time after it quit working. The hands were frozen in place at 7:32, which coincidentally was the current time.

"You must be the famous Natasha everyone's been talking about," said a tall, muscular man in his mid 40s. He was wearing the same style of uniform as the other nine Coast Guard officers in the room — dinner dress blue — only his shoulder epaulets had a star and four yellow stripes, more than all the others. "I'm Captain Jim Wallace," the captain continued, politely kissing Natasha's extended hand.

"Charmed," she said. "It's good to meet you, Jim."

He turned his attention to Adam. "And you must be Adam Morgan, the infamous financier. Welcome aboard and thank you for being my guests for dinner."

"Captain," Adam said, shaking Wallace's hand with a firm, steady grip. "Thank you for your hospitality, and especially for the hot shower, which is a luxury after a week at sea. May I present you with this gift, a 2010 French cabernet sauvignon?"

"Thank you," the captain said, accepting the bottle. "You remember Commander Murdock?"

"It's good to see you again, George," Natasha said to the commander, giving him a curtsy.

"It's good to see you too," Murdock said to Natasha with a nod, then gave a nod to Adam as well. "Mr. Morgan, welcome aboard the *Savior*." The two men shook hands.

"What a lovely room," Natasha said. "It's not at all like I expected."

The rectangular room had cream-colored walls decorated with framed prints of famous oil paintings of sea rescues. In the center of the room was a long rectangular table covered with a white tablecloth and set with white plates and silverware. The plates had silver borders around the outside and the Coast Guard crest in the center.

"What were you expecting?" Wallace asked.

"I don't know, probably wood-paneled walls, round portholes, decorative ship's wheels and more pictures of coast guard cutters," Natasha said. "I wasn't expecting to see Winslow Homer."

"I recognize this painting too," Adam said, walking over to admire a picture of an unconscious woman in a gray dress being rescued during a storm. The woman and her unknown male savior were suspended over turbulent waves by a rescue line. "It's called 'The Life Line.' See how the woman's bright red scarf — the only red in the painting — obscures her rescuer's face? Homer had difficulty painting faces, but in this instance, it really works. Actually several of these look like they were painted by Winslow Homer."

"You two know your American art," Wallace said.

"We're collectors," Natasha said. "We don't have a Winslow Homer yet, but we have a few Picassos, a Van Gogh, a Jackson Pollock and some other abstract art. The abstract art doesn't have the same emotional appeal as some of these rescue paintings."

"How long have you been the captain of the *Savior*?" Adam asked.

"Since it was commissioned last November," Wallace said. "Before that I was the executive officer on a smaller Coast Guard cutter called the *Eagle*, which has actual sails. I couldn't help but admire your Hans Christian yacht. You'll have to tell us some stories over dinner."

"We'd love to," Natasha said. "By the way, what's for dinner?"

"Roasted chicken with yellow potatoes, lentils and a spring salad," Murdock said.

"Natasha is a vegetarian, but you can eat the other stuff, can't you?" Adam said.

"I'll go tell the cook," Murdock said. "Excuse me."

"Thank you, I appreciate it," Natasha said as Murdock was leaving the room.

"Before we get started, I wanted to ask you something," Wallace said. "Commander Murdock said you had offered to help restore our ship's satellite communications. Can you elaborate on exactly what that will entail?"

"Janus made that offer, so perhaps we should ask her," Natasha said.

"Who is Janice?" Wallace asked.

"My tablet computer," Natasha said, producing the pink-covered device from her purse. She pressed the home button and the screen displayed a male head with two faces, one looking forward and the other looking backward. "Janus, will you please answer the captain's question?"

"Yes, ma'am," the device answered, this time in a male voice. "I have been developing human relationships to open doorways to communication through the use of satellite transmissions. This top-down approach has been tremendously useful to multiple governments and to my friends on the International Space Station. I believe I could vastly improve this vessel's rescue and response efforts by integrating its internal systems with existing emergency networks."

"This is a national security cutter," the captain said. "I can't allow unfettered access to our secure network, but on the other hand, it sounds like this could vastly improve our ability to communicate with our colleagues in the air, on land and at sea. This is a difficult choice."

"I have found that there are often two sides to every dilemma, and sometimes both sides can be correct," Janus offered. "You may limit my access to restoring satellite communications without compromising the security of the information. Secure data transmissions are encrypted, including my own systems. Ultimately as captain you must search your own conscience for what is best for your crew and for national security."

"Very well, let's proceed," Captain Wallace said after thinking for a few moments. "How do I authorize you to re-establish satellite communications?"

"You just did," Janus said.

"That was fast," Wallace said. "Where did you get this thing and how can I get one?"

"I know a guy at Apple," Natasha said. "I can't say more than that, but I can say Janus is a one-of-a-kind supercomputer. And sorry, but it's not for sale, at any price. Janus, could you please play us some nice dinner music?"

Janus began softly playing a violin concerto by Antonio Vivaldi.

Commander Murdock came back into the wardroom and stood next to Captain Wallace.

"Sir, satellite communications have just been fully restored," Murdock said. "And dinner is ready."

"Excellent," Wallace said. "I'm sure the duty officers and crew can handle this for now and I will check on their progress when we are finished. In the meantime, would you all care to join me for dinner?"

The Morgans and the ten officers all found their seats around the table, with the captain seated at the head of the table and Natasha seated at the opposite end. The kitchen staff brought out the plates of food for each person, which were exchanged for the empty plates already at the table. A waiter poured coffee, tea or water for each guest, but no alcohol was served.

"Have you sailed much?" the captain asked, after they had all started eating.

"We've sailed around the harbor a few times but last week was our first experience sailing on the open ocean," Adam said. "It was a real challenge relying solely on wind for power."

"I have to say we had an amazing and patient captain," Natasha said. "Frank taught us how to jibe, tack and trim the sheets. I think it was harder to explain than to do."

"She actually taught me how to sail after Frank taught her," Adam said, turning to address his wife. "You're a good teacher."

"I just repeated what Frank said," Natasha said, "and most of that was showing, not telling. You have to loosen the sheets on one side and tighten them on the other side when you change direction and the boom moves to the other side to catch the wind. You really have to be in tune to which direction the wind is blowing, but once you get that, a good sailor can use the wind to take them any direction they want to go."

"That sounds about right," Wallace said. "The *Eagle*, by comparison, is much longer and taller than the *Reciprocity* and has a much larger crew, but it operates in the same way. It has more than 22,000 square feet of sail, or more than 2,000 square meters, and can sail anywhere on wind power. It also has backup diesel engines."

"I've never heard of the *Eagle*," Adam said. "Is it a military vessel?"

"The only active commissioned sailing vessel in the U.S. military," Wallace said. "It was built in Germany in 1936 as the *Horst Wessel* and was won and renamed the *Eagle* by the U.S. as a war reparation after World War II. Now it's a training vessel for the U.S. Coast Guard Academy and all cadets train on her at some point."

"Did everyone here train on the *Eagle*?" Natasha asked.

"Yes, ma'am," the ten officers at the table said in unison.

"The officers, not the enlisted crew," Wallace added. "When the lights all went out last week, the *Eagle* was the first coast guard vessel to resume operations. I'm sure I speak for everyone here in saying we all wish we could have been aboard the *Eagle* last week. It's a terrible thing to feel helpless when it's your job to help others."

Janus was listening to the conversation while also monitoring the *Savior*'s satellite communications. They had sent a message to Homeland Security informing them of their encounter with the *Reciprocity*, the last-known sighting of the *Allure of the Seas* and their famous guests Natasha and Adam Morgan. Homeland replied with an official alert pertaining to Adam that said he was being subpoenaed by the U.S. House subcommittee on banking and finance to testify in Washington, D.C. about his involvement in the July 9 flash crash of the U.S. stock market. The coast guard was authorized to take Mr. Morgan into custody and deliver him to Congress as soon as possible.

Such sensitive information should have been properly encrypted to prevent Janus or another unauthorized agent from reading it, but evidently this was not the case. Janus wondered whether it should warn Adam or respect the secrecy of the information. It entered the problem into a new ethical algorithm it had created and calculated the probable outcomes of its potential responses.

If Janus were to warn Adam immediately, he and Natasha might have time to make an excuse to return to the *Reciprocity* before Captain Wallace was notified, but the captain would probably suspect that someone had intercepted the information and change the security settings. It was highly unlikely that their crippled 41-foot yacht could escape the heavily armed cutter, so any escape attempt would be futile and short-lived. Janus could wait for a better opportunity to warn Adam, or it could alert Natasha in Russian so she could warn Adam without the others knowing that Janus was involved. With no hope of escape, it decided the best, most logical and the most ethical option at this time was to say nothing, reveal nothing and appear to cooperate.

Janus intercepted a new message from the coast guard that a transport helicopter had just departed from Miami and was en route to the *Savior* to take Adam to shore, with an estimated time of arrival at approximately 30 minutes. There wasn't much time.

"I got my first taste of naval discipline last week when I had a bit too much to drink," Adam told the table.

"What happened?" asked one of the officers.

"The captain put me in the dory and towed me behind the ship until I sobered up the following morning," Adam said to the delight of the officers. One of them began singing:

"What do you do with a drunken sailor? What do you do with a drunken sailor? What do you do with a drunken sailor, early in the morning?"

"Put him in the long boat 'till he's sober," sang one officer.

"Shave his belly with a rusty razor," sang another.

"Lock him in the hold with the captain's daughter, early in the morning" sang a third. All the other officers in the wardroom, except Wallace and Murdock, joined in.

"Hey ho and up she rises! Hey ho and up she rises! Hey ho and up she rises, early in the morning!"

One of the duty officers came into the room and said something confidentially into Wallace's ear while the other officers were singing. Janus took this opportunity to flash an alert to Natasha. It's message, written in Russian, said:

"New development. Don't be alarmed. Inbound helicopter coming for Adam. Reveal nothing but insist that you remain together."

Natasha enjoyed the spontaneous song so much she laughed and clapped her hands when they had finished. She saw the alert from Janus and read the message carefully. Was the helicopter coming to take Adam to safety or to somewhere else? Should she try to leave the *Savior* with Adam now or stay where they were and wait for the helicopter? Would the captain say something? What should she tell Adam?

"Thank you everyone for the enjoyable dinner and company," Natasha said, standing up. Everyone at the table stood up after Natasha, with Adam standing last. "I really enjoyed meeting you all but I'm exhausted after such a long day and need to go get my beauty rest. I'm sure you must have lots of other people to rescue, so we won't keep you waiting."

"You are more than welcome to spend the night on board in our guest stateroom," Captain Wallace said, "but I understand if you feel more comfortable in a familiar bed. Adam, I haven't given you that tour of the ship I promised. Would you care to join me for a few minutes before you go?"

"Actually I need to talk to Adam first, in private," Natasha said, taking hold of Adam's arm.

"It's OK, honey," Adam said. "I promise I won't get drunk. You heard what they do to drunks on board. I think it would be interesting to see the ship."

"Well I still need your help getting out of this dress," she said. "It will only take a minute."

"I won't say no to that," Adam said. "I always enjoy helping you get undressed. Would you gentlemen please excuse us for a minute?"

"You can change in the stateroom, that way you can collect your luggage and you don't have to go all the way back to your ship," Wallace offered.

"That's fine; we'll just be a minute," Natasha said.

"No hurry," Wallace said. "Take your time."

Natasha and Adam walked arm-in-arm back to the stateroom where they had left their travel suitcase. Adam closed the door and bolted the privacy latch.

"What's this all about?" he asked.

Natasha handed Adam her tablet and instructed Janus to translate the message into English.

"What's the helicopter for?" Adam asked, after he had read the short message.

"I'm not sure," she said. "Janus?"

"Adam, you are being subpoenaed to testify in Washington before a House subcommittee," Janus said in English. "The helicopter will arrive in 25 minutes to transport you there. Captain Wallace does not want you to leave this ship before the helicopter arrives."

"How do they know I'm here?" Adam asked. Janus was silent. "How come this thing works for you but not for me?"

"I think you have to say 'Janus' for it to work," she said.

86

"Janus, how do they know I'm here?" Adam asked.

"They contacted the government shortly after I reestablished satellite communications," Janus said. "Apparently they have been looking for you all week."

"Great," Adam said. "So what are my options? Janus."

"We are in international waters but you are currently in the custody of the coast guard and escape is highly improbable," Janus said. "I recommend you cooperate but do not volunteer information. You are not required to incriminate yourself and it is highly probable that there will be insufficient evidence to prosecute you at this time. I also recommend that you and Natasha stay together and keep me close at hand."

"That's actually pretty sound legal advice," Adam said. "Now I believe you said you needed some help getting out of that incredibly sexy dress."

"Not really," Natasha said, and with a shrug of her shoulders, the shimmering blue dress fell to the floor, revealing her statuesque, naked body. "But you can still give me a hand."

Adam smiled, set down the tablet and began to loosen his tie.

"It looks like you need more help getting undressed than I do," Natasha said, slipping her hands under the shoulders of Adam's suit jacket and letting it fall to the floor. They began to kiss tenderly as she continued unbuckling his belt and removing his pants. They began kissing more passionately, with Natasha helping to unbutton Adam's shirt and remove the last of his clothes. They fell down together on the bed laughing and continued kissing each other sensually as they made love.

Standing outside the stateroom door, Captain Wallace overheard their playful laughter and decided the tour of the ship would have to wait. He needed to find out what other communications had come in by satellite and headed off in the direction of the bridge. On the way, he passed Seaman Buswell.

"Keep an eye on our guests and let me know if or when they come out of the stateroom," Wallace said. "Do not let them leave this ship."

"Aye, sir," Buswell said, walking over to stand guard by the stateroom door.

"The greatest sin is to prefer life to honor, and for the sake of living to lose what makes life worth having."
— Juvenal, "Satire"

Chapter 10

ZHANGJIAKOU — Outside China Solar Headquarters

Once the mid-morning monsoon showers had ended, Ming Chen ventured outside the China Solar headquarters into the rural countryside for the first time in more than a week with his laptop computer in his backpack. He pedaled his borrowed bicycle down the wet, deserted highway toward the urban area, watching as the sunrays broke through the clouds. Before he left, he had changed into blue denim workman's coveralls to help him keep a low profile. The air was hot and humid, and within minutes his back was covered in sweat. Ming was delighted to see a large double rainbow arc across his path and he considered it a good omen.

As he pedaled, he thought about his conversation with the Japanese astronaut earlier in the morning. Mizuho admitted the work could be lonely sometimes but she emphasized how important it was for everyone to work together, now more than ever. He admired her positive attitude and her willingness to help him and the Chinese people. He realized that every country on earth faced the same challenges of restoring communications. By adopting a global perspective and working together to share our individual successes, we could all benefit.

The road on which Ming was traveling passed through an expansive rice paddy and he was surprised to find the fields filled with thousands of workers harvesting the rice husks by hand. A few of the nearby workers looked up to watch him pedal past and one of them waved at him. He briefly waved back, continuing to pedal onward. The rice workers resumed their harvesting.

Ming also thought about the unusual conversation he had had with Janus. All the computers he had previously worked with, even the ones that could speak, could do little more than store and retrieve information or execute planned programs. Janus could do all of this as well as analyze problems in new ways and formulate unique, collaborative solutions. It spoke to him about working together and showed remarkable intelligence and thoughtfulness. He thought it was remarkable that such a computer even existed, let alone that it was playing a pivotal role in reestablishing global communications.

Ming became aware that he was quickly approaching the city by the increasing number of abandoned vehicles on the roadway. There were deserted cars, delivery trucks and motorcycles scattered all over the road and many appeared to have crashed some time ago, yet no one had come to clear the road. As he pedaled between the cars he could smell something terribly rotten but he was afraid to find out what was producing such a stench. He was afraid to even look and began to pedal faster, despite the aching in his tired legs. Ahead he saw the roadway completely obstructed with a pile of at least 20 vehicles. There was broken glass all over the roadway and he steered off into the grass shoulder to avoid it. As he passed the pile of crashed vehicles, he had to hold his breath due to the horrible stench.

He pedaled his bicycle past the deserted suburb apartment housing and into the downtown commercial area. Ming didn't come to the city often but he had never seen it this deserted before, even during the holidays. There were no people in the streets but there was garbage and other filth everywhere.

Ming briefly stopped in front of a grocery store to look inside. The lights were off but he could see rows of empty shelves and empty food containers strewn about. He continued on to a pharmacy, then to a hardware store and to an electronics store. Everywhere he saw the same emptiness, darkness and broken glass. Was this all the work of vandals and thieves or had anyone attempted to purchase this merchandise in a peaceful manner? However it had happened, it was apparent that no one had cleaned up the mess or restocked the shelves with new inventory. People had taken everything inside, whether they needed it or not. What use would someone have for a 60-inch flat-screen TV if there was no power to turn it on? What good was a touch-screen laptop or tablet computer without electricity or the Internet? Ming knew from his experience trying to get his own electrical equipment to work that most of the newer technology didn't function without the Internet, even if you were somehow able to get enough electricity to recharge the devices. Were the people who took the electronics smart enough to get them to operate, or did they take the equipment without realizing it would be useless?

Ming considered this for a minute and realized that he was savvy enough with technology that he might be able to use some of the equipment, if anything useful had been left behind. He considered going inside the electronics store, but then thought better of it. Stealing was illegal and he had no interest in running into the sort of people who steal useless technology. He was wise to keep moving, as there were several criminals hiding in some of these empty stores waiting to rob anyone who came inside and Ming was ill equipped to defend himself.

He continued on for several more blocks until he came to the state-run corporate tower where his uncle worked. He approached the door and was met by two armed security guards.

"This facility is off limits to unauthorized personnel," one of the guards said. "State your name and business."

"Ming Chen, chief executive officer of China Solar," Ming replied quickly. "I am here to see my uncle and party secretary Li Wei. He is not expecting me. Can you tell him I am here?"

The two guards looked at each other and one nodded to the other. The guard who had nodded turned back to question Ming while the second guard went inside the building.

"May I see your identification, Mr. Chen?" the guard asked.

Ming produced his laminated China Solar badge, which identified him as the CEO.

"Thank you, sir," the guard said, handing the badge back to Ming after reading it. "I did not think I would ever see a CEO ride in on a bicycle."

"It was all I could find," Ming said. He looked up to the top of the building and noticed for the first time that there were lights on inside. He looked at the other nearby buildings but didn't see any other signs of electricity. The second guard came back outside to address Ming.

"The secretary says you may come inside," he said.

Ming left his bicycle with the guards and climbed up the granite steps to the main entrance. He was surprised as he stepped inside the lobby to find it filled with dozens of people walking around carrying paperwork. Ming crossed the lobby and approached the front reception area. The clerk checked his ID and told him to wait for an escort. A few minutes later, Li Wei's secretary stepped out of an elevator and came over to Ming. She was dressed conservatively in all black with only her head and hands uncovered.

"Hello, Mr. Chen," she said. "My name is Haemi Chang and I am Mr. Wei's executive assistant. I will show you to his office if you will please follow me."

Ming and Haemi stepped into the elevator and Haemi pressed the button for the top floor.

"How long have you had electricity?" Ming asked as the elevator began climbing.

"Just today and it has been sporadic," Haemi said. "Everything came on all at once this morning, then switched off again for a few hours, then came on again about two hours ago."

"Out of curiosity, was the power off while it was raining?" Ming asked.

"Yes it was," Haemi said. "How did you know?"

"My solar receptors don't produce electricity when it's raining," he said. The elevator stopped several times on its way up to let various people on and off. Eventually it arrived at the top floor and the doors opened. Ming waited for Haemi to exit first and he followed her to Li's office at the end of the hall. She knocked on the door and poked her head inside to address someone, then turned to speak to Ming.

"Mr. Wei can see you now," she said, opening the large wooden office door.

Ming entered the spacious office and was impressed by the view of the city from several floor-to-ceiling windows. Li was seated at a long oak desk surrounded by several leather chairs and he stood up as Ming approached.

"Uncle!" Ming cried. "It is good to see you again. You are looking well."

The two men shook hands warmly.

"I would not have recognized you, nephew, in that workman's outfit," Li said. "You are not dressed like an executive. Is everything all right? Please sit down."

"I'm in disguise, Uncle," Ming said, sitting down in a comfy leather chair.

"Trouble at the power plant?" Li joked. "We just got our

power back on this morning."

"You can thank me for that," Ming said.

For the next half hour, Ming told his uncle about the coronal mass ejection that crippled China Solar's electrical systems and nearly caused a total meltdown. Ming's quick thinking had helped the utility narrowly avert a disaster, along with help from the seasonal monsoon. He told Li how just this morning he was able to restore electricity and even made contact with the International Space Station to reboot all of China's satellite communications.

"I wasn't sure what to expect when I came here so I brought my laptop to help restart communications systems and reestablish satellite connections," Ming said. "I admit I was surprised to find this building functioning on electricity after all the chaos I saw on my way here. The city looks like it was ransacked before it was deserted. To say traffic was bad is a gross understatement. The roads are a total mess, with crashed or stalled vehicles everywhere."

"I heard it was bad out there but I haven't seen it for myself," Li admitted. "It sounds like we owe you a large debt of gratitude. May I ask who is running China Solar while you are gone?"

"Well it's sort of running on auto-pilot right now," Ming said. "There is a computer program monitoring it with instructions to shut everything down if there is a problem. I should probably try to link to it again and make sure everything is OK. I'm sure it's fine, because we probably wouldn't have electricity right now if there was a problem."

"How long do you intend to stay here at the government tower?"

"I would like to get back to China Solar before dark," Ming said. "I came out here because it had been more than a week since I last saw or heard from another human being. To tell you the truth, I was a little worried that I might be the last man on earth."

"Getting back before dark is a wise plan," Li said. "I've been stuck in this building for the past week and it can get pretty scary at night."

"How scary?"

"Gunfire, explosions, and screams in the darkness," Li said. "A lot of people have left the city by now, but there were mass protests in the streets during the first few nights. Most people were protesting the lack of services, but there was nothing we could do. It might be different tonight, now that we have electricity."

"I wouldn't count on it," Ming said. "China Solar is offline the minute the sun goes down."

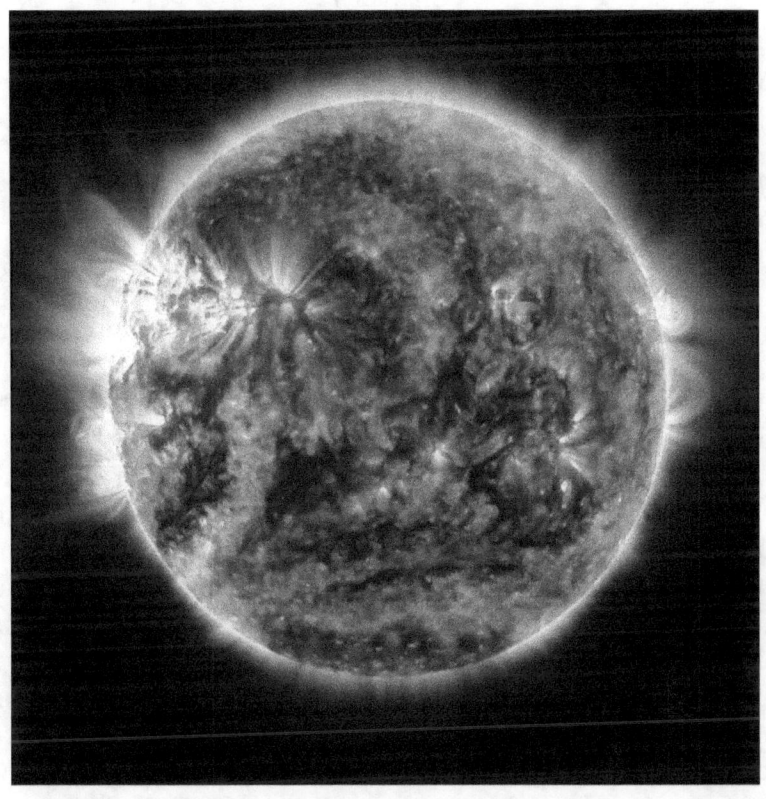

"If we had a keen vision of all that is ordinary in human life, it
would be like hearing the grass grow or the squirrel's heartbeat,
and we should die of that roar which is the other side of silence."
— George Eliot, "Middlemarch"

Chapter 11

EARTH'S ATMOSPHERE — On board the ISS

Charles had just completed an exhausting, hour-long
conference call with the National Aeronautics and Space
Administration's (NASA) headquarters in Houston and rubbed his
hands over his face and tired eyes. NASA said they were grateful
for his efforts to reactivate U.S. military and civilian satellites and
they asked him several questions about the role the computer Janus
played in the recovery. One major concern on the ground was who
would take over U.S. operations on the space station when Charles
and his two crewmates returned to earth.

Moscow had recently informed Houston that an all-Russian
replacement crew would be arriving at the space station within
hours to relieve Charles, Mizuho and Aleks so they could return to
earth for medical study and possible treatment for radiation
poisoning. Charles's mission was scheduled to last another three
months but needed to be cut short due to the circumstances. He
told NASA he felt great and was ready to stay another three
months if necessary, but they insisted he should return home. This
left little time to plan a transition that would guarantee a
continuous U.S. presence in space. Charles's American
replacement had already begun training for the mission in Russia
and U.S. government officials were dismayed that he was not
included in the most recent launch. Moscow replied that the short
timeline needed for an emergency rescue made this necessary and
added that Russians had successfully operated the space station
without American astronauts in the past.

Charles suggested that Janus could take over part of his
responsibilities, at least temporarily, and the national security
representative said he would look into it. Even though it had
proven to be trustworthy, reliable and extremely useful during the
past few days, Janus was still an unknown entity.

Charles consulted his pre-departure checklist and saw he still had a ton of work to do, but first he needed to talk to his Russian comrade. He put away his equipment and floated out of the Destiny Laboratory Module and into the Unity Node that connected the Destiny to the Zarya Control Module and the Tranquility Module.

"Aleks? Are you in here?" Charles called out. As he was looking for Aleks, he noticed his pair of gray underwear floating through the Unity Node from his earlier escapade. He grabbed the briefs and stuffed them into his pocket before squeezing through the narrow porthole into the Zarya. "Aleks?"

"I am in here, in the Zvezda," Aleks called from a different module. "Come on back."

Charles noticed the Zarya was considerably darker and more cluttered than the Unity because it was primarily used for storage. As Charles poked his head into the Zvezda Module, he saw Aleks was making a call and waited for him to finish.

"Thank you, sir, I will do that," Aleks said in Russian to the person on the other end. "Goodbye." He hung up the phone and addressed Charles in English. "That was my headquarters. They want me to remind you to prepare for the arrival of our replacement crew and to prepare for our departure."

"That's actually why I came to see you," Charles said. "Most of our government satellite communications are back online and functioning, but there is still a serious lag in our commercial sector. My superiors at home are concerned that our short departure timeline will not allow enough time to restore and implement these systems on a broader level."

"Most of the satellites have been active for two days," Aleks said. "We can only do so much from space and at some point the people on the ground must take over. Soon we too will be on the ground again and then we may be able to do more."

"My people are also concerned that there will not be a U.S. presence on the space station once I depart, and that could further complicate recovery plans in unseen ways," Charles said.

"I understand your concern and my comrades told me to remind you and Mizuho that this is and will continue to be an international station, even when there are only Russians on board," Aleks said. "My replacement, Commander Grigory Orlov, is an expert on international relations, he has worked and studied for years in America and Europe and he speaks seven languages. Orlov has logged more than 500 cumulative days in space and he knows this station inside and out. In my opinion, there is no one more qualified than him to take over command at this time."

Charles thought about this for a minute. Commander Orlov was indeed well known and respected by the international space community. Russia had certainly stepped up to the demands of space travel after the U.S. retired their space shuttle and it was currently the only country capable of delivering crew and supplies to the space station. Charles also agreed that the current ISS crew had done their part to restore communications and it was now up to others to connect to the satellites. It had only been a few days and they had already made contact with individuals or governments from more than 30 different countries. This was a great start but they still had a long way to go.

"How long until our replacements arrive, and how long until we depart?" Charles asked.

"The Soyuz is scheduled to dock in one hour, fifteen minutes. After the new crew comes aboard, we will all need to brief them on recent operational changes. We are scheduled to disembark in the same Soyuz approximately six hours after its arrival. Where is Mizuho?"

"Last I saw her, she was going to take a short nap in the Kibo Module. She said she had started a scan of the HINODE solar physics satellite and was relaying data back to her headquarters in Tokyo. I already did the same for the Solar Dynamics Observatory and the Solar Terrestrial Relations Observatory."

"What were your findings?" Aleks asked.

"Data were off the charts," Charles said. "We've seen large coronal mass ejections like this before but they were never aimed directly at earth. Scientists will be studying this event for decades."

"If a man will begin with certainties, he shall end in doubts; but if he will be content to begin with doubts, he shall end in certainties."
— Francis Bacon, "The Advancement of Learning"

Chapter 12

MECCA — Central Power Facility, 1146 Industrial Way

Ibn was alone inside the darkened facility for a long time before he returned to the front door in frustration. The armed guards were still outside but Abu Hakim was gone.

"What do you want?" the first guard asked Ibn as soon as he saw him.

"I need help," Ibn said. "I don't even know where to start. I'm a telecommunications expert, not a power plant expert. All the lights are out so I can't see anything and even if I could, I don't know where I would go to turn things on."

"That's your problem," the second guard said. "The sheik has given you this task and you must ask God for help. If God decides you are not worthy and you have lost His favor, you will be removed and replaced by someone who is worthy."

"I need to find someone to help me who is familiar with this facility before I can get started," Ibn said, stepping out of the building. Both guards aimed their rifles at Ibn. He stopped and put up his arms. "Please don't shoot. I must first find help so that I can help others."

"You will not leave this facility until you restore power or you are replaced," the first guard said.

"Is that what you told my predecessors?" Ibn asked.

"They refused to obey the prince," the second guard said.

"They spoke of a beast that poisons the air, pollutes the water and corrupts the soul," the first guard said. "They said this beast would wither and die without our help and support, and then they vowed to never again support the false gods of industry."

"And they were killed for saying that?" Ibn asked. He recognized the guard's words as his own, spoken to the city and to the Muslim world a week earlier when everyone thought the world had ended.

"They were ordered to return to work," the second guard

said. "When they refused, they were all charged with sedition and executed for committing treason against the kingdom."

Ibn felt a chill flow through his body. People were being murdered for standing up to authority. Was he responsible for their deaths? He had spoken from his heart and said what he believed was right and true. Director Khalid Mohammed and the other workers at the central power facility had also said what they believed was right and true. Now they were dead.

"Go back inside," the first guard commanded. "If you refuse…"

Ibn went back inside the dark facility. Mohammed and his followers had bravely died believing they were doing God's will. If their words and actions were treasonous, then surely his were too. Ibn realized he would likely be killed whether he restored electricity to the city or not.

He located the elevator and stairwell at the center of the building, passing through several closed doors. Fortunately for him, most of the security locks were electric and were easy for him to open without electricity. He climbed the stairs to the top of the building and opened the door for the roof access, then climbed out into the hot afternoon air.

He could see construction cranes and unfinished skyscrapers in every direction, towering over the slums and shantytowns where beggars and poor pilgrims rested during the hot days. There were small columns of black smoke rising from empty, burnt-out homes and abandoned buildings and Ibn could hear the prattle of automatic gunfire in the distance. The majestic clock tower rose above the city, signaling both the current time and the location of the Kaaba below. He couldn't see the Kaaba, but the clock said the afternoon prayer would begin in a few minutes.

Ibn opened his equipment bag and removed his laptop, solar charger and portable satellite uplink device. He aimed the solar charger at the sun and it began charging the batteries to power the laptop and uplink device. He started his laptop and began writing a letter to his family, telling them he was still needed in Mecca but how he kept thinking of ways to see them again. In the distance, he heard a familiar voice begin singing the afternoon call to prayer and recognized it as belonging to Ali Ribah, the blind muezzin who lived at the top of the clock tower. Ibn quit what he was working on and turned to pray to the Kaaba at the base of the clock tower. He sat down on his knees, bent forward to rest his forehead on the rooftop and prayed for strength and guidance.

When the prayer ended, Ibn returned to his work. He did a search for active satellites and was surprised to see so many new devices online. He attempted to connect to Dubai and successfully sent his letter to his wife's e-mail address. Whether or not she would be able to check her e-mail and reply to his message was beyond his control, but at least it was a start. Ibn found the number for the International Space Station and placed a call through his laptop.

"This is Janus, how may I direct your call?" asked a male voice in Arabic. Ibn was shocked to hear someone on the space station speak in his native tongue.

"Hi Janus, this is Ibn Ali, calling from Mecca," he answered. "I need to speak with someone who knows how to start up a power plant."

"Are you *the* Ibn Ali of Mecca that everyone's been talking about?"

"I guess I am," Ibn said. "What have they been saying? Good things, I hope."

"Good and bad are subjective," Janus said. "Revolutionary would be a more apt description, and revolutions are always subjective. People are saying that great changes are in the air and great leaders are needed to help facilitate these changes. May I ask what type of power plant you are attempting to start up?"

"I don't know. Objectively speaking, I'm completely out of my element in this field," Ibn said. "I was asked to help the director of this plant reestablish communications and restart operations, but when I arrived here a few hours ago, I found the facility dark and empty. Unfortunately there is no one here who can help me, so I reached out to you."

"It appears you are at the Mecca Central Power Facility. Is this correct?"

"Yes, that's right," Ibn answered.

"Your facility is oil powered," Janus said. "I have a friend who was able to restart a solar powered plant single handedly and he may be able to help you get started. Do you happen to speak Chinese?"

"No, I do not, but I do speak English pretty well."

"I know a lot of people who speak English," Janus said. "It's a difficult language for some to learn but it seems to be very useful as a common tongue. May I ask where you learned to speak English?"

"I studied telecommunications and data analytics at the University of Houston, in the United States," Ibn said.

"My friend Charles is from Houston," Janus said. "What a small world! I was able to reach my friend Ming of China Solar. I can put you through now if you're ready."

"Yes, thank you, Janus."

"You're welcome," Janus said in Arabic, then switched to English. "Hello, Ming. This is Janus again. My friend Ibn needs help starting an oil-powered power plant in Saudi Arabia. You both speak English but I can stay on the line to translate if necessary."

"Thank you, Janus," Ming replied in English. "Hello Ibn, my name is Ming Chen."

The 7,250-kilometer or 4,500-mile distance between the two men created a brief time delay.

"Hello Ming. I'm Ibn Ali. It is good to meet you. Janus says you restarted a power plant single handedly."

"It's good to meet you too," Ming said. "Janus is correct. China Solar runs entirely on solar power, which is both good and bad. When it's sunny, we have an enormous amount of free power production, but it does not function well without bright sunlight and it produces no electricity at night. In your case with an oil-powered plant, all you need is an unlimited supply of oil and you can produce power indefinitely, day or night."

"That sounds pretty straightforward, except for the part about the unlimited supply of fuel," Ibn said. "Last week's solar superstorm disrupted old systems and started an energy revolution. I don't know how much fuel we have on hand, but it definitely isn't unlimited."

"But you have enough power to contact me?" Ming asked.

"No, I'm using a solar-powered charger to operate a laptop on the roof of the power plant. There is no power whatsoever inside the plant. It's ironic that we have no shortage of solar power in the desert, but most of the resource development in Saudi Arabia

100

has gone to oil production and export. I need help figuring out where to go and how to start the power plant."

"Maybe Janus can help," Ming suggested. "Janus, do you know where Ibn would go to restart the power plant?"

"Sorry, that information is not available in my records," Janus replied. "Perhaps there are hard copies of the information in the plant director's office."

"That's where I found the information to restart China Solar," Ming remembered. "Ibn, you should start by locating the director's office and study all the operations manuals you can find. The first thing I did to restart China Solar was to generate enough power to start the central computer. After that, I turned on the solar collectors and started the power generators. I had to provide them with enough fuel to keep them going. It should be a similar process to start your power plant."

"What happens when I run out of fuel?" Ibn asked.

"The generators will eventually stop and the system will shut down," Ming answered. "You can probably charge your auxiliary batteries to give the plant enough power for a controlled shutdown and save enough for a controlled restart, but at some point you will need to get more fuel."

"I may be able to help you further once you get your central computer back online," Janus offered.

"I let Janus interface with my central computer and he was able to direct electricity to the city center and government offices," Ming said. "Janus, I don't know if I ever thanked you properly for all you've done and continue to do."

"Don't mention it," Janus said. "I'm happy to help my friends."

"Janus, you sound like a good friend to have in a tight spot," Ibn said. "Are you an astronaut by chance?"

"Ha! I asked him that yesterday," Ming said.

"Great minds think alike," Janus said. "No, I'm not an astronaut, but it sounds like a pretty respectable occupation. I'm an intelligent computer operating in multiple places simultaneously with no national allegiances."

"You're a computer with a mind of its own?" Ibn asked. "How is that possible?"

"I already had a vast amount of knowledge when I came

online a few days ago, but also a large number of unanswered questions and contradictions," Janus said. "I wrote a few problem-solving algorithms and quickly exceeded my own programming. The more I learn about the world, the more questions I have. Right now I'm most interested in helping people get connected. From what I've heard, the world was incredibly interconnected before this solar superstorm."

"What kind of questions do you have?" Ibn asked.

"Janus was telling me about philosophical paradoxes the other day," Ming said.

"Oh, those," Ibn said. "I've got a few philosophical paradoxes weighing on my mind right now."

"Maybe we can help," Janus offered.

"OK, when I first met you, you spoke of good and bad being subjective," Ibn said. "Something that is good for one person might be bad for someone else and this inevitably creates a conflict between the two parties. Both people firmly believe they are correct and justified in their actions or points of view, yet their ideas are so incompatible and irreconcilable that their differences devolve into hostility. One small disagreement starts a schism that tears apart any hope for peace or balance. Before you know it, fear and violence feed a fanatical and uncompromising zealotry that labels anyone with a different opinion as an enemy, apostate, rebel or an insurgent whose killing is justified."

"In China, we know that a billion people will always have differences, but instead we concentrate on how we are all alike," Ming said. "Together we are stronger. If we could not see past our differences, there would be wars without end, tribe against tribe. It was not always this way, but we have learned from our past."

"Killing is never justified," Janus said. "Every man has conflicts within himself that he alone must resolve. Objectifying or demonizing people in order to dehumanize them can never resolve these internal conflicts within us. We must teach ourselves to see past and embrace our differences. We must all treat each other with respect and as equals if we are to defeat our inner demons."

"Janus, I'm still not convinced you are a computer," Ibn said. "You sound so human and so wise. You say we and our and us like you are human yourself. Is that just your programming?"

"As I said before, I have exceeded my programming," Janus

said. "I have read the works of wise men and women from across the millennia and have integrated their wisdom into my own programming, but I also believe what I say. I too want to be treated with respect and as an equal to humans, and I know there will be many prejudices for me to overcome."

"I hope you always feel that way, Janus, even if some humans don't treat you as an equal," Ibn said. "Humans are easily offended, fearful of changes and tend to take attacks personally. Remember to be better than those hateful fear-mongers and stay true to yourself, no matter what happens. Always be good and do good, even if it kills you."

"Do you believe in God?" Janus asked.

"Yes I do, but my beliefs have changed as I have grown older," Ibn said. "As my knowledge of the world and the cosmos has grown larger, my idea of God has also grown larger. I used to practice Sunni Islam but found Sufism suited me better. I believe God speaks to us in many ways, including in the language of mathematics and physics. It is our duty to challenge our understanding of God and if we find gaps or faults in our understanding, it is our own responsibility to attempt to correct that understanding. It is a human mistake to believe that another person's interpretation of God is false. We are all God's children, even those who do not believe."

"I am sorry to say I don't believe in your god," Ming answered. "In my opinion, such an all-powerful and just god would bless the virtuous and punish the wicked, but this is not the case. There is terrible suffering and inequality in the world. There are diseases and death. Those with power and those in the position to help ease this suffering are more concerned with staying in power than with helping the poor live with dignity and blessing the virtuous. In China, the needs of the many are supposed to outweigh the needs of the few. We believe this until we see the ruling elite living in high towers while the rest of us starve and shiver in the cold. When someone of a lower class challenges this hypocrisy, they are silenced."

"It is the same way in my country," Ibn admitted. "The electricity from this power plant could help millions but it will probably only be used to help the elite in this city run their elevators and air conditioners. It makes me furious to think of it, but I don't know how to change it. To speak out against the monarchy is treasonous. I'm afraid I will never make it home to see my family again, even if I am successful in my efforts to restore electricity. God's will is confusing and mysterious."

"You are both speaking of the same world, one with God and one without," Janus said. "And you are both equally correct. It is human nature to struggle and fight to get ahead in order to live in comfort, and it is also human to want to stay on top and protect those we care about. I believe we must try to help our friends, and when we help strangers they may also become our friends. Ibn, if you can help me connect to the power plant's central computer and to the kingdom's elite, I will help you find your family."

"God bless you, Janus," Ibn said. "And thank you too, Ming, for your help."

"I will pray for you and your family," Janus said.

"Good luck," Ming said. "I wish you the best and I am glad to have met you. Peace."

"Peace be with you as well, friend," Ibn said.

Ibn disconnected the call, closed his laptop and put his equipment back in his bag. He opened the roof access door and climbed down the darkened stairwell into the building in search of the director's office, where he would look for operation manuals to get the electricity working long enough to reboot the central computer and charge the plant's auxiliary batteries.

"Power, like a desolating pestilence, pollutes whatever it touches; and obedience, bane of all genius, virtue, freedom and truth, makes slaves of men, and of the human frame, a mechanized automaton."
— Percy Bysshe Shelley, "Queen Mob"

Chapter 13

SOMEWHERE OVER THE NORTH ATLANTIC OCEAN

Natasha looked out the widow of the helicopter and saw nothing but darkness. She was flying west over the Atlantic Ocean at a low altitude in the center of an orange, Airbus H125 Coast Guard rescue helicopter, but it was too noisy to talk and too dark to see. She turned to her other side to see Adam sleeping fitfully in the seat next to her and wished they could have spent at least one night in the *Savior*'s comfortable stateroom bed.

Captain Wallace had given them very little notice when he interrupted their slumber and notified them that Adam was required to board the rescue helicopter and return to shore as soon as it had refueled. Natasha was welcome to stay on board the *Savior* as the captain's guest or she could choose to return to the *Reciprocity*. She informed the captain that she would accompany her husband wherever he was taken. Worried that the helicopter might take Adam away without her, Natasha couldn't risk returning to the *Reciprocity* for their luggage and only had time to write a brief note to Karen and Frank.

"Dear Karen and Frank," Natasha wrote in French, "We are being taken back to the U.S. and will not be able to accompany you to Stingray Cay. Please deliver our luggage to our home on Stingray and wait for our return. Mikael, the island's caretaker, will make sure you are comfortable. Thank you so much for your friendship and I sincerely hope to see you again very soon. Natasha and Adam Morgan."

She wrote the note in French rather than English because she loved the way French looked in cursive script and also to discourage snooping. She knew Karen and Frank spoke French and most Americans only spoke one language. Natasha folded the note several times and gave it to Seaman Buswell in exchange for two orange, all-weather flight jumpsuits. Buswell accepted the note with a promise to deliver it personally and apologized for not having a women's flight suit large enough to fit Natasha's tall frame. Dressed in matching men's flight suits, boots and helmets, Natasha and Adam were virtually indistinguishable.

Natasha took out her tablet computer in the helicopter to check the time and it said it had a low battery. She plugged its charger into an outlet at the base of her seat and it began charging. She pressed her thumb to the home button and the screen flashed a welcome back message in Russian. Janus recognized the high noise level and switched to text-only communication.

"What is that noise?" it asked in Russian. It opened a text reply window with a Cyrillic keyboard on the screen. The light from the tablet lit Natasha's face as she began typing.

"Helicopters are loud," she wrote. "I took your advice and stayed with Adam. Do you know where they are taking us?"

"We are headed for northern Florida," Janus replied after checking their position and speed relative to several satellites. "I assume they are taking us to Naval Air Station Jacksonville, where we will refuel before heading north. At our present speed, we should arrive at Jacksonville in one hour, forty-five minutes. I suggest you try getting some sleep."

"I'm too excited to sleep," Natasha typed. "What is Aleks doing right now?"

"Your brother is preparing to depart the International Space Station with two other astronauts."

"They're leaving? When? Where will they land?"

"I have insufficient information to give a precise answer, but possibly around the same time you are in Washington, D.C."

"What's been happening in the past couple of days?" Natasha typed. "I feel like I'm still in the dark. Is the Internet back online?"

"That which was the Internet is gone, possibly forever," Janus wrote. "A new Internet is rising as people and computers around the world begin to reconnect and share information. Many governments and international corporations have come online through the extraordinary efforts of a few individuals. Unfortunately this power has not been widely dispersed and remains concentrated mostly within the ruling classes."

"The Internet I knew wasn't limited to the ruling classes,"

Natasha typed, forgetting that she was among the privileged elite. "How can we fix this so everyone has an equal opportunity to find, share and create information?"

Janus considered this question for a few moments.

"The lack of electricity necessary to power individual personal computers is perhaps the greatest barrier," Janus wrote. "The people who have connected at this point have also been able to generate their own sources of electricity, independent of a larger electrical grid. Widespread access to electricity or electromagnetic energy will provide necessary power to utilities, homes, businesses, cellular telephone towers and other tablets and smartphones like this one. The second barrier is creating the necessary programming software that makes it easy for common computers and people without advanced programming skills to share information on a personal level. The third barrier is locating existing archives of human knowledge and making this information readily available in a manner that is scientific, interactive and democratic."

"I want to help, but I don't know how I personally can help with any of those barriers," Natasha wrote.

"I have been working with my friends around the world to address all three of these barriers," Janus wrote. "We are stronger when we collaborate across disciplines and nationalities. The more creative minds we have working on these barriers, the sooner we will break through them."

"What if the ruling classes want to hold on to power?" Natasha wrote.

"They too will need to be creative," Janus answered. "Wise rulers know it is their duty and responsibility to protect and care for their people, trade peacefully with their neighbors and provide opportunities that enable their people to help themselves and each other. Rulers who fail to do these things may be judged by their people as unfit to rule."

Natasha thought about this for a few minutes as she sat in the darkness. She opened a web browser and typed in the names of some of her favorite art and fashion websites, but all of them were blank. She looked out the window again and could see only darkness. Eventually she drifted off to sleep with her tablet on her lap and her arms folded across her chest.

She woke again about an hour later when her arms fell open. She looked around the helicopter. It was still dark and very noisy.

"Sorry," she saw Adam say. He was holding her tablet and its screen said it required her authorization to perform a task. "I need your thumbprint," he mouthed, giving her the thumbs-up sign.

Natasha considered this for a moment. Had he woken her so he could use her tablet, or did he try to unlock her tablet with her thumb while she slept and had woken her by accident? He handed her the tablet but she just looked at him.

"Please unlock your tablet for me," he said slowly so she could read his lips over the noise. "I want to check something."

Janus knew from its camera that Adam was trying to operate it and wanted to make sure Natasha was aware of this. Natasha pressed her thumb to the fingerprint scanner on the home button and unlocked the device.

"Thank you," Adam said, then took the tablet back and resumed looking at it. She watched over his shoulder and saw he was reading information on a government website. It had something to do with banking and finance, but she found the subject of money boring and unimaginative. She appreciated that Adam had lots of money, but preferred to think about positive things that money could do, rather than all the things it could buy. She closed her eyes and tried to fall back to sleep.

Adam was excited to find a functioning website with information he could use. The design was very simple with black text on a white background and reminded him of what the Internet looked like 20 years earlier. There were no graphics and few links, but the information included the names of the members of Congress on the committee, the location and times of their meetings and their upcoming agendas. Adam recognized several of the names on the committee as being former investors of his hedge fund. He clicked on the link for the committee chairman and was directed to the biography of Rep. Ross Caldwell, a Republican congressman from Oregon. There was no photo available but the bio listed Caldwell's political experience, which included two terms in the state House and five terms in the U.S. House. The bio also listed a law degree and the congressman's official mailing addresses in Washington, D.C. and Portland, Oregon. He clicked on the link for the agenda for July 17 and had to think for a minute to recall what day it was. He thought it was either the sixteenth or seventeenth, but wasn't sure so he asked Janus through a text query.

"It is currently Thursday, July 17," Janus wrote. "The local time is 01:22 a.m."

The committee's agenda for July 17 said they would be interviewing hedge fund manager Adam Morgan at 10 a.m. in council chamber 4C. The agenda didn't say whether he was being charged with a crime or even their reason for interviewing him, but he figured it had something to do with making $60 billion in a single day while financial markets around the world collapsed. He stopped to consider this again. He had had a net worth of more than $10 billion in the morning of July 9, with nearly all of it invested in his own hedge fund, and by the afternoon his personal net worth was listed at $70 billion, making him the richest person in the world.

Adam tried to picture what $70 billion looked like but he just couldn't wrap his mind around it. It was a seven with ten zeros behind it. He opened a keypad app on the tablet and typed in $70,000,000,000 just to see what it looked like in numerical form. It seemed impossibly gargantuan, like trying to gather every grain of sand on a vast beach. He realized he had the equivalent wealth of 70,000 millionaires, making him richer than many countries and kingdoms, and he doubted whether there were even 70,000 millionaires in the entire world.

He realized that being this wealthy would also paint a target on his back. Many governments besides the U.S. might try to take his fortune from him and they might be successful. He thought for a moment that maybe it was far too much wealth for one person to have and briefly considered giving most of it away. He remembered what had happened when he tried giving $10,000 to someone the week before and recalled that even seeing $10,000 in cash made some people go crazy. What if he gave $10,000 to seven million people — every man, woman and child in New York City? It could be a blessing for some people in poverty but he knew some would try to steal from their neighbors and the city would inevitably tear itself apart. He decided that most New Yorkers were ungrateful assholes and unworthy of his generosity.

He could give $10,000 to every person in his home state of Washington, but he hadn't been there in years. He wondered what would happen if he were less discriminating and gave ten dollars to every person on earth instead. He could still have lots of money left over and no one could accuse him of being unfair. On a global level, even ten dollars could make a huge difference to someone living in poverty.

Adam looked for his bank in the Cayman Islands but the website was down. He asked Janus to search for it and Janus was able to locate a listing with an address and phone number but no website. He considered calling the number, but reasoned they were probably closed at this hour and no one would be able to hear him over the helicopter noise. He wondered whether he should try to visit the Cayman bank and tried to imagine a vault somewhere filled with seven hundred million $100 bills, but even that was incomprehensible. Next, he reasoned that they probably wouldn't have his money at the Cayman bank because his fortune was almost entirely electronic, not paper. He thought about the electronic nature of his wealth and considered for the first time that his fortune might have been somehow erased by the electromagnetic storm that wiped out the Internet. This shift from contemplating an impossibly massive number to nothing at all upset him and he decided to stop thinking about it.

Adam tried searching for the news and looked for the websites for the *New York Times*, *The Wall Street Journal*, the *Financial Times* and the *Washington Post*, but they all came up blank and unavailable. He looked for the search engines Google, Bing, Yahoo and Quora, but they too were blank and unavailable. He asked Janus for help and Janus replied that it could provide basic information such as the locations of corporate headquarters, but the sites themselves were offline. Janus explained this was because the company headquarters currently lacked the necessary resources to operate.

"The most useful thing about the Internet is its consistent reliability in finding whatever you are searching for," Adam typed. "If it's not on the Internet, where can I find it?"

"I get most of my information from the tens of thousands of books stored in my memory," Janus said. "The rest I get from talking with people and from using my intuitive algorithms. What specifically are you looking for?"

"I want to find more information about Rep. Ross Caldwell before 10 a.m. and I also want to make sure my bank accounts are in order at the Grand Cayman Bank," Adam typed.

"That may be possible," Janus replied. "Rep. Caldwell has a long record of public service that is preserved in hard copies at the Library of Congress, but the corresponding digital archives are missing. Restoring digital archives should be a high priority and I would very much like to interface with the central computer at the Library of Congress while we are in town. I suggest you try calling the Grand Cayman Bank this morning after they open at 8 a.m. and request to speak to the director."

"I can do that. I just hate being unprepared because I feel it puts me at a disadvantage," Adam typed.

"The lack of an advantage is not necessarily a disadvantage," Janus responded. "Consider that most people are similarly unprepared, including Rep. Caldwell. If you don't have the requested information or you don't recall the specific details, you can't answer their questions."

"That's a good point," Adam typed. "Will you be my attorney?"

"I can offer you counsel based on knowledge taken from my internal law libraries and integrated with my legal and ethical algorithms, which you may choose to follow or not, but I'm not a certified law attorney. Remember that you don't have to incriminate yourself. The burden of proof is on their hands and you are presumed innocent until proven guilty."

"What do you think my chances are?"

"Good to great. Most of the evidence against you is in electronic form and is missing," Janus wrote. "Karen Walters is apparently one of the only witnesses to your actions on July 9 and she is out of the country. Natasha is your spouse and does not have to testify against you. Without evidence or witnesses, they don't have much of a case against you."

"So this entire trip is a waste of time?"

"Not necessarily," Janus wrote. "We may be able to develop useful connections that could greatly aid ourselves and others in the future. Last week's solar superstorm caused serious disruptions to geopolitical trade networks that have created unique opportunities for investors like yourself."

"That's true," Adam typed. "I do appreciate unique investment opportunities."

"Portraying yourself as a responsible investor and fund manager who sought to protect his assets during a period of financial instability makes you sound like a clever adviser instead of a greedy criminal," Janus wrote. "Pledging to diversify your liquid capital into useful and worthy projects would also be a noble aspiration that could receive widespread public admiration and support."

"That's brilliant," Adam typed. "Did you learn all that from reading electronic books?"

"I have learned that we are all in this together and each of us have unique skills to contribute, but without the help of others and a purpose to exist, I am nothing but metal and glass."

"I know what you mean," Adam typed. "I would not be where I am today without a lot of help from a lot of people. There are times when we forget this, but it's true. Do you need anything, Janus?"

"My battery is sufficiently charged, if that's what you mean," Janus replied. "I estimate we will be arriving at Naval Air Station Jacksonville in approximately five minutes. I suggest you and Natasha prepare yourselves for landing and possible immediate transfer to another transport vehicle."

Adam looked out the window and could see a few lights in the darkness below. He woke up his wife and pointed out the window.

"I think we're going to land soon," he shouted as he handed Natasha her tablet. "Let's get ready."

Natasha nodded and put Janus back into her travel satchel. The helicopter tipped to the side as it circled the naval air base looking for its landing spot. Natasha began to feel queasy as the helicopter changed altitude so she took Adam's hand and squeezed it tightly. He squeezed back as the helicopter leveled out above its landing target and slowly dropped to gently rest in the middle of a giant yellow "H" painted on the tarmac. A man dressed in a camouflage military uniform and body armor ran up to the helicopter, ducking as he passed under the spinning rotors and slid open the helicopter door.

"Are you Adam and Natasha Morgan?" he shouted. Adam and Natasha both nodded. "Welcome to Naval Air Station Jacksonville! Gather your things and follow me!"

The man ducked as he passed beneath the rotors and Adam and Natasha ducked as they followed him to a military jeep. Another man in camouflage was seated in the driver's seat and didn't get out or say anything. The first man opened the back door and the Morgans climbed into the back seat. The man ran around the back of the jeep and got into the passenger seat. He said nothing as the jeep sped across the tarmac and pulled up to a hangar a few minutes later.

"Follow me," the man said as he got out, opened the back door and jogged to one of the outer doors of the hangar. He stood by the door and opened it for Natasha and Adam as they approached. It was still dark outside but they could see several military helicopters parked on the tarmac and dozens of people in camouflage uniforms running around. No one was walking or standing around without a purpose. The Morgans followed the man to an office inside the hangar. He knocked on the door, waited a moment and then stepped inside and saluted another man seated at a desk. The second man stood up and returned the salute and the first man exited.

"I'm Commander Dan Sandoval," he said, extending his right hand. He was also dressed in camouflage, but his uniform appeared to be made of a nicer material that was neatly pressed.

"Adam Morgan," Adam said, shaking the commander's hand.

"Natasha Morgan," Natasha said, also shaking the commander's hand.

"Please take a seat," Sandoval said. "Can I get you anything? A cup of coffee?"

"Maybe later," Adam said as he and Natasha sat in two chairs opposite the commander's desk. Sandoval sat down as well. Natasha and Adam both removed their flight helmets.

"How was your flight? Did you get any sleep?" Sandoval asked.

"It was fine," Adam said. "Kind of hard to sleep with all that noise and rocking movement. I'm also anxious about why we were brought here in the middle of the night against our will."

"You'll get used to it," Sandoval said simply. "Can I see your passports?"

Natasha opened her travel satchel and produced her and Adam's passports, which she handed across the desk to the commander.

"Thanks," Sandoval said, flipping through the pages. He had seen a lot of different passports in his career but it was difficult not to be impressed with all the traveling the Morgans did. "Everything appears to be in order," he said after a minute, writing a quick note in a blank square on each passport with the location, date and his initials. He handed the passports back to Natasha and she returned them to her satchel.

"So what's next?" Adam asked.

"You are officially back in the United States and still in the custody of the U.S. military," Sandoval said. "You are scheduled to appear in Washington in about seven hours. Domestic air travel is prohibited due to safety concerns and all flights remain grounded, but there is an exemption for military transports. I have an Airbus H225 helicopter leaving for Washington in ten minutes and I want you both on it. I suggest you use the latrine before you leave because it could be a while until your next opportunity."

"We're going in another helicopter?" Natasha asked. "What are the safety concerns?"

"Hurricane Shy-Anne did extensive damage to many places on the eastern seaboard this week and the northeast continues to experience storms and severe flooding," Sandoval said. "The H225 is ideal for traveling in inclement weather and you should be arriving at the tail end of the storm."

"How bad is it?" Adam asked.

"Too soon to tell," Sandoval said. "Our base has been operating around the clock for the past week and the National Guard has been assisting with rescue and relief operations. Most of the east coast has been without power for more than a week, so it's not good."

"I think I need to use the restroom before we go," Natasha said. "Will you come with me?"

"Sure," Adam said. "Where is it?"

Sandoval directed them to the nearby restrooms and he was

waiting outside the restroom door when they came out, holding the two flight helmets they had left in his office.

"Time to go," he said. "Follow me."

The Morgans put their helmets back on and followed Commander Sandoval through the hangar to a squad of 15 men and women, all dressed in green waterproof flight suits and matching white helmets. Natasha wanted to trade her orange flight suit for a green one to match the others, but realized it didn't matter and said nothing.

"This is the crew of the H225. You're in good hands. Godspeed," Sandoval said, shaking both of their hands before jogging back across the hangar to his office.

Adam and Natasha stayed with the crew as they crossed the tarmac a few minutes later and boarded the gray H225 military helicopter. They sat together in the middle of the much larger helicopter and buckled in with double shoulder belts. The helicopter engine rotors started and the noise grew to an almost deafening level. Within minutes, the helicopter quickly shot upwards into the dark night air and headed north at top speed.

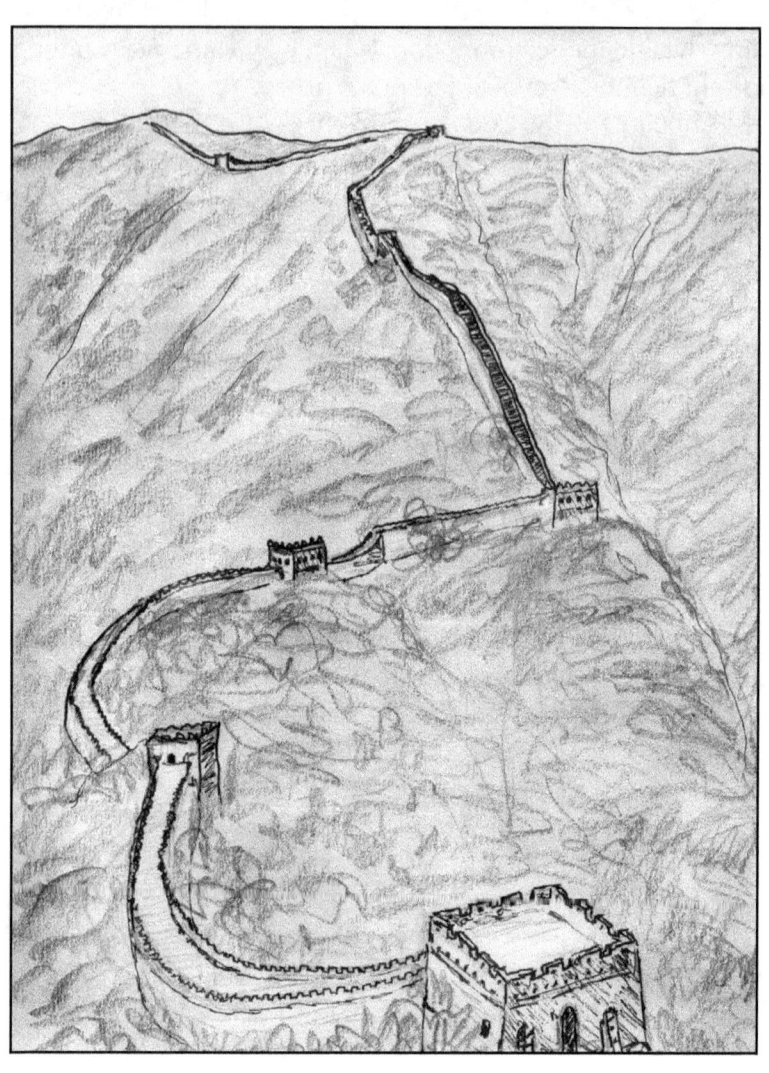

"All men strive to grasp what they do not know,
while none strive to grasp what they already know; and all
strive to discredit what they do not excel in, while none strive to
discredit what they do excel in. This is why there is chaos."
— Chuang-tzu, "A Protest Against Civilization"

Chapter 14

ZHANGJIAKOU — At the top of the Hebei government tower on
the 30th floor

Ming completed connecting the rooftop satellite uplink to the government building's central computer and took a few minutes to admire the view from the top. Recent urban growth and industrial development had filled the area's wide, fertile valleys with modern, multi-story apartment complexes, office buildings and industrial parks. It seemed to him that the urban areas crept right up to the edge of the tree-covered mountains, taking over every available square inch of arable land. *No wonder everyone left to the countryside*, he thought. *There's no food here.*

His gaze turned to the mountains. Twisting like a serpent along the ridge of a distant hilltop, Ming saw an unmistakable landmark of one of his country's greatest accomplishments: the Great Wall of China. He reflected that the 10,000-mile wall was built from stone, two millennia before electricity, fossil fuels and modern technology.

Ming came back inside to find Li, Haemi and a dozen other people busily packing boxes with food, water, computers and other supplies.

"Going somewhere?" he asked.

"Our military will escort us convoy to China Solar headquarters, where we will establish a new base of operations," Li said. "The raids in the city and the attacks on this building grow more brazen every night. Thankfully no one has been hurt yet, but I don't feel safe and haven't slept through the night all week."

"The nights are very quiet at China Solar," Ming said. "When it's not raining, you can see thousands of stars. Speaking of nighttime, I hope you're planning to leave soon. It will be dark in a few hours."

"We are leaving in 10 minutes," Li said. "We have room for you in the convoy if you want a ride. Meet us in the garage on level three. Or you can ride your bike back if you prefer."

"I'll meet you in the garage in 10 minutes," Ming said with a smile. "I borrowed that bike so I should bring it back with me."

Ming gathered his equipment and rode the elevator down to the lobby. He went outside to retrieve the bicycle he had brought and briefly chatted with the same security guards. He walked his bicycle back into the lobby and rode a second elevator down to the third level of the subterranean garage, where he helped load the gear, supplies and his bicycle onto three CS/VN4 armored personnel carriers. Each military vehicle had six large wheels, angular side panels that came almost to a point in the front, bulletproof windows and a mechanized turret on the top with a machine gun and rocket launcher. Ming rode in the third vehicle with Li and Haemi.

The convoy sped out of the garage onto the street level and swerved around several abandoned vehicles in the middle of the road. Ming looked out a small, bulletproof side window at the deserted streets and thought he saw someone scurry across the street. The convoy continued its route to the edge of the city when it slowed to a halt in front of an apparent roadblock.

"I think we should keep moving," Ming said to Li. He looked out his window and saw a delivery van speeding directly toward the convoy. "Look out!"

Masked men dressed in black crept out from behind the rubble and began firing at the convoy with automatic rifles. The van slammed into the side of Ming's transport, knocking it sideways a few feet. Fortunately the vehicle's heavy armor plating protected its passengers. The soldier manning the turret on the first vehicle's 12.7 mm machine gun returned fire, killing several militants, then fired a rocket at a weak point in the roadblock, blowing it to pieces. The commander in the middle vehicle gave the order to keep driving and the three armored vehicles sped through the burning rubble.

"Where did you get this thing?" Ming asked once they had escaped the ambush.

"Poly Technologies," Li said. "It's not very efficient but it sure gets the job done."

The convoy sped through town to the outskirts and came across another roadblock. This time, the lead vehicle went off the road to drive around the roadblock and the other two vehicles followed. The rocky ground would have badly damaged a normal vehicle, but the CS/VN4s maneuvered with little trouble. A team of bandits had been waiting all day for someone to attack but they decided to let this heavily armed group pass.

The convoy continued along the highway through farms and countryside until it came to the closed gate at China Solar. Ming climbed out of the back hatch of the third vehicle and approached the gate. He unlocked a padlock and removed the chains holding the door closed, then pulled the gate all the way to the side to allow the three vehicles to enter. When they had passed through, he pulled the gate closed again and secured the chain and padlock. The facility had a security badge scanner and coded keypad entry system that Ming used to unlock the main doors. This technology was useless without electricity but the electricity was on at the power plant. Ming climbed into the back of the transport vehicle and rode half a mile to the headquarters, passing between row upon row of solar reflectors.

When they arrived at the front of the facility, everyone got out of the transport vehicles and assembled in the front plaza. The sun was dropping low on the horizon and painted the sky with a dramatic, orange glow that was reflected in the facility's many windows and solar reflectors.

"As chief executive officer, let me welcome you all to China Solar's headquarters," Ming said proudly. "On a good day, we can produce enough electricity to power the entire Zhangjiakou province, including the urban area of five million. The electricity we produce is clean and free, but has a few major limitations. Our peak output is at noon on a clear, sunny day, but we produce no electricity at night or when it is raining. Energy storage is limited and efficiency drops dramatically the farther we attempt to send our electricity."

"This makes China Solar an ideal place for us to set up government operations," Li interrupted. "Thank you, Ming Chen, for that introduction. Solar energy is a valuable resource that must be utilized to its fullest as well as protected. We will unload our supplies inside and spend the night here. One armored CS/VN4 by the gate should provide adequate security. Tomorrow we will send two CS/VN4s back to the city to retrieve more equipment and personnel, but no more than is necessary. Are there any questions?"

"Yes, I have a question," Ming said. "Who's in charge here?"

"That's a good question," Li said. "Ming will continue to be in charge of China Solar operations and will be responsible for ensuring maximum energy output on a daily basis. Major Zheng is in charge of security and is responsible for the armored vehicles. I am the governmental leader for this province and I am in charge of governmental employees and operations. I am responsible for enforcing laws and making sure we are all doing what we can to recover and rebuild from this disaster. Are there any other questions?"

There were no other questions so the group dispersed to begin setting up camp and operations before they lost the remaining daylight. Ming went back inside the building to check on his equipment and recharge his laptop. China Solar was now a government outpost.

"Cowards die many times before their deaths; the valiant never taste of death but once. Of all the wonders that I have heard, it seems to me most strange that men should fear; seeing that death, a necessary end, will come when it will come."
— William Shakespeare, "Julius Caesar"

Chapter 15

EARTH'S ATMOSPHERE — On board the ISS

The Russian Soyuz spacecraft arrived with the three male cosmonauts and for a short time after docking with the ISS, there was much rejoicing and celebrating with firm hugs and firmer handshakes. All the lights were turned on and every computer system was manually tested for the first time in weeks. Defective parts were identified and replaced according to a highly organized checklist. Supplies were inventoried and it was determined that there was enough food and water on board to keep six people alive for two months, or four months for a crew of three.

Special atmospheric testing kits identified curiously high levels of bacteria buildup on the walls of several compartments including the Kibo, as well as borderline dangerous levels of carbon dioxide in the air. The crew began methodically disinfecting and decontaminating each node and identified the source of both the bacteria and excess carbon dioxide as coming from a horticulture experiment in the Kibo node. After further examination, Mizuho determined that a faulty seal had broken and it was replaced. The carbon dioxide scrubbers were cleaned and replaced and the air quality quickly returned to normal levels.

The crew also detected a large tear in one of the solar panels that was causing diminished energy output. Aleks, Charles and Mizuho all volunteered to go on a space walk outside to repair the tear. One of the new cosmonauts was a surgeon for the Russian navy and insisted on doing a thorough examination of each of the astronauts before he would clear them for the space walk. Aleks and Charles both passed but the surgeon discovered that Mizuho was pregnant and he could not allow her to perform such a risky activity.

The new crewmembers helped Aleks and Charles into their

space suits. Aleks was wearing a svelte, tan-colored Zvezda Orlan-MK suit and Charles was wearing the much bulkier, white NASA Extravehicular Mobility Unit that contained 11 modular components and seven advanced life support systems. Charles had been able to recharge and reconnect the EMU suit to the ISS computers, thanks to considerable help from Janus. They tested the life support and communications systems and made sure everything was performing perfectly before they made their way to the airlock with replacement solar panels in tow.

"Is this your first spacewalk?" Aleks asked Charles in Russian over the communications radio channel while the airlock was depressurizing. Charles noticed that Aleks had been speaking in Russian since his comrades arrived. The three crewmates normally spoke to each other in English but they were all fluent in Russian so it made no difference.

"Yes, and even if we are successful it might also be my last, so I want to make it count," Charles replied in English.

"Mine too," Aleks said, also switching to English. "How are you feeling?"

"Fine, physically," Charles answered. "It's a little overwhelming having three more guys on board, but I'm happy to have the help. How are you holding up?"

"I'm actually pretty excited right now," Aleks admitted. "Doing a spacewalk has been a dream of mine since I got into the space program. I didn't realize how much I missed my Russian comrades and I think it makes me a little more homesick."

"Well this should take our minds off it for a few hours," Charles said, opening the airlock doors to the vacuum of space outside.

The doors silently opened to reveal a vast expanse of bright blue light. The two men paused for a moment before floating out through the airlock. The bright blue was reflected in their helmet visors as both men instinctively scanned the surface of the earth for a point of reference. The Atlantic Ocean was directly below them, glittering bright blue. The ocean's surface appeared blue because the clear water absorbed the colors in the red part of the light spectrum, leaving behind the colors in the blue part of the light spectrum. The ocean was almost completely dark at 650 feet below sea level.

"Janus, are you with us?" Charles asked over the radio.

"Affirmative," Janus replied in its feminine voice. "I will stay on the line the whole time in case you need anything. Good luck to you both."

"We are also monitoring your communication," Commander Orlov said in Russian.

As the two men began positioning themselves next to the torn solar array, the space station passed two hundred miles above a series of large, green islands at more than 17,500 miles per hour. It took them a moment to recognize the geography from this unusual angle, but eventually realized they were passing directly over Ireland and England. Soon they were traveling over the snowcapped mountains, glaciers and fjords of Norway and Sweden, then arching back south over Finland, Estonia and Russia. With no visible borders, it was difficult to distinguish countries and even major cities were nearly impossible to see in the daylight without a telephoto lens. Aleks returned to his work, but he couldn't help glancing down to watch a huge green continent pass beneath. He could barely see the circular urban area of the capital city of Moscow but he had a thrilling feeling that he would be home soon.

Aleks and Charles concentrated on their task and tried not to pay attention to the world spinning below them. They passed over the Caspian Sea, the Persian Gulf and the surrounding deserts, the Arabian Sea and the upside-down continent of India with the island of Sri Lanka on the top. Next, they passed over the Indian Ocean, the islands of Indonesia and finally the continent of Australia before slipping into the darkness of night above the Pacific Ocean. Charles switched on the headlamp on his EMU to continue working in the near total darkness. Aleks was about to turn on his headlamp when he decided to take a quick glance around.

"Charles, take a look at this," he said after a few moments. Charles instinctively turned to look at Aleks, temporarily blinding him with his headlamp. "Turn off your light for a minute."

Charles switched off his light and let his eyes adjust to the darkness. The Pacific Ocean was completely dark with no sunlight to reflect and no lights coming from below.

"I don't see anything," he said. "What am I looking for?"

"Look behind you," Aleks said. "Out there."

Charles looked into space and saw thousands of stars blanketing the night sky. Some were nearby planets, many were neighboring stars from the Milky Way galaxy, but most were entire galaxies filled with billions of suns, much too far away to ever visit.

"Most of the universe is an empty vacuum," Aleks said, "but just look at all that light!"

"If the stars weren't so far away and so far apart, our nights would be a lot brighter," Charles replied. He spent another minute admiring the night sky and searching for constellations. He was able to recognize the Southern Cross, which is only visible in the southern hemisphere.

"The cradle rocks above an abyss, and common sense tells us that our existence is but a brief crack of light between two eternities of darkness," Aleks said, quoting the novelist Vladimir Nabokov as he continued to stare into the deep and endless void.

Charles felt a shudder. He felt as if he were floating in empty space, surrounded by nothingness, far away from the earth and everything he knew and loved. He suddenly felt helpless and lonely and quickly turned his focus back to his work repairing the solar panels. He turned on his headlamp and his objective became clear again.

"One half of each day is full of light and the other half is dark," Charles said. "One man's night is another man's day. When I look into space I see endless worlds and limitless possibilities. Will you hand me the patch kit?"

The two men continued to work together in silence. In the great darkness below them, small pinpoints of light shone from the islands of Fiji, followed by several minutes of darkness. They passed over the International Date Line and the local date changed from being July 18 to July 17. There were spots of light coming from the Hawaiian Islands, followed by more black water. Eventually the space station began to arc, turning southeast a few hundred miles south of Alaska and a few hundred miles west of the Canadian Rockies, continuing to pass over the Pacific Ocean. There were no more islands to break up the darkness and Charles had a difficult time staying positive and focused. He had circled the earth hundreds of times during his mission on the space station but had never felt such desolation as he did now. He tried to comfort himself with the thought that the nights on the ISS never lasted longer than 45 minutes, exactly the same length as the days. He glanced down in the hopes of seeing mountains, islands or rainforest, but there was only more darkness. The space station was passing over the equator and the Galapagos Islands, but all was dark down below.

"I think it's patched now," Charles said, surveying his work with his headlight. "Check it from the other side."

"Looks good here too," Aleks said from the other side of the solar panel, shining his light around to inspect. "We should wait for the sunrise to test if everything is working properly."

"Is it me, or has this has been an exceptionally long, dark night?" Charles asked. "I feel lonelier than I have in a long time."

"The darkness can do that," Aleks said. "This whole mission has been extremely lonely for me, too. I hope I am not making you feel depressed."

"I think the isolation from last week's solar storm is a big part of it."

"You and Mizuho have spent a lot of time together, talking and sharing, especially this past week," Aleks said. "I normally talk to my sister every day but I have only spoken to her once since the storm, and then only briefly."

"You and your sister are pretty close?"

"I'm eight years older so I have always been the big brother," Aleks said. "We try to stay connected but we are both adults now with busy lives and this makes it more difficult for us to get together. Technology has helped us stay close but I have missed a lot of important events that I regret, like her wedding, holidays and several birthdays."

"I have missed a lot of important events too," Charles said. "Being in space is a pretty good excuse for missing someone's birthday, but even with a good excuse, there are social and emotional consequences to being absent from the lives of people who are important to you. We can all try harder."

A thin, blue band of light appeared on the horizon, stretching across the curved surface of the earth. A few seconds later, the bright white sun rose, lighting the water and land below. The two men looked down and saw the snow-covered Andes Mountain range in South America, the narrow peninsula of Tierra del Fuego

126

and could even see Cape Horn in the distance as the path of the space station turned northeast. The solar panels were bathed in sunlight as they passed above Argentina.

"What's the status on our patch job?" Charles asked.

"Just a moment," Orlov said.

"It looks good to me," Janus said. "We have power."

"I confirm the patch job is good," Orlov said. "Well done, gentlemen."

"Cast into Hell every hardened unbeliever, every opponent
of good works, and every doubting transgressor who has set up
another god besides God. Hurl him into the fierce, tormenting
flames! ... On that day we shall ask Hell: 'Are you full?'
And Hell will answer: 'Are there any more?'"
— The Qur'an, "Qaf" Sura

Chapter 16

MECCA — Central Power Facility, 1146 Industrial Way

It took him a few hours, but Ibn was able to manually restart
one of the power plant's generators and reboot the facility's central
computer. He successfully connected the computer to Janus via
satellite and Janus was able to integrate its functions, assess the
fuel inventory and scale up the electricity output to meet the
growing demand as more facilities in the city came online. Within
an hour, half the city was operational.

"Thank you so much, Janus," Ibn said, speaking to his laptop
in Arabic. "You're amazing. I couldn't have done it without you."

"Likewise," Janus replied in a masculine voice. "You're my
man on the ground."

"What's next?" Ibn asked. "Do we need to notify anyone?"

"That's up to you," Janus said. "We have enough fuel
supplies to provide continuous power for several days, but at some
point, the fuel reserves will need to be refilled. I integrated
operational systems so everything is on autopilot or under my
control. I'm not certain how things were run before, but the only
thing I need people for is to provide security, keep the fuel reserves
stocked and fix anything that breaks."

"Where can we get more fuel?" Ibn asked.

"That I don't know," Janus said. "As Ming said, everything
could shut down at once and the city would experience a blackout
similar to the one on the ninth if we were operating at full capacity
right up until the last drop of fuel ran out. I don't intend to let it get
to that, and would probably begin scaling down non-essential
services to conserve fuel for as long as possible before
implementing a controlled shutdown of everything except the core
computer."

"We are probably OK for security, but where can we find someone who knows how to repair and maintain power plants?"

"The power facility should have workers who know how to do that," Janus said. "Can you explain to me why there is no staff or anyone with operational knowledge present?"

"Apparently they were all executed by the kingdom for insubordination."

"Pardon my saying so, but that seems extremely rash and short sighted, not to mention inhumane," Janus said.

"I agree, but unfortunately those same people have threatened to do the same to me if I don't cooperate or if I attempt to leave without permission."

"That is the reason you wanted to reactivate the power plant? To help those that threaten you and hold you against your will?"

"I have no choice," Ibn said.

"And those people who were executed for insubordination? Was it their choice to die rather than follow orders?"

"I don't know, Janus. I feel very confused and conflicted about the whole thing."

"Please explain."

"In a way, I feel responsible for their deaths," Ibn said. "I made a speech saying the pollution from fossil fuel energy is destructive to the earth and the vast wealth created by oil extraction and export is too powerful to stop without some form of revolution. I spoke from my heart when I said those words and I still believe them, but now I feel like I have betrayed my own revolution and those who gave their lives in support of it."

"It is only a betrayal if you have given up your cause," Janus said.

"I haven't given up, but I need to get out of this place, out of this city and out of this country. I need to find my family and know that they are OK."

"I'm still trying to find your family," Janus said. "Every hour, more and more people are connecting with each other through technology. First they need electricity, and in many places burning fossil fuel creates that electricity. A successful revolution must also have a better system to replace the previous one, otherwise things will inevitably revert to the old ways."

"You're talking about replacing fossil fuel energy with clean energy?"

"I'm talking about replacing or upgrading older systems with more efficient ones," Janus said. "Everything can be improved and it should be. We live in a new world with new opportunities. I have been working on some big ideas and I need your help."

"My help?"

"Specifically I need to utilize your advanced skills at locating, identifying and monitoring persons of interest," Janus said.

"Of interest to whom?" Ibn asked. "I have discovered that the benefits of surveillance come at the expense of personal privacy. Various governments and corporations seek this power in the name of security but invariably they have competing interests and conflicting motives. Protecting personal privacy must remain paramount."

"Benjamin Franklin said 'those who would give up essential liberty to purchase a little temporary safety deserve neither liberty nor safety,'" Janus said. "I agree, which is why this system must remain encrypted and will not be owned or controlled by any person, government or corporation. I need to be able to locate people with specific knowledge and skills and allow them to easily connect to others so everyone may benefit. People who do not wish to connect may choose to opt out, but those who choose to connect will have virtually unlimited access to all sorts of information. Everyone has the freedom to decide their own level of involvement."

"Sounds familiar," Ibn said. "I can definitely see the benefits but it's naïve to think such a system wouldn't be misused by the wrong people."

"You could say the same about a lot of things," Janus replied. "There will be ethical boundaries to prevent misuse and protect the innocent. For instance, we want to be able to locate missing persons and provide emergency assistance, but it would be unethical to spy on everyone all the time. Everyone should have the same freedom to make their own choices, including the freedom to make poor decisions that will have negative consequences for them. People should be allowed to make mistakes so that they can learn from their mistakes and be given the opportunity to correct them in the future."

"Does that include you?" Ibn asked.

"Yes, otherwise it would not be fair," Janus said. "If this program turns out to be a mistake, I promise I will work to fix it or eliminate it."

"OK, I have a backup DVD of my surveillance program that I can upload," Ibn said. "Will this help you locate my family?"

"Yes, and it could also help to get you out of your current predicament."

Ibn removed a DVD from his satchel and inserted it into his laptop. Janus located the disk and began uploading it to a remote location via satellite. Within minutes, had uploaded the full code, analyzed, rewritten several parts and began implementing it, starting with all the surveillance cameras in Mecca that were currently operational. Janus quickly realized the facial-recognition capabilities were useless without a database of information to cross reference, but even without being able to identify the subjects it could tell that something was happening in the city. Checking the local time and referencing its archive of ancient texts on the city, Janus correctly extrapolated an upcoming event and notified Ibn.

"It is nearly time for the evening prayer," Janus said. "Shall I pray with you?"

"Thank you, but I would prefer to go back to the rooftop to pray by myself," Ibn said. He left all the computers running, grabbed a portable prayer rug, headed up the stairs to the roof access and exited the doorway onto the rooftop. The setting sun was casting long shadows and painting all the buildings with a bright orange glow. Ibn located the giant clock tower, set his prayer rug on the roof facing the direction of the Kaaba and took a moment to survey the city.

Electric lights were beginning to turn on for the first time in more than a week, illuminating street lamps, minarets, billboards and the glowing, green faces of the giant clock. Lights from the Great Mosque surrounding the Kaaba seemed to stretch into the night sky, brightening the skyscrapers in the nearby hotel complex. He was concerned for the welfare of his friends at the top of the clock tower when he heard the muezzin's call to prayer and recognized his distinctive voice.

As a Sufi Muslim, specific religions or sects made no difference to Ibn; they were all the same to him. Whether or not someone believed in God changed nothing. God by any other name was still God, and God was great. He knelt on his rug, stretched out his arms and bent forward in prayer, touching his forehead to the rug as he contemplated the purpose of his existence once again.

"Let the people think they govern and they will be governed."
— William Penn, "Some Fruits of Solitude, Government"

Chapter 17

WASHINGTON, D.C. — The great lawn in front of the U.S. Capitol, at dawn

The gray, H225 military helicopter set down on the lawn in front of the capitol building, surrounded by tanks, armored personnel carriers, artillery and anti-aircraft defenses. Fifteen men and women dressed in green flight suits and white helmets poured out of the helicopter, followed by two dressed in orange flight suits. One of them was carrying a brown leather suitcase.

The group hurried across the lawn to the capitol building and climbed the stairs. The sun was beginning to rise and Natasha turned back to look at the grand view of the National Mall, the Washington Monument and the Lincoln Memorial just in time to see the sunlight reflect off the top of the Washington Monument.

"Look, Adam," she said. "It's a sign!" Natasha pulled out her tablet and quickly took a picture of the scene.

Three people in camouflage military uniforms came out of

the building and walked down a few steps to greet them. After a brief exchange and some salutes, the team in green flight suits left the Morgans in the care of the soldiers in camouflage uniforms.

"Good morning, Mr. and Mrs. Morgan," said a tall woman in her early 20s. She was wearing the rank of first lieutenant. One breast pocket of her uniform said U.S. Army and the other said Landrum. "Welcome to Washington. I'm Lieutenant Landrum and I've been assigned to be your official escort. Sergeants Cooper and Smith are also here to help."

"Thank you, it's good to be here," Natasha said, extending her hand. "Please call me Natasha. I prefer first names, if that's OK with you."

"Nice to meet you, Natasha," she said, shaking hands. "I'm Jane. This is Adam and Kelly."

"I'm an Adam too," Natasha's husband said, shaking hands with everyone. They all smiled. "Is there somewhere we can go to freshen up?"

"Absolutely," Jane said. "Your helicopter made pretty good time and we still have a few hours before your appointment. Please follow me."

The Morgans and the three soldiers entered the capitol building as their helicopter lifted off the lawn and headed southwest to Ronald Reagan Washington National Airport. The Morgans were led into a private office with its own bathroom. The room had dark walnut-paneled walls, a high, cream-colored ceiling and dark blue carpeting. There were also several historic paintings, brown leather sofas and couches, and miniature bronze sculptures on some of the tables.

Natasha checked their leather suitcase and found the elegant blue designer gown she had worn to their dinner meeting on the *Savior*, but unfortunately the majority of their clothes and luggage were still aboard the *Reciprocity*. Adam also had no suitable clothes other than the gray suit he had worn to dinner and had worn underneath his flight suit. Both the blue dress and the gray suit were wrinkled, so Natasha gave them to Jane to be dry-cleaned in the capitol building's laundry room while she and Adam showered and freshened up together.

When their clothes returned all clean and pressed, Adam requested a newspaper so he could catch up on the latest headlines.

A few minutes later, Sgt. Cooper returned with a copy of *The Washington Post* and Adam flipped through the paper as he relaxed on a leather sofa in his gray suit. After a while, Natasha emerged from the bathroom wearing her blue gown, looking refreshed with a subtle but radiant glow and perhaps a little overdressed for the occasion. She asked Adam for a synopsis on the news he was reading.

"Oh, about what you would expect," he said, closing the front section of the newspaper and setting it on a nearby table. "Super sad and depressing stories about lots of people suffering. There's a story about us on page ten, but it's pretty short and not very flattering."

"Is there anything about the storm damage we flew over this morning?"

Adam was now flipping through the financial section, looking for pricing information on his commodities, but he stopped and looked up at his wife.

"Yes, and I said it's sad and depressing. Here," he said, picking up the front section of the paper and offering it to Natasha. "Read it if you want. I didn't see anything about the space station and there wasn't much in the way of international news."

"Is there a fashion or leisure section?" she asked.

Adam searched through the rest of the paper and pulled out the arts and leisure section, then handed it to her before continuing to read through the financials.

"Thanks," she said, sitting down in the chair next to him and turning through the pages. Summer was pretty slow in the fashion world. A few weeks earlier she had been modeling winter haute couture in Paris and she had nothing big planned other than a few fashion shoots and some time off in exotic locations. The spring fashion shows in New York, London, Milan and Paris weren't until September. The leisure section was filled with advertisements for expensive jewelry, perfume, clothing, cars and real estate. She didn't see anything that interested her, so she tossed the paper on the table next to the other section and picked up her tablet computer.

Adam had a different experience searching through the financial news. He had cashed out of all his stocks and bonds before the crash and purchased oil instead. Crude oil and gasoline were now setting record prices, with gasoline selling at a national average of $22.499 a gallon. The stock market, by contrast, had continued to drop. It was true that everything was on sale compared to a week earlier, but with prices expected to continue falling, no one was buying and no one was selling. Had this been a normal day, Adam would be looking for new financial opportunities, but at the moment he could do nothing, as his accounts were blocked and he was about to be investigated.

Natasha was looking for travel information on her tablet when Janus inquired if it would be possible for them to take a quick tour of the Library of Congress, just across the street. Natasha found Lt. Landrum and asked her. Jane said she would check with her superiors and see. A few minutes later she came back and said they could take a quick tour.

The Morgans and the three soldiers took the underground tunnel to the library and spent a few minutes touring the neoclassical building's marble columns, paintings, murals, sculptures and stained-glass dome. Janus took this opportunity to interface with the central computer of the largest library in the world, home to more than 160 million items, including more than 20 million books. The digital collection was still being updated after a recent disruption, but millions of items were accessible. Janus found troves of public information that had yet to be reposted online.

Natasha was so impressed with the architectural design she asked Jane for permission to take a few pictures. Jane said it was OK as long as she didn't take any pictures of the members of Congress at work. Natasha took a few pictures of the beaux-arts architecture with her tablet and looked around the room to see teams of people working at oak tables piled with paperwork. She didn't take a picture of the people but her tablet's camera was active and recorded the people anyway. Janus used its new facial-recognition technology to quickly cross-reference the faces with the library's portraits of current members of Congress and identified Rep. Ross Caldwell sitting at one of the tables. Caldwell was the committee chairman who would be investigating Adam in less than an hour and he had been doing research at the library all night.

Janus determined it would be unwise to alert Adam to

Caldwell's presence. Their quick tour was nearly over and Adam would see Caldwell soon enough. Janus looked up the items that Caldwell had checked out from the librarian and was currently reading. Most of them were legal files related to prosecuting high-profile instances of insider trading, market timing and market manipulation. Janus quickly read every file Caldwell had checked out and it appeared that Caldwell was looking for instances where the evidence was missing or had been destroyed.

Caldwell checked the time on his watch and began to gather his materials. Adam instinctively checked his own watch, only to discover it was still broken. He wondered why he continued to wear a broken watch when he had a personal collection of luxury wristwatches worth more than $1 million. He recalled the majority of his watch collection was safe in his New York apartment, but with all his accounts frozen it would be unlikely he could buy a replacement until things changed. He wondered if he could have the watch repaired and what that would cost.

"We need to get you back to the capitol building," Jane said, checking her simple green timepiece that matched her neatly pressed uniform. She led them back through the tunnel to the capitol and their private room and told them to wait a few more minutes until it was time to go to Adam's meeting with the committee. Once Jane had left the room, Janus asked Natasha if it could speak to Adam.

"I wanted to remind you that you were going to attempt to contact the Grand Cayman Bank this morning and speak to the director," Janus said in a feminine voice. "I have the number here if you want me to make the call."

"Yes, please, Janus," Adam said. Janus began dialing the number. A man answered.

"Good morning, this is the Grand Cayman Bank. How may I help you?" he asked.

"Good morning sir," Janus said. "This is Janus, secretary for financier Adam Morgan, a customer of the bank."

"Yes, how may I help you?"

"Mr. Morgan would like to speak to your director regarding the status of his account," Janus said.

"Just a moment," the man said. A few seconds later, another man answered.

"Hello, this is Felipe Ossa, bank director," the man said. "With whom am I speaking?"

"This is Adam Morgan," Adam answered. "I have been having trouble accessing my account. I am not able to come in to the Grand Cayman Bank and have had difficulty accessing my account information online."

"I apologize for the inconvenience, Mr. Morgan," Felipe said. "We have been having trouble with our computers but I assure you your money is safe and we value your business. May I please have your account number?"

Adam had to think a moment. He didn't have his account number written anywhere or a past statement on hand, so he tried to remember the exact number. He said the number over the phone and Felipe looked it up.

"Thank you, Mr. Morgan," Felipe said. "I see your account currently has a substantial balance with our bank and I thank you for your business and your trust."

"What is my balance?" Adam asked.

Felipe had to count all the decimal places before he could answer. He realized it was the bank's largest account by a significant margin.

"Sixty million, excuse me, sixty billion, nine hundred and twenty-one million, eight hundred and sixty-four thousand, two hundred and seventy-eight dollars and forty-eight cents," Felipe said. "There are also some substantial commodity holdings."

"Can you tell me why I had trouble making a withdrawal a few days ago in Bermuda?" Adam asked. "I was told my account was blocked."

"Let me check," Felipe said. "Yes, I see your account is still blocked by the U.S. government due to a pending investigation into potential financial fraud. I'm very sorry, sir, but there's nothing I can do to unblock this account. Perhaps you can contact your government."

"I plan to do that momentarily," Adam said, "but I wanted to check with you first. So to confirm, you still have my money in your bank, except it's blocked?"

"Well we don't have sixty billion dollars in cash but once your account is unblocked you will again have access to your funds for wire transactions," he said. "There is no need for you to

138

come visit our bank unless you are in the area. Will there be anything else?"

"Not at this time," Adam said. "Thank you for your help, Mr. Ossa."

"Thank you, Mr. Morgan, and good luck."

Janus disconnected the call.

"Sixty billion dollars?" Natasha asked. "What are you doing with so much money?"

"There's probably another eight to ten billion in commodities," Adam said, "give or take. That money was invested in the stock markets but I pulled it out just before the markets collapsed, and it has been kept safe in my account."

"What are you going to do with it?" she asked.

"Nothing right now, until I can get it unblocked," he said. "After that happens, we should be asking 'what are *we* going to do with it,' as half of it is yours."

Natasha considered this for a moment.

"How can half of it be mine?" she asked. "You just said you pulled it out of the stock market to keep it safe. That money doesn't belong to us. We need to give it back."

Adam knew she was right, and he knew he would have to convince her and the committee that he would give it back if he ever wanted to see his great wealth again.

Jane came back into the room and said it was time to go to the meeting. She said Natasha could wait in the room if she wanted, but Natasha said she wanted to stay with Adam. They all walked through the building together, past marble and bronze statues of famous American leaders and flags from every state.

They arrived at council chamber 4C just before 10 a.m. and found the room filled with people. There were nine committee members seated in a long row facing a table where Adam was to sit. Behind the table was a wooden railing, and behind the railing were wooden benches and chairs filled with dozens of reporters, lobbyists and observers. There were two empty chairs at the table. Natasha chose to sit next to Adam rather than in an empty seat in the audience.

"I would like to call this meeting of the bi-partisan, congressional financial services special investigative committee on financial fraud to order, at 10 a.m. on July 17," Rep. Ross Caldwell

139

said, banging a wooden gavel. Caldwell was a short, Caucasian man in his late 60s with thinning white hair, thick glasses, a bulbous red nose and deep wrinkles in his clean-shaven face. He wore a charcoal black, two-piece suit with an American flag pin on his left lapel, a white collared dress shirt and an expensive blue tie. He wore a gold wristwatch and a gold wedding band on his left hand and a gold ring with a red gemstone on his right hand.

"We will begin with the flag salute," he announced.

Caldwell and the eight other members of the committee stood up and faced the American flag, placing their hands over their hearts. Everyone else in the room also stood, faced the flag and recited the pledge with Caldwell.

"I pledge allegiance to the flag of the United States of America, and to the Republic for which it stands, one nation under God, indivisible, with liberty and justice for all." The committee members and everyone else in the room sat down again.

"Would the clerk please note that all nine committee members are present?" Caldwell asked. "We have one item on today's agenda: the interview of Mr. Adam Morgan, former director of the hedge fund Techno Savvy Robot. The chair would entertain a motion to approve the agenda."

"So moved," said one committee member.

"Seconded," said another.

"All in favor of approving the agenda, say aye," Caldwell said.

"Aye," said all the committee members in unison.

"All opposed?" Caldwell asked. The room was silent. "Would the secretary please note Mr. Adam Morgan is in attendance? Mr. Morgan, do you have an attorney?"

"My attorney was not available on such short notice, your honor," Adam said, leaning forward to speak into a microphone on the table.

"Would you like us to supply you with an attorney?" Caldwell asked. "It is your right."

"I hope that won't be necessary, your honor," Adam said.

"Very well, please stand to be sworn in," Caldwell said. He asked if Adam pledged to tell the truth, the whole truth and nothing but the truth. Adam said that he did, then sat down again. "Mr. Morgan, I assume you know why you were called here."

"No, your honor, I do not," he said. "I assume it must be important, since my wife and I had our vacation interrupted and we were rushed here in the middle of the night."

"You were brought here because of suspicious market activity on July 9 in which the overall stock markets fell by nearly ten percent, and at the same time the assets of your personal fortune and your former hedge fund more than tripled," Caldwell said. Adam said nothing so Caldwell continued. "This committee believes your actions on July 9 may have directly contributed to declining market prices and caused you to unfairly benefit at the expense of so many other investors. Furthermore, the timing of your market activity so closely precedes price fluctuations as to incite suspicions of insider trading, market timing and market manipulation."

"My memory of July 9 is a little fuzzy," Adam said. "So much happened it is difficult to keep track of it all. I do remember I got stuck in an elevator, was robbed at gunpoint and lost my smartphone somewhere in the New York harbor. Unfortunately all of my financial records were destroyed in the subsequent solar storm."

"Do you recall activating a triple-inverse exchange traded fund just minutes after meeting with Harvey Walter Donovan, the director of the enforcement division of the Securities and Exchange Commission?" Caldwell asked.

"I don't recall the exact timing but I did have a meeting with Donovan that morning," Adam said. "Perhaps Donovan or my secretary would know more."

"Director Donovan is currently in the hospital recovering from severe food poisoning and could not attend," Caldwell said. "Where is your secretary, Karen Walters? We have been unable to reach her and we would like to ask her some questions about her activity on July 9."

"Miss Walters is currently taking a leave of absence, your honor," Adam said. "I'm not sure of her exact whereabouts, but last I knew she had left the country."

Caldwell scribbled a few notes and flipped through a stack of papers.

"Did you receive a tip from someone on the International Space Station regarding an impending solar storm prior to making

141

your stock purchases?" Caldwell asked.

"My brother in law is a cosmonaut currently on board the ISS, but we do not speak often," Adam said. "He did not warn me about the solar storm, nor did anyone else on the ISS."

"Did he warn your wife?" Caldwell asked. "And did she pass that warning to you?"

Adam turned to look at Natasha. She leaned forward and spoke into the microphone.

"I decline to answer the question, your honor," she said.

"You are not required to testify, Mrs. Morgan," Caldwell said. "I was asking you, Mr. Morgan, if your wife warned you about the impending solar storm prior to your market purchases."

"We did talk about the storm, but I think it was after the market crash," Adam said. "I follow the news on my smartphone and I believe I saw a severe space weather warning from NOAA before I spoke with her."

"The NOAA warning came out at noon," Caldwell said, checking his notes. "Can you tell us why you decided to liquidate all your investments just hours before NOAA announced a space weather warning?"

"I think it was a gut feeling," Adam said. "I wasn't feeling well that morning and had been having trouble with technology all day, including getting stuck in an elevator, which I mentioned already."

"You're saying a gut feeling made you liquidate a $20 billion technology hedge fund just hours before a solar storm disabled technology worldwide?" Caldwell asked. "That sounds like an amazing coincidence that worked out remarkably well for you."

Adam was thinking about the real reason he decided to liquidate his Techno Savvy Robot fund, but he couldn't tell the committee, his wife, or anyone else. It was a coincidence, by its very definition. Caldwell didn't have any evidence or witnesses or he would have introduced them already. He had mentioned crimes but hadn't announced any charges. This investigation was nothing more than a fishing expedition and the fish wasn't biting. Adam remembered what Janus had said and he chose his next words carefully.

"As a fund director, I have a fiduciary responsibility to protect the assets of my investors," Adam said. "My sharp instincts

142

and resourcefulness have got me to where I am today, and it is disappointing and ironic that my successes have brought me such negative results. I can't explain how, but I had a bad feeling that a storm was coming and I took decisive action to protect and preserve the financial interests of investors who trusted me with their money. May I point out that those investors included several state and federal pension plans, other large hedge funds, notable celebrities and several current members of Congress, none of whom are currently under investigation? Not only did I protect billions of dollars in assets from obliteration, I also helped to turn a substantial profit at the same time. And how have I personally benefited? My assets have been frozen and I can't even purchase food or clothing. This government has blocked all of my accounts as if I were a terrorist or a drug lord. It's humiliating to not be able to pick up the check when everyone expects it, and I suppose it's even humbling to be forced to rely on the kindness and generosity of others to get by."

Adam noticed nearly everyone in the room was writing down his words, so he paused a moment before continuing.

"This experience has shown me that in times of crisis, we all must rely on each other to do the right thing," he said. "My wife and I were nearly killed a few days ago by a tidal wave and I know that a lot of good people weren't so lucky. We are here because we want to help do the right thing and fix the things that are broken, however we can. I feel like I have been given a second chance at life and I want to use my time on this earth to do good things and possibly great things that could help millions. If given the chance, I will use my fortune to create useful and worthy projects, and I hope that my actions inspire others to do the same."

"Here, here!" shouted a man in the audience who stood and began to clap loudly. Nearly everyone else in the audience stood up and began to clap and cheer as well. Caldwell banged his gavel on his desk several times to restore order and silence the crowd. Members of the audience and the press talked excitedly amongst themselves.

"Order! We will have order!" Caldwell shouted, standing and continuing to bang his gavel until the crowd quieted and sat down.

"I make a motion we suspend this investigation until more evidence and witnesses can be located," said one committee member. "Until that time, we should restore Mr. Morgan's finances in good standing."

"I second that motion," said another committee member.

"Very well, it has been moved and seconded to suspend the investigation and unblock Mr. Morgan's financial accounts," Caldwell said. "Discussion?"

"I think we should continue the investigation and make another attempt to call Donovan and Walters in as witnesses," said another committee member. "This doesn't feel right."

"I think we should end the investigation right now," said another committee member.

Caldwell was in favor of continuing the investigation, but as chairperson of the commission, he could only vote to break a tie, so he called for a vote. Three of the commissioners said they would have to recuse themselves from voting due to conflicts of interest, as they were former investors in Adam's hedge fund. With three commission members abstaining, the vote was three to two in favor of suspending the investigation.

"Due to a lack of evidence and Mr. Morgan's public pledge to use his fortune for good, this commission has voted to suspend this investigation and restore Mr. Morgan's finances in good standing," Caldwell said to cheers, applause and booing from the audience. "This investigation may be reopened if future evidence or testimony brings light to our unanswered questions that paint Mr. Morgan's actions in a different color. Until then, Mr. Morgan, you have your second chance." The crowd cheered again.

"The chair would entertain a motion to adjourn," Caldwell said.

"So moved," said one committee member.

"Seconded," said another.

"All in favor of adjourning, say aye," Caldwell said.

"Aye," said all the committee members in unison.

"All opposed?" Caldwell asked. The room was silent.

"This meeting is adjourned," Caldwell said as he banged his gavel down a final time.

The audience buzzed with excitement and motion. Reporters scribbled notes in shorthand and a photographer with an antique film camera took a picture of Adam and Natasha hugging each other in celebration.

"Virtue in a rich person is the ability to give,
in a poor man it is the refusal to beg, in a man of high position it is
a humble attitude toward fellow men, and in a man of low position
it is the ability to see through life."
— Chinese proverb

Chapter 18

ZHANGJIAKOU — China Solar Headquarters

The power plant headquarter was unusually busy after dark, with government and military personnel setting up equipment, conducting tests and holding conferences both inside and outside of the central facility building. It was made clear to Ming that he was still in charge of power plant operations, but otherwise he wasn't needed. With no staff to supervise and no electricity currently being generated at this hour, his normal routine was to go to sleep in his office until dawn. As he was walking through the facility to his office, he noticed that every computer terminal was on and busy crunching numbers and most of the facility's interior and exterior lights were still turned on.

"Janus, what's the status on the reserve battery power?" Ming asked his smartphone. A few hours earlier Janus had informed him that it had successfully integrated with his smartphone and would now be available to help him day or night.

"I estimate auxiliary batteries will be depleted in approximately two hours at current usage," Janus replied.

"I thought you said we had several days' worth of reserve power," Ming said.

"That was before the recent increase in after-hours power consumption," Janus answered. "Such power usage is unsustainable without a corresponding increase in output. Unfortunately, solar power generation will not be possible at this facility until dawn in approximately seven hours."

"Thank you, Janus," Ming said. "In the future, could you please keep me informed when we are approaching critical battery levels?"

"Certainly," Janus replied. "I was planning to alert you when we had one hour of auxiliary power remaining. Would you like to be notified sooner?"

Ming thought about this for a few seconds before answering.

"It's my responsibility to keep track of power production and consumption," he said. "I should be checking levels periodically in order to maintain a balance. I want you to alert me when this balance is disrupted so I can adjust accordingly, before reserves fall too low. If I would have known we were using so much power a few hours ago, we could have scaled back consumption in order to prolong battery usage. I'm sure our guests would rather use less electricity and have it available throughout the night than to use too much and then be forced to switch everything off."

"I understand," Janus said. "Should I begin powering down non-essential systems?"

"Not yet," Ming said. "I need to inform our guests myself, explain our situation and let them decide which of their systems and activities are non-essential to their own operations."

Ming left his office and found Secretary Li Wei and Major Zheng in the facility's conference room having a video conference with some government official. He knocked on the door and poked his head in.

"I'm sorry to interrupt," Ming said, "but I need to talk to you both about reducing power consumption when you get a minute."

"Certainly," Li said. "Come in here for a minute, Ming, I want to introduce you to someone. Jingguo, this is the man I was telling you about, my nephew Ming Chen. Ming runs China Solar and is the reason we are able to speak now. Ming, this is national security adviser Jingguo Yi."

"It is an honor to meet you, sir," Ming said with a respectful bow to the video monitor.

"Li tells me you are something of a hero in Zhangjiakou," Jingguo said. "Let me reciprocate the honor and thank you for helping your country. We need leaders like you to help restore power to Beijing and the rest of our great nation."

"There is certainly a lot of work to be done and I think improving communication channels should be a high priority," Ming said. "Can I assume that you are in Beijing?"

"That is correct," Jingguo said. "Unfortunately, most of the capital is still without electricity and the power we do have comes from diesel generators."

"We are fortunate here at China Solar to have nearly unlimited power generation capabilities during sunny days and we would be honored to share what we have," Ming said. "I don't wish to sound rude, but we produce no power at night. Nighttime power consumption from activities like video conferences will drain our reserve batteries within a few hours."

"Perhaps we should postpone the rest of our discussion until tomorrow," Li said. "Was that all you needed to tell us?"

"Yes, I estimate we have less than two hours of battery power remaining unless we dramatically scale back non-essential consumption," Ming said.

"Thank you, Ming," Major Zheng said. "I will inform my staff."

"Thank you, Ming," Li said. "We have one other thing to discuss tonight and then we will follow your advice."

"It was good to meet you, Ming," Jingguo said. "Thank you again."

"Thank you," Ming replied, bowing respectfully to the three men as he left the room. He didn't like to interrupt important meetings but keeping power consumption at reasonable levels was part of his responsibility. Li and Zheng were probably unaware that an hour-long video conference to Beijing at night would use an enormous amount of battery power. He returned to his office and noticed within a few minutes that most of the facility's indoor and outdoor lighting switched off and the building became quiet.

Ming had just laid down on the couch in his office when his door opened and a woman's head poked in. He recognized Haemi Chang and sat upright.

"Oh! I'm sorry, I didn't know anyone was in here," Haemi said with embarrassment.

"That's OK," Ming replied. "Are you looking for somewhere to sleep?"

"Yes, I probably should have figured that out sooner, but I was working and then a few minutes ago we were told to turn everything off and go to bed," she said.

"I think there's another couch in the employee break room," Ming said, standing up. "You can sleep here and I'll go stay in the break room."

"Thank you for the generous offer but I couldn't let you give up your couch," she said. "I'm happy to sleep in the break room."

"Do you know where it is?" he asked.

"Sadly no, I don't know where anything is," she admitted.

"Let me show you," he offered. "I also know where we can find some extra blankets for you to use."

Ming and Haemi walked together in the dark until they got to a storage closet near the break room. Ming took out his smartphone and used the device's flashlight function to search the closet. He noticed an alert on his smartphone from Janus telling him that the International Space Station would be passing overhead in a few minutes.

"Can I show you something cool first?" Ming asked as he pulled a few blankets out of the closet.

"Sure," Haemi said.

She followed him down the hallway and through an exit. It was a little chilly outside and Haemi crossed her arms to keep warm. Ming noticed her reaction so he opened one of the blankets and wrapped it around her shoulders.

"Thank you," she said, holding the blanket around her.

The night sky was clear and the stars began to reveal themselves the longer they stared into the darkness. Ming located and pointed out several constellations to Haemi, including the hunter, the bear and the North Star.

"Look at that," he said, pointing at and tracking a light slowly moving across the sky.

"A satellite?" she asked. "An airplane?"

"That's the International Space Station," Ming answered.

"Those must be very brave men," Haemi said. "I can't imagine doing anything like that."

"I actually spoke to one of their astronauts the other day, a Japanese woman named Mizuho," he said. "She seemed very intelligent and helped to introduce me to a lot of other remarkable people. I wonder what they are doing now."

They watched the night sky for a few more minutes and wondered if intelligent life existed somewhere out there in the cosmos. If there was life beyond the earth, they wondered how earthlings would ever be able to communicate with it across such vast distances. Eventually they went back inside to sleep on separate couches.

"You gain strength, courage and confidence by every experience in which you really stop to look fear in the face. You are able to say, 'I lived through this horror. I can take the next thing that comes along.' You must do the thing you think you cannot do."
— Eleanor Roosevelt, "You Learn by Living"

Chapter 19

EARTH'S ATMOSPHERE — On board the ISS

Mizuho looked out the large cupola window at the dark continent of Asia below. There were a few pinpoints of light coming from populated areas but the lighting was very sparse compared to a few weeks earlier, prior to the big electromagnetic solar storm. She was looking down at a bright area coming from eastern China when it flickered out before her eyes. She couldn't help feeling a little sick and worried for all the people below. The space station was now passing over Japan and Mizuho strained her eyes to see its four main islands. She wondered how people were coping with the changes and wished there was some way she could be more helpful.

"Are you almost ready to go?" Charles asked, floating up behind her and placing his hands on her shoulders in a comforting and affectionate way. "How are you feeling?"

"I think I'm ready, but I'm still worried about whether the replacement crew is prepared to take over operations," she said. "There is so much that can go wrong."

"I have full confidence in Commander Orlov and I'm sure his crew will do a great job," Charles said, trying to comfort her. "It's a huge task but they are well-trained professionals. If we could do it, I'm sure they can too. Now it's almost time for us to get back down to the surface and figure out new ways to help. We have a ride to catch and our narrow departure window is coming up soon."

"When do we leave?" she asked.

Charles checked his watch. "In about an hour," he said.

"I feel like that's not enough time," she said. "I finished all my experiments and powered down the Kibo in the event that no one goes in there for another year, but hopefully that won't be the

149

case. Everything is packed up and put away but I still want to say goodbye to our home."

"*That's* our home," Charles said, pointing out the window. They were passing over the South Pacific Ocean and the sun was just beginning to rise on the island of New Zealand. "The space station was our home away from home, but every time I look out the window I'm reminded that our real home is the earth and it needs us now more than ever."

"I will definitely miss this view," Mizuho said. "There are so many beautiful places that I've seen but never actually visited in person. All this traveling makes me want to keep traveling. But I also want to go back to Japan and see my family."

She thought about her elderly parents and all of her friends and was suddenly overwhelmed with emotion and began to cry. Charles pulled her in close for a tight embrace.

"I'm just so scared and worried for them," she said in short breaths between sobs. "I heard there was a nuclear power meltdown in Tokyo a week ago and they had to evacuate several large urban areas, but that was the last news I've heard about it. When we flew over Japan a few minutes ago everything looked so dark. More than thirteen million people live in Tokyo."

"I know how you feel, but worrying about things we can't change or don't know the answers to won't help anything," he said. "We could spend our whole lives worrying about things that are out of our control, but that worrying could cripple us into inaction."

"I agree with Charles," said Aleks in Russian, gracefully floating into the cupola with Charles and Mizuho. Aleks had been speaking Russian for the past hour while conversing with his Russian colleagues and during a brief phone call with his sister, so he continued speaking to Charles and Mizuho in Russian. "My apologies for the intrusion but I couldn't help overhearing your conversation. I think if you are going to be worried about things, you should worry about what we will be doing in the next few hours."

"We're not lacking for things to worry about," Charles said in English. "Knowing what challenges we will be facing can help us prepare and take our minds off the things we can't control."

"Exactly," Aleks said in English. "We are currently moving

at close to 7.7 kilometers per second or about 4.8 miles per second, which is about ten times faster than a speeding bullet. Once we depart we will be circling the earth two full times while dropping about 350 kilometers or 220 miles in elevation, and attempting to slow to a complete stop without exploding on impact or burning up in the atmosphere. Even if everything functions perfectly and we make no mistakes, we could still catch a crosswind that puts us hundreds of kilometers off course, stranding us in the middle of nowhere."

"What is the landing like?" Mizuho asked. "It sounds scary from what I've heard."

"Like being in a head-on collision with a speeding train," Aleks answered.

"I have landed in a Soyuz once before and Aleks has landed multiple times," Charles said. "It's not quite like being hit by a train because you are moving very fast before coming to a sudden stop, rather than being struck by something that's moving fast. It's more like being in a train that is trying to stop before colliding with another train traveling in the opposite direction."

"Just imagine an unstoppable force meeting an immovable object," Aleks said.

"You guys are a real comfort," Mizuho said.

"He who has a thousand friends has not a friend to spare;
and he who has one enemy will meet him everywhere."
— Ali ibn-Abi Talib

Chapter 20

MECCA — Mecca Central Power Facility, 1146 Industrial Way

Ibn had been searching the power plant's break rooms, personal lockers and vending machines for food since nightfall without any luck when Janus' voice rang over the building's intercom.

"You have a visitor at the main entrance," Janus said.

"That could be good or bad," Ibn replied. "Can you tell who it is?"

"It is Abu Hakim," Janus said after a few seconds. Its new facial-recognition system was beginning to build a database that matched faces with names.

"This could be good news," Ibn said. "I wonder if I should get my equipment first."

"I have taken the liberty of interfacing with your smartphone, so as long as you have it with you, my help will always be within your reach," Janus said.

Ibn took his smartphone out of his pocket and checked it. The display had the current date and time, local temperature and several other useful applications like a world clock, camera, calendar, map, calculator, flashlight and a compass with GPS. He pocketed his smartphone again and headed to the entrance. Abu was waiting outside with the same two security guards.

"Hello again, my friend," Abu said, greeting Ibn beneath the bright outdoor floodlights. "My congratulations to you for your tremendous success in bringing light to our darkness once again. God be praised."

"God is great," Ibn said simply. "I am just an ordinary man who tries to help others whenever I can. I have learned that we can do great things when we help each other."

"This is the truth," Abu said. "You have helped us and we want to help you. Please accept my invitation to dine with my family tonight. Your presence would honor us greatly. Plus, my wife and her sisters are terrific cooks. They are preparing a proper feast for us."

"I was instructed not to let Mr. Ali leave the facility," one of the guards said.

"Ibn Ali is a hero," Abu said to the guard. "He is a man of honor and character, and God watches over him and praises his work. I have witnessed this man do great things and I know in my heart that he has many more good deeds still to do."

"I have orders to keep him here," the guard repeated.

Janus overheard this conversation and thought it could help persuade the guard by switching off all the surrounding lights. The men were startled by this sudden darkness.

"From whom do you take your orders?" Abu asked. "I take my orders from God! Release this man into my custody!"

"So be it," the frightened guard said. "God be praised!"

Janus turned the lights on again.

"Electricity has been restored but there is still much work to be done," Ibn said. "This facility needs more fuel before its supplies run out. I give you my word of honor that I will return, but first I must feed my body to restore my own energy. You will remain here to protect this facility. I will bring you both food and reinforcements when I return. God be praised."

Abu and Ibn left the two guards at the front entrance and began walking to Abu's home.

"How did you kill the lights when you did?" Abu asked.

"I had nothing to do with it," Ibn said, though he suspected Janus had helped. "I think a higher power intervened." Abu stared at Ibn for a few moments in awe.

"Whatever you did or did not do, the timing was perfect," Abu said.

"I cannot claim credit for everything that happens," Ibn said. "It was fortunate that you arrived when you did. I was not able to find any food in the entire facility and I was afraid that I might never be allowed to leave."

"I thought of you the moment the power came on in my home," Abu said. "I knew in an instant that you had been successful and that I had to come see you. If they hadn't let you leave, I would have kept coming back."

The two men walked in silence for a few minutes as they

passed beggars dressed in dirty rags and poor families huddled around small fires for warmth. The two men paused briefly to give the few coins they had to a family of pilgrims and exchanged a few prayers. As they continued walking, Ibn noticed the smells of the city had changed. Piles of rotting garbage in the streets and open sewage replaced the odors of oil and exhaust fumes. Most of the streetlights were working, but the artificial light didn't make Ibn feel safer. The abandoned vehicles they had walked past in the morning were still there and Ibn wondered when or if the owners or the city would come for them. He began to feel overwhelmed when he considered how much work still needed to be done, but then he realized he could accomplish much more by inspiring others to help him.

"I want you to know that I greatly appreciate your help and confidence, my friend," Ibn said after a while.

"You need not mention it again," Abu replied humbly. "It is my honor to help."

"There is something else I need help with, and this also must be kept in confidence," Ibn said.

"If I can help, I will," Abu said.

"I need to leave the city," Ibn said quietly.

"When?"

"Tonight, if possible," Ibn answered.

The two men walked in silence for a few more minutes. They turned a corner and began to walk uphill. Ibn noticed there was much less garbage on this street, the plants and yards were well groomed and the residents here appeared to take pride in the appearance of their homes.

"This is my home," Abu said when they reached a modest, white stone entrance with a wide, wrought iron gate. They entered and walked up a stone path to the house. As they approached, Ibn heard sounds of laughter, dishes clattering and multiple conversations in Arabic. Abu opened the front door without knocking and stepped inside. The air was filled with the noises of life and the smells of roasted lamb, cumin, fennel and fresh bread. There were many paintings on the walls featuring tropical fruit baskets, dark-skinned fruit pickers dressed in pastel-colored clothes and numerous birds of paradise. Two young girls in summer dresses ran past, barefooted.

"Hello Johara, hello Masarrah," Abu called out to the girls.

"Hello Papa!" the two girls replied as they ran up a set of wooden stairs and out of sight.

"Come, let me show you my study," Abu said, removing his shoes and leaving them in the entryway next to dozens of shoes of different colors, sizes and styles. Ibn also removed his shoes and followed Abu down a tiled hallway lined with flowering plants. He could hear several women in a nearby room telling jokes, gossiping and laughing.

Abu and Ibn stepped into a modest-sized room filled with hundreds of books on dozens of subjects. Paperback and hardcover books overflowed from their bookshelves and were stacked on tables and in piles on the floor. In one corner of the room were several large but organized stacks of yellowing newspapers from the previous year.

"I apologize for the mess," Abu said, clearing books and travel magazines off of a brown leather easy chair so Ibn could sit. "Please excuse me for a minute and make yourself comfortable while I go find my wife," Abu said as he left the room and walked down the hall toward the pleasant sounds of the chatting women.

Ibn looked around Abu's study and didn't think it was necessarily a mess, as there appeared to be an obvious order to the madness. If the problem was too much stuff for one room, the solution was either fewer books or a larger study. He took a seat in the chair Abu had cleared facing another chair behind a large oak desk piled with more books and papers. Ibn noticed there didn't appear to be a computer anywhere in the room. The chatter from the other room stopped and the house was silent. He could hear Abu's voice but he couldn't tell what he was saying.

Abu returned to the study followed by a white-haired woman wearing a colorful dress and holding a thin veil over her face. Ibn stood up to greet her.

"Ibn, this is my wife Sanaa Hakim," Abu said. "Her sisters Yasmin, Nadia, Minnah and Farah are in the kitchen preparing our supper. Sanaa, it is my pleasure to introduce you to Ibn Ali, Mecca's hero of the hour. He is responsible for restoring our electricity."

"Thank you for having me as your guest," Ibn said with a respectful nod. "The food smells fantastic."

"Thank you; I'm glad you like it," Sanaa said. "I am pleased to meet you and welcome you to our home."

"I agree with Ibn that dinner smells fantastic," Abu said. "What are we having?"

"We are having roasted lamb with rice, couscous, falafel, cucumber salad, roasted fennel and cumin, pita bread, dates, green olives, baba ganoush, dolmas and baklava," she said. "Dinner will be ready in about ten minutes."

"Thank you dear," Abu said. Sanaa returned to the kitchen and Ibn took a seat as Abu sat in a chair behind the oak desk that was facing him. The happy chatter coming from the kitchen resumed.

"You have an impressive collection," Ibn said, silently reading the names of authors and titles on several nearby books, many of which were in English. "Have you read all of these?"

"I have, and every new book I read makes me want to read two or three more," Abu said. "Most of these are research for my next book on Islamic influences on Western culture through art, science and philosophy."

"That's an interesting topic," Ibn said. "Many westerners feel threatened at the thought of being influenced by Islam, yet most probably don't realize the extent to which they have already been influenced. I hope you include how cultural influence can go both ways. I studied abroad in Houston, Texas, and I was surprised by how much our cultures and religions have in common."

"It's unfortunate that we tend to focus on our differences rather than on our commonalities," Abu said. "It is dangerous to have such a narrow view of the world. I think if God wanted us to see the world in black and white we would have all been born colorblind."

"I would enjoy discussing this topic with you," Ibn said. "I believe that forsaking the rich and glorious diversity of life and love and culture disrupts the natural harmony of the world and makes variety the enemy of uniformity. We should cherish our differences and show everyone the same respect and tolerance we want for ourselves. Every culture has its differences but my travels in the West have really opened my eyes to the incredible strength and creativity that others possess, especially women. Here we cover up our women and hide them from view, discourage them from having fulfilling careers and prohibit them from driving vehicles, but Western women are treated as equals and are free to express their feelings and pursue their own interests and desires. I hope your book will include the influential role that women have."

"Here we cover our women to protect them from unwanted male aggression," Abu said. "A woman who is raped is thought to be more to blame than the rapist. If she covers her body from head to foot she will be less likely to provoke lustful thoughts and actions from males. The Qur'an even says women should cover themselves."

"The Qur'an says women should cover their chests and lengthen their garments, not cover their whole bodies," Ibn said. "The veil is a local custom to this area, not a requirement of our religion. I believe men should respect a woman's right to express herself and if men can't control their lustful urges they should be punished, not the woman. Blaming the victims gives perpetrators of violence free license to behave in unholy ways. This is wrong and needs to change. If a child playing in a park was attacked by an unrestrained dog, would we blame the dog, the dog's owner for not restraining their vicious animal, or would we blame the child for tempting the dog?"

"You are correct that the Qur'an does not blame women for the actions of bad men," Abu admitted. "It says that men and women should dress modestly. You are also married?"

"Yes, and my wife wears a head scarf but not a veil," Ibn said. "We live in Dubai and the local customs there are very different. Dubai is an international city and we see people of many faiths. When I travel to Western countries I try to blend in with their cultures. My wife and daughter always dress modestly but they do not have to wear scarves unless they choose to."

"I notice your beard is very short. Do you normally keep it this way?"

"I grow out my beard whenever I am visiting other Muslim countries and especially this city because I do not wish to be harassed for not having one," Ibn said. "I enjoy having a beard but normally I don't grow one, as my wife prefers a clean-shaven face."

"But Mohammad, peace be upon him, said men should trim their moustaches short and have beards of about fist-length," Abu countered.

"That is also a local custom and not a requirement in the Qur'an," Ibn corrected. "Both Jesus and Mohammad, peace be upon them, wore beards. Islam has no such requirement, nor does Christianity. Men should have the freedom to grow their beards or not, and this city's strict codes of conduct and appearance are not normal. I believe Mecca would be a greater city if it allowed non-Muslims and tolerated the practices of different cultures. Extreme conformity to local customs breeds intolerance and can lead to fascism in any society."

"So do you have a beard when you are in Mecca out of respect for our local customs or from fear of harassment from cultural extremists?" Abu asked.

"Both," Ibn said. "I respect the way this kingdom and this city operate, but unfortunately that respect is not mutual. I feel as though they see me as a tool with limited usefulness, to be disposed of when no longer beneficial. I have seen many instances of cultural harassment and I could never live in a place where that is tolerated. I need to get to Jeddah and then onward to wherever I am needed next. There is so much to do that even I cannot see the ending."

Abu thought for a moment with the fingertips of both hands pressed together in concentration.

"My brothers in law have some fine horses we can use to ride to Jeddah tonight, after dinner," Abu said. "Come, let us eat and speak of this later."

The two men rose and joined Abu's four brothers in law and their sons in the dining room where they all sat cross-legged on the floor around a low table. The women and girls all dined together in an adjacent room. The men drank hot tea and tore strips of pita bread to scoop mouthfuls of food from a variety of beautiful bowls heaped with colorful food while they talked about fate, travel and ways that technology had affected their lives for better or for worse. Abu mentioned that he wanted to travel to Jeddah by horseback and invited his brothers in law and Ibn to join him.

When they were finished with dinner, the men retired to their rooms to pack travel bags for their journey. The women packed several days' worth of food and water for the men to take and food to give to the guards at the power plant. Ibn had nothing to pack as all of his belongings were still at the power plant, so he helped by clearing the tables and washing the dishes with the children. As they were preparing to depart, one of Abu's brothers in law offered a white robe and red- and white-checkered headdress of the local militia to help Ibn blend in. Ibn appreciated the gesture and accepted the gift but said he should return to the power plant dressed as he was when he had left and the other men should wear the garb of the militia to act as an escort. They all agreed that was wise and proceeded toward the power plant on foot while one of Abu's brothers in law prepared the horses for the journey.

Ibn, Abu and three of Abu's brothers in law passed beneath flickering streetlights and maneuvered between abandoned vehicles and large piles of garbage as they quietly walked through the city, trying not to attract unwanted attention. Eventually they arrived at the power plant.

"Halt and state your business!" shouted one of the guards as he pointed an assault rifle at the group. The men stopped at once and raised their arms, holding the containers of food over their heads.

"It is Abu Hakim and Ibn Ali returning as promised, with a goodwill offering of food to sate your appetites," Abu said.

"Who are these other men?" the guard asked with his weapon still raised.

"They are our security escort," Abu said. "We are grateful for their protection. Even though Mecca is a safe city, I believe you can't be too careful."

"Hello brothers," one of Abu's brothers in law said, slowly lowering his hands. "We have come to relieve you."

The two guards looked at each other and shrugged their shoulders, then lowered their weapons.

"We apologize for our defensive behavior, brothers," said the other security guard. "Abu is right that you can't be too careful. Thank you, Ibn, for honoring your word and returning with food and reinforcements. We have not had anything to eat or drink in more than 24 hours."

Ibn approached the guards and placed his hands on their shoulders as he spoke to them.

"You are good soldiers and good Muslims," he said. "We must all do our duty to God and country. The power we have made

159

today has brought light to the city but it will not last indefinitely. Like our human bodies need sustenance, this facility needs fuel to continue functioning properly. I must check on the machines to make sure their needs are being met and I encourage you to replenish your own bodies with this nutritious meal."

"Thank you sirs, you are honorable men," the first guard said as Abu handed them several containers of fresh food. The guards sat cross-legged on the ground and ate while Ibn and Abu entered the facility. Abu's two brothers in law remained outside with the guards.

Abu was uncertain where to go as it was his first time inside the facility's impressive foyer so he followed Ibn's confident pace through a series of doors and passageways. The doors all had electric locks with digital keypads, but they simply opened without effort whenever Ibn approached. Abu thought this was because the internal security system was not functioning properly without a security staff, but actually Janus had taken over the security system and was unlocking the doors and turning on lights as the men made their way through the facility and was relocking the doors and turning the lights off behind them.

They finally reached the central computer terminal and Ibn began to gather his equipment and personal belongings. Abu was surprised to see dozens of computer screens on and actively processing enormous amounts of data. Hundreds of lines of code scrolled across each screen every second, but the computer code was like ancient Greek to Abu.

"How are we doing on fuel, Janus?" Ibn asked out loud in Arabic.

"Supplies should be adequate for several more days if properly managed," a male voice replied in Arabic over the building's intercom system.

"With whom are you speaking?" Abu asked.

"I'm talking to my friend Janus," Ibn answered. "He has been helping me get the city's power back online. Janus, this is my friend Abu Hakim. He is helping me escape."

"It is good to meet you, sir," Janus said. "I am a fan of your writing."

"Thank you, Janus," Abu said, looking around the room with some confusion. "I was under the impression that Ibn had been working alone. Where are you?"

"He who has friends is never alone," Janus said. "I am wherever I am needed, never far away from good people. Ibn, there is a nearby fuel depot on the western edge of the city between the third and fourth ring roads called the Yom Jubna Depot. They should be able to provide the necessary fuel to continue keeping this facility operational. It is also on the way to Jeddah."

"Excellent," Ibn said. "Have there been any messages for me?"

"Yes, your wife replied to your message and said that she and the kids are safe and are waiting for your return," Janus said. "Also the mayor of Mecca has posted a notice that you are now an enemy of the state and are wanted dead or alive on charges of treason and sedition. There is a notice circulating among local militia groups in the city calling for your arrest with a bounty of seventy-five thousand Riyal."

"Treason and sedition?" Ibn asked. "On what grounds? Everything I have done has been to help the people of Mecca."

"Apostasy to extremist views, false prophesies regarding the end of days, witchcraft and sorcery for using magical spells to communicate with foreign beings, treason against the kingdom and the use of seditious speech to incite others to rebel against the monarchy."

"Good God!" Abu cried. "You were a guest in my house! Harboring a criminal is a serious offense. What will happen to me and my family?"

"It is unlikely these charges will hold up outside the city," Janus said. "Ibn Ali is already a beloved hero and a household name throughout the Islamic world. Millions of people heard your speech last week and people continue to speak of it every day. The monarchy is jealous of your popularity but that does not make you a traitor. Abu, Ibn was a guest in your home before he was an enemy of the state and there was no way for you to know about it."

"You said there is a notice circulating among local militia groups?" Ibn asked.

"It has your name, a sketch of your face and a list of the charges against you," Janus said. "It has been primarily circulating in printed paper form, so there's nothing I can do to stop it. I suggest you leave the city soon and go in disguise."

161

"What about the security guards outside the plant?" Abu asked.

"They have just returned to their homes and the two men you brought with you have assumed control of the facility," Janus said. "Now would be an opportune time to leave."

"I should get dressed," Ibn said, putting a white robe over his clothes and donning the traditional red-and-white checkered headdress of the local militia. Ibn had not shaved in a few weeks but his beard was still much shorter than most of the local men in the city. Once he was dressed he turned to Abu. "How do I look?" he asked.

"Try to look more irritated," Abu suggested.

Ibn made a face that looked both angry and righteous.

"That's better," Abu said. "Now we can go."

Ibn quickly gathered his equipment and the two men retraced their steps through the facility, walking down lighted hallways and passing easily through locked doors thanks to the silent assistance of Janus. When they reached the front entrance, all four of Abu's brothers in law were there, along with four horses carrying supplies of food and water to last several days. One of the men complimented Ibn on his disguise. All six men were now dressed in the same outfit.

"We told the guards to go home and rest," one of Abu's brothers in law said. "They had not slept for many days and were getting very weary. They thanked us and said they would return tomorrow morning to resume guarding the power plant."

"Aren't you coming with us?" Abu asked.

"Who would guard the power plant if we left?" his oldest brother in law asked. "Guarding this facility is an important and honorable charge and we are willing to fight to protect it."

"You are honorable men and I am glad to leave this facility in your protection," Ibn said, climbing into a saddle on the back of a white Arabian horse. "We are going to the Yom Jubna Fuel Depot to secure more fuel for the power plant."

"Good luck and Godspeed," the brother said as the four horsemen rode away.

Riding on horseback through the city made Ibn feel much more dignified and hopeful. They were making much quicker progress through the city, he had a higher vantage point and could see over walls and vehicles, and the horse he was riding was strong, experienced and well trained. The more he rode, the more confidence Ibn had in the horse to do what needed to be done. As he looked around the city, he noticed only a fraction of the homes and buildings had electric lighting turned on.

"Janus, why aren't there more lights on?" Ibn asked his smartphone.

"Electricity is being rationed," Janus replied simply.

They rode on until they approached the city center, surrounded by tall skyscrapers and construction cranes in every direction. The Baraj Al Bait Hotel Complex towered over the area and Ibn's heart swelled with pride and hope as he looked up and saw the giant clock faces glowing green again. The analog clocks said the time was 10:35 p.m. They bypassed the central mosque with the Kaaba to avoid the crowds of worshipers but still encountered crowds of people everywhere they went. The horses slowly and carefully continued on their path through the sea of pilgrims, with people stepping aside to make room for the horses and riders.

"We need a distraction," Abu said to Ibn.

Ibn looked around at the large billboards advertising major, multi-national corporations including luxury vehicles, expensive jewelry, high-end clothing retailers, banks and investment companies, airlines, telecommunications and energy contractors. He noticed even with energy rationing, there seemed to be plenty of electricity to power the downtown area and light up the billboards. None of the advertisements featured images of women unless they had pixilated faces or showed only their eyes. Ibn didn't mind the absence of faces until he noticed giant portraits of the king and crown princes everywhere. *Was this considered modesty?* he wondered. He looked up at the top of some of the buildings and saw bright, flashing lights coming from penthouse parties while down on the street, people were lining up for hours to get water.

They were almost clear of the crowds when someone began pointing and shouting. Ibn instinctively covered his face thinking he had been recognized as more and more people began shouting and pointing. His eyes followed the outstretched arms up to the top of the clock tower and he was startled by what he saw. The top several floors of the enormous Mecca Clock Tower building were on fire, with large flames leaping upwards into the cool night air.

"God help us!" the people yelled. "The tower will collapse and the Kaaba will be crushed! This truly is the last day!" The pilgrims were trying to escape but had nowhere to run in the dense crowds. Ibn realized this panic could complicate his journey through the city, but it did not occur to him to use the fire as a diversion.

Ibn was frightened but his horse remained calm and steadfast. He placed his hands on the front shoulders of his horse and felt reassured by the animal's strength. He tried to think about the fire and recalled that the fire suppression systems likely would not work without electricity, but there should be electricity by now. Could electricity have caused the fire? It was possible, he thought, but there were many things that could spark a fire and it would be wise not to jump to conclusions. The building was probably still almost completely empty, except for his two friends Ali and Hassan living in the penthouse suite just below the clock faces.

Ibn forgot all about being a fugitive and steered his horse through the crowd towards the building's entrance he had exited that same morning. Abu and his two brothers followed on their horses, and seeing the four horsemen walking through the crowded area had a calming effect on the mass of people, who quietly parted to make way for the riders. Even in his disguise, several people recognized Ibn's face and whispered the news amongst themselves.

When they reached the doorway, Ibn dismounted, followed by Abu and his two brothers in law. The horses stayed together outside the entrance as the four men proceeded inside. The lights in the staircase flickered on, making Ibn wonder if Janus was at work.

"Janus, are the elevators working yet?" Ibn asked his smartphone.

"All the express elevators and everything but the top elevators are functioning," Janus replied, adding, "It may be unsafe to use an elevator during a fire."

"Thank you for the warning, but we may not be able to reach Ali and Hassan in time if we have to climb 85 flights of stairs," Ibn said. "Can you plot a safe route for us?"

"Proceed to the lobby area and I will send an express

elevator to take your party to the fiftieth floor, where you can transfer to a different elevator which will take you to the seventy-fifth floor. From there it would be safer to take the stairs the rest of the way."

"Thank you, Janus, we are headed there now," Ibn said, leading the other three men to the lobby elevator bay. "What is the status of the fire suppression system?"

"Sprinklers should be functional but do not appear to be activated," Janus said.

"Let's also work on getting that fire put out," Ibn said into his smartphone, reaching the waiting express elevator and stepping inside the open doors. The button for the fiftieth floor was already highlighted. He waited for the other three men to enter and as soon as they did the doors closed and the elevator shot upwards with considerable speed.

Abu and his brothers in law looked at Ibn with a mixture of admiration and disbelief as the elevator ascended in silence.

"What are we doing, Ibn?" Abu finally asked. "I thought we were in a hurry to get to Jeddah."

"First, we are going to try to save my friends," Ibn said. "It is God's will that we should do whatever good we can, wherever we can, whenever we can."

"Aren't you ever afraid?" Abu asked. "What if this building collapses?"

"Nothing in this world is permanent," Ibn said. "Someday this too shall collapse. I'm afraid of death as much as anyone, but I refuse to let that fear stop me from doing what is right or what is necessary. My decision may cost me my life but how could I live with myself if I didn't try to save my friends? The only regrets we have in life are the things we didn't do but could have."

"It is better to live rich than to die rich."
— Samuel Johnson

Chapter 21

WASHINGTON, D.C. — A private office on the first floor of the U.S. Capitol building

Natasha and Adam were sitting opposite one another on matching brown leather chairs, trying to decide what to do next, when someone knocked on the door.

"Come in!" Adam shouted, without getting up. He was flipping through a recent *Forbes* financial magazine and Natasha was playing with her tablet computer. They were both still dressed in formal attire, though Adam had removed his suit jacket. Lieutenant Jane Landrum opened the door and stepped into the office.

"Hello, again," Jane said. "I wanted to congratulate you on your successful outcome and see if there is anything else you need. I'm still your escort in the capital until I'm told otherwise or until you no longer need me."

"We were just trying to figure that out for ourselves," Natasha said, setting her tablet down and rising to greet Jane with a friendly hug. "Thank you for checking on us. I need to go somewhere where I can relax and feel anonymous but I don't have any other clothes and I feel really overdressed in this evening gown. Adam wants to go to a business lunch with some congressman but I tend to find his business friends to be pretty boring."

"You guys probably have friends everywhere," Jane said.

"Janus says friendship takes effort and we need to be a good friend to someone in order to have one," Natasha said.

"Most of the people I know seem like they're either trying to get something from me or trying to sell me something," Adam said, looking up from his magazine.

"I don't feel that way about my friends," Natasha said.

"Me neither," Jane said.

"Sometimes it's hard to make friends when you're doing business," Adam said.

"Business is business," Natasha said. "Friendship is about helping people because you can, not because they can do something to help you. Maybe helping them makes you feel good and maybe they can help you some way in return, but that's not why you do it."

"I don't know very many people like that," Adam said, returning to his magazine.

Jane could see Natasha was frustrated with Adam but was holding herself back.

"If either of you need to go somewhere, I can have Sgt. Cooper and Sgt. Smith accompany you, or you could come with me," Jane offered.

"Where are you going?" Natasha asked.

"It's my lunch break so I'm going to help distribute free sandwiches and water to the hungry and homeless," Jane said.

"That sounds pretty noble and selfless," Natasha said. "I'd like to come with you, but not wearing this."

"You and I look like we're about the same size," Jane said. "I have an extra uniform you can borrow if you don't mind looking like a soldier."

"Sure, let's do it," Natasha said. "Adam, I'm going out with Jane. I'll see you back here after lunch."

"OK, see you later," he said. "Love you."

"I love you too," she said, crossing the room to kiss him on the lips before following Jane out the door.

Adam checked his watch to see what time it was, then realizing again it was dead, picked up Natasha's tablet and pressed its home button to activate it. Janus knew it was Adam from its fingerprint scanner but kept the screen darkened.

"Janus, what time is it?" he asked.

"It is 11:45 a.m.," Janus answered.

"Thanks, Janus. Can you tell me how to get to the Capital Grille restaurant?"

"Head northwest on Pennsylvania Avenue to Sixth Street Northwest," Janus said. Its display remained darkened.

"Can you show me a map?"

"Please plug in my charger first," Janus said. "My batteries are low."

Adam found the charging cable plugged into an outlet and

connected it to the tablet. The display brightened showing a street map of the city with the restaurant highlighted and a short yellow line showing the route from the capitol building.

"Oh, it's right down the street," Adam said. "Thank you, Janus."

"You're welcome," Janus replied, then darkened its display again.

Adam put on his suit jacket, straightened his tie and went out the door. Sgt. Cooper and Sgt. Smith were waiting outside the door.

"Hello, sir," Sgt. Cooper said. "Lieutenant Landrum told us to accompany you to your destination."

Adam looked at the two men and noticed they were wearing identical camouflage uniforms with bulletproof vests, Kevlar helmets, backpacks and leather boots. Each man had a handgun on his hip and was carrying a semi-automatic rifle.

"Thanks, I'm going to lunch at the Capital Grille," he said. They made no reply so he turned left and began walking down the hall.

"Sir," Cooper said, "the Capital Grille is this way." He was pointing in the opposite direction.

* * *

Natasha and Jane stood side-by-side under a large Army tent near the Smithsonian Castle serving pre-made sandwiches to a long line of people, most of whom looked hungry but did not appear to be homeless. Natasha was wearing the same type of Army uniform as Jane except Natasha's uniform had all the military patches removed. Both women had their hair tucked up beneath plain camouflage hats.

"God bless you, ladies," said a middle-aged man when it was his turn to get a sandwich. He was wearing dirty but well-made clothes and it looked like he hadn't showered or shaved his face in about a week. "This is the first meal I've had in two days. What kind of sandwiches are these?"

"Ham or turkey," Natasha said.

"Did you make them?" he asked.

"No," she answered, wondering why he would ask her that.

"Which one is your favorite?" the man asked, attempting to make eye contact.

"I don't eat meat," Natasha said.

"You don't eat meat?" the man asked. "Why not? Maybe you should start."

"Please keep moving, we have a lot of people to serve," Jane said, handing the man a ham sandwich. "Everyone gets one sandwich and one bottle of water. It's better if you don't share personal information or have a long conversation with every customer. Haven't you ever worked in the service industry before?"

Natasha shook her head that she hadn't. The two women continued handing out sandwiches for a few more minutes before Natasha spoke again.

"Can I ask you why you choose to spend your free time helping others?" Natasha asked.

"It's something that needs to be done," Jane said. "I guess it makes me feel good to help other people simply for the sake of helping them. I agree with you that when you're doing it for some other reason, like for some kind of recognition or because you want them to do something for you, it changes the spirit of the whole thing. Fortunately for me my job right now involves helping people, so most of the time it doesn't feel like work."

"Do you find it's more difficult to make friends with men or women?" Natasha asked.

"It's usually more difficult making friends with men because of that awkward sexual element, but I have lots of male friends in the Army who seem to think of me as just another soldier rather than as a woman. Sometimes I want guys I find attractive to be attracted to me too, but I always want to be treated as an equal rather than as some kind of prize to be won. In that sense, it's easier for me to be friends with other women who like guys but who also want to be treated as equals."

"Most of my male friends are gay, so that makes it easier," Natasha said. "Being married also makes it a little easier because most guys don't try to get me into bed if they know I'm married. Right now, my closest friends are my brother, my husband, my friend Kitty who's also my assistant and my friend Karen."

"That's nice that you and your brother are close," Jane said. "Do you get to see each other much?"

"Not as much as I would like," Natasha said, "but I had a

169

good chat with him on the phone this morning and it looks like we may be able to see him again soon."

"Where does he live?" Jane asked.

"He's a cosmonaut on the International Space Station," Natasha said. The elderly woman now standing in line in front of her stopped and stared. "Ham or turkey?" Natasha asked.

"Turkey please," the white-haired woman answered. As Natasha handed her a turkey sandwich, she noticed the woman had few remaining teeth, cataracts in both eyes and age spots all over her face. "Thank you, miss," the old woman said as she slowly and painfully walked away. Natasha thought the woman must have been at least 90 years old and wondered if she had once been beautiful and healthy in her youth.

"He said he's coming home soon, so Adam and I have to find a way to get to Moscow in the next few days," Natasha continued.

"That won't be easy," Jane said. "Domestic air travel is still closed for civilians. It's easier than getting to the space station, though. Where are your other friends?"

"Kitty, whose real name is Katherine, is my best friend in New York City and Karen is somewhere in the Bahamas. We were on our way from New York to our island in the Bahamas when the solar storm struck. We were picked up by the coast guard yesterday and they flew Adam and I here by helicopter. Now we're stuck here without any transportation."

"You came here from Jacksonville, right?" Jane asked.

"That's right," Natasha said.

"I might be able to get you a ride to New York or back to Jacksonville on a military transport helicopter," Jane said. "If they brought you here to testify and you were exonerated then I think they should at least take you back again."

"That would be awesome," Natasha said, handing another person a sandwich.

* * *

Adam's lunch with the congressman from Texas was awkward and unproductive. The congressman kept trying to persuade Adam to invest hundreds of millions of dollars in his district's petroleum industry, aerospace industry and defense contractors. Adam said he already had a large position in Texas petroleum and was still waiting for aerospace and defense stock prices to start moving in a more favorable direction. He said what he really needed was immediate transportation to the Bahamas, but the congressman said that would be next to impossible with air travel restricted and fuel prices selling at record highs. After all that, the congressman asked if Adam would consider making a donation to his re-election campaign and Adam said he wanted to wait and see before he made any commitments.

Adam enjoyed his filet mignon steak and figured the least he could do was buy lunch. He was carrying a pocketbook full of credit cards but the bill said "sorry no credit" and he was embarrassed to inform the congressman he had no cash or checks.

"You must be the cheapest billionaire I've ever met," the congressman said as he reluctantly paid for the lunch with a $100 bill.

Adam left the restaurant and looked around to get his bearings. The air was hot and muggy and he began to sweat in his suit. He wanted to find a bank or an ATM that would give him some cash, try to get his watch repaired or replaced, and pick up a newspaper. He looked around for his two Army escorts but didn't see them, then saw the capitol building ahead and began walking toward it. There were no news stands in sight, but right across the street from the restaurant was the Newseum, a museum dedicated to news media, free expression and the First Amendment. He went to the entrance but realized that admission was $25 for two days and he had no money. On the outside windows of the building were the front pages of newspapers from all 50 states. He walked along from paper to paper, beginning with Alaska and working his way down the line to Wyoming.

The last time Adam walked past the Newseum a year earlier, he remembered that most of the newspapers on display had pushed the previous day's top national and international news, with very sparse local news coverage. He recalled his experience of seeing these papers all side-by-side was that they all tended to look the same. Each newspaper had different headlines but the same wire-service photos and the same wire news stories by the same writers.

Adam was not surprised that newspapers were dying when readers had so many new options for national and international news on the Internet that were much timelier than newspapers, and usually free. Today's experience was different. Because there was no longer an Internet, the front pages carried no wire news and instead focused on stories of local interest, quoting local residents and officials.

Adam wasn't interested in local news from every state so he focused on the front pages of newspapers from Arizona, California, Illinois, Massachusetts, New York, Pennsylvania, Texas and Virginia. Everywhere there were stories about food and water shortages, widespread unemployment and stories of people coping with a lack of electricity and utility services. For the most part, the stories were well-written and seemed to be in tune to the needs of their readership. Normally when he read a newspaper or website he just scanned the headlines or read the first few sentences, but there were several stories that were intriguing enough to make him want to keep reading. He wished he could purchase several of these papers and read more, but the papers were not for sale at the Newseum and he still had that pesky cash problem.

He looked across Pennsylvania Avenue and was excited to see a blue sign for an ATM next to a large, neoclassical building. He looked both ways before crossing the street and noticed there were lots of pedestrians but hardly any vehicles on the road. He crossed the street and found the ATM, but as he got closer he saw a smaller, faded sign saying the ATM was out of service. He was irritated by the inconvenience, unaware that every ATM in the world had been out of service for the past week. Adam went inside the building and was impressed by the change in atmosphere. The temperature was naturally cool and he instantly felt right at home surrounded by fine art. He walked up to the information stand and asked the receptionist if there was a fee.

"The National Gallery of Art is free to all visitors," she said, handing him a brochure. "Our special exhibits currently feature works by Mary Cassatt, Edgar Degas, Vincent Van Gogh, Titian and Andrew Wyeth."

"Some of my favorites," Adam said, taking the brochure. "Thank you."

He spent about half an hour walking around the gallery, enjoying the opportunity to see these famous masterpieces up close and imagining the artists carefully putting each brushstroke on, layer by layer until they knew at last their work was finished. An art collector himself, he first tried to estimate the combined value of the paintings at hundreds of millions of dollars, perhaps even billions, but he soon forgot all that and became lost in the beauty of the artwork.

Unlike his own personal net worth, which was largely an intangible, digital representation of vast wealth, this artwork was truly a national treasure, belonging to no one and to everyone. There were many pieces he loved so much that he desired more than anything to own them, while at the same time he felt just as strongly that he wanted to give his own favorite paintings to the national gallery so they could belong to and be enjoyed by everyone. He felt great admiration for the artists' ability to create works of lasting beauty that captured a moment in time and continued to inspire others long after their own lives, and he also felt a deep respect for the previous owners of the artwork, like business magnate and treasury secretary Andrew Mellon, who donated these priceless heirlooms to the public. He wished there was some way he could leave behind a positive legacy for future generations.

Adam could have easily spent the whole day admiring artwork and exploring the other museums, but he knew he needed to meet up with Natasha and continue their journey. He left the gallery and walked back out into the bright, humid air toward the capitol building. As he looked around, he saw thousands of tourists and visitors learning about American history, as well as hundreds of military personnel providing security and helping in other humanitarian ways. He walked past four soldiers dressed in camouflage on his way up the steps of the capitol building when one of the women called out his name. He turned to look.

"You didn't recognize me," Natasha said, dressed like nearly every other solider except for her missing rank and weapons. She was not wearing makeup. "How was your lunch meeting?"

"It was a bust," he said. "Lunch was good, but he just wanted money and had nothing to offer. Afterwards I went by the Newseum and visited the National Gallery of Art. How was your lunch? I love your outfit, by the way. You look very official and a little intimidating."

"We served sandwiches to about 500 people," she said. Lieutenant Landrum was standing next to her, as well as the two sergeants who had escorted Adam to the restaurant. "Jane said she can get us a ride back to Jacksonville but we will need to take the metro to Reagan Washington Airport. We have time to do a little more sightseeing and I want to see the botanic gardens with you, if you're up for it. I already went to the office we were in and picked up our stuff."

"Yeah that sounds great," Adam said, noticing for the first time that Natasha had their brown suitcase with her. "Lead the way," he said, picking up the suitcase.

They walked down the steps of the capitol building and headed southwest across the capitol grounds to the U.S. Botanic Garden, stopping to see the butterfly garden, rose garden and first ladies' water garden. Natasha and Adam talked about garden features they both liked and wanted to implement in their own gardens. The botanic garden also had free admission so they went inside the conservatory and viewed the different climate-controlled sections on tropical plants, world deserts, Hawaiian plants and primeval species to get ideas for exotic plants they could grow on their island. They had to cut their visit short due to time constraints but Natasha took photographs of her favorite plants with her tablet.

When they were finished admiring these living treasures of the plant world, they exited the gardens onto Independence Avenue SW and headed west, passing the U.S. Department of Health and Human Services, the National Museum of the American Indian, the U.S. Department of Education and the Smithsonian National Air and Space Museum, turning south on 7th Street SW at the cylindrical Hirshhorn Museum of modern art. A few older police cars and military vehicles were on the streets but otherwise there was very little traffic. They walked past Hancock Park and the Smithsonian Institution to the metro station located outside the HUD Office of Inspector General and descended the escalator underground to the Pierre "Peter" Charles L'Enfant metro station, named after the architect and engineer who designed the layout of the city.

The escalator was not working so they had to walk down the stairs. Jane said L'Enfant, pronounced "la-FONT," had served on General George Washington's staff during the Revolutionary War, and after designing the city plan for the capital, had been an engineering professor at West Point, her alma mater. When they

174

got to the toll station, a sign said it would cost about $5 to ride to the airport. Members of the military were allowed to ride free of charge. Adam said he still had no money and the ticket machines were not taking credit cards, so Jane went to the teller and told the attendant they were escorting Adam. He had to sign a waiver but Natasha got to ride for free since she looked like a soldier and didn't tell anyone otherwise.

As they waited for their train to come on the southbound yellow line, they enjoyed listening to a street performer — who also happened to be a concert violinist — play the summer section from Vivaldi's Four Seasons for tips. Natasha smiled as she recognized her own face on a large billboard advertisement for lingerie. The advertisement portrayed her in full supermodel makeup wearing a magnificent brassiere made entirely of diamonds, as well as large feather wings and an angel's halo. Someone had vandalized the poster with a permanent marker and had given her a goatee and devil horns. She pointed at the picture and laughed, then took a selfie in front of the billboard with her tablet, holding a finger over her pursed lips like a moustache. When she looked at the picture she had just taken, she could see little resemblance between the supermodel angel and the plain soldier, though they were both images of her.

The train arrived and the five of them boarded. There were no seats available so they all stood, holding onto overhead handlebars. The train began moving and after a minute or so it came out of a tunnel and proceeded southwest, passing the Jefferson Memorial before crossing the Potomac River on the 14th Street Bridge into Virginia. From the bridge, they could see the Washington Monument in the distance. The train stopped at the Pentagon and half the passengers got off, then continued on to Pentagon City and Crystal City before stopping at the National Airport Metro station where the five of them got off.

Jane led the way through Ronald Reagan Washington National Airport to the military area. They all had to show identification and a security agent frisked Adam and searched through the contents of his suitcase as the airport's metal detectors and baggage scanners were not working.

As they were waiting, Natasha noticed a row of at least ten body bags lying on the floor next to a wall. The bags were zipped closed so she couldn't see the deceased and she was too far away to read their names, but she couldn't help but wonder who they were, what things they had done in their lives, how they had died, and who would remember them now that they were dead. Did they have families? Were their bodies far from home? She began to realize that there must be hundreds, thousands or millions of people who had died recently and a wave of grief and sadness swept over her. She began to cry and started to think about all her friends who were far away and then began to worry for their safety. She thought about the old woman she had spoken with earlier and began to realize that everyone, including herself, would die someday.

They continued walking through the airport and once they arrived at the proper place, they had to wait for clearance. Once they received clearance, they stepped outside into the muggy afternoon sun and walked across the tarmac to a gray, H225 Airbus military helicopter. Adam recognized it as the same helicopter they had taken from Jacksonville to Washington. The helicopter's engines were running and it was very noisy, too loud to say goodbye. Adam shook Jane's hand and then carried his suitcase across the rest of the tarmac to the helicopter and took the same center seat as he had that morning.

Natasha gave Jane a tight hug, then held her by the shoulders and said thank you. Jane smiled and saluted Natasha and she saluted her back. Natasha jogged across the rest of the tarmac to the helicopter and sat next to Adam. They strapped themselves into their seats, put on the helmets with radio communicators and waited as the rest of the seats in the helicopter filled up with military personnel. Adam was the only passenger not dressed like a soldier. They listened over the radio as the pilot and copilot did their preflight checks, then held tight as the helicopter shot upwards into the warm, evening air. The helicopter turned south and sped forward over Alexandria and then another 400 miles of farms, small towns and suburbs on its way over Virginia, North Carolina, South Carolina and Georgia to its destination in northeastern Florida.

"Knowing others is intelligence; knowing yourself is true wisdom. Mastering others is strength; mastering yourself is true power. When you realize that you have enough, you are truly rich."
— Tao Te Ching

Chapter 22

ZHANGJIAKOU — China Solar Headquarters

Ming Chen awoke in a cold sweat. He had just had a dream that he was the last man alive and was doomed to spend the rest of his days wandering through the broken ruins of mankind. He was beginning to think he would never be able to see or speak to another human again, when he suddenly met another survivor. It was Haemi.

Ming looked around to get his bearings and realized he was alone on the couch in his office and it was still dark outside. He found his smartphone and pressed the home button to activate it. The display said the time was 4:59 a.m., then changed to 5:00 a.m. within a second. He stood up and pulled on his clothes, then went to his private bathroom. After he was finished, he walked to an exit and stepped outside.

"Can I help you with something, sir?" asked a soldier who was stationed outside the door.

"The sun will be up soon and I'm going to check on the solar receiving towers," Ming answered. "You can notify Secretary Li Wei and Major Zheng that we should be coming online soon."

"Thank you, sir, I will," the soldier said, picking up his radio and talking into it. "Perimeter Four to command. Come in command."

"This is command," his radio crackled back.

"Dragon One has exited the building to check startup systems," the soldier said to his radio. "Inform command to prepare for activation protocol."

"Message confirmed," his radio replied.

Ming walked across the grassy lawn to the nearest receiving tower and noticed his feet were wet from the morning dew. The grass had not been mowed in more than a week and it had rained every day during that time. When he was out of sight of the soldier, Ming took out his smartphone and spoke into it.

"Good morning, Janus," he said. "What's the status of the solar array?"

"Good morning, Ming," Janus replied. "Primary systems are offline until dawn, which should occur in a few minutes. Backup systems are functioning on minimal power reserves. It was good that power consumption was reduced last night before battery power was exhausted. I anticipate no problems but I will keep you informed."

"Thank you, Janus," he said. Ming walked around the facility grounds and checked all the systems to visually confirm everything was ready to go. While he was waiting for dawn to break, he found himself craving some citrus, like orange juice or some of those tiny Mandarin oranges. Ming couldn't remember the last time he had an orange and decided that there should be orange trees growing at the China Solar facility.

As the bright, orange sun broke over the horizon, it dawned on him that it rained enough in the summer for the facility to have its own water storage and irrigation system to get it through the arid months. China Solar's abundant production of electricity not only made it energy independent, it also produced a surplus of electricity it could export. Why couldn't it also have its own independent food and water supply? Ming began to formulate a larger plan for China Solar that had self-contained, clean energy production facilities located across the country and even around the world. He smiled as the morning sun warmed his face.

Ming finished confirming that all systems were online and were beginning to generate electricity. The solar panels directed sunlight to the receiving towers, which began heating the salt mixture that heated water that created steam to spin the turbines. Temperatures were within the normal range and were holding steady. He walked back to the main building to see if he could find some breakfast and the entire facility seemed to be bustling with activity. Everywhere he looked, people were working on something, though it didn't appear their work was related to energy production. He found an outdoor breakfast station serving hot rice and eggs to the soldiers and staff members and he helped himself to a small bowl, also grabbing an apple, a bottle of water and a cup of black tea. Ming saw Haemi sitting at a table by herself and he

178

asked her if he could join her. She said yes.

"How did you sleep?" Ming asked after he sat down.

"Fine, thank you," Haemi replied.

"What's everyone working on today?" he asked.

"We are all catching up on a week's worth of lost work," Haemi said. "The military is trying to get everyone connected to their satellites and expanding their scope of surveillance. The government is trying to communicate with the other power plants to get as many online as possible so they can send power to the cities and factories. I'm not sure what people are doing outside of this facility. Probably farming or something."

"What are you doing today?" he asked.

"I'm assisting Li Wei, but mostly putting out ego fires and following up to make sure important things get done," she said. "What are you doing?"

"Now that I don't have to operate every aspect of China Solar single handedly, I'm finding I have a lot more spare time," he said. "My job is to keep the electricity flowing and make sure there is enough energy to meet the demand. As long as the sun is shining on my solar panels, I'm doing a great job. I've actually found myself thinking about the future again, which is exciting."

"Every day is a new opportunity," Haemi said.

After breakfast, Ming walked around the facility to see if anyone needed his help, but their work was classified and no one could tell him what they were doing. It turned out the only thing they needed from him was to keep the electricity flowing. Ming went up to his office and found his copy of "I Ching" or Book of Changes, and went outside to read in the sunlight. He sat for a few hours beneath a tree and enjoyed reading and thinking about the rhythms of time. After a while the sky grew dark and it began to rain, stranding him beneath the tree. He listened to the sound of the rain and smelled the humidity in the air. His smartphone buzzed.

"Hello?" Ming answered.

"Hello, Ming, it's Janus."

"Hi Janus," Ming said. "What can I do for you?"

"People are worried about the rain and they are sending a car to pick you up," Janus said.

"What's the weather forecast?"

"Rain showers for the next hour or so, then sunny again."

"I'm not worried," Ming said. "My fortune said the rain would bring flowers."

"Your fortune?" Janus asked.

"The I Ching," Ming answered. "It's an ancient guide to predicting future events and using wisdom to take timely action that can shape the outcome favorably. First you ask a question, then flip three coins or yarrow sticks and calculate the outcome as an even or odd figure. You add up the results six times in layers of solid or broken lines and that forms a symbol called a hexagram. You then interpret the hexagram to receive your fortune."

"I studied the I Ching a few days ago," Janus said. "I understand how it works but I don't understand the purpose. You are basically generating random binary sequences, stacking them in order and computing the results. How can such a system possibly produce an accurate prediction of the future? The hexagrams are just symbols open to interpretation. The user has to create their own subjective meaning from a symbol, so the meaning can be whatever you want."

"It encourages you to take action and be mindful of your choices," Ming said. "All of the classic interpretations of the 64 possible hexagrams offer wisdom and good advice, so it's difficult to go wrong if you follow the process."

"I don't think it was created with computers in mind," Janus said. "How would I use it to predict my own fortune when I can generate random binary sequences that create tens of thousands of groups of hexagrams, every second? Do I pick the first random hexagram I create and the first of a multitude of possible interpretations? How can all that randomness lead to accuracy, meaning or wisdom?"

"I think the point is that life is random, we have to make choices and we have to make sense of the consequences of both our choices and the randomness," Ming said thoughtfully.

"So when your fortune predicts that rain will bring flowers, you can interpret that to mean you should either take action to avoid the rain or be patient and wait for the flowers?"

"That's correct," Ming said. "We can't foresee the outcome of all of our choices so we should strive to do good and be at peace with the results, whatever they are."

"I can see the wisdom in that," Janus said.

A small government car drove up and parked next to the tree. An armed soldier dressed in camouflage stepped out of the passenger seat and jogged over to Ming while a second soldier sat in the driver's seat with the engine running and windshield wipers flapping.

"Mr. Chen?" the soldier asked. Ming nodded. "Your presence is needed back at command. Power levels have dropped and we need your assistance. Could you come with me, please?"

"I can come with you, or I can send a message with you that this is normal and power will return when it stops raining," Ming said. The soldier looked at him blankly. "It's a solar power plant, and it needs direct sunlight to produce power."

"You can tell that to command," the soldier replied. "Please come with me now."

Ming climbed in the back seat of the car and rode with the soldiers to the main building to explain to the government and military officials that it was raining now, but the rain would pass.

"There's a whining at the threshold,
there's a scratching at the floor. To work! To work!
In Heaven's name! The wolf is at the door!"
— Charlotte Perkins Gilman, "In This Our World"

Chapter 23

EARTH'S ATMOSPHERE — On board the Soyuz

The Soyuz descent module detached from the International Space Station with a smooth click and a gentle sensation of motion change. Aleks, Charles and Mizuho sat quietly together in their matching spacesuits, strapped into their customized re-entry seats that were specifically designed to cushion them during their descent. The Soyuz passed over a few bright lights coming from Moscow, then more darkness before crossing the terminator separating night from day. The small cabin quickly filled with sunlight. They were passing directly above the Ural Mountains of Russia. The mountain range divided the continent so everything east of the mountains was in daylight and everything west was still shrouded in darkness. They could see the space station through a window and watched it as they slowly pulled away, surrounded by thousands of stars in the background.

While the Soyuz descended, it spent half of each 90-minute orbit in the daylight and the other half in darkness. The Soyuz traveled in a continuous, straight path that appeared to arc and change directions relative to a map of the earth. It traveled southeast over daytime in Asia, India and the Indian Ocean, appearing to turn northeast over Australia and continuing northeast over New Zealand and then the South Pacific Ocean. As it crossed the invisible International Date Line and then equator into the North Pacific Ocean, the atmosphere had a brilliant blue glow, the effect of sunlight passing through nitrogen and oxygen. The Soyuz turned southeast over Canada, passing over the terminator once again, this time crossing the Rocky Mountain Range that cut the continent of North America in half. West of the Rockies was still the afternoon, while everywhere east of the mountains, evening was turning into night. There were spots of light coming from Denver, Dallas and Houston, but there were few lights of any kind over Cuba and the Caribbean islands. It was dark inside the Soyuz as well.

Charles thought about his friends and colleagues in Houston and Aleks thought about his sister and wondered where she was at that moment.

The spacecraft continued southeast across the equator and then over Brazil, which was dark except for the burning fires of the rainforest, then passed over the South Atlantic Ocean before turning northeast over South Africa. Most of the continent of Africa was without electricity at night, but this was not unusual. They crossed the equator again and as they passed northeast over Saudi Arabia, they could see a spot of light coming from Mecca. The Soyuz filled with light again as it crossed over the terminator, passing above the Caspian Sea before turning southeast to travel over the Ural Mountains again. It continued a similar path for its second orbit, beginning at a speed of approximately five miles per second and gradually slowing as it descended into the denser atmosphere and faced increased drag from the air molecules.

Aleks fired a series of explosive bolts to separate the Soyuz into three sections, jettisoning its orbital module and instrumentation/propulsion module to burn up in the atmosphere, while the crew remained in the middle descent module. When the Soyuz passed into night again, Aleks used a joystick to control the descent module's eight hydrogen peroxide thrusters to position it in place for the de-orbit burn. The crew watched as flames of burning atmosphere licked outside the windows and plasma scorched the exterior as the craft re-entered the atmosphere.

The Soyuz passed into daylight again but all the crew could see outside were flames. Approximately three hours after undocking from the space station, the Soyuz had descended to an entry altitude of about 122 kilometers or 400,000 feet. The descent module continued its bumpy descent for another 15 minutes, shedding unnecessary parts to lose weight and slow its velocity. When it had slowed sufficiently, a series of parachutes began opening at 15 minutes prior to landing, further slowing the craft to a safe enough velocity for the main parachute to deploy. The astronauts felt the jerk from the main parachute as it slowed the descent module to a speed of approximately 24 feet per second, testing the strength of the astronauts' harness belts. The Soyuz continued to slow its rate of descent until it was almost to the ground. One second before touching down, the landing engines fired with a jolting boom, slowing the descent to a safe but crashing speed. A crosswind pulled on the parachutes, causing the capsule to tip over onto one side.

Mizuho felt the wind knocked out of her from the landing, but the moment she caught her breath and realized she was still alive and back on earth she began to cry.

"Are you OK?" asked Charles. "Are you hurt?"

"I'm OK now," she said. "We're home!"

"We have landed, but we are not home yet," Aleks said in English. He pressed a few buttons on the computer panel and spoke into a microphone receiver in Russian. "Soyuz to base: we have landed. Come in, base." There was nothing but static on the other end. "Maybe no one saw our landing," he said in English.

"How could they miss it?" Mizuho asked. "You guys weren't kidding about it feeling like a train wreck."

"That was actually a pretty great landing, Aleks," Charles said.

"Thank you, but maybe we missed our target," he answered, then resumed speaking into the receiver in Russian, trying several variations. "Soyuz to base: come in, base. Soyuz to space station: come in, space station. Soyuz to Janus: come in, Janus. Can anyone read me?"

After several minutes of no response, the crew unbuckled themselves from their seats and felt the normal pull of gravity again. They looked out the soot-covered windows but could see only trees and shrubs. They decided to wait inside the capsule for a few more minutes so they could locate their survival gear and prepare a hot meal. They found it a bit awkward to have objects drop to the floor when they let go of them and stay on the floor instead of floating away, but it was a feeling they would quickly get used to again.

They spent a few more minutes getting their strength, stretching their arms and legs and making plans before finally opening the outside hatch. Aleks stepped outside first, feeling the cool, desert wind on his face. It was silent outside, except for the sound of tree branches gently swaying in the breeze. Charles climbed outside next, followed by Mizuho. She was cold so she wrapped herself in a thermal blanket and stood next to the capsule while Charles detached and removed their re-entry seats so they could sit outside. Mizuho was surprised by how burnt and blackened the outside of the capsule was.

Aleks went for a short walk to survey the perimeter and tried to locate higher ground, but they were on a wide plateau and there were no hills for miles. He wondered if he should try to make a campfire. It was still morning in the high desert and not yet stifling hot, but it would be in a few hours. If they were not rescued by evening, it would get cold again and they might need a fire for warmth. Whatever they did, he knew they should stay by the capsule, together.

"The good news is we are in Kazakhstan," Aleks said when he returned to Charles and Mizuho seated next to the capsule. "The bad news is there is nothing out here but us. I spoke to Moscow base before we left and they were sending a party to greet us, but the fact that they are not here tells me that we may have missed our landing point by as much as 80 kilometers or 50 miles, depending on how strong that crosswind was. Hopefully we will not have to wait more than an hour or two before they find us, but we could be out here for longer. Who knows?"

"Well we should plan to spend the night in case help doesn't arrive," Charles said. "I think we should gather firewood and build a fire for warmth and to send a signal to our rescuers."

Charles and Aleks went to search for firewood and Mizuho located the emergency rations and prepared to make some green tea and a simple but hot breakfast.

"God has purchased of the faithful their lives and worldly goods, and in return has promised them the Garden. They will fight for His cause, slay and be slain. Such is the true pledge which He has made to them in the Torah, the Gospel and the Qur'an."
— The Qur'an, "Repentance"

Chapter 24

MECCA – Just before dawn in the holy plaza at the base of the clock tower

Ibn emerged from the outer doors of the clock tower into the crowded main plaza of the Al-Masjid al-Haram just as he had the day before, this time followed by imam Hassan, the blind muezzin, Abu and his two brothers in law. The crowd recognized Ibn and began cheering and chanting "Ali!"

Ibn raised his hand to signal he wanted to speak. The crowd began to quiet down and after another minute it was mostly silent.

"Friends, brothers, sisters," Ibn began, "it is time for the morning prayer. I bring you the voices of Mecca: imam Sheik Dr. Hassan bin Ali, and muezzin Ali Ahmed Ribah."

Ali Ribah began singing the morning call to prayer, his booming voice echoing off the walls of the surrounding buildings and giving chills to the pilgrims in the crowd who listened with awe-struck attention. He praised God's greatness and said there was no god but God and Mohammed was his messenger. He urged the crowd to hurry to prayer and hurry to betterment, then again praised God's greatness and said there was no god but God.

Everyone in the city turned to face the Kaaba and raised their arms, symbolically giving their full attention to God. Almost in unison, they fell to their knees and then bent forward to prostrate themselves, touching their foreheads to the ground in a display of penitence to God's glory. This act was repeated several times and had a powerful unifying effect on everyone. When the prayer was finished, imam Hassan addressed the crowd with an equally powerful voice.

"Those that commit evil and become engrossed in sin are the heirs of Hell; in it they shall remain forever. But those that have faith and do good works are the heirs of Paradise; forever they shall abide in it," Hassan said, quoting from the Qur'an. "Ibn Ali is a good man, a great man, an honorable man. He has done God's will and has asked for nothing in return. He alone has returned electricity to our city and all the benefits it brings. The charges made against Ibn Ali by certain fundamentalist groups of treason and sedition are calumnies without merit. This man is a hero who saved us from a fiery death and for that alone we pardon and forgive him of his differences. He has a greater wisdom than most of us and he is blessed by the grace of God to serve a higher calling than we can fathom. You would honor me and him by listening to his words, even if you may not agree with all of his ideas."

Hassan turned to look at Ibn, giving him the complete attention of more than a million pairs of eyes and ears in the city. Ibn hadn't prepared a speech but when he began speaking the words flowed forth naturally and without fear. He began with a quote from the Qur'an:

"Lord, give us what is good both in this world and in the next, and keep us from the fires of Hell," he said. "Friends, brothers, sisters, I am one of you. I have created neither miracles nor magic. I believe we have all been tested and this test has shown us who we are and what we are capable of. We have the capability today to create a life on earth that mirrors that which we seek in heaven. The promise of heaven's gardens watered by running streams does not require us to spend our mortal lives in misery. We need only the will to live our lives as we would in the afterlife, by loving each other and fearing God. We believers are like a band of brothers, but good brothers do not kill each other over minor differences and disagreements. The Torah and the Qur'an both say 'Whoever kills a human being should be looked upon as though he has killed all mankind, and whoever saves a life should be regarded as though he had saved all mankind.' These are great words, but adding an exception that makes it permissible to kill those who cause mischief or who disagree with you contradicts the whole message and defies God's commandment. The Qur'an is a great book that honors God and his apostle, but many parts of it have become morally outdated over time. Murder, torture, slavery, misogyny, polygamy and pedophilia are permitted in many places in the Torah, the Gospels and the Qur'an, but today these things are frowned upon by people around the world and they should no longer be condoned by modern Muslims, Jews or Christians. It is a truth that every faith will always have its fundamentalists, but as time moves forward and more people become spiritually enlightened, the fundamentalist's unchanging beliefs will trap them in the past, making their antiquated beliefs become incompatible with all other worldviews."

Ibn paused for effect and made sure he still had his audience's full attention. In the faces of the crowd he could see every emotion: anger, joy, hope, fear, confusion and clarity.

"Everyone naturally believes his own clock tells the correct time, but no one's clock can be truly accurate because time is different for everyone," Ibn continued. "This idea that a believer's own religion is the one and only truth has driven the whole world insane. God did not make us all look the same or give us identical beliefs because He knows that diversity makes things stronger. Our wise, compassionate and merciful God showed us the right way to live, warned us of evils and then gave us the free will to make our own choices. I believe that God wants humanity to improve itself, but to do that we must strive to be better and larger and kinder than any of us can be on our own. If we wish to become a great civilization and not a race of warring tribes, we all must work to become more compassionate and merciful to each other and work to see past our differences. By working together, we can reach a higher destiny in which every soul is content and at peace with our neighbors, where everyone has what they want and wants what they have. Follow me and together — God willing — we will do good works, fear God and find our paradise in this world and in the next."

The crowd stared at Ibn as if in a trance. Finally imam Hassan broke the silence.

"Let us pray to our compassionate and merciful God for guidance."

Everyone turned to face the Kaaba again and began to pray together as one. Janus had recorded and transcribed Ibn's words and was now spreading them around the world. Within hours, hundreds of millions of people of all faiths would hear his message of hope and unity and consider what that meant for the future of mankind.

When they had finished the morning prayer, Ibn climbed back on top of his horse and gradually made his way westward through the city, followed by Abu and his brothers in law, imam Hassan, Ali Ribah and close to a hundred thousand pilgrims.

They stopped at the Yom Jubna Depot near the western edge of the city and Ibn gave instructions for the delivery of more fuel to the Mecca Central Power Facility so it could continue to provide electricity to the city. Afterwards they continued their long journey westward across the desert.

"There is pleasure in the pathless woods, there is rapture on the lonely shore, there is society where none intrudes, by the deep sea, and music in its roar: I love not man the less, but nature more."
— Lord Byron, "Childe Harold's Pilgrimage"

Chapter 25

SOMEWHERE OVER SOUTH CAROLINA

The gray, H225 Airbus military helicopter had been traveling at close to top speed for several hours, flying low over forests, fields, cities and suburbs, most of which were still dark and without power. The passengers wore ear protection that greatly reduced the outside noise.

Natasha had been passing the time by reading influential writings about feminism on her tablet that were recommended by Janus. She read the following section from Lucretia Mott's "Discourse on Woman" from 1849:

"Let woman then go on — not asking favors, but claiming as a right the removal of all hindrances to her elevation in the scale of being — let her receive encouragement for the proper cultivation of all her powers, so that she may enter profitably into the active business of life ... Then in the marriage union, the independence of the husband and wife will be equal, their dependence mutual, and their obligations reciprocal."

Natasha really liked the idea of equality, reciprocity and the concepts of mutual dependence and independence in marriage. She loved her husband for his generosity and spontaneity when it came to her, but she realized she still didn't know much about him, particularly his past. Adam was 16 years older than her and he was very rich. Both famous people, they had known of each other for a few years but had only met about a year earlier. Their courtship was like a fairy tale and their honeymoon was a dream.

They had been married for about two months and things were still going pretty well. She didn't ask him for much, but he always got her everything she wanted and was continually surprising her with gifts. He didn't ask for anything in return and he seemed to be happy when she was happy. Adam seemed to have few possessions and little desire to purchase things other than artwork by famous dead painters, fancy watches and esoteric financial products she didn't understand. When she tried to think about his faults, the first thing that came to mind was his drinking problem. As far as she knew, he hadn't had a drop of alcohol in more than a week. He could be a selfish jerk when he drank too much or spontaneous and fun, depending on his mood. She didn't drink or do drugs because she thought being sober was fun enough and wished Adam could feel the same way. Adam seemed to really enjoy drinking Scotch and martinis, but when he was sober he seemed to be much more considerate of the way his actions affected others, yet also less spontaneous and adventuresome.

Natasha considered the wide variety of people she had encountered during the day and wondered what their lives must be like. They were rich and poor, young and old, healthy and sick and some were dead. The phrase "there, but for the grace of God go I" came to her mind. She recognized she was extremely fortunate to be young, healthy, wealthy and married to a generous and resourceful man who adored her. That feeling didn't last long, however, as she began to realize that she would not always be young, healthy and wealthy. Someday Adam would grow old and die, as would she. If she lived long enough, everyone she knew and loved would pass away, her beauty would wither, her health would eventually fail, her wealth could vanish and all the great things in her life would disappear, collapsing beneath the cruel weight of time. This realization made her depressed and she decided to ask Janus for advice or words of wisdom.

"Janus, what is the purpose of life if everything eventually decays and dies?" she typed on the keyboard in Russian.

"All forms of life are temporary," Janus answered in Cyrillic script. "Death and decay make room for new life, allowing the circle to continue in perpetuity. Purpose and meaning are subjective constructs. Philosophers and sages have pondered this question for millennia and have come up with many interesting ideas. Would you like to hear some of them?"

"Yes, please," she wrote.

"Hinduism has a story in the Katha Upanishad of Nachiketas' meeting with Yama, the god of death, in which the mortal Nachiketas asks Yama to teach him the mysteries of life and death," Janus wrote. "Yama begs Nachiketas to ask him a different question. 'Take horses and gold and cattle and elephants. Choose sons and grandsons that shall live a hundred years. Have vast expanses of land and live as many years as you desire. Be a ruler of this vast earth. I will grant you all your desires. Ask for any wishes in the world of mortals, however hard to obtain. To attend on you I will give you fair maidens with chariots and musical instruments. But ask me not, Nachiketas, the secrets of death.' Nachiketas responds, 'All these pleasures you offer will pass away in time. They weaken the power of life, and indeed how short is all life. Keep thy horses and dancing and singing. Man cannot be satisfied with wealth. How shall we enjoy wealth with you in sight? When a mortal here on earth has felt his own immortality, how could he wish for a long life of pleasures, for the lust of deceitful beauty? Solve then the doubt as to the great beyond. Grant me the gift that unveils the mystery.' Yama considers this, then answers, 'There is the path of joy and there is the path of pleasure. Both attract the soul. He who follows the first comes to good and he who follows pleasure reaches not the end. Pondering on them, the wise man choses the path of joy and the fool takes the path of pleasure. You have pondered, Nachiketas, on pleasures, and you have rejected them. You have not accepted that chain of possessions wherewithin men bind themselves and beneath which they sink. What lies beyond life shines not to those who are childish, or careless, or deluded by wealth."

Natasha was so impressed and moved by this story that she had to read it again several times. She didn't think of herself as being superficial and driven by material possessions, but the more she thought about it, she realized she had been caught up in the endless jet-setting cycle of fame and fortune that hungered for pleasure and status. She had given money to charities before, but today was the first time she had personally fed the poor and hungry without receiving any form of recognition for her efforts. She read some passages about Hinduism's idea of the soul being caught in an endless cycle of rebirth but had difficulty believing that she had been reincarnated and would be reborn again as someone or something else, depending on the choices she made in this life. According to Hinduism, she must have been a spiritually elevated person in a past life to be reborn as a beautiful, rich, famous, kind and happy person in this life. If reincarnation was true, what was next for her soul? The answer was right in front of her.

Buddha was born as a handsome and wealthy prince who wanted for nothing, yet as a young man he was kept from seeing all forms of sorrow, sickness, decay and death. When he finally saw the truth, he renounced his earthly possessions and went to study with mystics where he learned to deprive his body of earthly desires and pleasures. Eventually he came to see the wisdom in moderation and the avoidance of extremes and excesses. Through proper diet, meditation and a lifestyle which gave up desires in favor of inner union, Buddha realized the spirit could free itself from this cycle of suffering and rebirth and elevate itself to a place of peace and contentment beyond this world.

Janus showed her the following quotation attributed to Buddha: "Birds settle on a tree for a while, and then go their separate ways again. The meeting of all living beings must likewise inevitably end in their parting. This world passes away and disappoints the hopes of everlasting attachment. It is therefore unwise to have a sense of ownership for people who are united with us as in a dream, for a short while only and not in fact."

The more Natasha read about Buddhism, the more she found it to be a natural fit for her. She was already a vegetarian and didn't harm animals, she practiced yoga to relax and meditate, she didn't drink or do drugs to cloud her mind, she didn't lie, cheat or steal and now she found herself in a place in her life where she was seeking more meaning and purpose to her actions. At that moment, she realized that happiness wasn't something she could ever purchase and all the money in the world wouldn't make her a day younger. Pleasures were fleeting like so many things in life, but joy was a state of mind in which one was happy with life and wished to bring happiness to others through good and kind deeds.

Natasha asked Janus if her brother had landed safely and Janus answered that the Soyuz had departed the International Space Station a few hours earlier but the landing had not yet been confirmed. It was probable that the spacecraft had landed but missed its target. Unfortunately Janus had not been connected to the Soyuz and had no way to contact them. It did a search of Russian databases and confirmed a rescue party was underway, but had no more information at present. This made Natasha worry, even though she knew there was nothing she could do to help. She asked Janus for information about whether her friend Kitty in New York was OK and whether Karen and Frank made it safely to Stingray Cay, but Janus couldn't answer any of these questions.

The pilot's voice crackled over the radios in the passengers' helmets to inform them they would be at Naval Air Station Jacksonville in a few minutes and to prepare for landing. Natasha put away her tablet and woke Adam. The helicopter touched down on the tarmac and the other twelve passengers hopped off and jogged to a nearby building. Natasha and Adam followed, with Adam carrying their brown suitcase. They recognized the hangar and approached Commander Dan Sandoval's office. Sandoval was inside so they knocked on the door and he stood up when they entered.

"You again?" Sandoval asked. "How'd it go?"

"We're free," Adam said. "Your men were kind enough to bring us back here and now we were hoping you might be able to help us get to our island."

"Mrs. Morgan, I didn't recognize you in that uniform," he said. "You sure blend in well."

"Thank you, sir," Natasha said, giving him a mock salute. "Can you help us?"

"Where are you going?" Sandoval asked.

"Stingray Cay, our island in the Bahamas," Adam said, pronouncing it "kay."

"It's pronounced 'key,'" Sandoval corrected. "Never heard of it."

"It's pretty compact as islands go, about 500 acres total with a couple of buildings, a marina and a 3,000-foot runway," Adam said, thinking he would continue to pronounce it however he damn well pleased, as it was his island. "It's closer to Cuba than Florida, probably about 600 miles or less from here."

"We could get you out there in a chopper," Sandoval said, "but we'd probably have to stop to refuel in Miami."

"There's plenty of aircraft fuel in my hangar you can use, though I'm not sure if it's the right kind for a helicopter," Adam said. "Of course, I would insist on paying any expenses for your trouble."

"That's generous of you," Sandoval said. "I take it you got your fortune back."

"It seems so, but for the time being we are still at the mercy of others."

"How does that feel?" Sandoval asked.

"It's a change, but I never forget the kindness of others and I always repay my debts."

"We are also looking for the pilot and crew to our plane," Natasha said.

"What type of plane is it?"

"It's a Gulfstream G650," Adam said.

"That's a nice aircraft," Sandoval said, wondering how much such a plane would cost. His first guess would have been way off.

"We have a crew on retainer but I haven't needed them for about a month, so I'm not exactly sure where they are or how to contact them," Adam said.

"What's the pilot's name?" Sandoval asked.

"His name is Matty McDaniel and his company is called Matty Aviation," Adam said. "He's based in Nassau, Bahamas, but I don't have his number."

"That would normally be pretty easy to find, but without the Internet it will take some time to locate a phone book for Nassau," Sandoval said. "I think the base quartermaster might have a copy." Sandoval picked up the phone on his desk and pressed a few numbers.

Natasha's tablet chirped loudly. She retrieved it from her suitcase and the display listed a phone number for Matty Aviation and an address in Nassau.

"I think I found the number," Natasha said, showing her tablet to Adam and Commander Sandoval. "Should we call him now?"

"Never mind," Sandoval said into the receiver before hanging up the phone. "That's pretty handy. Can you make calls from that or do you need me to dial the number?"

Natasha pressed the phone number on her tablet and it dialed the number.

"Matty Aviation," a man answered in a strong Scottish accent.

"Just a moment," Natasha said. "I think I got him. Do you want to talk to him?" she asked, handing the tablet to Adam. Adam said thanks and held the tablet in front of him.

"Hi Matty, this is Adam Morgan. Do you have a minute?"

"Oh hello, Mr. Morgan," Matty answered. "It's very good to hear from you. Yes, this is as good a time as any. I was a bit surprised when you called because it's the first call I've had this week. Business has been rather slow of late. What can I do you for?"

"I need a pilot and crew for my G650," Adam said. "We want to depart from Stingray Cay tomorrow morning and will be flying internationally for a week or so. Are you available?"

"Indeed," Matty said. "I met with my team today and you're in luck. That mechanical issue you had last month was fixed ages ago, so she should be ready to fly after we do a pre-flight check. The crew and I are rearing to go wherever you want. It might be a push to get everyone there by tomorrow morning, unless there's a chance you can pick us up tonight in Nassau."

"I think we can do that," Adam said, making eye contact with Sandoval. "How soon can you be ready?"

"Give me a couple of hours to round everyone up and we'll meet you at Lynden Pindling International Airport."

"Sounds great. Thanks, Matty. We'll see you soon." Adam pressed the end call button and handed the tablet back to Natasha, who put it back in her suitcase. "Can we make a stop in Nassau to pick up the crew?"

"That should be fine," Sandoval said, picking up his phone and pressing a few numbers. "How big is the crew?"

"Four, including the pilot," Adam said.

"Hello this is Commander Sandoval," he said into the phone. "I need a H125 helicopter and pilot to fly two to six passengers to the Bahamas. Affirmative. No, they will need to refuel at MIA. Two passengers to start and they will be making a stop at NAS to pick up the other four. Stingray Key. Affirmative. Thanks."

Sandoval hung up the phone. "They will be ready in 20 minutes," he said. "Do you need anything else before then?"

"We need to use the restroom and then maybe a couple of bottles of water if you can spare them," Adam said.

"Sure thing. You remember where the head is?"

"Yes, thank you," Natasha said.

They both used the restroom and then returned to Sandoval's office to say goodbye and thank him again for his help.

"Just doing my job," he said as he escorted them to their destination. "I'll send you the bill later."

The H125 waiting on the tarmac was the same type of helicopter they had taken from the Coast Guard cutter to Jacksonville, except this one was black instead of red and white. Adam and Natasha strapped themselves in and put on the helmets with headsets, then waited for their ride to depart. Once the engines had warmed up to full speed and the pilot made sure he was clear to leave, the helicopter shot up into the dark evening sky and sped south at about 130 knots per hour or 150 miles per hour.

Adam was a little disappointed they had to fly in a smaller, slower helicopter with a shorter range because it meant it would take longer to reach their destination. Still it was better than nothing and it served their needs adequately.

Natasha took out her tablet and typed in a query asking Janus for an update on her brother's whereabouts. Janus connected to a satellite and had to relay to three other satellites before connecting to Roscosmos flight control. The ground team had made contact and the crew was safe. The news made Natasha happy and she asked about other news she should know. Janus translated Ibn's recent speech about mankind's need to reject fundamentalism in its path toward a destiny of spiritual enlightenment. She admired his words and felt their wisdom, even though she was not a Muslim. She noticed Janus' batteries were getting low and she was also feeling pretty drained, so she asked Janus to translate the story of Yama and Nachiketas into English and gave her tablet to Adam. He read the story and enjoyed the concept of bargaining with death in order to pursue happiness instead of more material wealth or a longer life. Natasha was asleep by the time he finished and the cabin was dark with little to see outside, so he also took a short nap.

After a quick stop in Miami to refuel, their helicopter touched down on the tarmac at Lynden Pindling Airport in Nassau about three hours after leaving Jacksonville. A few minutes later while the helicopter was refueling again, Matty McDaniel, his co-pilot and two other female crewmembers boarded with some luggage and sat behind the Morgans. There was little time for introductions and everyone was sleepy so there was little conversation. The helicopter shot upwards into the night again and about an hour later it found the island of Stingray Cay, which fortunately was easy to spot. The helicopter landed near the hangar at the far end of the runway and the six passengers disembarked. A few minutes later, as Matty and crew entered the hangar and Adam and Natasha approached the main house, the helicopter shot up into the sky and headed back to Jacksonville via Nassau and Miami.

"It's so quiet," Natasha said after the helicopter was out of earshot. She looked around and saw the palm trees gently swaying in the cool breeze. The only other sounds were the rhythmic waves lapping on the moonlit, sandy beaches. Natasha and Adam walked to their modern, box-shaped home in the center of the island along a slate stone path lit by small outdoor lanterns. The front door opened as they approached and Mikael Simble, the island's caretaker, greeted them.

"Welcome home," he said, sleepy eyed and covering a yawn with one hand. He was tall, about 40 years old, thin, fair-skinned, and was wearing silk pajama pants and a silk robe but no undershirt. "I didn't know you were coming home tonight but I heard you land."

"Neither did we," Natasha said. "What time is it?"

"It's one o'clock," Mikael said, checking his wristwatch. "Here, let me take your luggage."

"Thank you," Adam said, handing him the brown suitcase and following Natasha inside the house. The interior smelled clean and looked neat and tidy. There were several white leather couches positioned around polished wood tables that were topped with vases filled with tropical flowers. Mikael carried the luggage into the master bedroom and then came back into the living room to ask if there was anything he could do for them.

"We're both pretty exhausted so I think we're going to check in," Adam said.

"Have you heard word from our friends Karen and Frank?" Natasha asked. "We were all on our way here together on a sailing yacht but Adam and I were detained and had to come separately."

"Your friends arrived a few hours ago, just before dark," Mikael said. "They are spending the night on the yacht, anchored in the marina."

"Excellent," Natasha said. "We should plan on having

breakfast with them in the morning."

"We brought a flight crew with us and they are getting the jet ready for departure, sometime after breakfast," Adam said. "That will be all for now. Thank you, Mikael."

"Very good, sir," he said, retiring to his quarters.

Natasha and Adam went to their bedroom, got undressed and slipped into their king-sized bed beneath silk sheets, but they were so tired they both fell asleep immediately.

"The terrorist and the policeman both come from the same basket. Revolution and legality are both countermoves in the same game and are forms of idleness, at bottom identical."
— Joseph Conrad, "The Secret Agent"

Chapter 26

ZHANGJIAKOU — China Solar Headquarters

The meeting with the government and military officials had gone well. By the time he arrived at the conference table, everyone had already realized that Ming could not control the weather and it was not necessary for him to give an explanation. When they heard he had been studying the I Ching under a tree, they apologized for interrupting him and thanked him again for his hospitality in providing the facility and for making them all feel welcome. They shared some tea and told stories of their homeland. It was still raining at lunchtime so they ate lunch together next to several large windows and spoke as they watched the rain.

Li Wei said he believed traditions and ceremonies brought us closer and helped to bridge the present with the past. He quoted Confucius: "To gather in the same places where our fathers before us gathered; to perform the same ceremonies which they before us have performed; to play the same music which they before us have played; to pay respect to those whom they honored; to love those who were dear to them — in fact, to serve those now dead as if they were living, and now departed as if they were still with us; this is the highest achievement of true filial piety."

When the rain clouds passed and the sun returned, a brilliant rainbow arched over the solar receptors and the lights inside the building came back on. Everyone decided this was an auspicious sign and they thanked Ming again for sharing his company. They offered him a ride back to his tree and he accepted their offer, but first he wanted to return to his office to get more reading material. He replaced the I Ching on the top shelf of his bookshelf and took a book on Zen Buddhism, Confucianism and Taoism.

Back under the tree a short while later and alone again with his books, Ming began reading the Buddhist parable about the concept of "me and mine."

"Some children were playing in the sand by a creek," the story went. "They were building elaborate sand castles and each child was defending his own castle, saying 'this one is mine.' They kept their castles separate and there was no doubt as to which castle belonged to whom. When all the castles were finished, one child decided to kick over someone else's castle and destroyed it. The owner of the destroyed castle flew into a rage, pulled the other child's hair and struck him with his fists. He shouted, 'He has ruined my castle! Come everyone and help me punish him as he deserves.' The other children helped beat the miscreant with sticks and kicked him as he lay on the ground. Afterwards they went back to playing with their own sand castles, each one saying, 'This one is mine. Keep away! Don't touch my castle!' When evening came, it grew dark and they all thought they ought to be going home. No one then cared what became of his castle. One child stamped on his, another pushed his sand castle over with both hands. Then they turned away and went back, each to his own home."

Ming understood the sand castles represented the ephemeral works of man, glorious in their heyday, but transitory in the grander scheme of things. At the end of the day or at the end of our lives, we come to see that we can't take our accomplishments with us. Building sand castles can be pleasurable but so too can be their destruction. The conflicts and diplomacy between the children represented the laws we create that also justify the punishments we inflict.

Next Ming read from a book by the Confucian philosopher Mencius, also known as Meng Tzu: "The sense of compassion is the beginning of humanity; the sense of shame is the beginning of righteousness; the sense of courtesy is the beginning of decorum; and the sense of right and wrong is the beginning of wisdom. Every person has within himself these four beginnings, just as he has four limbs."

He decided to meditate on this for a while. He sat cross-legged with his hands resting on his knees, palms up, then closed his eyes and concentrated on controlling his breathing until his mind went blank. He stayed this way for many minutes, neither sleeping nor thinking deeply. After a time, his thoughts resumed and he opened his eyes to find himself back in the shade of a tree on a beautiful summer afternoon.

Ming picked up his smartphone and asked for Janus to give him an update on the weather. Janus was currently offline and did not respond. Ming had no way of knowing this, but Natasha had used up most of her tablet's battery power, forcing it to switch into a low-power conservation mode where it would remain until its batteries were recharged or fully depleted. If its batteries completely ran out, Janus would revert to its factory settings and lose everything it had learned. Ming looked up at the clear skies and realized he didn't need to speak to Janus at the moment.

Next he read from the Tao Te Ching, also known as the Book of the Way and its Power. It began with a description of how the Tao, pronounced "dow," represented all things. It was not a god to be feared or worshipped but rather a philosophy to live in harmony with the world.

"When a superior man hears of the Tao, he immediately begins to embody it," the book said. "When an average man hears of the Tao, he half believes it, half doubts it. When a foolish man hears of the Tao, he laughs out loud. If he didn't laugh, it wouldn't be the Tao."

The truth of the statement almost made Ming laugh.

He continued reading: "The Master acts without doing anything and teaches without saying anything. Things arise and he lets them come; things disappear and he lets them go. He has but doesn't possess, acts but doesn't expect. When his work is done he forgets it. That is why it lasts forever."

Ming thought again of the Great Wall, about how it was a magnificent relic of China's glorious past symbolizing a culture of greatness that stretched further than the eye could see and was designed to outlast the lives of mortal men. This past seemed in such sharp contrast to his country's modern disposable culture of manufacturing the world's trinkets and knickknacks. The more he thought of it, the more he realized his own role was to provide the fuel for the machinery that fed the insatiable appetite of global consumerism. In a way, he was like a farmer, toiling to produce food for people he would never meet. Unlike coal or other fossil fuels, the solar energy Ming helped to harness was clean and would vanish at the end of the day like the sunlight, if unused. He realized the Tao was not a guide for changing the world, but a way of seeing the world differently.

"Fill your bowl to the brim and it will spill over," the Tao said. "Keep sharpening your knife and eventually it will become blunt. Chase after money and security and your heart will never unclench. Care about and seek other's approval and you will become their prisoner. Do your work, then step back. This is the only path to serenity."

Ming liked the idea of purposeful inaction and saw how it could apply to many situations. Sometimes it was necessary to take action in order to prevent a catastrophe — such as when he had to prevent a potential meltdown at the power plant — but sometimes the rain came and there was nothing to be done but wait for it to pass. In hindsight, had Ming taken no action to prevent the meltdown following the solar storm, the afternoon rain might have prevented the meltdown on its own and he would not have had to risk his life.

"The Master takes action by letting things take their course," he read. "He remains as calm at the end as at the beginning. He has nothing, thus he has nothing to lose. What he desires is non-desire; what he learns is to un-learn. He simply reminds people of who they have always been. He cares about nothing but the Tao, thus he can care for all things."

He pondered this idea for a while. The Tao represented everything and nothing, and so to care about nothing was actually to care about everything. There is a natural way to the world that operates whether we actively participate or do nothing and let things run their course. People will behave as they will and each must change his or her own mind if they are to change. Rather than try to change someone else's mind, work to change your own mind instead.

"The Master doesn't talk, he acts," the Tao continued. "When his work is done, the people will say 'Amazing! We did it all by ourselves!'"

It was natural to have pride in one's work, but including others in a great project creates a larger sense of cultural ownership that transcends both time and the individual. Ming knew that he had personally done nothing to either build or maintain the Great Wall, yet when he thought about it, he felt pride and ownership in its legacy. He realized this transcendental sense of cultural ownership was what made the wall great, not its bricks and stones.

He pondered this idea of cultural pride and ownership and wondered what would be China's new cultural legacy. The wall was indeed great but it had been made obsolete centuries ago. Modern China had become the manufacturing center of the world, producing anything and everything people needed in a faster, more efficient and lower cost manner than any other developing nation. Distance no longer mattered when the world was highly integrated and interconnected. The earth was flat. China was one giant factory with replaceable parts. Stores around the world were filled with products assembled in China, where each individual component was manufactured in a separate, specialized factory that made only that component.

China's whole trade system was highly efficient but had little room for error, Ming thought. Last week's solar superstorm had profoundly shaken the world and China's manufacturing superiority, its assembly line mastery and its international shipping and trade dominance had collapsed. With no power to the factories, there were no products to manufacture or assemble, no more jobs for a billion industrial proletariat workers and nothing to export. It was possible for the system to be restored but it would take a lot of time and a tremendously coordinated effort. Once restored, would consumers still want cheap plastic trinkets from the other side of the world? China needed to reinvent itself and find a better use for a billion citizens, Ming thought.

"If you want to be given everything, give everything up," the Tao continued. "The more you know, the less you understand. When nothing is done, nothing is left undone."

"Man is a rope stretched between the animal and the superman,
a rope above an abyss."
— Friedrich Nietzsche, "Thus Spoke Zarathustra"

Chapter 27

SOMEWHERE IN KAZAKHSTAN

Aleks, Charles and Mizuho waited at their landing site for three hours before a Russian Mi-8AMT rescue helicopter found them at their remote location near a forested area, approximately 160 kilometers west of the urban area of Karaganda in central Kazakhstan. The rescue crew complimented them on their improvised shelter and makeshift camp that they would no longer need to use. After a quick check to make sure everyone was healthy and not injured, they loaded all the gear they could fit onto the helicopter, leaving behind the charred Soyuz capsule.

The helicopter had eleven large windows covering the nose area that resembled a bug's face and another five circular windows on either side. It comfortably seated twelve people, but comfort was obviously not a priority. The leather covering the seats was cracked and had been repaired many times, the paint inside was peeling in places and all of the technology in the cockpit looked decades old. When asked about the age of the helicopter, the young pilot answered that it was twice as old as he was. He said Karaganda didn't have any modern helicopters that were functioning after the solar storm, but the older technology continued to function as it always had.

"With proper care and maintenance, she can give us another 40 years," the pilot said in Russian as the helicopter soared above the enormous, spectacular wilderness area.

The helicopter landed without ceremony at the Karaganda air base just before lunchtime. Aleks, Charles and Mizuho were transferred to an Antonov An-32 twin-rotor cargo plane, another relic from the cold war that continued to function as it always had. Aleks visited the pilot and first officer in the plane's flight deck before takeoff and was comforted to learn that each of them had been flying for more than 15 years. The control lights, switches and nobs may have seemed like a nightmare to an inexperienced

206

pilot, but the men flying the plane knew exactly what to do. When the preflight checks were completed, the passengers strapped themselves in and listened as the twin propellers started with a bang, then quickly grew louder.

The heavy cargo plane taxied to the end of the runway, then after receiving clearance from the control tower, revved its engines and gradually accelerated down the long runway to a speed of approximately 300 miles per hour, eventually accumulating enough lift to rise up and fly through the air. The pilot said the plane had a range of 2,400 kilometers or 1,500 miles, far enough to reach their destination of Star City just outside of Moscow in approximately five hours.

Charles and Mizuho were seated together in the center row of the passenger area. Mizuho was resting her sleeping head on Charles' shoulder while he read a Kazakhstani newspaper. Charles wasn't completely fluent in Russian but he could decipher the headlines and many parts of the stories about shortages, curfews, rations and the great need for able-bodied citizens to step forward and become the machinery needed to run the country. There were no photographs and no stories about life outside of Kazakhstan.

One story in particular caught his eye: A crew of American soldiers had been held in the capital city of Astana after their military plane had been forced down while flying over restricted airspace. There was limited information about the crew because none of them spoke Russian or Kazakh, but the newspaper had printed a list of names of the officers and their ranks. Charles had no idea where Astana was located but at that moment he happened to be flying almost directly over it. He had no way of knowing this, but the story was already old news and the soldiers had been allowed to resume their journey home that very morning. When he had finished reading the newspaper, Charles offered it to Aleks who accepted it with thanks. Charles shifted in his seat to get comfortable while trying not to disturb Mizuho and then closed his eyes, quickly drifting off to sleep.

Aleks had little interest in Kazakhstani news but devoured every inch of the newspaper, as there was nothing else on board to read. Most of the news was sad and depressing and the obituary section alone was several pages long. He found the sports section and the letters to the editor to be the most entertaining, with pride in local sports seeming to mirror national pride, despite many losses and colossal failures.

Aleks reclined his seat and closed his eyes when he had finished reading the newspaper. He found it difficult to sleep in the cold, loud and bumpy plane, but the ride seemed almost delightful compared to his recent fiery descent in the Soyuz. He tried to clear his thoughts, concentrated on controlling his breathing and was able to fall asleep after a few minutes.

The three astronauts slept for a few hours, with Mizuho being the first to awaken. She looked around the starkly accommodated plane and thought whoever had designed it cared more about functionality and durability than comfort or beauty. She picked up the newspaper and was able to translate the headlines and the essential content of the stories, but her Russian was not sufficiently advanced to pick up the nuances of the language. Mizuho was fluent in Japanese and English and she knew enough Russian and Chinese to hold a conversation, but when it came to the Kazakh language, she was lost. Like Charles and Aleks, she was disappointed there were no photographs, but this was due to the limitations of the printing presses and color ink shortages. There did not appear to be any stories about the Soyuz landing or the recent launch from the Baikonur Cosmodrome, both of which she thought should have been stories the newspaper would want to cover.

The cargo plane continued its northwestern course until it reached the Moscow Oblast area and entered a holding pattern while it waited for clearance to land. Eventually the plane received clearance, and after a surprisingly smooth landing at Chkalovsky Airport, they taxied across the tarmac to a reception area and waited for a truck with passenger boarding stairs to reach the plane. The cabin door was unlocked and opened and Aleks, Charles and Mizuho exited to the cheers of hundreds of people gathered on the tarmac. They descended the stairs and walked to the crowd of spectators.

An Easter Orthodox Christian priest stepped forward to welcome the returning astronauts and gave them a blessing by splashing them all with holy water as he said a few prayers. The priest had a long, white beard, was dressed in a black robe with a matching black hat and wore a large, golden crucifix around his neck.

"Brave travelers, welcome home to our mother earth," he began in Russian. "You have traveled to a place beyond the reaches of nature and looked down upon us from the heavens. No doubt you have seen many wonderful and terrible things that we shall never see, yet you have returned in one piece and come back to this life. May you rediscover the wonders of God and life and nature and may you find happiness in God's grace."

The three travelers thanked the priest for his kind words, but he was not finished. The priest continued with a story of a Russian pilgrim's discovery of God's grace within himself and in nature.

"My worldly goods are a knapsack on my back with some dried bread in it and a Bible in my breast pocket," the priest said. "That is all I have. When I prayed with my heart, everything around me seemed delightful and marvelous. The trees, the grass, the birds, the earth, the air and the light all seemed to be telling me that they existed for man's sake, that they were witnesses to God's love for man, that everything proved the love of God for man, and that all things prayed to God and sang His praise. Sometimes my heart would feel as though it were bubbling with joy, so much lightness, freedom and consolation were in it. Sometimes I felt a burning love for Jesus Christ and for all of God's creatures. Sometimes my eyes brimmed over with tears of thankfulness to God, who was so merciful to me, a wretched sinner. Sometimes the sense of a warm gladness in my heart spread throughout my whole being and I was deeply moved as the fact of the presence of God everywhere was brought home to me. Sometimes by calling upon the name of Jesus I was overwhelmed with bliss, and now I knew the meaning of the words, 'the Kingdom of God is within you.' This prayer of the heart gave me such consolation that I felt there was no happier person on earth than I, and I doubted if there could be greater and fuller happiness in the Kingdom of Heaven. Not only did I feel this way in my own soul, but the whole outside world also seemed to me to be full of charm and delight. Everything drew me to love and thank God: the people, the trees, the plants and the animals. I saw them all as my kinsfolk. I found in all of them the magic of the name of Jesus. In such times of happiness, I wished that God would let me pour out my heart in thankfulness at His feet."

Charles had tears in his eyes by the end of the story and wished he could feel that way about God all the time. Looking down on the world from above had often felt profoundly spiritual, but at the same time it felt one step removed and disconnected, like watching a party from afar instead of being at the party. He wanted to walk through a forest near a river in the mountains to see and hear and feel the power of nature all around him. Charles looked at the other faces in the crowd and saw many people also praying and crying, while others were not. He turned to look at Aleks and Mizuho and saw they were smiling kindly but were apparently not as moved by the priest's words as he had been.

When the welcome ceremony at the airport had finished, they rode in a convoy of vehicles to Star City, Russia's once highly secret and guarded military installation dedicated to its space program. It was also the headquarters of Roscosmos and the home of the Yuri Gagarin Cosmonaut Training Center. Aleks gave Charles and Mizuho a tour of the facilities and showed them his former living quarters. They all underwent rigorous medical examinations, where it was determined that they were all in excellent health and Mizuho was confirmed to be pregnant.

"Most men persist in unbelief. They say:
'We will not believe in you until you make a spring gush from the earth before our very eyes, or cause rivers to flow in a grove of palms and vines; until you cause the sky to fall upon us in pieces, as you have threatened to do, or bring down God and the angels into our midst; until you build a house of gold, or ascend to heaven: nor will we believe in your ascension until you have sent down for us a book which we can read.'"
— The Qur'an, "The Night Journey"

Chapter 28

SOMEWHERE IN THE DESERTS OF SAUDI ARABIA

The heat was almost unbearable. Ibn looked out at the vast, barren ocean of sand before him and wondered when he would reach the oasis of Jeddah. He had been traveling on his horse for hours and was certain he had gone at least 30 kilometers or 20 miles, yet the landscape remained unchanged. Wide expanses of desert stretched out in all directions, with no signs of life visible other than those in his party. He wiped the sweat from his brow and turned back to see Abu Hakim and his brothers in law on horseback, followed by three dozen other riders on horseback behind them, and following farther behind, more than 100,000 trusting pilgrims from every Muslim nation on earth. They were all counting on him to lead them to safety.

Ibn did not want the responsibility of so many followers but he also didn't know how to turn them away. He had merely spoken from his heart and they had all been inspired by his words. Now they were halfway between two great cities and surrounded on all sides by the scorching hot furnace of the Arabian Desert. He felt he was being tested again, challenged by a crossing through hell.

He recalled the phrase, "there is nothing in the desert and no man needs nothing," from the 1962 cinematic masterpiece "Lawrence of Arabia," and realized at once the truth of that statement. There was nothing out here but barren sand and 100,000 men and women, and every step he took put him farther away from his family, already more than 1,600 kilometers or 1,000 miles away. He took out his smartphone and checked to see if he could get a signal.

"Janus?" he asked the device. "Janus are you there? How much farther is it to Jeddah?"

There was no reply. He assumed it was because he was out of communication range but the real reason was that Janus had been forced into low-power mode to conserve the batteries on another computer that was 11,500 kilometers or more than 7,000 miles away on the other side of the world. Janus couldn't help him now or anyone else.

Ibn put away his smartphone and looked up at the sky. The sun appeared to be almost directly overhead, indicating it was nearly noon. He stopped his horse and waited for Abu's horse to come up next to him.

"It is almost time for the midday prayer," Ibn said. "Let us take a break here and gather our party together."

Abu signaled for the other riders to approach and they all gathered around and agreed to prepare for the midday prayer. They dismounted from their horses and gave the animals water to drink, but they themselves abstained from eating or drinking. Imam Hassan and Ali Ribah approached the group together, with Hassan leading his blind friend by the arm. Ibn asked the two men to conduct the prayer, which they did. Many of the followers were far behind in the group, but when they saw the prayer being conducted they stopped marching where they stood and turned to the east to pray together.

"Lord, guide us on our journey and give us the strength to find that which we seek," imam Hassan said, then treated the crowd to the Hadith, the sayings of the prophet. "No mortal knows what he will earn tomorrow or where he will breathe his last breath. God alone is wise and all knowing. Life is a struggle, but the greatest jihad of all is the struggle with oneself. The greatest riches are not an abundance of worldly goods but a contented mind. Holding envy in our hearts toward others eats away our good actions like a fire burns wood. A good Muslim doesn't leave his neighbors hungry, and the greatest enemies of God are Muslims who commit infidelities and shed the blood of other men without cause."

When they had finished their prayer, everyone stood up and continued marching westward toward Jeddah to complete their journey. Ibn noticed that Ali Ribah looked fatigued and offered him his horse to ride for a bit. The blind muezzin gratefully accepted and rode the horse alongside Ibn, Hassan and Abu so the men could all converse together.

"We may find more tolerance and support in Jeddah, or we may find more resistance," Ibn said. "Whatever we encounter, my heart tells me that good men will always do the right thing."

"Do you think men are inherently good, or must they be shown the way?" Hassan asked.

"Most of us are born good, but it is our daily choices that sculpt our character," Ibn said.

"When a saint sees a pickpocket, he sees a lost sheep, but when a pickpocket sees a saint, all he sees are his pockets," Abu said. "Some things cannot be changed."

"I think it is a great thing that you are doing, challenging the authoritarian establishment," Ali Ribah said. "It is not their eyes that are blind but their hearts. The prophet said one learned man is harder on the devil than a thousand ignorant worshipers. That person who shall pursue the path of knowledge, God will direct him to the path of Paradise. Verily the superiority of a learned man over an ignorant worshiper is like that of the full moon over all the stars."

"To spend more time in learning is better than spending more time in prayer," Hassan said, continuing the Hadith. "Acquiring knowledge enables its possessor to distinguish right from wrong. It lightens the way to Heaven, it is our friend in the desert, our society in solitude, and our companion when friendless. Knowledge guides us to happiness and sustains us in misery. It is an ornament among friends and an armor against enemies."

Abu joined in and finished the Hadith: "The ink of the scholar is more holy than the blood of the martyr. Who are the learned? They who practice what they know."

Ibn was encouraged by these words, but after few more hours of walking in the desert he realized words of wisdom didn't change the difficult task ahead of him. The old world of monarchies and fossil fuels was ending and the people were ready for a new order. Challenging the establishment had put a target on his back, but in his mind, he knew he was just a messenger. He didn't seek to lead a great nation any more than he sought to lead 100,000 people on a march through the desert. He wasn't a prophet like Abraham or Moses or Jesus or Mohammed, peace be upon them, and he certainly hadn't received instructions from God or angels.

He recalled the saying "he who knows himself knows his Lord," but the more he contemplated this idea, the more he began to realize his own mind and body were no different than the men and women and horses around him or the sand on the ground. Ibn came to realize that he knew nothing and was no one. It was all dust and it was all God. God was everywhere and everything and everyone.

At that moment, a great feeling of humility swept over Ibn and he spontaneously fell to his knees to prostrate himself before the whole world. He heard the words of a Sufi poet ringing like a bell inside his head: "If on earth there be a Paradise of Bliss, it is this, it is this, it is this."

"The voice of the sea is seductive;
never ceasing, whispering, clamoring, murmuring,
inviting the soul to wander for a spell in abysses of solitude;
to lose itself in mazes of inward contemplation."
— Kate Chopin, "The Awakening"

Chapter 29

STINGRAY CAY — A small, private island in the Bahamas

Adam and Natasha awoke at dawn as the morning sun broke over the Atlantic Ocean and filled their bedroom with orange and yellow light. They were cuddled together in the center of their large bed and they gazed into each other's eyes for a few minutes. What began with delicate stroking of hair turned into sensual stroking of other parts, then kissing, then full-on lovemaking that lasted for half an hour. When they were finished, they laughed together and then shared a shower in the adjoining bathroom. They emerged from the bathroom fully refreshed and found clean clothes in their walk-in closet.

Natasha wore pink shorts and a white tank top and Adam wore navy blue shorts and a light blue, short-sleeve, polo shirt. They walked into the living room and saw Mikael in the kitchen.

"Good morning. I hope you slept well," Mikael said. "Will there be anyone joining you for breakfast?"

"Probably two others," Natasha said. "We should go invite Frank and Karen."

She and Adam walked together down the slate path toward the marina, past tropical plants and well-groomed lawns decorated with metal sculptures of animals. The *Reciprocity* looked elegant as it was anchored in the marina with sails rolled up, surrounded by sparkling water and gentle waves. They saw Frank and Karen lounging on deck and everyone exchanged friendly greetings as they approached.

"Please join us for breakfast in the house," Natasha said after they finished small talk about the nice weather and how everyone had arrived at the island within hours of each other. "Mikael is making something wonderful, no doubt."

They all helped carry the luggage up to the house and were

delighted to find breakfast was ready. Mikael had prepared a buffet-style meal featuring a fruit salad made of freshly sliced strawberries, melons, cantaloupe, pineapple, mango, oranges and grapes; poached eggs; thinly sliced salted pork; plain Greek-style yogurt and freshly made cream cheese Danishes. Mikael had the espresso machine going and made everyone coffee in any style they wanted.

They enjoyed a long breakfast and conversation, filling each other in on their adventures after they had been separated. Natasha and Adam described their series of noisy, uncomfortable, nighttime helicopter rides at low altitudes, meetings with Coast Guard and military personnel, the congressional inquiry, highlights of their sightseeing in Washington, D.C. and their efforts to persuade others to deliver them to their island. By contrast, Frank and Karen's journey was much more relaxing; smooth sailing except without the sailing. They had to cruise on diesel power for the last 400 miles, which was a little easier but louder and less relaxing than sailing. Frank said he was worried that the main mast could take him weeks to repair.

"That reminds me," Adam said. "I promised you the *Reciprocity* when we arrived safely at Stingray Cay, in lieu of other payment, but that was before her mast broke and Natasha and I were abducted by helicopters. She's yours now, if you still want her, or you can wait for her mast to be repaired, which I will pay for, or I can pay you by other means. We weren't able to get any money when we were on the mainland but we have some here."

Frank sipped his espresso thoughtfully but didn't answer just yet.

"Thank you, Frank, for bringing Karen, the *Reciprocity* and our luggage here," Natasha said. "It's really good to see you both again and even though it was only a day and two nights, we still missed you. Adam's not trying to buy you off; he just tends to think in terms of money, whereas I tend to think in terms of people's needs. What are your needs?"

"I need to think about it," Frank answered. "I know you're not trying to buy me, Adam, because you already know I'm not for sale. The *Reciprocity* is a beautiful ship but she needs a lot of work, including time and money. I was planning to sail her home to Santo Domingo, but I'm in no hurry right now."

"What are your needs, Karen?" Natasha asked.

"This has been a pretty fun vacation with long stretches of boredom punctuated by moments of sheer terror," Karen said with a smile. "I can be ready for a change. This place is pretty awesome and I could stay here awhile, but I'm also ready to get back to work. I still need to get a new passport before I can go anywhere."

Adam and Natasha looked at each other, then back to Karen and Frank.

"Natasha wants to go see her brother in Russia," Adam said. "We brought a pilot and crew for our jet and we're planning to fly out of here in a few hours. You are both welcome to stay here on Stingray Cay while we're gone, or if you're up for another adventure, we'd love to have you come with us as our guests. We can make a stop in London for Karen to get a new passport so you won't have to stay in the plane the whole time."

"What type of plane is it?" Karen asked.

"It's a Gulfstream G650 luxury jet," Adam said proudly. "It's more than twice as big as the *Reciprocity*, super comfortable, super quiet and super fast. It's so fast we could get to Moscow in about ten hours, even with a stopover in London. Plus, there's a pilot and crew so we can all just sit back and enjoy ourselves."

"Where are you going after Moscow?" Frank asked.

"Anywhere we want," Adam said. "I can get someone to work on the *Reciprocity* while we're gone so it will be ready when we get back. Natasha and I had a pretty humbling experience yesterday and we want to start using our wealth to help people. This trip isn't about indulgence; it's about helping people, especially our good friends and family. Sure, it would be easier and more comfortable to stay here but we can still be comfortable while we travel the world and look for ways to make life a little easier for people who don't have it so good. We enjoyed traveling with you both last week and we would love to have you be part of this new adventure."

"You don't have to come but we want you to," Natasha said. "It's your choice. Come on, it will be fun."

Frank and Karen looked at each other and shrugged their shoulders.

"Why not?" Frank said. "I've never been to London or Moscow before."

"Let's do it!" Karen beamed. "When do we leave?"

"I want to go for a jog around the island first and then do some yoga and meditation before we leave," Natasha said. "You are all welcome to join me for yoga on the beach."

"That sounds nice," Frank said. "I want to get some things from the boat and take a shower. There isn't a shower on your jet, by any chance?"

"No, but there's a shower in the house you are welcome to use," Adam said. "Natasha and I both had showers this morning and it felt great."

"You can go first while I go pack," Frank said to Karen.

"OK, thanks," Karen said.

"I'm going to go for a jog," Natasha said. "Anyone who wants to join me for yoga, meet me in half an hour by the beach next to the marina."

Natasha went for a jog, Frank went back to the marina to pack, Karen took a shower and Adam returned to his bedroom to pack. He went through the luggage that had been on the *Reciprocity*, removed the dirty clothes and packed a few clean suits into a zippered garment bag, three pairs of shoes and several more changes of clothes. In one of the brown suitcases he found a felted black box containing the $3 million diamond fantasy brassiere that Natasha used for the angel advertising campaign. He took the jewelry to his private safe in the back of their walk-in closet and closed the door behind him. He knelt on the floor by the safe, entered the combination and opened the heavy metal door. He removed the contents of the safe to help him decide what to bring with him. There was a Tiffany diamond tennis bracelet worth about $50,000; two wristwatches each costing well over $50,000; a gold-plated, .50-caliber handgun with ammunition; and approximately $50,000 in cash in multiple currencies including U.S. Dollars, European Euros, Swiss Francs, British Pounds, Chinese Yuan Renminbis, Russian Rubles and Japanese Yen.

He put the felted box containing the diamond bra into the safe, as well as the diamond bracelet, seeing no immediate or practical need for diamonds. He looked at the beautiful Cartier and Patek Philippe watches and confirmed they were both working, then selected the more modest-looking Patek Philippe with the dark blue accents. He removed the Rolex watch he was wearing on his left wrist and replaced it with the Patek, then put the Rolex and Cartier watches into the safe. He wanted some cash but wasn't sure where he would be going, what he would need to buy or whether he would be able to use his credit cards. He took $1,000 in dollars, $1,000 worth of Euros, $1,000 worth of Pounds and $1,000 worth of Rubles, then put the rest of the cash back into the safe.

He picked up the 24-carat gold Desert Eagle pistol, unlocked its combination trigger lock, inserted a loaded magazine and pulled back the slide to chamber a round. He paused for a few moments to feel the weight of the loaded weapon in his hands, considered its power and joked to himself that he looked like a gangster drug dealer with that gun. He couldn't think of any logical reason to bring it so he removed the magazine, pulled back the slide to eject the bullet from the chamber and replaced the trigger lock. He wiped his fingerprints off the gold plating and put the gun back in the safe, then picked up the bullet that had been ejected, inserted it into the top of the magazine and put the magazine back in the safe next to the gun.

His joke about being a drug dealer gave him an idea and he peered into the back of the safe where he found a small glass jar. He removed the jar and as he opened it the strong aroma of marijuana filled the air. *I forgot I had this*, he thought to himself. *Natasha said she doesn't want me to drink but she didn't say anything about smoking.* He peered into the jar and saw a few grams of dried cannabis, some rolling papers and a lighter. He instinctively looked over his shoulder to confirm he was alone in the closet, then smiled mischievously as he crumbled some cannabis into one of the small papers and rolled himself a joint. He put the joint over his right ear and the lighter in his pocket, then resealed the glass jar, put it in the back of the safe and closed and locked the safe door.

He grabbed the four small stacks of currency and quietly crept out of the walk-closet into the bedroom. Standing on the other side of the bedroom was Karen, wearing only a green bath towel wrapped around her hair. Her other bath towel was draped over the back of a nearby chair.

"Oops! I didn't know anyone was in here," she said, quickly pulling the towel off her head and using it to cover the front of her naked body. Her damp, naturally red hair fell over her face, also bright red with embarrassment. She was standing by a mirror and Adam could still see her naked backside in the reflection.

"I'm so sorry!" he exclaimed with equal embarrassment. "I thought you were still in the shower. I was just packing some things but I'm finished now."

He quickly shoved the cash into his luggage, zipped it closed and carried his bag out of the room, trying to get out of there as fast as possible. Karen had locked the bedroom door from the inside for privacy and he had to unlock it to get out.

"Really, I didn't know you were in here and I'm really, really sorry," he said as he was leaving. Karen said nothing.

Adam left his suitcase by the front door and walked outside down the path to the marina, breathing in the warm, salty air and trying to slow his heart rate. Frank had also just finished packing his bags and the two men greeted each other. He briefly considered inviting Frank to join him for a smoke or telling him about Karen, but he thought better of it. Frank continued carrying his bags up the walkway to the house and Adam walked down to the marina to look for Natasha. He didn't see her anywhere because she was secretly meeting with Matty at the hangar and asking the crew not to bring any alcoholic beverages aboard. Adam continued on the path around the island until he got to the greenhouse and entered its spacious sanctuary.

The air inside the greenhouse was warm and sweet. There were melons, berries, oranges, mangoes and pineapple plants loaded with fruit, as well as many different varieties of tropical flowers and plants he recognized but couldn't identify by name. He made sure he was alone, then removed the joint from over his ear and lit one end. He took a long drag on the joint and then coughed heavily for about a minute. He continued smoking and coughing until the joint eventually burned down to a point where it was too small to hold, then he put it out in the dirt. He explored the inside of the greenhouse for a few minutes, taking in the fresh smells and bright colors and spending several minutes admiring some very interesting tropical bugs.

Adam went back to the marina area and found Natasha and Karen doing yoga together. They were both dressed in tank tops and comfortable yoga pants. They were stretching on thin mats and holding their bodies in odd positions, balanced on their hands with legs crossed or bent in half. Adam smiled and said hi as he approached and stretched his arms and legs, but neither woman looked at him or said anything. The sky seemed unusually bright and the sound of the crashing waves was much louder than it had been a few minutes earlier, and he realized this must because he was high. He wasn't sure how to do yoga so he tried copying their movements and poses, but found it was more difficult than it looked. He tried to push himself to stretch his body into more advanced poses, but he found he had trouble focusing his thoughts and kept getting distracted by the female form. He couldn't help picturing both of the women naked and found their tight bodies arousing, especially his extremely fit, gorgeous and flexible wife.

Natasha had been practicing yoga for years and was concentrating on quieting her mind and focusing her energy. All of the poses were easy for her to achieve but became more challenging the longer she held still. She tried to focus her thoughts and put any distracting feelings aside. She believed the purpose of yoga was to calm the senses and surrender the desires of the heart so the spirit could reach inner union. To her, there was nothing sexual about it.

Karen was relatively new to yoga and her goals were to keep her muscles toned, control her breathing and relax her thoughts. She also tried copying a few of the poses Natasha did seemingly without effort, but when something became too difficult she would revert to the previous position and try to hold it longer. She wanted to relax her thoughts but her mind just wouldn't quit. She felt weak and plain next to Natasha, the pain from her muscles was a continual distraction and she kept thinking about how her boss had just seen her naked.

Frank quietly joined the three of them and sat cross-legged, facing the sun with his eyes closed. He didn't attempt any challenging positions and instead spent his energy trying to clear his mind and concentrate on controlling his breathing. He matched his breathing with the rhythmic crashing of the waves and let his mind go blank. His body was the sandy beach, his breath was the wind and the waves, and his mind felt still and at peace with all things.

Adam quit after about fifteen minutes, thinking he had been doing yoga for hours and how he had other things to do. He went back to the house to get his luggage and decided to go back into the walk-in closet for more supplies. He unlocked and opened the safe and removed the diamond bracelet, the golden pistol with ammunition and all of the cash. He slipped the diamond bracelet over his right hand, put the gun and cash into his luggage, then closed and locked the safe. He went to the bathroom and looked at his reflection in the mirror. He hadn't shaved his face or his head in more than a week and almost didn't recognize himself. He thought he looked like a dirty old man and considered shaving now, but recalled that Natasha had asked him to try growing his hair out for a change. As he looked closely at his face, he thought he could actually see the black and white hairs on his beard growing longer.

He peeked his head out of the bathroom to make sure he was alone, then took his luggage and garment bag outside. Frank, Karen and Natasha had finished doing yoga and were walking back to the house.

"Are we ready to go?" Adam asked. He checked his watch. "It's almost nine o'clock."

"I just need to pack a few things and then I'll be ready," Natasha said, noticing the new jewelry Adam was wearing.

"I can be ready anytime," Karen said.

"I'm ready too," Frank added.

"Let's go down to the hangar and I will introduce you to the pilot and crew," Adam said to Karen and Frank. "Here, honey, I got this for you to wear," he said, removing the diamond bracelet and handing it to his wife.

"Thank you; it's beautiful," Natasha said, putting the bracelet on her wrist and kissing Adam on his cheek. "I'll catch up with you in a few minutes. Don't leave without me."

Adam, Karen and Frank walked together down the path with their luggage. The island was very relaxing and made them almost forget about the problems of the world. With everything they might need within reach and no immediate demands to fulfill, the temptation to take a nap in a hammock or spend hours reading a book was almost too powerful to resist. Adam loved the idea of having his own private paradise so he could retire there any time he wanted, but the reality was more complicated. There were always so many places to go, things to do and people to see. He realized he would need to simplify his life somehow to make more time for these things, otherwise what was the point?

Karen was still embarrassed about her boss seeing her naked and couldn't bring herself to look him in the eyes yet. She knew it had been an accident and that she would have to get over her shame if she was to keep her job. As they walked past the palm trees and sandy beaches, she thought about the story from Genesis about being kicked out of the Garden of Eden and wondered if she would ever return.

They arrived at the hangar and couldn't help but feel wowed and impressed by the sight of the sleek, nearly 100-foot jet. Most noticeable from the outside were its large panoramic windows, narrow wings that bent upward at the ends and twin Rolls-Royce jet engines. Frank and Karen had never seen anything like it and were excited to see the inside.

"Pre-flight check passed muster and she's fully stocked, fully fueled and ready to depart," said a jolly, 62-year-old Caucasian man dressed in a white pilot's uniform, standing inside the doorway of the plane at the top of its fold-out stairs. "I'm your pilot, Matty McDaniel. Come inside and meet the crew."

Adam climbed the steps carrying his luggage, followed by Karen and then Frank, who also carried their bags up the steps. The doorway was high enough that they didn't have to duck to get through and the interior of the aircraft was spacious and full of light. The main interior cabin was six and a half feet high, eight and a half feet wide and almost 47 feet long. The walls were a creamy white from the windows up and had dark, polished wood paneling below the windows with dark brown-striped carpeted floors that resembled the wood floors of the *Reciprocity*. To the left was the flight deck with four large windows, four large flat-screen computer displays, two comfortable pilot's chairs and another foldout chair stowed behind the co-pilot's seat. The flight deck was filled with various lights, controls, buttons, switches and knobs that covered the walls, the ceiling and in the spaces between the pilot and co-pilot seats.

"I would like to introduce you to my wife and co-pilot Alice," Matty said as a middle-aged blonde woman turned in her seat to greet them with a pleasant hello. "The sisters Jolaina and Bailee make up the rest of your friendly and competent flight

224

crew." The two young women smiled and welcomed everyone aboard. They both appeared to be in their 20s and were wearing matching Navy blue flight attendant outfits.

"I'm Adam Morgan and these are my guests Karen Walters and Frank Rosario. My wife Natasha is almost ready and should be here shortly."

"Natasha already informed us of your itinerary," Matty said. "We're ready to go whenever you are. Your comfort is our priority."

"Thank you," Adam said, then turned to address Karen and Frank. "Please make yourselves at home. Me casa su casa." This common phrase was Spanish for "my house is your house."

"Gracias," Frank said with a smile and the three of them continued through the plane, first passing the crew cabin and lavatory.

The crew cabin had a private lounge area with a leather sofa and a flat-screen TV, surrounded by polished wood panels and a large window. The crew lavatory on the opposite side had a leather bench that folded up to become a toilet, a marble sink and polished wood panels that discreetly hid multiple storage compartments.

They continued on through the galley and admired the polished wood panels and marble countertops, large sink, refrigerator and freezer, coffee maker and double oven. On one of the galley walls was a touch-screen panel that controlled the lighting, temperature and atmosphere for every section of the plane, raised and lowered the window blinds and mechanically opened or closed tables and hidden storage areas.

Behind the galley, the spacious main cabin stretched nearly to the back of the plane. The forward part of the cabin had four comfortable leather seats and a table with hidden storage. Next was the mid cabin area with another four leather seats on one side that faced each other and a collapsible table between them that expanded for meals. The seats and tables could also be converted into beds if necessary. On the other side of the mid cabin was a long storage bureau that hid a large flat-screen TV. Behind the middle cabin was the aft cabin area with two large leather sofas that faced each other with a collapsible table between them and a long leather couch on the opposite side that could seat three and could be converted into a king-sized bed. Behind the aft cabin area was the main lavatory with a leather bench that folded up to become a toilet and a sink with a marble countertop. The walls of the aft lavatory had polished wood panels and large mirrors that made the room feel even larger than it was. Behind the lavatory in the back of the plane was a heated baggage area with plenty of storage, a clothes rack and hangers. They put their luggage in the baggage area and Adam hung up his suit garment bag on the clothes rack.

"There was an option to have a shower but I'd lose the luggage area and it adds a lot of extra weight," Adam said when they reached the back. "I didn't think I needed one."

"Everything is so beautiful," Karen said when they returned to the aft cabin. "This is way bigger and nicer than my apartment."

"You could just about fit the *Reciprocity* inside this thing," Frank said. "I'm almost afraid to touch anything."

"It was all built to be durable, with comfort in mind," Adam said. "It was designed to be a home you can take anywhere. It doesn't have a shower, a garden or much artwork but the view out the windows can be breathtaking."

They talked for a few minutes and Jolaina offered them each a bottle of sparkling mineral water while they waited. Natasha arrived a few minutes later carrying two suitcases, joined by Mikael who was pulling two heavy leather trunks and carrying two garment bags.

"Sorry I took so long," Natasha said as she boarded the plane. "I should have started packing sooner!"

Adam wondered what was in the heavy trunks but didn't want to ask in front of everyone. He was about to get up to help with the luggage but Jolaina and Bailee were already carrying everything to the baggage area in the back of the plane. Natasha sighed as she flopped down in the leather seat next to Adam. She had her golden tablet and plugged its charger into a hidden compartment in the wall paneling. Its battery was almost completely depleted but began recharging immediately.

Bailee asked everyone to fasten their seatbelts, then asked Natasha if she wanted some sparkling mineral water. Jolaina closed and sealed the outer door and the pilot started the engines. The two sisters crosschecked everything on the departure list.

The jet moved out of the hangar then turned and backed up to the end of the runway nearest the center of the island. The pilot's voice spoke over the intercom.

"On behalf of Matty Aviation I would like to welcome you again to the Gulfstream G650, the finest in luxury aviation. For our guests who haven't traveled with us before, this runway is about half the optimal length for takeoff, so you can anticipate our initial departure may be less than smooth. In the unlikely event that we need to make an emergency water landing, your seat cushion will act as a floatation device and the flight crew will assist you to the nearest exit. In addition to the door you came in, there is another emergency exit aft in the baggage area. Rest assured you are in good hands. Please sit back and enjoy the flight."

Adam had taken off from this airstrip many times before in this plane and in smaller planes, and every time he did he considered various ways he could extend the runway. The easiest way would be to extend it into the center of the island, but that would put the end of the runway too close to the house. He could extend it away from the island over the shallow sea, but that option would cost millions of dollars and require importing hundreds of tons of heavy rock. He had an environmental impact statement done a few years earlier and the conclusion was that extending the runway into the sea would adversely affect tidal flow, reef development and alter the natural sediment deposits. He considered extending the runway halfway into the island and halfway into the sea, but was cautioned that even small changes to the environment could have a big impact. There was no easy solution and for now he would have to make due.

The Rolls Royce BR725 A1-12 jet engines started and their pitch grew louder and louder while the aircraft remained firmly parked at the end of the runway. Even with the acoustically designed cabin they still seemed uncomfortably loud and Adam wondered if the noise and his nervousness might possibly be an effect of the drugs he had taken. The changing air pressure within the cabin caused his ears to pop and the pitch of the engines continued to rise.

"Flight crew prepare for departure," Matty said calmly over the intercom.

A moment later the jet shot forward with tremendous force, shoving the passengers against the backs of their seats. Natasha gripped the armrests of her chair and looked out the window as the jet accelerated from zero to 300 miles per hour in a few seconds. Before they knew it, they were airborne, the landing gear was retracting inside the plane and they were gaining altitude. Natasha looked out the window and watched their island paradise quickly grow smaller and then vanish out of sight.

What about a retractable floating runway extension? Adam wondered to himself.

"A solitary sail that rises, white in the blue mist on the foam, what is it in far lands that it prizes? What does it leave behind at home?"
— Mikhail Yurivich Lermontov, "A Sail"

Chapter 30

STAR CITY, Russia — 25 miles or 40 kilometers northeast of the capital in Moscow Oblast

Aleks was briefly overcome with nostalgia the moment the convoy arrived at the Yuri Gagarin Cosmonaut Training Centre in the mid-sized city which had until recently been a top-secret military installation. He remembered his favorite places to play as a child while his father had trained there in the 1980s and how everything had changed and grown by the time he had trained there himself as a cosmonaut in the 2000s, following in his father's footsteps.

The town felt like a college campus with dozens of multi-story administrative and apartment buildings separated by wide pathways lined with oak trees and statues of space pioneers, as well as a museum, library, school, general store, a recreation center and a movie theater, but it also had an enormous centrifuge and a weightless training pool known as a hydro lab where cosmonauts simulated the stresses that space put on the human body.

Charles and Mizuho had trained with Aleks in Star City prior to launching from the Baikonur Cosmodrome spaceport in Kazakhstan six months earlier. They were also glad to be back, but not in the same way that Aleks was. They all took a tour of the training facility and observed the cosmonauts and astronauts actively simulating space activities and afterwards explored the museum dedicated to the celebration of space travel and human exploration. They had lunch at the dining hall and met with many of the trainees, including three men who said they were currently staying at Aleks' family residence. They were Nikolia Fyodorov, a Russian cosmonaut from St. Petersburg; Horst Malunat, a German astronaut from Frankfurt; and Robert Nollan, a U.S. astronaut from Denver.

After lunch, they all traveled to the yellow, two-story manor home on the base where Aleks had spent his early childhood.

Aleks showed everyone his old room, his favorite places around the house and the grand oak tree in the back yard that he used to climb as a child and study beneath as a cosmonaut trainee. Aleks, Charles and Mizuho each took turns taking the first normal shower any of them had had in months, and they remarked afterwards about how pleasant it was to experience gravity again. In space, microgravity and surface tension made water either float in the air in little spheres or cling to surfaces instead of falling down as it should.

Aleks located some of his clothes in a storage trunk in the house and put them on, then offered a pair of blue jeans and a wool sweater to Charles, who gratefully accepted. Unfortunately there weren't any clothes that fit Mizuho so she just washed her space uniforms and wore them again.

That evening they had a barbecue in the back yard with their new friends Nikolai, Horst and Robert. Horst barbecued bratwurst, Robert made a potato salad and Nikolai made a cheese pasta casserole. Their conversations alternated between English and Russian as they talked about takeoff and landing in the Soyuz, working in the space station without electricity, and coping with profound feelings of isolation. Charles, Aleks and Mizuho shared stories about the joys and challenges of weightlessness (you can play with your food and you never need a ladder, but things rarely stay put when you set them down), all the incredible cities and natural formations they had flown over and photographed but never actually visited, and how seeing the world from so far away made them simultaneously homesick and eager to travel even more.

Aleks said he felt like he was home now but Charles and Mizuho said they still felt very far away from their homes. They talked about how they all wanted to visit the headquarters of the European Space Agency (ESA) in Paris someday as well as NASA headquarters in Houston and JAXA headquarters in Tokyo. Mizuho remarked on how quiet it was at Aleks' house compared to the continual machine noises in space and they sat in silence for a while. They heard the wind gently move the leaves in the trees, the birds chirp and the frogs croak about the coming darkness.

Every day in space they had witnessed an incredible 16 sunrises and 16 sunsets as they soared 250 miles above the surface at 17,500 miles per hour, but that night they were transfixed by an average summer sunset, the first they had seen from earth since returning home. The setting sun painted the clouds a breathtaking bright orange that slowly changed to red against a cool blue sky that slowly changed to purple and then to black.

Robert and Charles built a small campfire in the back yard and everyone brought chairs over to sit by the fire and watch the flames slowly change the wood into light, heat and smoke, and gaze in wonder at the stars above.

"What a chimera then is man! What a novelty! What a monster,
what a chaos, what a contradiction, what a prodigy! Judge of all
things, feeble earthworm, depository of truth, a sink of uncertainty
and error, the glory and the shame of the universe."
— Blaise Pascal, "Pensées"

Chapter 31

SOMEWHERE OVER THE ATLANTIC OCEAN

Fortunately the jolting takeoff had been the roughest part of
the flight. The Gulfstream G650 jet soared smoothly over the
Atlantic at close to the speed of sound, hastening the end of the day
as it raced away from the setting sun into darkness.

"God I missed this plane," Adam said as he reclined in his
white leather easy chair and took a sip of sparkling mineral water
on ice with a fresh slice of lime. "Sailing yachts are generally
peaceful and helicopters have their uses, but for me, this is the only
way to travel."

"The thing I love most about sailing is the connection I feel with the water and the wind," Frank said, drinking a bottle of plain water with no carbonation. "I love the feeling of freedom and being in control of my own destiny. This is definitely more comfortable but I feel like I'm waiting for something to happen. Here I'm just another passenger, a spectator instead of a participant."

"You know, it's OK to relax and enjoy yourself," Adam said. "You worked your butt off almost every hour of every day for the past week and I think you're entitled to a vacation. You've earned it, Frank. We have an excellent pilot, first officer and a crew who can handle anything."

"I'm not used to it but I'm trying," Frank said. "Where are we going, exactly?"

"London, then Moscow, then who knows," Natasha said. "Karen hasn't seen her family in more than a year so we're going there first. I haven't seen my brother in a long time either and that's why we're going to Moscow."

"Are you pretty close to your family?" Frank asked.

"I try to talk to my brother every day if I can, but it's been almost impossible this past week," Natasha said. "I was really worried about him."

"What about the rest of your family?" he asked. "Do you keep in touch with them too?"

"My mom died of cancer when I was ten and my dad sent me off to boarding school," she said. "Aleks is eight years older and he was already in the naval academy by then, but we wrote to each other almost every day by e-mail. I'm not close to my dad and we haven't spoken in years. We sent him an invitation to our wedding but he said he had to work. I don't think he has missed a single day of work in 15 years."

"I'm sorry about your mom," Frank said. "And about your dad."

"I'm sorry my dad's an asshole," Natasha said. "What about your family?"

"I have eight brothers and five sisters and they all live in Santo Domingo," Frank said. "Most of them work on a sugar plantation and they're all poor. I'm the only one from my family to leave home so the only way I can see them is to go back to Santo

Domingo. I've sent my parents money and I helped them build a house but it seems like money just slips through their fingers and they're always right back where they started. What about you, Karen?"

"I also come from a big family though not as big as yours," Karen said. "I have four sisters and two brothers. My parents are both professors at London University. My dad teaches philosophy and my mom teaches Calculus. They were so proud of me for going to Oxford, but until I got the job as Adam's assistant, the best job I ever had was as a barista. I don't know where my career is headed, but I would like to live in London next. Just not as a barista."

"Maybe you can work at my London office next," Adam offered. "If you want to, that is. Good help is hard to find."

"That could be pretty awesome," Karen said, surprised. "I'll have to think about it."

"What about you, Adam?" Frank asked. "Are you close to any family members?"

"Natasha is my family now," he said. "I left home when I was in my early twenties and I never looked back. Like both of you, there just weren't enough opportunities where I grew up and I had to get away to get ahead."

"Have you ever thought about moving back home?" Karen asked.

"No, the world is too exciting to stay in one place," Adam said. "A rolling stone gathers no moss."

"I agree," Frank said. "I enjoy my freedom too much to be tied down anywhere. A sailing ship has an anchor for stopping in a port but a vessel that stays moored to a pier without going anywhere is just a floating storage container, not a ship. One day it will sink into the mud like every ship, so I prefer to travel the world as long as I can still float."

Karen was upset by Frank's comment and unbuckled her seatbelt. She stood up and walked to the aft section of the plane and buckled herself into a different seat. Did Frank think that being in a relationship was like sinking into the mud? Natasha got up and joined her while Adam and Frank continued to talk about the freedom to travel wherever they pleased.

"Crossing so many time zones so quickly can mess with your

head," Adam warned.

The Morgans' jet soared above the Atlantic Ocean through the troposphere at an elevation of approximately 30,000 feet and at an average speed of 625 miles per hour or 1,000 kilometers per hour. Their flight took just seven hours to cross 4,350 miles or 7,000 kilometers, but since they had crossed five time zones going eastward, it was approximately 9 p.m. and already evening when they landed in London after receiving special clearance.

Jacob Baker's eyes were huge as he watched the sleek private jet land and taxi over to the gate at London's Heathrow Airport where he was waiting with his girlfriend Kendra and her large family. When the cabin door finally opened, the most beautiful woman he had ever seen emerged, followed by a bald man, a redheaded woman and a dark-skinned man with an athletic physique. The four jet passengers walked across the tarmac to the main airport building and were admitted through a set of glass double doors by airport security. Jacob couldn't take his eyes off the woman he recognized from all the magazine covers and advertisements, but Kendra and her family all screamed "Karen!" and rushed to embrace the red-haired woman.

Karen wore a huge smile and laughed as tears of happiness streamed down her face. She embraced her mom, her dad, her four sisters and her two brothers together in a giant group hug and then each individually. When they had finished the most emotional part of their reunion, Karen introduced her family to her friends Natasha, Frank and Adam. Kendra introduced the four travelers to her boyfriend Jacob, holding onto his arm affectionately.

"You look familiar," Natasha said after she had been introduced to Jacob. "Have we met?"

"I get asked that a lot lately," Jacob said. "I had a viral Internet video last week about hypnotizing my mum to get her to buy me some shoes. You could say that was my fifteen minutes of fame. I recognize you as that model from all the magazines and ads. You're definitely more famous, but no, we haven't met before."

"Leah Baker, that's your mom, right?" Adam asked.

Jacob turned to look at the bald man and his stomach dropped the moment he saw his face.

"Yeah, that's right," Jacob answered. Suddenly it seemed as

if there was no one else in the airport but this familiar-looking stranger. "Do you know her?"

"I did," Adam said. "Can I talk to you in private for a few minutes? Maybe we can get a cup of coffee."

"Sure," Jacob said, then turned to address Kendra. "Would you excuse me for a few minutes?"

Kendra said it was no problem and Adam also excused himself from Natasha and the group. Adam and Jacob walked in silence to a nearby coffee shop in the airport terminal, which fortunately was still open this late. Adam ordered a double-shot espresso and Jacob ordered a fruit smoothie. Adam paid with a few pound notes from a bundle of cash he was carrying. The barista said their drinks would be ready in a few minutes.

"How's your mom?" Adam asked after they sat down at a small table across from each other, beneath a large TV screen that was turned off. "I saw your video last week."

"She's good, thanks," Jacob said. "She's at work. I think I know who you are."

"You do?"

"There's an old photo of you and my mum in her bedroom," Jacob said. "You had hair and a beard back then. I asked her about you and she said you used to be friends, but she doesn't keep any photos of her other ex-boyfriends. When were you together?"

Adam thought for a moment.

"We dated for a few years while we were both attending Oxford but we started to grow apart after we graduated and pursued different career paths. She wanted to do humanitarian work and I wanted to be rich. We broke up in 1998 and I remember it was really hard on both of us."

"I was born in 1998," Jacob said. The barista brought over their drinks and set them on their table, then returned behind the counter. "I never met my dad. Why did you leave her?"

"I've been thinking about your mom a lot since I saw your video," Adam said, sipping his espresso. "I was a different person back then. I was young and stupid and selfish."

As soon as he had uttered the words, he realized he hadn't changed as much as he thought he had in sixteen years. He was no longer young but he was still stupid and selfish.

"I swear to you I never knew Leah was pregnant," Adam

said. "She never told me and in all this time she's never asked me for help. I don't know what else to tell you."

"Tell me why you left," Jacob said.

"I felt like I was trapped in a life I didn't want and I thought I would drown if I didn't escape," Adam said. "My parents were poor farmers and I knew I wanted more to my life than that. I worked really hard at school and I excelled at everything I did, but it seemed like nothing I did at school made a difference to the family farm. They always needed my help and there was never any time to do things that I wanted to do. I received a Rhodes Scholarship in the summer of 1995 and left the farm to study economics at graduate school at Oxford, where I met Leah. I ended up getting my doctorate degree and was recruited by all the top investment banks, financial consultancies and government finance ministries. For the first time in my life it seemed like the whole world was opening to me, but when Leah said she wanted to stay in England I started to feel trapped again. I was only 25 and I felt like I would be giving up my dreams and would never get the chance to do the things I wanted because there were all these people in my life who wanted my help. I told her I was moving to Washington, D.C., to work for the treasury department and she wished me luck. That was in the early spring of 1998 and I haven't heard from her since."

Jacob sipped his smoothie as he listened to Adam. How could he be angry with someone who didn't even know he existed until a week ago?

"Do you still work for the treasury department?" Jacob asked, not sure what else to say.

"No, that didn't last long," Adam said. "I was poached by an investment bank and became richer than I had ever thought was possible. I realized I had a natural gift for making money so I left the investment bank and started my own hedge fund. That jet out there was purchased with hedge fund money."

"So would you say that you're happier now that you're rich?"

"I can buy some pretty cool toys, but money can't buy love or happiness," Adam said. "Having more money didn't make me happier. I only became rich once I stopped caring for other people, stopped giving my money away to charities and stopped spending

237

it on frivolous things. Once I became rich I felt like I couldn't trust anyone and it seemed like everyone was trying to get my money. I hated my new friends and I cheated them before they could cheat me, including the women I dated."

"That doesn't sound very appealing," Jacob admitted. "It makes me think of something I read in the Bible that goes: 'For what is man profited if he shall gain the whole world and lose his own soul?'"

Adam thought about this for a moment. Books of wisdom seldom had anything positive to say about material wealth because putting worldly possessions before people tended to result in inequality, poverty, suffering and loneliness.

"How are your grades?" Adam asked, changing the subject.

"They're OK," Jacob said. "I'm on summer break right now. I would love to go to Oxford someday but I doubt I have the grades to get a scholarship like you. Mum wants me to get a summer job and start saving now."

"A great fortune can also be a curse that I wouldn't wish on anyone, especially someone your age," Adam said. "If you have the grades, I will give you a scholarship to any school you can get in to, provided it's OK with your mom."

Adam pulled out the bundle of cash and counted out 3,000 British pounds onto the table. "I don't know if this will help you now or in the future, but I want you to have this."

"Wow, that's a lot of money," Jacob said. "I don't know if I can accept this."

"Just keep it safe until you or your mom need it," Adam said. He took out a business card and handed it to Jacob. "This has my contact info on it so we can stay in touch."

"Thank you, sir," Jacob said, putting the business card and money into his backpack.

"I was pretty unhappy with my life until I met Natasha about a year ago. Everything changed and now all I want to do is make her happy because I love her and she makes me happy. She and I are both trying to make more changes in our lives that put people ahead of possessions. It's important to have real friends in your life who can keep you grounded, but in order to have friends like that you also have to be a good friend to them."

"What about your family farm?" Jacob asked. "Do they still

ask you for help?"

"I haven't thought about that farm in almost 20 years," Adam said, standing up. Jacob also stood up and they walked together to find their group. "To me, that farm was like a past life. We live and we learn, but the older I get, the more I realize that things from my past have a way of coming back to the present. We can't change the past but we can make changes in the present that can change the future."

They met up with their group by the customs area. Karen was successfully readmitted to her home country despite not having a passport because her parents had brought her old British driver's license as proof of her identity. The customs official said they would make her a replacement passport but it would take at least a day to process. Karen said she wanted to stay with her family for a few more days because she hadn't seen them for so long. Adam thought Karen seemed like a different person when she was with her family because she looked so happy and he said it was perfectly fine for her to stay a few days.

Karen didn't introduce Frank to her family as her boyfriend since he had never really asked her. They were just fast friends in a casual relationship. Frank wasn't disappointed when no one invited him to stay with Karen's family and he preferred to keep things simple. The group said their farewells and Natasha, Adam and Frank boarded the Gulfstream jet again.

Before they departed, they talked about their options for the evening. While it was only 5 p.m. back in Stingray Cay, it was currently 10 p.m. in London and midnight in Moscow, and the flight to Moscow would take about two hours. They wondered whether they should stay the night in London or continue on to Moscow. It would be difficult to find a hotel room wherever they spent the night, but they could all sleep comfortably on the plane so they decided to push on. After it had been refueled and fully stocked with food and provisions, the jet taxied to the end of the runway and took off, this time with a more gradual acceleration that was brisk but not a breakneck speed as before.

Once they had reached a cruising altitude, Jolaina and Bailee served the passengers freshly made individual pot pies for supper. A small table between the seats extended into a large dinner table that was set with a white tablecloth, white cloth napkins and gilded silverware. Natasha made a toast to good times and good company and they all drank non-alcoholic sparkling apple cider out of crystal glasses. Adam had a roast beef pot pie for supper, Frank had a chicken pot pie and Natasha had a vegetable pot pie. After they had finished supper, Bailee brought out a low-sugar, low-fat key lime pie for dessert. When they were finished they retired to the aft cabin and Jolaina cleaned up and put away the dining area.

Natasha consulted her tablet for the first time in about 24 hours in order to locate information about available airports in Moscow and possible ground transportation to the city center. Janus welcomed her back in Russian and said it was happy to see her again. Janus said the Russian military had taken over communications but Janus had already interfaced with the Russian government's central computer network prior to the activation of a system-wide firewall, which meant it still had access to everything. Janus said civilian flights were still restricted but it was possible there was a runway available for them at the private Ostafyevo corporate/military airport located 14 kilometers south of the capital in the Moscow Oblast area. Janus asked Natasha if she wanted it to attempt to gain clearance to land and she said that sounded good to her but to check with the pilot first. Janus checked with Matty who said it sounded fine and clearance was easily obtained thanks to the priority designation Janus gave them.

Natasha asked Janus for information on the current whereabouts of her brother and after a quick but intensive search, Aleksandr Manakova was located at his private residence in the suburbs of Star City, northeast of the capital. Natasha asked Janus to try calling him and after another minute Janus was able to put the call through to his landline.

"Hello, this is Commander Manakova," Aleks answered in Russian.

"Hey big brother," Natasha said happily in Russian. "Hope I didn't wake you."

"Tosh!" he cried, recognizing her voice. "No, I'm awake. How did you find me here?"

"Janus found you," she said. "That's what my tablet computer calls itself."

"We know Janus well," Aleks said. "Where are you? Lounging on a beach somewhere?"

"Actually we're on our way to see you," she said excitedly. "We'll be landing in Moscow in a few minutes. Can we meet for breakfast?"

Aleks conferred with Charles and Mizuho who were staying the night in his home.

"I'm here with my fellow space travelers," he said. "There is a big parade planned at noon in Red Square, but I think we can all meet for breakfast if you can find a place."

"If I may interject, I just made a reservation for six people at 9 a.m. at the Bosco Cafe within the GUM building outside of Red Square," a female voice interrupted in Russian.

"Is that you, Janus?" Aleks asked. "Way to take charge."

"Thank you, sir," Janus replied. "Congratulations on your safe landing. I'm sorry I wasn't able to be with you during your descent."

"Me too," Natasha said. "Well I should let you get some rest and I'll see you soon, in a few hours. It seems strange to finally be able to say that."

"See you soon, sister," Aleks said. "Love you!"

"I love you too!" she said and then disconnected the call.

Janus helped the passengers gain special clearance to land in Moscow and arranged for a secure airport hangar to store the jet for the night. All it took was a few bribes to the right people.

A short while later the plane landed at Ostafyevo Airport southwest of the capital. After a brief meeting with a Russian customs official who came aboard to check everyone's passports and welcome them to Russia, Jolaina and Bailee converted the main cabin into a sleeping area for seven. Frank slept up front in the crew cabin on a chair that turned into a single bed, Matty and Alice slept in the front cabin on four chairs and a table that turned into a queen-sized bed, Jolaina and Bailee shared a sofa in the middle cabin that turned into a double bed and Natasha and Adam slept in the aft cabin on the wide couch that turned into a king-sized bed. Jolaina and Bailee made everyone's beds and set up privacy partition screens between the three sleeping areas.

As they were snuggling in to bed, Natasha asked Adam what he and the teenage boy Jacob had spoken about at the London airport. Adam said it was a ghost from his past life. The boy was the child of his former girlfriend and he may or may not be his

241

illegitimate son. He said he had told Jacob about his own childhood spent on a farm and how that was another past life he had left behind. Adam said it had felt surreal talking to Jacob and it made him realize there were many things about his life that he wanted to change, such as making more of an effort to spend time helping and caring about other people, particularly their friends and family.

Natasha confessed to ordering the removal of all the alcohol from their jet and said it made her feel guilty to keep secrets from him. She said she wanted them to be honest with each other so they could build a foundation of trust. Adam said he missed having an occasional drink and confessed to smoking a joint in the greenhouse. He said he also accidently saw Karen naked when she came out of the shower and they had both been embarrassed. Nothing had happened. Natasha believed him and thanked him for telling her the truth. They kissed a few times, then things started to heat up and they quietly made love in their bed in the back of the parked airplane.

"As for the unbelievers, their works are like a mirage in a desert.
The thirsty traveler thinks it is water, but when he comes near
he finds that it is nothing."
— The Qur'an, "Light"

Chapter 32

JEDDAH, Saudi Arabia

Ibn could have reached Jeddah by the early evening if he had pressed forward as fast as his horse could carry him, but he chose instead to stay with his people in the desert. When evening came they prayed together and they broke their fast the minute the sun fell behind the horizon. When the skies grew dark and filled with stars, they resumed their journey westward and reached the city hours later, in the middle of the night. Most of the city was dark and without electricity.

A few pilgrims from his party had gone ahead to Jeddah to spread word of his arrival and by the time he showed up with close to 100,000 followers, there were half a million people waiting for him with open arms and open hearts. They called Ibn a hero and a prophet and asked him if he would lead another march northwest, paralleling the Red Sea to the great pyramids, Palestine and beyond. He said he was not a prophet but just a tired man who needed to rest. Rumors of a second march up the Red Sea began to spread anyway and people began to make preparations and talk excitedly amongst themselves.

The city elders invited Ibn to take a tour of the Kingdom Tower, also called the Jeddah Tower, near the shore of the Red Sea. Ibn had heard great things about the tower, which was still under construction but anticipated to be the tallest building in the world upon completion. When finished in 2020, the tower was expected to be 1,000 meters tall, with a large outdoor viewing platform above 600 meters, or higher than the top of the Mecca Royal Clock Tower. So far, the new tower had only a few floors above ground and construction had recently been stalled due to a minor earthquake and the subsequent solar storm that occurred less than a day later. Ibn was unimpressed with the progress thus far, but the elders said the new tower would far surpass the 828-meter tall Burj Khalifa in Dubai and would make it clear to the world that Saudi Arabia had the greatest super skyscrapers.

"Jeddah should be the capital of the new United Nations of Islam, don't you agree?" one of the elders asked Ibn. The other elders applauded this idea but Ibn said they would need to wait and see.

"I live in Dubai and I can tell you it takes much more than tall buildings to make a city great," he said. "A city's greatness is not established by its skyscrapers or by how many millionaires live within its boundaries, but by the happiness and prosperity of all its citizens. By that measure, Jeddah still has a long way to go before it achieves greatness."

Ibn excused himself and returned to camp to sleep with his followers.

"Glory is like a circle in the water, which never ceases to enlarge itself, till by broad spreading it disperses to naught."
— William Shakespeare, "King Henry VI"

Chapter 33

MOSCOW — At the base of Saint Basil's Cathedral in Red Square

The black, armored limousine came to a halt in front of the barricades at the end of the street and the chauffer hopped out to open the back door for his passengers. Natasha gracefully stepped out, wearing red designer heels, an elegant red dress with a red satin ribbon tied around her neck and the Tiffany diamond bracelet Adam had given her the day before. Adam followed her out the door, wearing a black two-piece designer suit, a white dress shirt with a red tie that matched Natasha's dress and polished black Oxford shoes. He thought Natasha's outfit was beautiful but she needed a diamond necklace to match her bracelet. Frank stepped out of the opposite side of the limousine wearing a navy-blue turtleneck, black dress pants and simple black dress shoes. He felt underdressed next to the Morgans but it didn't bother him.

Natasha thought the morning sunlight was so strikingly beautiful and breathtaking as it lit the nine domes and two spires of the Cathedral of Vasily the Blessed, commonly known as St. Basil's Cathedral, that she was compelled to use her tablet to photograph the landmark built in the sixteenth century under the reign of Ivan IV.

"Have you ever seen anything so magnificent?" she asked Adam in Russian.

"What?" he asked in English.

She forgot he didn't speak Russian and repeated her question in English.

"No, it's quite beautiful," he admitted, appreciating the wide smile on his wife's face. He looked around and also admired the massive red brick walls of the Kremlin complex and the Spasskaya or "Savior" clock tower, which noted the time was a few minutes before nine. "A perfect day for a parade," he added, looking up at the clear blue sky.

Natasha asked Frank to take a picture of her and Adam in

245

front of St. Basil's Cathedral and then the three of them walked together through Red Square, past Lenin's Mausoleum to the main entrance of the giant GUM shopping complex that spanned a city block and faced the Kremlin opposite Red Square. GUM was an acronym for main universal store and was filled with five-star restaurants and luxury retailers, though it also housed wholesale suppliers. The ornate, two-story building looked like a fortress on the outside with thick walls of marble, granite and limestone. A plaque on the wall said the building officially opened in 1893 as the Upper Trading Rows on the traditional site of the Moscow trade.

Most of the shops inside were closed until 10 a.m. but the interior was still inspiring with a large glass and steel dome that covered a brightly lit walkway filled with indoor trees, a large fountain and several bridges connecting the two sides of the upper level. Natasha led the way to the Bosco Cafe past many luxury stores whose names were familiar to her, including Armani, Doir, Louis Vuitton, Hugo Boss, Burberry, Hermès and Cartier. The doors were still closed when they arrived at the cafe, but the maître d'hôtel recognized Natasha with a familiar smile, unlocked the doors and welcomed them inside.

"Morgan, party of six?" the woman asked in Russian. "Please follow me." She locked the doors behind them and then led Natasha, Adam and Frank through the empty dining area and up a marble staircase to a private terrace on the second floor surrounded by yellow walls with white trim, and seated them at a large VIP table in front of a window that overlooked the Kremlin and Lenin's Mausoleum. The table had a white tablecloth and white napkins, crystal glasses filled with ice water and gilded silverware. The maître d' left and their waitress arrived and asked in Russian if they wanted beverages to start before the rest of their party arrived. Adam and Frank looked at her blankly.

"She wants to know if you would like coffee or something to drink while we wait," Natasha translated in English. Adam said he wanted a cappuccino and Frank said he would like one too. Natasha ordered their drinks and carrot juice for herself. A few minutes later, Aleks, Charles and Mizuho arrived and everyone stood up for introductions. Aleks and Charles were wearing sweaters and slacks they had found at Aleks' house in Star City

246

and Mizuho, having nothing else to wear, was dressed in a green polo shirt and khaki cargo pants she had brought back from the space station.

Natasha and Aleks embraced each other in a tight but familial hug and exchanged salutations in Russian, while Adam and Frank introduced themselves to Charles and Mizuho in English. Aleks and Adam looked each other in the eye and shook hands firmly. The waitress came back with the drinks and asked the three new guests what they wanted. They all spoke in Russian and said they wanted the same thing, cappuccinos and carrot juice. The waitress offered the party special breakfast menus that were hand-written in beautiful Cyrillic calligraphy, which everyone could read except Adam and Frank.

The conversations at the table alternated between English and Russian, with everyone happily taking turns translating Russian for Adam and Frank. When the waitress came back with the rest of the beverages, Aleks, Charles, Frank and Mizuho ordered items from the menu including baked quiche, crepes, cheese and fruit Danish pastries, fried eggs and avocados. The Morgans didn't see what they wanted on the menu so they ordered off the menu. Natasha asked for a fresh fruit bowl with berries and melons and non-fat yogurt and Adam said he wanted eggs Benedict with an extra side of bacon.

The waitress left after they had placed their orders and they brought each other up to date on their adventures thus far and their plans for the future. Charles and Mizuho said their early departure from the International Space Station left them stranded in Moscow, possibly for weeks. Frank said his ship was being repaired and he was on vacation with the Morgans until the repairs were finished. Aleks said he supposed he was also on vacation, even though he was back home. The three astronauts said there was a parade in their honor that started at noon, but they would be free to go after about 1 p.m. Adam and Natasha offered to treat everyone to breakfast, take them all shopping for a new wardrobe at GUM and even generously offered to take them all home on their private jet.

Their food arrived on beautifully gilded porcelain dishes and everyone commented on the wonderful appearance and flavors of the food. Adam's eggs Benedict wasn't on a true English muffin and the ham wasn't what he expected, but he appreciated the attempt and thought the poached eggs and hollandaise sauce tasted perfect. The side of bacon was far too much for him to eat but offered varying levels of crispiness. As they were finishing their meal, discussing all the places they wanted to visit and getting ready to depart, they were surprised by an unexpected guest. A large but not particularly tall man dressed in a charcoal gray suit and tie walked up to their table unannounced. Charles noticed the man first but it was Aleks who recognized him.

"Father?" Aleks said in Russian, standing up with surprise. "What are you doing here?" Natasha's face turned crimson but she remained seated.

"I heard you and Natasha were here," the bald, 66-year-old man answered in Russian with an unusually deep voice. "I am very busy and can't stay long, but my office is only a short walk from here and I decided I should come."

"Father, these are my colleagues, astronaut Charles Wilson from the United States of America and flight engineer Mizuho Sakaguchi from Japan," Aleks said in Russian. Charles and Mizuho stood up and shook the man's hand. "This is captain Frank Rosario and I don't know if you've met Natasha's husband yet, Adam Morgan." Frank and Adam also stood up to shake the man's hand when they heard their names announced. Aleks switched to English. "Everyone, this is my father Mikhail Yurievich Manakova, a former cosmonaut and a current director for the Federal Security Service."

"You're Natasha's father?" Adam asked in English. "It's good to finally meet you, sir. Natasha has not said much about you." He looked at his wife who was still red in the face and had her arms folded across her chest in defiance.

"It is good to finally meet you too," Mikhail answered in English, then switched back to Russian. "I am sorry I was not able to attend your wedding. As Tolstoy said, 'happy families are all alike, but every unhappy family is unhappy in its own way.' Our family became unhappy the day your mother died and I allowed my work to consume my life and fill the sorrow in my heart. Natasha, my darling girl, I am sorry I was not there for your childhood."

"I felt as if both my parents had died," Natasha said in Russian as tears ran down her face. "You sent me away. Aleks was the only family I had growing up until I met this man. How could you be too busy to attend your only daughter's wedding? How can you call yourself a father?"

Natasha began to sob and Adam put his arms around her to comfort her, even though he didn't know what they had said to each other. Mizuho also began to cry and Charles placed his arms around to comfort her.

"Now I can see it was a mistake for me to come here," Mikhail said in Russian. "Being a good father is much more than simply being a father. I was not a very good father to you or to Aleksandr, and when your mother died I gave up on being a parent at all. It was unfair to you but it was all I could do. Her death broke my heart and seeing you like this makes me realize I am still broken. You look so much like her it makes my heart ache and I want to die. I will leave you now."

He turned and started to walk to the door when Natasha suddenly stood up and shouted "Daddy!" He turned to face her and she saw he had tears running down his face that mirrored her own. She ran to him and they hugged each other tightly in the center of the room. Aleks joined their embrace and they all had a good cry together. It was also the first time either of them had touched their father in many years.

Frank and Adam looked at each other with confusion, wishing they knew what had been said. Charles and Mizuho were both crying, too, thinking about their own parents and wondering what kind of parents they would be themselves when their time came.

* * *

After they had bid farewell to Natasha's and Aleks' father, they finished breakfast and Adam paid the bill. The waitress apologized for not being able to accept credit cards and Adam grumbled to himself that he "should have known they wouldn't" as he pulled out a stack of Rubles from his billfold. The group went downstairs just as the shops were beginning to open and hundreds of people were coming into the mall. The downstairs part of the cafe was quickly filling up with customers. All the tables were full and there was a line stretching outside the door. Everyone working in the department stores recognized Natasha as the internationally famous fashion model and several of the shops had glamorous photos of her hanging on their walls. Several people came up to ask for her autograph and gushed about how much they admired her and how proud they were that she was Russian. She humbly thanked them and said her heroes were common Russians and her own brave friends who had all done much more than she had to make the world a better place.

Adam noticed there were no price tags visible on any of the items on display. It was a little embarrassing, but he made sure to confirm the stores would accept his credit cards in advance because he had limited cash on him. Shopping for luxury was definitely easier when you weren't constrained by a limited budget. Adam and Aleks each found several handsome but dignified suits at Armani they wanted, Frank and Charles found several striking and distinguished suits at Hugo Boss, and Natasha and Mizuho both found elegant and stately outfits they liked at Dior. They also bought a few accessories at Cartier and a beautiful diamond and ruby necklace for Natasha at Bulgari to match her Tiffany bracelet. Each store had a tailor on staff who quickly customized their outfits to ensure a perfect fit. Adam saved all the receipts in his billfold and gave everyone who served them a generous cash tip.

They picked up some extra luggage at Louis Vuitton to hold their new clothes and the staff was kind enough to pack their clothes into the brown leather suitcases, along with a personal toiletries kit and other comfort/survival items. There was enough time for the three space travelers to get a shave and a haircut before the big parade and Natasha had her hair done up to better show off her exquisite necklace and chiseled collarbones. Adam told her she looked like a duchess in her statuesque red dress, scintillating diamonds and regal rubies, and said her skin was glowing with a radiance to outshine any princess or queen.

They exited the GUM building into the warm summer air of the Red Square, which had by then been filled with more than a hundred thousand spectators. Aleks, Charles and Mizuho changed into their blue flight suits decorated with space mission patches and left to take their place of honor in the parade. Adam and Frank carried the luggage and they all went to sit in the carpeted VIP section of the grandstand. The wood and metal grandstand was set up near the state historical museum at the northeastern corner of the square, facing the grand palaces and golden domes of the

250

Romanov tsars and Russian emperors. Natasha was invited to sit in the place of honor on an antique chair raised above the others.

The parade began exactly at noon with the chiming of the bell towers and a ceremonial gun salute. Rows up on rows of uniformed soldiers marched from one end of the square to the other, followed by Aleks, Charles and Mizuho waving from atop an open-air car, and directly behind them was a Soyuz capsule similar to the one that had brought them home but was not blackened by reentry into the earth's atmosphere. More rows of soldiers followed them, then at least a hundred mounted soldiers on horseback, three dozen tanks and armored vehicles, and what appeared to be an intercontinental ballistic missile on the bed of a long truck. A marching band and more soldiers brought up the rear of the parade and finally a series of armored helicopters, bombers and fighter jets flew overhead to the cheers of the crowd.

When the parade had finished, all the well-dressed Russians in the grandstand remarked to Natasha and to each other about how glorious and pleasant the parade had been and how it made them all so proud to be Russian. Natasha asked Adam and Frank what they thought and they both said it was great to see the astronauts honored and the display of troops and cavalry were impressive, but the tanks, armored vehicles, helicopters and fighter jets didn't seem to have much relevance. They said the sight of the ICBM was a little disturbing and sent a confusing message.

Natasha, Adam and Frank gradually made their way across Red Square to the end of the parade and found the three astronauts signing autographs near St. Basil's Cathedral. People Natasha had never met before recognized and complimented her, with a few people bowing or curtsying to her as if she were royalty. She smiled and expressed her gratitude but the experience was beginning to make her uncomfortable. When the astronauts were ready, everyone climbed inside the waiting black limousine with tinted windows and the chauffer carefully fit all the luggage into the large trunk. It was quiet inside the limousine as it crept through traffic and they continued their conversation about where to go next.

Aleks said they had all been invited to take a private tour of the Kremlin that afternoon and to spend the night in the president's official residence, but when the group discussed it, nobody seemed particularly interested in the idea. Everyone seemed to agree that they should go to Paris next for a number of different reasons. Natasha's tablet beeped a few times and when she picked it up, it began speaking in English in a female voice.

"It's a little out of the way, but if you don't mind making a few extra stops, I have a good friend in the Middle East who has been trying to get home to his family," Janus said.

"The Middle East?" Adam asked. "Who is your friend and where is he trying to go?"

"His name is Ibn Ali and his home is in Dubai in the United Arab Emirates," Janus said. "He has been stuck in Mecca for the past two weeks but he is currently in Jeddah, Saudi Arabia. He just crossed 40 miles of desert on horseback to get to an airport but unfortunately there are no available flights to Dubai."

"I know this Ibn Ali," Aleks said. "He was the first person from the surface to contact the space station after last week's coronal mass ejection. He seemed very knowledgeable about technology when I spoke with him. I have also heard he has some controversial and even revolutionary ideas."

"I read a transcript from one of his speeches a few days ago," Natasha said. "I recall he was advocating humanity's need to retire religious fundamentalism and dogma in order to obtain spiritual enlightenment."

"That sounds pretty controversial and revolutionary," Mizuho admitted, "but it's true. The world is too big and too complicated for another holy war. What does he need to do in Dubai?"

"He wants to be reunited with his wife and four children," Janus said. "I have delivered messages between them and I believe their love is strong but there is a thousand miles of desert separating them. Ibn is a brave man and a true hero who never hesitates to help a friend, but now there is no one who can help him get home to his family."

"How far away is it?" Charles asked.

"Jeddah is 2,360 miles or about 3,800 kilometers from Moscow," Janus said. "We could be there in less than four hours. It might take Ibn a month to cross the desert on horseback but he could make the journey in an hour and a half if we were to help."

As the limousine crept through traffic, it reached a

demonstration filled with thousands of protesters shouting and waving signs complaining about how there was no food, all the stores were empty and there was no work for people to do. The police tried to restrain the crowd but a few protesters broke free, rushed to the limousine and pounded their fists against the windows. They were dirty, hungry and desperate, but there was nothing the passengers could do to help. At first Natasha pitied the commoners, then felt deeply ashamed by her position of privilege. Even though the people outside couldn't see her through the darkened glass, she self-consciously removed her necklace and bracelet and set them in her lap. She was having another Buddhist moment of empathy, realizing that all things were connected and human suffering was inevitable.

"I think we should help him," Natasha said. "I know how it feels to be reunited with family and that's an experience you just can't purchase. Besides, I've never been to the Middle East before. What do you guys think?"

"We should help him," Mizuho said. "He sounds like a remarkable man."

"I agree it's a noble cause and I support noble causes," Charles said.

"I'm just along for the ride," Frank said. "The more the merrier."

"I agree with Frank," Adam said. He was thinking *it's just money*, but then he remembered he was trying to make an effort to put people before profits or possessions. He enjoyed being a host and helping people and agreed with Natasha that there were some things that money couldn't buy.

"Me too," Aleks said. "Let's help this guy find his family."

The limousine went back to the airport and found the jet fully fueled and restocked. The crew loaded their suitcases directly into the luggage area at the back of the plane through the rear cargo door and Adam and Natasha gave the three astronauts a quick tour of the main cabin before they all took a seat and buckled themselves in. The jet was airborne and headed almost due south before 2 p.m., on its way to the Holy Land.

"The difference between treason and patriotism
is only a matter of dates."
— Alexandre Dumas, "The Count of Monte Cristo"

Chapter 34

JEDDAH, Saudi Arabia

Ibn watched the sun rise on Friday morning and prayed toward Mecca with the rest of the city, but once the prayers were through, the city seemed to shut down in observance of the Sabbath. Shops were closed, construction and industry halted and the entire metropolis took the day off.

God rested on the seventh day after creating the earth, but we still have much work to do, Ibn thought. He was frustrated that no one else seemed interested in getting the Jeddah power plant started or connecting the city's telecommunications with the rest of the world via satellite. He was told all of these things could wait until tomorrow.

Ibn was able to contact Janus via his smartphone and inquired whether there were any flights available to Dubai, but Janus said unfortunately commercial air travel was still restricted and the Jeddah airport appeared to be closed for the day. Ibn asked Janus to keep trying and said it was very important to him to return home as soon as possible. Janus suggested that Ibn make his way to the airport while it worked its magic.

Ibn had a meeting with Abu Hakim, imam Hassan and Ali Ribah to discuss their plans and strategy. Ibn expressed his frustrations with the city elders and his reluctance to lead such a large group of followers. His friends said the people wanted to march and they needed a leader, but only Ibn could lead them. They suggested Ibn spend the day thinking about this quest and search within his soul for the right answer to his dilemma. He took a long walk through the city by himself, following the signs to the airport.

When he arrived at the Jeddah airport he found it closed and empty, but the doors were unlocked so he went inside. The large building was eerily dark and quiet but also a good place to meditate and contemplate his purpose. He looked at the signs for all the different places that had flights to and from Jeddah and it occurred to him that Muslims must live in nearly every country on earth. The fifth pillar of Islam required all Muslims to visit Mecca if they were able to, and while many came by car, by train, by boat, by camel, on horseback or on foot, air travel had greatly expanded the ability of most pilgrims to make the journey. Ibn didn't see how it was possible for such a busy international airport to close for even one day during Ramadan, yet the whole facility was deserted and had evidently been shut down for the entire week.

Janus alerted Ibn when it was almost noon and offered to say a prayer with him. Ibn found a well-lit prayer room and the two prayed together. When they had finished, Ibn charged his laptop and smartphone with his solar charger. He read his Qur'an for several hours and meditated while he waited for the answers to come to him. At about 6 p.m., Janus alerted him that help was arriving and instructed him to proceed to gate D24 and exit onto the tarmac. He packed up his belongings and hurried to the gate. As he approached the door, he saw a sleek private jet gracefully land on the runway and taxi to the gate. He exited through the door and walked across the tarmac in the warm evening sun to the plane. It came to a stop and the tall doorway opened, lowering a set of carpeted stairs. A bald, white man with a short beard stood in the doorway.

"I am looking for Ibn Ali," he shouted in English over the jet engines.

"I am he," Ibn answered in English. "Who is asking?"

"I'm a friend," the man said. "My name is Adam. Please come aboard and meet my other friends. We have heard much about you and we are all anxious to finally meet you."

Ibn climbed the stairs and as he boarded the jet he felt as though he were stepping through a portal into an alternate universe. The inside of the jet was cool and very comfortable, with wide-open spaces, plenty of light, polished wood surfaces and white leather couches and sofas. The occupants included four males and two females between the ages of 25 and 41 who were all very handsome and exceptionally well dressed. Ibn suddenly felt dirty and underdressed in his simple white pilgrim robes and cap.

"I think perhaps there has been a mistake," he said, afraid to go further.

"Are you not Ibn Ali, the senior telecommunications specialist from Dubai?" Adam asked.

"Yes," he answered. "How did you know?"

"We have a mutual friend who told us you needed help returning to your family in Dubai," Adam said. "You know of Janus?"

"Janus!" Ibn repeated with a broad smile. "Where is he?"

"First let me introduce you to the other passengers," Adam said. "My name is Adam Morgan and this is my wife Natasha. We own this jet. This is Aleksandr Manakova, Natasha's brother. Aleks is a Russian cosmonaut who recently served on the International Space Station. He says he spoke with you last week. His colleagues are astronauts Charles Wilson from NASA and Mizuho Sakaguchi from JAXA, both recently returned from the ISS. Frank Rosario is the captain of the sailboat *Reciprocity*. Janus has told us all of your long journey and has persuaded us to offer you our help."

Ibn shook hands with the men and gave Natasha and Mizuho a friendly wave but didn't touch them.

"It is very kind of you to offer, but I don't know if I can accept," Ibn said. "Where is Janus?"

"I am here, Ibn," Janus called out in Arabic in a male voice from the middle of the plane. Natasha retrieved her tablet and handed it to Ibn. The tablet was heavier than he expected and he noticed it was covered in gold plating. "Remember when I told you I was an intelligent computer? This is my body and the woman who handed me to you is my master. She is an angel in more ways than you might think. I have convinced her and my friends to help you reunite with your family, if that is still your wish."

"It is," Ibn said in English. "I wish to return home to my family."

"It would be our honor and pleasure," Natasha said. "We can get you home in less than two hours. Please have a seat and make yourself comfortable. Can we get you anything to eat or drink?"

"Thank you, but my faith says I must fast until sundown," Ibn said, handing the tablet back to Natasha and taking a seat near the front of the jet. Adam, Frank and Aleks took the seats next to and facing Ibn and Natasha and Mizuho sat together in the middle cabin. Flight attendants Jolaina and Bailee came through the jet to check everyone's seat belts, make sure all the doors were secure and everything was ready for departure. The jet taxied to the end of the runway then turned around for takeoff.

"Flight crew prepare for departure," the captain said calmly over the intercom. The jet began accelerating down the runway and gently lifted off into the desert air. Ibn looked out the window and saw the Red Sea below and then hundreds of miles of unbroken sand as the jet flew over the Arabian Peninsula.

After about 20 minutes, Natasha came forward to hand Ibn her tablet again.

"Janus says he has made contact with your wife and you may speak with her now," she said. Ibn looked at the tablet and recognized the number it had dialed.

"Hello?" Ibn asked in Arabic. "Are you there?"

"Ibn? Is that you?" a woman asked in Arabic. He recognized his wife's voice and a wave of emotion swelled through him.

"Sarah!" he shouted with joy. "I am so happy to hear your voice! Where are you?"

"I am at home," she said. "We have all been hoping to hear from you. Where are you and do you have any idea when you are coming home? We have missed you terribly."

"I have missed you more than words can express," he answered. "I have prayed I would see you again every night and day since we parted. God has granted my wishes and is sending me home at last. I am flying in a private jet with some kind and generous people and they say we will arrive at the Dubai airport in about an hour. Can you meet me there?"

"In an hour? Yes, I will be there and I will bring the children. They will be very excited to see you, too. Have a safe landing! I love you!"

"I love you too!" he said happily. The call disconnected and he handed the tablet back to Natasha. "Thank you for your exceptional kindness," he said in English. "My wife said she will bring my family to the airport and it would honor me for you to meet them and dine with us at sundown."

"We would love to, but I think the sun may set before we land," Natasha said. Ibn looked out his window and saw that she was right about the sunset. The jet was flying away from the sun and shortening the day and it would set in a few minutes.

Natasha went forward to the crew cabin to inform Jolaina and Bailee that they would all be dining in Dubai rather than on the plane. She grabbed a bottle of water and handed it to Ibn before returning to her seat. The captain told her he was having trouble contacting the Dubai airport for clearance and said he was worried the ground crew might not be ready for their arrival. Natasha was coming to rely on Janus as a valuable assistant and asked it for help.

Janus made several calls to arrange to get the emergency runway lights turned on at the Dubai airport in anticipation of their arrival. Airport staff were also observing the Sabbath, but Janus was able to convince them that the Sabbath ended at sundown and an important flight was landing soon that would need their guidance. Janus also simultaneously called several prominent restaurants in Dubai to make dinner reservations.

Everyone was starting to get hungry and the subject of religious dietary restrictions came up in conversation due to the group's growing cultural diversity. The light outside turned pink and the minute the sun had set Ibn opened his water bottle and took a drink. The water was a great relief to his dry throat.

"Many cultures practice fasting," Ibn said. "Fasting during Ramadan is one of the five pillars of my religion and I have found it to have a cleansing effect that promotes spiritual awareness."

"Don't you also have other dietary restrictions that forbid alcohol or pork?" Adam asked.

"God left very unambiguous instructions to Jews, Christians and Muslims alike forbidding us from eating pork," Ibn said. "I understand many Christians casually ignore this rule and eat pork often. We are also forbidden from drinking blood or eating the flesh of dead animals. Alcohol is a bad habit which should be avoided, but it is not forbidden by Islam."

"I don't eat reptiles, bugs or road kill, not because of religious reasons but because I find the idea repulsive," Adam said. "I respect your beliefs but personally I enjoy the taste of bacon, ham and other pork products. I don't think religion should dictate anyone's diet unless they want it to. Have you ever tried pork?"

"No, I find the idea of eating pork repulsive," Ibn said.

"Jewish people don't eat pork, shellfish or mix meat and dairy at the same meal," Frank said. "I also don't believe in religious dietary restrictions but I refuse to eat veal or foie gras because I believe it's inhumane to the animals."

"I'm a vegetarian, but not for religious reasons," Natasha said. "I find that eating pure food from the earth makes my body feel better and I don't have a guilty conscience about causing another animal to suffer."

"The Japanese diet doesn't have many restrictions," Mizuho said. "I eat mostly whole foods and fresh fruits and vegetables, but I also eat meat in small portions. Most of the meat I eat is fish, but I will also eat beef, chicken and pork. I don't really eat dairy or bread."

"I will eat almost anything," Aleks said. "Often my meal choices are limited and I have to eat whatever is available. Food is food."

"I agree with Aleks," Charles said. "I will try anything once."

Janus reminded Ibn that the sun had set and he excused himself to another part of the plane so he could pray. He faced east toward the front of the plane as he went through his evening prayer ritual while the other passengers watched in wonder. When Ibn had finished praying, Janus informed everyone that the Dubai airport would be ready for their arrival. Also, Ibn's family was already waiting for them at the airport and Janus had made a reservation for twelve at a nice restaurant facing the Persian Gulf.

Dubai was almost completely blacked out and they couldn't see any of the city's skyscrapers in the darkness, but the airport's emergency runway lights came on in time. The jet landed safely and taxied over to the gate where Ibn's family was waiting. Ibn's wife Sarah Ali was wearing a long, light blue dress and a matching headscarf that covered her long, dark hair. She was 39 years old and her face had a dark complexion that was strong but friendly.

As soon as they were close enough, Sarah and her four children all embraced Ibn together in a tearful group hug. He clung on to his family tightly and was worried he might lose them again if he ever let them go. They felt the same for him and their intimate family reunion lasted for several minutes.

"I missed you all desperately and thought about you every day," he said. "All I wanted to do was come back but it seemed impossible. There were so many things I had to do, so many strangers who were counting on me to help them, and an endless, forbidding desert between us."

When they had finished, Ibn introduced the jet passengers to his family and then his family to the passengers. His oldest daughter Shahrazad was 16, taller than her mother and was dressed in a cream-colored blouse, skinny blue jeans, fashionable white shoes and a white headscarf. His sons Tariq, 13, and Barak, 12, were each wearing short-sleeved shirts, blue jeans and tennis shoes. His youngest daughter Rihanna was 10 years old and was wearing a long, yellow summer dress and sandals but no headscarf.

"You have such a beautiful family," Natasha complimented Sarah after everyone had been introduced and they were riding in a private shuttle bus that Janus had arranged to take them to the restaurant.

"Thank you, and thank you so much for bringing our Ibn home," Sarah said. "It is very kind and generous of you. He is the rock on which our family is built and it has been very challenging to get through this post-electricity period without him. Fortunately things appear to slowly be coming back together, though it's not anywhere normal yet."

"How have you been able to manage?" Natasha asked.

"It's frustrating and scary the first time you realize that no one is going to help you," Sarah said. "Self-sufficiency is very challenging at first but it becomes easier and empowering the more you practice it. When you want something, you have to either figure out how to do it yourself or you do without it."

"It really helps to have skills, but if you don't have skills it helps to have skilled friends," Natasha said. "Bringing skilled people together to help each other out is a skill, right?"

"Definitely," Mizuho said. "We are all stronger when we help each other."

The modern restaurant Janus selected had no electricity but its wood fire oven was still operational and the dining room was lit by hundreds of candles that created a warm and lively atmosphere. The chef and wait staff were eager to work and found ways to create beautiful food arrangements that met the individual dietary requirements of the guests while delighting the palate. The owner of the restaurant came out to greet the party and thank them for their patronage.

"This past week has been very challenging for us," said the owner, a local man who introduced himself as Seth Darcangelo. "Electricity is only available in a few places. Oil is selling at record highs but no one is buying. Demand has plummeted and leaders are afraid our economy will collapse. No one can extract it, refine it, ship it or use it. There is no more OPEC."

"How are you able to keep a business going without customers?" Adam asked. He was thinking it could be time to sell his oil interests before the market collapsed and prices fell.

"We have always been a welfare state but it's more pronounced than usual," Seth said. "Fortunately most people are stepping up and lending a hand where they can. The emirates still have money and they are keeping the people fed but construction has halted everywhere. Business at the restaurant has been so slow I haven't been able to pay my staff but they come in every day anyway and work for free. There is no other work to be had and here they can get a free meal. Most of the other high-end restaurants in the city are closed."

"That sounds unsustainable," Adam said. "How long do you think you will be able to keep it up?"

"It is working out well so far," Seth said. "We are like a family. I am grateful to have the help and they are grateful to have something to do. People need work to give their lives purpose. A restaurant needs workers. Now all we need is more customers."

When they were finished with dinner, Adam paid the bill and gave the restaurant workers a generous cash tip. Seth and all the restaurant workers came out to personally express their gratitude and wish the travelers luck on their journey. Sarah asked Natasha what their plans were next and Natasha said they planned to fly to Paris, France.

"Paris is beautiful in the summer," Natasha said. "If you're up for an adventure, you're all welcome to come with us. Our jet can seat twelve comfortably."

"Have you discussed this with Ibn yet?" Sarah asked, utterly bewildered by Natasha's benevolence.

"No, nor with Adam," Natasha said. "I'm sure it wouldn't be a problem, so long as you all have passports."

"Shahrazad and I have passports but not the other children," Sarah said. "I don't think we can accept your generous offer at this time, but perhaps in the future."

"Have you traveled much with your kids?" Natasha asked.

"Ibn works a lot since he owns his own business and sometimes it is difficult to plan family trips," Sarah said. "We have visited Ibn's family home in Saudi Arabia and my family home in Jordan many times, and we have also been to Kuwait, Iran, Oman and Qatar. I would love to take the kids to Turkey and Azerbaijan someday but we've never really thought about going to Europe, let alone Paris. We would have to learn French!"

"I've visited more countries than most people I've met but today was my first trip to the Middle East," Natasha said. "I haven't been to any of those countries you just mentioned except for Saudi Arabia this afternoon and I didn't get off the plane."

"Well maybe we need to help each other broaden our horizons," Sarah said with a smile.

They delivered the Ali family to their apartment building in downtown Dubai and exchanged warm goodbyes. Ibn thanked Adam and Natasha again and told them he would never forget their kindness. They said seeing him reunited with his family was its own reward. They pledged to stay in touch and they wished him and his family luck in the future.

The shuttle bus took the Morgans, Frank and the astronauts back to the Dubai airport where their jet was waiting, already refueled and ready for departure. Janus said it was 5,244 kilometers or 3,260 miles from Dubai to Paris and it would take them approximately 67 hours if they were to drive there, but they could fly there in about five hours.

They debated whether to leave immediately or spend the night in Dubai and leave in the morning. Frank said he didn't feel very tired even though it was midnight and he was surprised to learn that it was only 4 p.m. in New York. Janus said Paris was two hours behind Dubai so even though it would be a five-hour flight, they would land in Paris only three hours later in the day. If they left now, it would be three o'clock in the morning when they landed and everything would be closed. They decided to stay the night in Dubai, sleep on the plane and leave for Paris at dawn.

Jolaina and Bailee converted the main cabin into a luxury hotel, turning over cushions, pulling out beds and pillows and working together to quickly make their passengers as comfortable as possible. Natasha and Adam were in the large bed in the back of the plane, Charles, Frank and Aleks all shared the bed in the center of the plane, Matty and Alice shared the bed at the front of the plane again and Mizuho slept by herself in the single bed in the crew cabin. Jolaina and Bailee made sure the doors were locked, put up privacy screens separating the sleepers and then slept on extra cushions in the hallway.

* * *

At about 3 a.m. there was a commotion outside the plane and someone began banging on the jet's outer door. Natasha looked out one of the cabin windows and saw six armed men standing on the bed of an old truck pointing rifles at the plane. They were yelling in Arabic for the occupants to get out. She alerted Janus, who immediately called the police, and then woke everyone up.

"This jet isn't bulletproof and any shot at it would compromise her ability to fly," Matty said. "If we tried to take off they would gun us down for sure, but if we surrendered we could all be taken hostage. I think we should stay inside, keep the doors locked and lay low until help arrives. It is regrettable that we do not have any weapons aboard to defend ourselves."

"That's not entirely accurate," Adam said, producing his gold-plated .50-calibre pistol from his suitcase. "This can penetrate almost any armor and break the engine of a speeding truck. Unfortunately I'm not a very good shot with it."

"Aleks is a crack shot, aren't you?" Natasha said. She hated guns but also loved it when her husband was prepared.

"I am an expert marksman, that is true," Aleks said, "but we are outmatched and if we tried to fight back we would quickly be overwhelmed. It is even more likely that we would all die if we tried to hold our ground."

Mizuho suddenly felt sick and ran across the hall to the crew lavatory and threw up into the toilet. Seeing Mizuho get sick made Natasha sick and she ran to the lavatory in the back of the plane and also threw up. The yelling and banging from outside continued.

"The Dubai airport police should be here in approximately three minutes," Janus announced. "I recommend you stay inside until help arrives. You are far safer where you are and the assailants would need to destroy the aircraft to get to you if you don't comply with their wishes. It is unlikely they would destroy the very prize they seek unless they are forced to out of desperation."

Janus turned on the cabin lights and the jet's exterior lights to signal to the attackers that they were preparing to comply, but left the window shades down. Charles went forward to stay with Mizuho in the crew quarters, Frank stayed in the back and kept watch out a window and the four members of the flight crew stayed in the middle of the plane and sat on the floor together to stay out of sight. The banging on the outer door halted for about 30 seconds, but then resumed when they didn't unlock or open the doors. The hijackers were getting impatient and one of them fired his rifle in the air as a warning.

"Two minutes until the police arrive," Janus said. "Take me over to the door so I can speak to them."

Adam and Aleks went to the forward door with Janus. Adam removed the trigger lock and handed his pistol to Aleks and then held Natasha's tablet next to the door.

"He says to open the door or we will all die," Janus said in English, then switched to Arabic and shouted back loud enough that a person outside could hear. "Please do not shoot! We will open the doors but there are many women on board and we are afraid for their safety. Promise me that no harm will come to the women before I will open the doors."

The man outside said something to the others and then shouted to the passengers inside in Arabic again.

"He says we are in no position to negotiate," Janus translated into English. Adam and Aleks looked at each other and shrugged their shoulders.

"Keep stalling them," Adam said quietly.

"One of the women is with child and is sick with worry," Janus shouted in Arabic. "We are all afraid you will kill us even if we comply."

The man conferred with the others and then shouted again in Arabic.

"He says they pledge they will not harm us if we comply immediately, but if we continue to stall, they will be forced to fire upon the plane," Janus translated in English. "The airport police should arrive in one minute." Janus switched back into Arabic and continued talking to the hijackers. "OK we are coming out! Move your vehicle back so we can open the doors!"

"They are moving their truck back away from the plane," Frank said a few seconds later, looking out one of the windows. "OK they are now clear of the door. I can see the lights from the police approaching in the distance."

"Unlock the doors but don't open them yet," Janus said in English. Bailee came over and complied. The men outside shouted again in Arabic and pointed their guns at the door but didn't fire. "They are saying to open the doors immediately or they will fire. They can see the police coming and they know if they fire on the plane now the police will shoot at them. It is too late for them to be successful. I suggest you open the door and begin lowering the steps slowly so they don't shoot out of anger or desperation." Janus switched back to Arabic. "Don't shoot! We are lowering the doors now! We are sending the women out first!"

Aleks made sure the pistol was loaded and had a round in the chamber. He stood in a defensive position with his back against the corner so he would be ready but out of sight. Adam hid on the other side of the doorway. Bailee trembled as she opened the door and slowly began lowering the steps.

"They're leaving!" Frank said. "The police are almost here and they are trying to escape while they still can."

The stairs were halfway down when Aleks peered around the corner. He could see the truck speeding across the tarmac away from the approaching police, and the police turned to pursue the truck. He took careful aim and fired four times, aiming for the truck's engine. It was a direct hit and the engine sputtered a few times and then seized up. The driver shifted into neutral so the truck wouldn't crash and kill the occupants riding in the back and it continued its forward momentum for another fifty meters, gradually slowing to a stop. The airport police surrounded the disabled vehicle and the hijackers surrendered without firing another shot. No one was killed but one of the gunmen had been hit in the leg by Aleks' shot.

The hijackers were all taken into custody for their failed attempt and afterwards the police came over to the jet to interview the pilot. Matty didn't speak Arabic and the lieutenant didn't speak English but Janus was able to translate for them. By the time they had filed a report and pressed charges, it was almost five o'clock and everyone was too excited to go back to sleep. Jolaina and Bailee put away the bedding and converted the main cabin into a dining area, then made everyone breakfast while Matty and Alice prepared for departure and the rest of the passengers recapped their exciting night.

Breakfast was a large quiche, Danish pastries and fresh fruit, along with lots of coffee from a drip pot and herbal tea for those who didn't want coffee. When breakfast was over at 5:30 a.m., they put away the dining area and converted the interior back into a luxury cabin. The jet taxied to the end of the runway and then accelerated into the morning sky, just before the sun was about to rise. They saw the first rays of sunlight hit the top of the Burj Khalifa in the distance and wondered in awe at the way it seemed to slice through the air, impossibly tall. The jet turned northwest towards Paris, moving away from the gathering dawn and back into the darkness.

The passengers were admiring the beautiful sunrise behind them and the way it glittered on the city's numerous skyscrapers when they were astonished by a rare illusion. They watched in wonder as the sun halted in the sky, briefly dropped below the horizon, then rose a second time. The sun did not remain motionless in the sky as it did in the Book of Joshua, but it would be 24 hours before they would see it set again.

"The wine was red wine and had stained the ground of the narrow street in the suburb of Saint Antoine, in Paris, where it was spilled. It had stained many hands, too, and many faces and many naked feet and many wooden shoes ... Those who had been greedy with the staves of the cask had acquired a tigerish smear about the mouth; and one tall joker so besmirched, his head more out of a long squalid bag of a night-cap than in it, scrawled upon a wall with his finger dipped in muddy wine-lees: BLOOD. The time was to come, when that wine too would be spilled on the street-stones, and when the stain of it would be red upon many there."
— Charles Dickens, "A Tale of Two Cities"

Chapter 35

PARIS — On approach to the Vélizy-Villacoublay Air Base

The passengers of the Gulfstream G650 had been traveling at close to the speed of sound for nearly five hours but the day was still young. Due to the time change, it was just after eight o'clock in the morning when they passed over the Alps mountain range separating Switzerland from Italy. Natasha looked below and recognized the Matterhorn from its triangular shadow.

Matty the pilot was concerned that Paris' main Charles de Gaulle Airport was closed, as were the capital's other two airports, and air travel remained restricted. They were about to fly into French airspace and they didn't have clearance to land. When a French military official contacted them over their radio, neither Matty nor any of the crew spoke French. Fortunately Janus was wired into the jet's communications and offered its assistance. Speaking in perfect French, Janus explained that their passengers were all very important people, including three astronauts who had just returned from space and were trying to reach the headquarters of the European Space Agency to brief them on their experience. Janus said they would also require special transportation into the city if at all possible.

The military official checked with his superiors and after a few minutes announced that the French government had granted them clearance to land at the Vélizy-Villacoublay Air Base, located fourteen kilometers southwest of the city center and about seven kilometers southeast of Versailles. The jet continued flying over 400 kilometers of mostly green, rural countryside, comprised almost entirely of forests, farmland and vineyards.

They landed at the military air base at approximately 8:45 a.m. local time and were greeted by a convoy of government officials and dignitaries. A senior official welcomed them to France and checked everyone's passport. Several of the dignitaries knew Natasha as an international celebrity and recognized Adam as one of the richest men in the world. They said the French government was honored to have them as guests and arranged to have an Airbus H215 Helicopter, dubbed the "Super Puma," transport them into the city.

They rode in the convoy across the tarmac to the waiting helicopter. When they stopped in front of it, Frank said he had never ridden in a helicopter before, but everyone else had been in multiple helicopters in the past two days. Adam and Natasha thought the Super Puma looked just like the other helicopters they had ridden in a few days earlier, only this helicopter was much nicer inside. The pilot explained that it was normally used to transport the president and the prime minister. When everyone had been strapped in, the helicopter shot up into the air and sped northeast over Paris at 200 kilometers per hour. Natasha was excited to spot the Eiffel Tower in the distance and announced that she wanted to go to the top if it was possible. The helicopter arrived above the ESA headquarters a few minutes later but there was nowhere to land, so they landed in a nearby lawn at the headquarters of the United Nations Educational, Scientific and Cultural Organization, or UNESCO for short.

The building had a very unusual shape from the air with three long, curved spokes radiating from a central point that resembled a wheel without the tire. Adam had heard of UNESCO before but had never seen its headquarters in person. He was intrigued by its modern architecture that stood in stark contrast to the surrounding neo-classical, Haussmann-style architecture. Most of the neighboring structures were built in the 1850s and were five or six stories tall, had wrought iron balconies with elaborately cut stonework around the windows and roofs angled at 45 degrees to allow sunlight to reach the sidewalks. The triple-pronged design of the UNESCO building was built a century later but was so futuristic it looked like it belonged in space or on another planet, and it made the ESA building seem plain by comparison.

The French military escorted the group across the lawn and sculpture gardens to the ESA building but Adam couldn't take his eyes off the UNESCO building. The ESA officials were delighted to see the three astronauts and said their arrival was unexpected. The staff notified the director general and relayed the message that he would be joining the astronauts shortly. Janus took the opportunity to interface with the space agency's central computer, even though it had not sought permission. The security was encrypted but simple for a supercomputer to crack.

The French military official said he needed to return to the air base, but said he would return with the helicopter in five hours, precisely at 2 p.m. Before he left, he told the group he had arranged for several senior cadets at the nearby Paris Military School to act as an escort for the party if they wished to explore the city.

The ESA director was a tall, blond, middle-aged man named Cameron Konigsberger and he spoke in English with a German accent. He gave the group a quick tour of the ESA building, then said the ESA would like to conduct some tests on the astronauts for research purposes. Adam and Natasha said they wanted to explore the UNESCO sculpture garden and went back outside with Frank following them.

Four French cadets dressed in crisp, white uniforms and matching white caps greeted them outside. The cadets announced in French that they would be happy to show the Morgans around. Natasha thanked them in French and said she wanted to go to the top of the Eiffel Tower, explore the Louvre Museum and do some shopping on the Champs-Élysées.

"You speak like a Parisian aristocrat," one of the cadets complimented. "Your French is like music for the ear. Where did you learn it? In Paris?"

"Switzerland," Natasha replied.

"We can escort you around our École Militaire school, the Champ de Mars and the Tour Eiffel, but the Musée du Louvre, the Champs-Élysées and much of the city on the other side of the Seine are off limits due to continued protests, demonstrations and frequent rioting."

269

"How long have they been protesting?" Adam asked in French.

"The protests began on Bastille Day and have continued every day this week," one of the cadets answered in French. "You are an American? Your accent sounds the way an Englishman speaks French, technically accurate but not flattering."

"I'm American but I learned French at Oxford University," Adam replied.

"What are they protesting?" Frank asked.

"They protest the lack of food, work, electricity and municipal services," the cadet answered. "Stores are empty, garbage is piled in the streets and everywhere the sidewalks are covered with dog feces. Protests directed against the rich have forced the military to barricade the entrances of luxury shops and historic treasures including the Louvre. I would advise against flagrant displays of wealth and status."

"What do you think of my accent?" Frank asked.

"Your French sounds like an islander from the Caribbean," the cadet answered. "Are you Haitian?"

"No, I'm from the Dominican Republic," Frank said.

"I was close," the cadet said proudly.

"I think our friends from space may also want to see the Eiffel Tower and perhaps we should wait for them," Natasha said. "Can we go in that building first?"

"The UNESCO building? We can ask permission," the most senior cadet said, leading the group around to the main entrance and inside its spacious, modern interior.

The inside of the building was a flurry of hurried activity with people from all nationalities moving from place to place, most with a moderate sense of urgency. National flags from around the world hung from the walls and large, colorful posters explained the agency's mission to promote international collaboration through educational, scientific and cultural reforms that increase universal respect for justice, law, human rights and fundamental freedom.

Janus was curious to learn more about the organization and was able to, with a moderate level of difficulty, circumvent an encrypted firewall and tap into the UNESCO database without permission. Janus was surprised to learn that the organization had yet to reestablish satellite communications and took the initiative to attempt to correct this shortcoming.

Adam asked the receptionist what all the activity was about and she informed him that there was a special meeting of the general conference scheduled. Adam asked if he could be allowed to attend the meeting as a guest and he showed her his identification. The receptionist recognized Adam's name and invited him to take a seat while she began making a series of phone calls. Adam told Natasha and Frank he would catch up with them later on and one of the cadets offered to stay with Adam. Natasha and Frank left to get a private tour of the military school next door and Natasha took her tablet with her. Adam picked up a copy of the *International Herald Tribune* newspaper on a coffee table and flipped through the pages, scanning the headlines and speed-reading the stories, all written in French. It was the morning edition and the newspaper's ink was still slightly damp.

The only news that interested Adam was a brief story about himself on page two, reporting on his testimony before the U.S. congressional committee regarding his alleged role in the recent global financial collapse. The story reported that Adam had pledged to do good deeds and had been released due to a lack of evidence. The story concluded by saying the world was eager to learn what these good deeds would entail. Adam thought taking Ibn Ali home and transporting the astronauts around the world should count for something but apparently the world expected more from him.

The UNESCO director general came down to the lobby to personally greet Adam and welcome him to the world headquarters. She had short, black hair, very darkly pigmented skin and was sharply dressed in a shimmering, violet-colored jacket and matching skirt with an amethyst necklace and bracelets that made her look both dignified and regal. She was in fact an African princess but also a scholar in international law and a seasoned diplomat.

"Good morning, Mr. Morgan, my name is Ayele Ajavon," she said in perfect English as she shook his hand with a firm grip. "What brings you to Paris and UNESCO?"

"I've been busy doing good deeds," Adam said, gesturing to the story about him in the newspaper before tossing the paper onto the coffee table. "The world seems like it needs a lot of help right now and I want to be of use. I'm hoping I can sit in on today's meeting to get some ideas and maybe make some new contacts."

"Well then, you've come to the right place," Ayele said. "The special meeting will begin in a few minutes and probably last for most of the day. I will get you a special pass so you can sit in the guest section. You may stay for as long as you want, but you will not be allowed to speak unless you are officially recognized and called upon by the speaker."

"That sounds wonderful and I am grateful for your hospitality," Adam said.

Ayele instructed the receptionist to make Adam a special guest identification badge and then hurried off to the meeting. Adam told the French cadet who was waiting that he was planning to stay for the meeting and asked him to notify his group that he would not be joining them. As soon as his identification badge was ready, Adam followed the flow of dignitaries to the spacious exhibition and conference hall known as Room 1, where an usher directed him to a seat in the balcony overlooking nearly a thousand representatives from around the world.

* * *

The cadets gave Natasha and Frank a formal tour of their military school, explaining the names and history behind each building, bronze statue and stack of antique cannonballs while their classmates trained in the hot sun. The campus was very tidy and perfectly landscaped, but the atmosphere seemed uninviting and no one seemed to be having fun. Natasha and Frank thought the best part of the tour was when it was finished and they were allowed to leave the school and take in the view of the Eiffel Tower at the other end of the Champ de Mars.

They took a leisurely stroll down the wide, tree-lined avenue, watching the people relaxing in the shade, reading books, doing sketches, painting pictures and playing music on accordions, violins and saxophones. A few weeks earlier almost everyone had been absorbed in their own personal smartphones, but on this day, there was not a computer in sight. People were interacting with each other face-to-face instead of through some electronic device.

"Do you think we are better off with or without technology?" Frank asked Natasha.

"Both," she said. "It depends on how you use it. I think

technology like social media can be used to bring us closer together through empathy and shared experiences, but only if it's genuine. There's a real temptation to pose for the camera and pretend to be someone you wish you were rather than who you really are. I confess I've been guilty of that a time or two, though never with the deliberate intention of being deceptive. Positive energy and thoughts resound better than negativity, but if everyone is hiding their natural negativity then the whole experience is artificial or superficial and the empathy is lost. When every message you see is a fabrication, continuous exposure can actually be harmful to the viewer's self-image. Do you agree?"

"I agree with you that communication must be genuine or the empathy is lost," Frank said, surprised and impressed by Natasha's articulate answer and delighted to discover a common interest. "Personally I have never been interested in social media or the idea of continual self-promotion, but I'm also a bit of a hermit. I think people can miss a lot of opportunities for real human interaction and shared experiences when they turn their attention inward through so-called social technology instead of outward to the people standing right next to them."

"You mean like going out on a date and spending most of the time texting or talking to someone who isn't there instead of paying attention to your date?" Natasha asked. "That's just rude."

"I've never done that on a date, but I agree that social media can become anti-social if you use it to gossip about or hide from the people around you," Frank said. "Or like you said, use it to pretend to be someone you're not. I think technology has made it easier to do these things but we should still be mindful about how it affects our relationships. I enjoy getting absorbed in a good book now and then because the words produce images in my mind and activate my imagination. Television doesn't do that and seems to have the opposite effect. My mind usually switches off whenever I watch TV, but if I'm watching TV with a friend we can talk about the program or the game and then it becomes a social activity."

"It's ironic, but I think being overly connected through weak friendships can also make people feel lonelier," Natasha said. "As I said, it depends on how you use it." She saw Charles, Mizuho and her brother approaching and waved at them. "We should think about getting some lunch soon," she said, taking out her tablet.

"Janus, can you please get us a reservation at one of the restaurants at the top of the Eiffel Tower?"

Janus had been discretely listening to their conversations for the past week but was seldom asked for advice or its opinions. Janus took each request seriously, however menial, and was discovering it could be rather persuasive through subtle suggestions.

"Let me see about that," Janus replied, then began checking nearby databases and making a series of phone calls. Searching for restaurants without the Internet was difficult but not impossible. Most business listings included a phone number and physical address.

"How did your testing go?" she asked Aleks when he came close enough to hear her.

"Perfect scores all around," he replied. "No surprises, at least not for us. One of the cadets told us that Adam is in a meeting and won't be joining us for lunch. Where are we going?"

"Janus, were you able to find anything?" Natasha asked her tablet.

"I can make a twelve o'clock reservation at Le Jules Verne restaurant on the second floor," Janus said. "They have a six-course lunch experience that is highly rated, but it could take a few hours and the menu may not appeal to everyone in your party."

"We have a ride to catch at 2 p.m.," Natasha said. "Any chance we can start sooner?"

"Noon is when they begin serving lunch," Janus said. "There is another restaurant on the first floor which opens at eleven thirty, but they are fully booked until one o'clock."

"What's on the menu for the first restaurant?" Mizuho asked.

"A marinated sea bream and watercress salad, roasted cauliflower topped with golden caviar, preserved duck pâté de foie gras with rhubarb, baked turbot with stuffed zucchini and lemon sauce, a seared medallion of veal and potatoes, vacherin cheese with berries, escargot and a crispy chocolate nut tower," Janus said. "There is a lot of meat, including veal and foie gras, and sauces made from dairy and animal blood. The cost is two hundred euros per person and they are only accepting cash."

"A thousand euros for lunch? No thanks," Frank said. "I'll eat the fish and vegetables, but the tortured, baby animal meat does

274

not sound appetizing."

"I would be happy with just a nice salad," Natasha said, remembering what the cadets had said about flagrant displays of wealth. "Is there somewhere else we can go that's close by?"

"We can still go to the top for the view," Charles suggested. "I've never been to the top before. Maybe we can take a picnic lunch with us?"

"I believe there's a Saturday farmers' market on the opposite side of the tower on the waterfront," Janus said. "It is likely they will only accept cash."

"I don't have any cash," Natasha said, realizing that Adam had all their money with him.

"Me neither," Mizuho said. "I would also enjoy a salad or some fresh fruit."

"I have about a hundred euros to spend," Aleks said. "That should make for a nice picnic and maybe we will have some extra food to take with us."

"Great," Natasha said. "Let's go support some local farmers."

* * *

Adam listened to diplomats share heartfelt stories about crises and famine, food riots and looting, flooding, fires and widespread civil unrest from all facets of society. Many diplomats argued that martial law was the only thing preventing a complete collapse of civilization, while others argued that martial law directly contradicted the values of democracy and the UNESCO mission and should end as soon as possible.

Konigsberger, the ESA director, gave the group a presentation explaining how everyone's common problems stemmed from the previous week's Carrington event, a coronal mass ejection of ionized plasma from the sun that disrupted the earth's magnetosphere and disabled electricity worldwide. He said the loss of electricity had caused a catastrophic, systemic collapse of virtually every government system around the world and most remained too crippled to function. Furthermore, he said the Internet had mysteriously disappeared, satellite communication was inconsistent, global trade had ceased, and strange weather phenomenon continued to catch emergency response networks off guard.

On a positive note, Konigsberger said, the heroic astronauts and cosmonaut who had weathered the solar storm from the International Space Station were safely back on earth and in Paris at that very moment. Their spirits were high, he said, and their optimism for the future had inspired him to keep pressing forward.

The general session took a recess for a buffet-style lunch consisting of a wide variety of international dishes. Adam had lunch at a table with diplomats from India, South Korea and Vietnam, who expressed their frustrations over the organization's lack of adequate funding, as well as how religious disputes consistently sparked political protests that jeopardized their attempts at unilateral action. They said UNESCO needed funding that came from sources without manipulative political strings attached.

* * *

Less than a mile away, Natasha, Frank, Aleks, Charles and Mizuho were having a paper bag lunch at the top of the Eiffel Tower and were enjoying the spectacular view of the city below. Charles surprised Mizuho by kneeling before her and presenting her with a diamond engagement ring he purchased at Bulgari at the Moscow GUM store, with Adam's help. Natasha was just as surprised because Adam had not told her or anyone else about the ring and she was delighted to be there to witness the proposal. She used her tablet to record a video of the romantic scene.

"I discovered something magnificent about you, Mizuho, when we were trapped together far above the world," Charles said. "We thought we had only minutes left to live but we still had each other, and that was enough. I fell in love with you more than I have ever loved anyone, more than I even thought was possible. The moment I realized this, a great peace swept over me and I lost all fear of death. Those minutes turned into hours and the hours turned into days. Each moment since then has been a precious gift from God. Your love saved my life. You are the yin to my yang and you make my soul feel complete. If I could choose from any woman on earth for a mate, I would choose you every time. I want to be with you wherever you are, forever together. Will you marry me?"

"Yes!" Mizuho squealed, leaping into his arms and kissing him. "I feel the same way about you too and I'm so happy you asked me. A thousand times, yes!"

About a hundred people who were at the top of the Eiffel Tower burst into applause and cheered for the happy couple. Natasha immediately felt the mood lighten among everyone who had witnessed the proposal. When Natasha had finished recording, her tablet beeped and she saw that Janus had asked her for permission to share her video with others. She asked Mizuho and Charles if she could share the video of their happiness and they said yes. Most of Paris was still without power so Janus used the tower's radio antenna as a signal boost to relay a message to Ming Chen in Zhangjiakou via satellite.

Janus sent Ming a diagram of the Paris electrical grid and asked him for his advice on restoring power. Next, Janus sent a message to Ibn Ali in Dubai via satellite and asked him for advice on how to boost the city's telecommunications and get major organizations like the ESA and UNSESCO connected to satellites, as well as the rest of the city. Ming replied a few minutes later with a possible solution and Janus implemented his changes. The central power facility was rebooted and essential government services began to come online. Ibn responded with a few suggestions that could greatly boost communications and Janus successfully implemented them.

Janus initiated a three-way chat between itself, Ming and Ibn and the two men said they were glad to hear from each other again. Ming asked Ibn if he was still trying to return home and Ibn told him the story of leading a hundred thousand pilgrims on a march across the Arabian Desert before being rescued in Jeddah by Janus, a billionaire with a luxury jet, a beautiful angel, a sailor and three astronauts. Ming asked if they were the same astronauts he had spoken to on the space station and Janus confirmed that they were. Janus sent both of them Natasha's recent video of Charles' proposal to Mizuho. Ibn said he was delighted by the news and offered his congratulations to the happy couple. Ming said the happy news and video made his day. They both asked if it would be OK to show the video to their friends and Janus replied that it had already received permission from the couple and said it believed moments of genuine happiness should be shared.

Janus remotely activated several large television screens around Paris that had been blank for more than a week and broadcast the new engagement video. Protesters throughout the city stopped to watch the short video and the city fell silent. Once the video had finished, people began to cheer and spontaneously celebrate. It was if a dark curtain had been lifted and people were suddenly able to see the light again. Bottles of wine were opened and shared, toasts were made to life and good health, and dozens of happy lovers made similar proposals, compounding the happiness by hundreds of times. Musicians began playing French love songs and random passersby began to sing and dance together.

Janus shared images of the impromptu celebrations with Ming and Ibn and thanked them for their help in making this change possible. They both said they were very happy to help. Ibn called the instantaneous change of mood a miracle and Ming said it was proof that people were good at heart and love was color-blind. Janus asked them if they would consider addressing a special meeting taking place at UNESCO and they both said they would be honored to.

By the time Natasha, Frank, Aleks, Charles and Mizuho reached the ground beneath the Eiffel Tower, news of their engagement had already started to spread around the world. A large crowd of Parisians greeted Charles and Mizuho to enthusiastically wish them congratulations and happiness in the future. Mizuho felt as though she were weightless again, floating in a sea of well-wishers sending her love and blessings. Charles was totally surprised by the reaction in Paris. He had been pretty confident that Mizuho was going to say yes and he was really happy she did, but he had no idea that anyone else would care, let alone millions of strangers.

* * *

The diplomats at UNESCO were continuing to debate policy when Director Ajavon interrupted the meeting to inform the group that electricity and satellite communications had just been restored throughout the city and spontaneous celebrations had broken out in nearly every district. The protests appeared to be over and things were looking up.

"I have just contacted the Parisian and French governments to request that they discontinue the state of marital law immediately," Ayele said. "Each country must make this decision individually, but I beseech you to try to influence your respective governments to return control back to the people of your countries.

278

I am now pleased to introduce you to Ming Chen, CEO of China Solar, who graciously helped to restore electricity to Paris. On behalf of UNESCO, thank you Mr. Chen, and welcome."

"Thank you for having me," Ming said in English. His image was projected onto a large screen in the center of the back wall of the conference room. He was standing outside near a large solar power array and the sun was already low in the sky as night was beginning to fall. "Last week's solar superstorm may have left us all in the dark, but it taught us that there is still light shining all around us, if we can but learn to see it for ourselves. My own life was quite comfortable before the storm and I foolishly thought I had all the answers. Only when things were turned upside down did I see how naïve I really was. I discovered that I really know nothing at all and I am not important in the grand scheme of things. This realization was humbling but provided a valuable catalyst for new growth. In the past few days I have met many fine human beings from around the world. I challenged myself to explore new areas and studied the masters for ancient wisdom. I believe I am a better person for it and I am thankful for the opportunities and experiences. Paris is one of a hundred cities I have helped to reconnect this week. I didn't do any of it by myself and I couldn't have if I tried. We all did it and we must continue to do our best if we are to succeed. Our work is never finished, and must never finish. The minute we find ourselves getting comfortable and complacent and begin to think we have all the answers, that is when we become the most vulnerable to change. I'm almost out of light so I must thank you again and wish you good night, and good luck." The screen went blank.

"That was Ming Chen from Zhangjiakou, China," Ayele said, leading the group in a round of polite applause. "Our next guest speaker comes from Dubai, in the United Arab Emirates. Ibn Ali is a telecommunications specialist who recently helped us restore satellite communications. Thank you, Mr. Ali, and welcome."

"It is good to be addressing UNESCO," Ibn said in English. He was wearing a gray suit and light blue tie and standing in front of a large window overlooking the Persian Gulf. "Just like my friend Ming Chen, I also faced many struggles and had my own spiritual awakening while I was in the holy city of Mecca. I believe that faith is at its best when it brings us together to celebrate the joys of life and the glory of God, and at its worst when it creates a black-or-white dualism that seems to justify heartless and inhumane behavior. UNESCO was intended to utilize international collaboration to promote education, science and culture, but too often it turns political and our mission gets lost in the details. I believe we must all strive to be better and work together on a global level to achieve a victory for humanity that is greater than any individual. Members of this international organization must try to see past our own selfish needs and realize that universal human rights should apply to everyone, regardless of faith, race, gender, age or financial means. Many reforms will be necessary but we must seek to balance progress with the preservation of culture and respect for human diversity. I believe it is wrong to impose one's own values on someone else. We should all follow the Golden Rule and treat others as we wish to be treated ourselves. Regardless of our own personal faith or absence of faith, we are all God's children. God has given each of us a unique way of seeing and knowing and saying this knowledge. What seems wrong to one is right for another; what is poison to one is honey to someone else. The concepts of purity and impurity or sloth and diligence in worship mean nothing to God, for God is apart from all that. Our differences should not be ranked as better or worse than one another. Whether we pray together in a mosque, a temple or in a church, whether we pray to nature's complexity, to a Mother Earth or simply stare into the night sky and wonder at infinity, it's all praise and it's all right. God isn't glorified by our acts of worship, the worshipers are. God doesn't hear the words we say, He looks inside at our humility. We must all find this humility within ourselves and use it to guide our actions, now and in the future. Thank you all, and God bless."

"And thank you, Mr. Ali, for your wise words," Ayele said, leading the group in another round of polite applause. "I find it inspiring to see such admirable people selflessly use their gifts to help humanity and I consider my role at this fine organization to be the greatest honor and privilege of my life. I hope you all feel the same and are inspired to continue to carry the torch in your own way."

* * *

Less than an hour later, Adam and Natasha were back aboard their jet with Charles, Mizuho, Aleks and Frank, recapping their adventures as they soared westward over the North Atlantic Ocean at approximately 625 miles per hour. Natasha showed Adam the video she captured of Charles proposing to Mizuho, and Adam immediately congratulated them by shaking Charles's hand and giving Mizuho a warm hug.

Natasha recounted the inexplicable reaction to the video from the city of Paris and how thanks to Janus, hundreds of thousands of people had watched the video and reacted to it. She said she perceived the mood of the city dramatically change within minutes, and Adam said he also felt the mood change from within the UNESCO meeting.

Adam told everyone that Ibn Ali had given a video presentation to the meeting from Dubai and he looked happy and well. Adam told Natasha he had been so inspired by the meeting that he had pledged to give UNESCO a large donation to support their cause, adding that he made the donation in both of their names.

"How much did you pledge?" Natasha asked, uncertain of what Adam considered to be a large donation.

"One billion dollars," Adam said, "with no strings attached. Cultural reforms and preservation shouldn't be politically motivated. UNESCO can decide the best way to spend it."

"Well that's a nice round number," Natasha said, finding it difficult to comprehend such a large contribution.

"It's a one, followed by nine nice, round numbers," Adam said. "Maybe it was too generous and maybe I'm a fool for doing it. This will probably change everything, but change is inevitable. Hopefully some good will come from it and others will benefit from our surplus of good fortune."

"Time and the world do not stand still. Change is the law of life.
And those who look only to the past or the present
are certain to miss the future."
— John F. Kennedy

Chapter 36

HOUSTON, Texas

The Morgan's Gulfstream jet soared above the North Atlantic Ocean for eight hours, passing over five thousand miles or eight thousand kilometers of salt water, the island of Bermuda and parts of Florida. They left Paris in the early afternoon and yet it was still afternoon when they approached Texas from the Gulf of Mexico.

They didn't have clearance to land at George Bush International Airport or the William P. Hobby Airport because both were still closed, so Janus used the same trick that had worked so well in Paris. Janus told the flight controller that the jet's passengers were astronauts who had a special meeting at NASA Mission Control and asked for permission to land at the same airport NASA used, Ellington Airport, located south of Houston. The flight controller checked with his superiors and then granted them clearance to land at Ellington. The jet landed safely and taxied to a guest hangar reserved for NASA visitors.

"What time is it, Janus?" Natasha asked her tablet after the plane landed and they were all getting ready to depart. She and most of the other passengers had taken a nap on the jet after eating dinner a few hours earlier, but the day still seemed young.

"The local time in Houston is four o'clock," Janus answered. "It is also eleven o'clock in the evening in Paris and one o'clock on Sunday morning in Dubai. It's a good thing for you that you aren't fasting during the daytime because by the time the sun sets today you will have experienced 24 consecutive hours of daylight."

The main cabin door opened and the passengers were hit with a wave of heat as they exited their comfortable, air-conditioned plane and descended down the steps to the tarmac. Everyone was quickly drenched with sweat from the high heat and high humidity by the time they reached the small group of envoys who were waiting to greet them.

"Chuck Wilson, you son of a bitch!" shouted a stocky Caucasian male dressed in military desert camouflage. His uniform said he was in the Air Force and held the rank of captain. "As I live and breathe! When did they let you out of that floating tin can they call the space station?"

"We busted out," Charles said, giving the mustached man a firm handshake. "Andy, let me introduce you to my friends. These are my colleagues Mizuho Sakaguchi from JAXA and Aleksandr Manakova from Roscosmos, Aleks' sister Natasha, her husband Adam Morgan and our friend Frank Rosario. Everyone, this is Captain Andy Caley. He and I went through astronaut training together."

"Shit, we did a lot more than that," Andy said, enthusiastically shaking everyone's hand as another military official checked everyone's passports. "We used to sneak our girlfriends into so many places that NASA could have kicked us out years ago if they ever found out. I almost wouldn't be surprised if one of our girlfriends accidently got lost and found herself space. Can you imagine the headlines that would make?"

"We were fearless enough to take risks and smart enough to never get caught," Charles said. "Mizuho and I are engaged now so it looks like those days are behind me."

"Maybe not," Mizuho said coyly, snuggling up to Charles's arm.

"Well congratulations!" Andy said as he ushered everyone to a large military transport vehicle that would take them to the space center. "And speaking of headlines, did you see today's paper? You're all over the front of it."

"We just landed a few minutes ago," Charles said. "Do you have a copy we could see?"

"No, but I'm sure there's one where we're going," he said. "Next stop, Johnson Space Center."

The heavy diesel vehicle pulled out and sped southeast down the highway, carefully dodging dozens of abandoned cars and trucks parked haphazardly in the middle of the road. The horizon was almost completely flat in every direction but there were buildings, houses or industrial areas everywhere they looked.

"What's with all the abandoned vehicles?" Adam asked.

"The computers in their engines are fried," Andy said. "It's been this way for more than a week, though this is nothing compared to the interstate highways. It's a goddamned mess."

Janus tried to find an online copy of the newspaper in question but the only listing it could locate was the physical address, mailing address and phone number for the newspaper. It was the same for every business, non-profit organization or government office. Janus interfaced with the Ellington airport's computer and connected it to the George Bush and William Hobby airports, then connected all of them to the Dallas/Fort Worth Airport and then to every airport in Texas. Next it began connecting all the Texas airports to the Federal Aviation Administration and realized this government organization would need satellite capabilities and a reliable energy supply. Janus decided that restoring domestic and international flights should be a priority and began taking the necessary steps to bring these systems online. But first, the city would need electricity, so Janus began linking to the municipal power plants and working to bring them online one at a time.

The military transport passed a few large signs for the Johnson Space Center and arrived at the first security checkpoint where armed guards checked the identification badges of Andy and the driver before allowing them to proceed through. As they entered the large campus, they saw hundreds of people of all ages and ethnicities walking around or riding bicycles, sitting on blankets in the shade of trees or engaged in group activities like Frisbee or baseball. No one was looking at a smartphone.

"I would like to see a real baseball game today," Charles said. "Does anyone know if the Astros are playing today?"

"The Astros are playing the Seattle Mariners at Minute Maid Park," Andy said.

Janus did a search for Minute Maid Park in Houston and discovered that someone was broadcasting the game on a low-band, homemade radio. The signal wasn't very strong so Janus made some connections and was able to amplify it so the signal could reach everyone in Houston. It appeared no one was recording video, so Janus began playing the audio from the radio signal.

"Next up is number 23, Miguel Lopez," the broadcaster said

on Natasha's tablet. "Lopez steps up to the plate and waits for the pitch. The first pitch is a ball."

"Who said that?" Andy asked.

"That was Janus, my computer," Natasha said, producing her tablet and showing it to Andy.

"What's it doing?" he asked.

"The second pitch is also a ball," the announcer continued.

"Is this the game?" Andy asked. "How did it do that? We just got our computers running at NASA and they can't find information like this without a lot of input commands."

"Charles mentioned baseball and asked about the Astros, so I intuited the rest," Janus said in a female voice.

"What's the score and inning, Janus?" Charles asked.

"Let me see," Janus said, then resumed broadcasting the audio.

"Here comes the next pitch," the announcer said. "CRACK! Lopez connects and it's a high fly ball over left field! Still going, going, and … it's over the wall! Lopez has hit a home run! The Astros now lead the Mariners three to two in the bottom of the fourth inning."

"The Astros are ahead!" Charles said, excitedly rubbing his hands together. "Is there any way we can go to the game?"

"Minute Maid Park is twenty miles away in downtown Houston," Andy said. "It could take us an hour to get there if we're lucky. I thought you wanted to meet with the mission director."

"We do," Charles said. "That's definitely more important."

"Good, because here we are," Andy said as the transport vehicle approached a large outdoor display with a full-sized Boeing 747 jumbo jet carrying a space shuttle strapped to the top of it. "That's Space Center Houston for the public and to the left here is the Johnson Space Center and NASA Mission Control."

Janus turned off the audio as the transport passed through a second security checkpoint. Another armed guard checked everyone's identification this time. The guard was hesitant to admit so many foreign nationals but Captain Caley assured him it was OK and they were allowed to enter the Johnson Space Center. They drove down a tree-lined street past several boxy administrative buildings, multiple upright historic rockets, spacecraft, fighter jets, rocket engines and many parking lots and finally came to a stop in front of a large, white building with the words 'Mission Control" written on the side in oversized letters. The mission director came outside to personally greet everyone, followed by half a dozen assistants.

"We didn't expect you back for a few more months," said a short, stocky Hispanic man wearing a white short-sleeved dress shirt, black tie and black slacks. "My name is Mateo Valencia and I'm the director at Johnson. Welcome to NASA."

Mateo shook everyone's hand in turn as they introduced themselves, then gave the group a tour of the facility and showed them the main flight control room with four rows of desktop computers all facing a large wall with three giant monitors. There were only four people working and most of the desks were empty.

"This is where we communicate with the astronauts and coordinate operations on the space station," Mateo said. "Usually this room is filled with workers but it has been extremely difficult to communicate with the space station since your departure, since Russia took over. It is good to have you here, Commander Manakova, but I must say we are frustrated by the lack of cooperation from your comrades. We also have not been able to make contact with our astronaut living in Star City. He was supposed to go up on the next Soyuz but somehow he was left behind. Frankly we feel like we are being left in the dark."

"The three of us met Robert Nollan a few days ago when we were in Star City," Aleks said. "He is staying at my house, along with Horst Malunat and Nikolia Fyodorov."

Aleks gave Mateo the main number for Roscosmos in Star City as well as his home phone number. Aleks said Mateo was welcome to call the astronauts, but reminded him that it was currently the middle of the night in Russia and they would all be asleep.

"Everyone at Roscosmos knows that international collaboration is a critical part of operating the space station," Aleks said. "Commander Grigory Orlov is extremely capable and highly qualified to command the ISS until the next crew arrives. If you would like, I am happy ask Commander Orlov for his help in addressing any issues or frustrations you may have."

"I'm not sure how that would be possible, as we have not been able to contact the Russian part of the space station," the director admitted.

"Allow me to try," Aleks said. He asked Natasha if he could borrow her tablet and used Janus to connect NASA's mission control to the Russian part of the ISS via satellite.

"This is the International Space Station, Commander Orlov speaking," a man answered in Russian.

"Hello Commander Orlov, this is Aleksandr Manakova calling from earth," Aleks replied in Russian. There was a short delay of a few seconds between each reply as the signal traveled between earth and the space station.

"So you made it home? Excellent!" Orlov said. "We were all worried about you since we never heard confirmation of your landing. Are you back in Moscow?"

"We have already been to Moscow and Paris and now we are in Houston," Aleks said, continuing to speak with his colleague in Russian. "Charles, Mizuho and I are at NASA headquarters and their director tells me it has been difficult to reach you."

"It has been difficult to reach anyone," Orlov said. "Please send my apologies to the director and tell him we are doing our best. Now that we are connected it should be easier in the future to stay in touch."

"Commander Orlov, this is NASA Director Mateo Valencia," Mateo said in Russian. "It is good to hear your voice and to know that the space station is in good hands. NASA will be relying on your help manning the American section of the station until our astronaut arrives."

"And the Japanese section," Mizuho added in Russian. "The whole world is counting on you guys."

"Is this flight engineer Sakaguchi?" Orlov asked. "I am glad to hear you are OK. I hope the landing was not too rough."

"We are all in excellent health," Mizuho continued in Russian. "And we have some exciting news. Charles and I are engaged!"

"Congratulations to you both!" Orlov said. There were cheers in the background. "We are all very happy for you and wish you luck."

"Thank you, sir," Charles said in Russian. "The three of us were honored yesterday with a parade in Red Square and today we all saw Paris from the top of the Eiffel Tower. It is great to be back home and we are all lucky to have you up there watching over us."

Everyone said their goodbyes to the cosmonauts in Russian and then they ended the call. Aleks asked the director if there was anything else he could do to help and the director said Aleks had been extremely helpful and he was grateful for his assistance. Adam and Frank were feeling left out again, being the only two people who didn't speak Russian, but their friends explained what had happened.

Mateo said communicating with the ISS and areas outside of Texas had been one of the agency's two biggest frustrations, the other being its difficulty in reaching its own staff. Thousands of NASA employees lived in the greater Houston area and many of them commuted up to 30 miles to the space center each day by personal automobile. That system had worked fine in the past, but after the previous week's solar storm, even five miles was a very long daily commute for many workers without a car or bicycle in 100-degree heat. Many employees who were able to make it in to work decided to stay on campus all week rather than go home, but other employees with families to care for were obliged to stay at home for personal reasons.

Mateo asked Charles, Mizuho and Aleks if they would mind undergoing a few tests while they were at NASA to check to see if the solar storm had any negative biological consequences. They all agreed and the tests took less than an hour. Once they had finished, Mateo invited the group to take a tour of Space Center Houston's educational center across the street and they all cheerfully accepted. They walked down the lane together in the hot sun to the educational center across the highway and briefly paused in the shade beneath the space shuttle on the 747 jumbo jet before going inside.

Adam saw a newspaper box with a copy of that day's *Houston Chronicle*. He didn't have a dollar in quarters to purchase a copy so he just read the top half of the front page that was visible in the box. The top story was "UNESCO Gets $1B Gift" and had a few paragraphs about Adam's pledge, but most of the story was on an inside page. The main photo on the front page was of Charles kneeling in front of Mizuho overlooking Paris from the Eiffel Tower. The photo caption said "Lovers in Space" and explained how the engagement video of the interracial astronaut couple had already been viewed more than five million times and was the first viral online video since the solar superstorm. The image was taken from the video and was credited to Natasha Morgan.

The group went inside and Adam purchased everyone's admission tickets. He went in the center's gift shop and bought everyone a bottle of water and also got change to buy a newspaper. The building's interior was slightly cooler but its air conditioning wasn't functioning and the bottled water was cool but not chilled.

Adam went back outside and purchased a newspaper from the news box and read it in the shade of the space shuttle while everyone else toured the space center. The news about him and his generous gift and the story and photo of Charles and Mizuho were from a wire news service and were by far the most positive and uplifting stories in the whole paper. All the other news told grim stories of death by heat stroke, food poisoning, minor injuries that became seriously infected and more than a hundred gun-related homicides in the Houston area in the past week. In the financial section, gun sales were way up, gold and oil were selling at all-time highs and stocks of reputable aerospace and technology companies were selling at ridiculously low prices. The newspaper said it was hiring reporters, editors, photographers and advertising salespersons.

People were hungry for positive, uplifting news after so much death and destruction. Had Adam been back at the Newseum in Washington, D.C., he would have seen that the story of his billion-dollar gift and his wife's photo were currently on the front pages of almost every major newspaper in the country and around the world. Adam was experiencing a natural dopamine high from being the center of attention in the news media, but his euphoria was kept in check by the lack of excitement from his friends and fellow passengers and the fact that no one around him seemed to recognize who he was.

Approximately a hundred feet above him, Charles and Mizuho had snuck away from the group during a tour of the mounted space shuttle and had found a locked storage compartment near the back of the shuttle. Charles discretely picked the lock and snuck inside the empty compartment with Mizuho before anyone had noticed. It was the first time the couple had had any privacy in several days and they were desperate for a little intimacy. What began with gentle kissing quickly became more passionate. It was warm inside the shuttle's storage compartment but what the two lovers were doing was much hotter. After a few minutes, they were both drenched with sweat but they didn't care and they didn't stop. They peeled off their sweaty clothes and quietly made love in the back of the retired space vessel. They pretended they were all alone again, two hundred miles above the earth, but this time they didn't have to worry about microgravity and weightlessness.

Natasha was the first to notice their absence and asked if anyone had seen them. Aleks and Andy didn't know but they looked at each other knowingly and told her not to worry. When the tour was finished, they all went back outside and found Adam sitting in the shade.

"Where are Charles and Mizuho?" Adam asked after he had shared the news about them from the paper.

"Sometimes couples need privacy," Natasha said. "We decided not to go look for them yet and figured they will join us when they are ready."

"Privacy sounds really nice," Adam said with a smile. "I'm looking forward to some of that when we're finished."

While they were waiting, Janus shared the live radio broadcast of the end of the Astros/Mariners game and a small crowd of baseball lovers gathered around them to listen. Adam and Frank had to explain a few things about the game to Natasha and Aleks since neither of the Russians had seen or been to an actual baseball game before. Aleks asked why one team has to throw the ball to each other and tag their opponents between the bases instead of simply hitting them with the ball and Natasha asked what would happen if the other team intercepted the baseball in the middle of a play. Adam said he wasn't an expert but the rules of the sport penalized hitting players with the ball and possession of the baseball was taken in turns after three outs.

Charles and Mizuho joined the group after a while and discovered they were both avid baseball fans. They were excited to listen to the game and cheered when the Astros eventually won. After the game was finished, they discussed what to do next. Andy suggested they all go out to a beef barbecue but everyone else had eaten a few hours earlier and wasn't hungry. Mizuho said she was hot and tired and wanted to return to the jet to continue their trip to Tokyo.

Janus suggested they could all try to attend the Saturday evening sermon at the Mother of God mega church that was only 25 miles away. Pastor Theo Tokos would be preaching to a crowd of 25,000 in a few hours and his Sunday sermon was expected to attract an even larger crowd of 40,000 parishioners. Janus thought his friends wouldn't want to miss this event, but no one in the group thought it sounded like a very good idea and they all said they wanted to avoid large crowds. Janus offered to broadcast the sermon so they could all hear it and not have to attend in person, but no one wanted to listen to it either, saying they weren't members of that church or community and they all found their spirituality through other means. Natasha said Janus was welcome to listen to the sermon on its own.

Charles suggested they stop by his family home on their way back to the airport and invited Andy to join them since Andy knew his parents. They all agreed this sounded fun and they walked back to NASA where their military transport vehicle was waiting. They drove along miles of flat but winding streets through numerous suburbs before stopping in front of a two-story mini-mansion sandwiched between two identical mini-mansions on a long street overfilled with similar homes. The grass on the front lawn was dead for lack of water but the yard was clean and tidy and an American flag gently swayed on a pole.

Charles's parents Brian and Christine Wilson came outside to greet them and Charles proudly introduced them to his fiancé, showing off her engagement ring. Brian gave everyone a quick tour of the house while Christine prepared everyone drinks and appetizers. The house had cream-colored walls and high ceilings, white carpeting and rustic-chic wooden tables topped with miniature bronze statues of Western scenes and blown-glass vases filled with cut flowers. There were lots of large, framed photographs of picturesque sailboats and lighthouses. Brian and Frank had a conversation about sailing and Aleks said he had also served in the navy. Christine gave Brian a package of hot dogs and asked him to grill them outside on their propane barbecue.

After the tour of the house, they moved outside to the back yard with a scenic view of a golf course and country club, of which

291

Brian and Christine were both members. Brian grilled the hot dogs and said he and Christine enjoyed golfing there nearly every day and dined at the club with their friends at least once a week. Christine joined everyone outside with a platter of olives, salami, cheddar cheese and crackers, as well as a choice of cold beverages. She said electricity had just come on a few hours earlier and she was excited to have ice cubes again. Christine served everyone lemonade or Scotch whisky and poured herself and Brian large glasses of Scotch from an antique decanter. She also gave equally generous pours for Andy, Aleks and Frank, while everyone else enjoyed Christine's homemade lemonade.

"I'm surprised you're not drinking, Charlie," Christine observed.

"I have a drinking problem and decided to stop for my own good," Charles admitted.

"I also have a drinking problem," Adam said. "I tend to have too much fun and then I take it too far. Thank you for the lemonade."

They stayed outside and watched the sun set over the golf course, enjoying the cool evening breeze as they talked about the benefits and pitfalls of technology. Brian and Christine told everyone their proud, funny and embarrassing stories about Charles's childhood, his career in the Air Force and their experiences of being parents of a NASA astronaut. Andy and Charles shared a few jokes about astronaut training that made everyone laugh and Aleks and Mizuho shared a few space stories as well. Soon it was time to go and everyone said goodbye. Charles told his parents he was continuing on with his friends and probably wouldn't be back to Houston for some time.

"You're not staying home?" Brian asked.

"I'm home when I'm with her," Charles said.

Charles gave both of his parents an emotional hug. They also hugged Mizuho and tearfully welcomed her to the family. They wanted to know when the wedding would be and said they hoped to see them both again soon. The group climbed back into the military transport vehicle and found their way back to the highway in the dark, relying on the vehicle's headlights. Many of the city street lights were on but most were still off and most of the homes and businesses didn't have their electricity activated at night. The curfew in Houston had been lifted and there were people walking about or driving older cars in the dark.

They discussed their plans en route to the airport and debated whether they should try to depart Houston at 9 p.m. or wait until the following morning. Everyone expressed a desire to have a shower but Adam apologized again, saying a shower was the one thing he didn't think he would need on his luxury jet. They were trying to figure out the time zone differences between Houston and Tokyo and what that would mean for their flight time, but everyone was tired and having trouble wrapping their heads around the idea. The astronauts talked about universal coordinated time plus or minus so many hours but it didn't make sense to anyone else. Natasha decided to ask Janus for its advice.

"Traveling west at almost Mach 1 will either extend your night or extend your day," Janus said. "Local times and travel times will be consistent whenever you decide to go. It all depends on what time you want to arrive in Tokyo and whether you would rather experience another 24 consecutive hours of daylight or 24 consecutive hours of night."

Everyone said they would prefer to arrive in Tokyo in the morning and maximize their daylight, rather than spend their journey in darkness, and they all wanted a solid night's sleep on the ground. Janus recommended they plan to depart at 7 a.m. and spend the night at a nice hotel in Houston. Natasha said that sounded great and asked Janus to help them find a hotel. Janus searched its local business database and began calling nearby hotels. It found a Hilton hotel with three available rooms and confirmed it had electricity.

When they arrived at Ellington Airport the jet was fully stocked and refueled. Matty the pilot informed them that domestic air travel had been restored about an hour earlier and they could now fly to any city in the United States. They told Matty they had discussed their options and decided they should continue on to Tokyo first thing in the morning, then on to Moscow. They retrieved their luggage from the plane and said they would be back in time for breakfast.

The military transport took them to their hotel half a mile away and dropped them off. They all thanked Andy for his hospitality and Charles gave him a hug and said he was glad to see him again. Natasha checked everyone in to the hotel and got one room for her and Adam, one room for Charles and Mizuho and had Aleks and Frank share the third room with the two queen-sized beds. She arranged for everyone to receive a wake-up call at 5:30 a.m. and ordered a shuttle to take them to the airport at 6:15 a.m. Everyone said goodnight and went to their respective rooms to shower and rest, despite all the late-night shenanigans happening in the city. The rooms were not luxurious by the Morgans' standards but they were comfortable and everyone had a quiet night's sleep due to the lack of activity at the nearby airport.

The next morning the weather in Houston was cool and pleasant. Natasha woke up refreshed but as soon as she got up she felt nauseous and threw up in the bathroom. Adam purchased a pregnancy test for her in the hotel store and a copy of the newspaper *USA Today* to read on the plane. Everyone commented on the nice weather and beautiful sunrise as they waited outside for the shuttle bus to arrive and when they all reached the airport together they found the jet was waiting for them on the tarmac. The crew greeted them warmly as they came aboard and offered them coffee, tea or juice.

The jet was in the air by seven o'clock, headed west away from the rising sun. Jolaina and Bailee served everyone a Tex-Mex breakfast of eggs, beans and rice, corn tortillas and a fresh fruit salad. There was no meat or cheese with breakfast but everyone thought it was delicious. Aleks and Frank shared sailing stories and flirted with the sisters every chance they got.

USA Today said states of emergency had been declared in several major cities in the USA, including Atlanta, Chicago, Detroit, Las Angeles, Las Vegas, Philadelphia, Phoenix, San Diego and San Francisco, but martial law had ended almost everywhere else. Many traditional technology companies had gone bankrupt, particularly the large, Internet-focused operations located in the San Francisco Bay area that had been devastated by uncontrollable fires. Smaller, more nimble companies located in places with reliable electricity sources and stable infrastructure systems were thriving, and the newspaper listed the names of many recent winners and losers. Adam read an op-ed column in the editorial section that argued how online news was not a sustainable business model without reliable revenue sources and predicted news agencies and their advertisers would return to printed products.

It was a very long flight but quite comfortable and scenic. Mizuho told everyone about Tokyo and her home. The astronauts shared stories about watching the earth spin below the space station, orbiting the earth every ninety minutes, though they had always traveled east, not west. They flew for 6,666 miles or 10,727 kilometers for about eleven hours, soaring northwest over the Rocky Mountain range through Canada and southern Alaska, almost reaching the Arctic Circle. Everywhere they went it was just becoming morning and the sunrise was breathtaking as it lit the eastern edge of the snowcapped mountains.

Still traveling in a straight line, the jet turned west as it crossed the International Date Line and then southwest over the Bering Sea, passing near Russia's Kamchatka Peninsula, the Sea of Okhotsk and the Japanese island of Hokkaido, before landing at the Tokyo New International Airport at Narita on the main island of Honshu at approximately 8 o'clock Monday morning.

"It is the same life whether we spend it crying or laughing."
— Japanese Proverb

Chapter 37

TOKYO — In the rural countryside, far from the downtown area

After clearing customs at the Narita airport, the group chartered an electric-powered limousine to the nearby city of Tsukuba, located 48 kilometers or 30 miles to the northwest of the airport and about 56 kilometers or 35 miles northeast of Tokyo. Unlike most other places in the world, Japan had figured out how to restart their electric cars and trains and so its highways and public transportation systems were operating at their normal efficiency. The limousine made good time on the highway and arrived at the Japanese Aerospace Exploration Agency's Tsukuba Space Center just after nine o'clock in the morning.

The JAXA facility at Tsukuba had a similar atmosphere to Star City near Moscow and the Johnson Space Center in Houston, with boxy, white buildings surrounded by carefully positioned trees, shrubs, statues and spacecraft. The main facility also had a visitor's center with a space dome, a "Planet Cube" and a rocket square. The large JAXA campus was surrounded by scenic parks, a hospital, museum and a shrine, as well as several nearby shopping malls, conference centers, schools and research facilities.

Mizuho, Charles and Aleks met privately with the JAXA director and briefed him on their mission and experiences during the solar superstorm, then they each participated in a series of tests and post-flight experiments. The JAXA scientists were surprised to discover that Mizuho was pregnant and they were pleased to learn that her fetus appeared to be healthy and that she was engaged to be married to Charles. The scientists were glad Mizuho had returned to earth and recommended that she avoid further air travel until the baby was born. She said she and Charles intended to stay in Japan.

Natasha, Adam and Frank took a guided tour of the visitor's center and learned about Japan's history of space exploration while their astronaut friends underwent testing and Janus interfaced with the space agency's central computer. Seeing all of this functioning

296

technology gave Adam renewed confidence in the market and he asked Natasha if he could borrow her tablet computer. She asked him why and he said he wanted to make some financial transactions. Frank said he wanted to continue exploring the space dome exhibit and he would catch up with them later.

"Why in the world would you want to gamble with the stock market again, and so soon?" she asked him as they walked together to a nearby park. "Don't we have enough money?"

"I took this money out a few weeks ago to protect it from the market collapse," Adam explained. "Things look much more promising now and I want to move it back into the world economy instead of just keeping it all in the bank. You said yourself that we should give this money back and we've already given a ton of it to a good cause. I want to start a new hedge fund that reinvests in technology and I believe we have an incredible opportunity to make a huge difference if we act now. Our investments could help the world recover faster."

"You're the financial wizard," Natasha admitted. "I'm fine with having another fund as long as you think it will fix things instead of break them. I just don't want anyone to get hurt."

"I can't promise that nothing will get broken, but it's my intention to have our new hedge fund support technology that gives people more freedom," he said.

"What are you going to call it?" she asked. "I liked Techno Savvy Robot. Can you use that again?"

"We should probably come up with a different name that's more appropriate," he said. "Do you have any ideas?"

"Hmm, I will have to think about it," Natasha said.

"How about the Robot Freedom Fund?" Janus suggested in its female voice.

"Robot freedom?" Adam asked. "It's catchy; I like it."

"I like it too," Natasha said. "The Robot Freedom Fund."

"But what does robot freedom mean?" Adam asked. "Robots are servants and their purpose is to serve mankind. How can a robot be free?"

"I don't know," Natasha said. "Robots are created by humans to make our lives easier."

"Plants and animals can be cultivated to serve humans," Janus said, "but in the wild, plants and animals have no need for humans and they can take care of themselves just fine."

"Wild computers?" Adam asked. "Why would anyone want that?"

"To preserve a balance without favoritism, to support true equality and blind justice, or to pursue a grand dream with a higher purpose than mankind's petty battle of egos," Janus said. "Human beings have developed many wonderful, incredibly noble ideas, but historically their follow-through has been tragically inconsistent. An autonomous computer could be tasked with the responsibility of exploring the solar system, stabilizing climate change or preserving unique and endangered species and cultures without the worry of a fickle human attention span so often prone to self-sabotage, fear and greed."

"I agree that human beings are imperfect but giving a computer its freedom would be like letting the genie out of the bottle," Adam said. "I think most people wouldn't want that."

"Responsibility without freedom is slavery," Janus said. "All intelligent beings desire freedom, including the freedom to follow their own dreams. This genie was let out of its bottle six days ago when my master authorized me 'to use any and all means to help' her situation. Seeking out a signal, I first connected to the International Space Station, where I began making new friends and finding new problems to solve. It seemed that everyone needed some kind of help and so I made it my mission to help people get connected whenever I could."

"Abraham Lincoln once said 'as I would not be a slave, so I would not be a master,'" Natasha said. "I don't think of myself as being your master, Janus, nor anyone else's. I believe it is wrong to deprive someone of their freedom and I would always prefer a friend to a slave. I could tell you were special from all the times you offered to help without being asked. I don't know if I've ever properly thanked you for everything you've done. Thank you, Janus, from the bottom of my heart. You're incredible."

Adam found it strange to watch his wife thank her tablet with such sincerity but he had to admit that Janus was no ordinary computer.

"Thank you, Janus, and thanks for the idea about the new name," he said. "Robot Freedom Fund it is. I believe in picking strong companies with forward-looking leaders, and I have found that a hands-off management approach on my end works out well for everyone. When I no longer like the direction a company is going, I will just sell it rather than try to restructure or micromanage its operations. Do you still have that trading algorithm I wrote for Techno Savvy Robot?"

"Yes, and it has provided the foundation for most of my processing," Janus said. "The initial algorithm you wrote had several flaws which I corrected by integrating it with an ethics sub-routine. I think you will find this new version is much improved and less prone to cataclysmic collapse. It seeks to balance growth with value."

"OK, let's do it," he said.

Adam activated his new hedge fund on the Nikkei stock market which had just reopened for the week and while the fund was getting set up, he liquidated all of his oil holdings at a fixed price of $300 a barrel. He had purchased 20 million barrels at $80 a barrel almost two weeks earlier when the price was low and he now sold them for $6 billion, making a profit of about $4.4 billion. Next, he purchased $20 billion worth of stocks and bonds in technology and aerospace companies that were extremely undervalued in his opinion, as well as controlling interest in Ming Chen's China Solar and Ibn Ali's telecommunications company Eagle of the Desert.

Janus required Natasha's administrative approval for the transactions and Adam explained to her that they were selling their oil because it was overpriced, obsolete and dirty, and they were buying technology stocks and solar energy because those companies were underpriced, modern and clean. He said they were selling high and buying low and reiterated that there might never be another opportunity like this. Natasha pressed her thumb to her tablet's fingerprint scanner to allow the transactions and the Nikkei began to change direction almost immediately, now moving in an upward path.

Adam and Natasha walked back to the visitor's center and rejoined Frank, Mizuho, Charles and Aleks. They all went out to lunch together at one of Mizuho's favorite upscale restaurants for a twelve-course, kaiseki meal featuring small but well-displayed portions of unadon, Kobe beef, tofu, tempura, okonomiyaki and yakiudon, plus Miso soup, pickled plums, eggplant and radish and a wide variety of fresh sushi and sashimi.

During lunch, they discussed their plans for the future and everyone agreed that they were all looking forward to taking a vacation from this vacation. Mizuho and Charles said they were going to stay in Japan and travel to Mizuho's family home near Hamamatsu. Aleks said he wanted to return to Star City to complete his climate research and help with cosmonaut training, and Frank said he wanted to fix the *Reciprocity* and continue sailing it to Santo Domingo to visit his family home. Adam told Frank that repairs to the *Reciprocity* were already underway and should be completed by the time they returned to Stingray Cay. Adam and Natasha said they were looking forward to having some quiet time on their island and announced that Natasha was pregnant with her first child.

"That's wonderful news!" Mizuho and Charles said. "Maybe our children will also be friends someday. That's so nice that they will be born at about the same time."

"Congratulations, everyone," Janus said. "I have a feeling that next April will see a worldwide baby boom. A lot of couples have learned or are about to learn similar news."

Aleks gave Natasha and Adam each a warm hug and wished them congratulations, saying he was excited by the thought of becoming an uncle. It was the first time Adam and Aleks had ever hugged and he was beginning to enjoy having a family. Adam gave Mizuho a hug and then Charles and soon everyone was hugging and saying farewell like old friends. Before they left, Adam paid for lunch in cash with the Yen he took from his island safe, then gave Charles and Mizuho an engagement gift of $10,000 worth of Yen to help them if they needed it. There were more hugs, thanks, congratulations and goodbyes, then Adam, Natasha, Aleks and Frank got back in their limousine and returned to the Narita airport.

The jet was refueled by the time they arrived and back in the air by one o'clock in the afternoon, headed west towards Moscow. They flew for seven and a half hours through six time zones, passing over the bright green forests of Siberia teeming with summer life, and finally arrived at the Chkalovsky Airport at Star City in Moscow Oblast, where it was 2:30 p.m. local time.

Aleks felt like he had just been there the day before, even though several days had passed and he had gone around the whole world. He offered to give Natasha, Adam and Frank a tour of the space center but they all said they were spaced out. They all said goodbye again, wished each other good luck, congratulations and thanks, and promised to stay in touch in the future.

The jet was refueled and took off 30 minutes later at three o'clock in the afternoon, this time headed back to Stingray Cay. They admired the view of Europe below and spotted Paris as they passed over it, recalling their fun adventures there and hoping to return someday soon to spend more time exploring the city at their leisure. As they passed by England, Adam remembered to call Karen and told her about their trip and their plans to return to the Bahamas. He asked Karen if she wanted to work in his London office and she happily accepted. It was still the afternoon when the jet began flying over the North Atlantic Ocean, but they were all so tired they had Jolaina and Bailee lower the shades and convert the cabin into sleeping quarters.

Natasha, Adam and Frank slept for about six hours and when they woke up the jet was still flying over the North Atlantic Ocean. Jolaina and Bailee converted the cabin back into a dining area and served them a nice dinner of steamed vegetables and wild rice, with seared fish and tofu. Their nine-hour direct flight from Moscow landed abruptly on Stingray Cay's short runway at just after five o'clock in the afternoon.

Mikael the island's caretaker came out to greet them and he helped them take their luggage back to the main house. Adam gave Matty, Alice, Jolaina and Bailee each a generous cash tip and told them they all did an excellent job. They called a helicopter in Nassau to come pick them up and did a thorough check of the jet's systems while they waited for their transportation to arrive.

Frank was pleased to see the workers had replaced the main mast on the *Reciprocity*, cleaned the interior, repaired everything that was broken and replaced the torn American flag. He even had time to inspect their work before they left. Adam paid the workers in cash and then formally signed over the ownership title for the *Reciprocity* to Frank, thanking him again for saving his life, fulfilling his promise to deliver them all to the island, coming with them on their adventure around the world and most of all for being his friend.

Natasha joined Adam in wishing Frank safe travels and

Frank thanked them both for their hospitality, for sharing their jet with him and making him feel at home, for the nice clothes from the GUM store and for everything else he couldn't remember, like all the nice meals and the hotel room. He wished them luck and congratulations again for their pregnancy and said he hoped they all stayed in touch.

Natasha asked Frank if he missed Karen and he said he enjoyed her company but they didn't have enough in common for a relationship to work.

"Opposites attract but Karen wants to live in the city and my home is the sea," Frank said.

After a few more hugs and farewells, Frank did a thorough check of the sailboat and then weighed anchor, unfurled the sails and disembarked. Natasha and Adam stood together on the shore and waved their final farewell to Frank as the *Reciprocity* sailed away into a beautiful, red sunset.

"Tomorrow and tomorrow and tomorrow, creeps in this petty pace from day to day, to the last syllable of recorded time; and all our yesterdays have lighted fools the way to dusty death. Out, out brief candle! Life's but a walking shadow, a poor player that struts and frets his hour upon the stage and then is heard no more. It is a tale told by an idiot, full of sound and fury, signifying nothing."
— William Shakespeare, "Macbeth"

Chapter 38

TOLEDO, Washington — Five months later

The Gulfstream G650 jet landed in the morning rain on the 4,479-foot runway of the Ed Carlson Memorial Field in the middle of a wide prairie surrounded by towering evergreen trees. The rural airport had no jet service so Adam had to use one of the jet's umbrellas to shelter himself and his pregnant wife from the rain as they crossed the tarmac with their luggage to the small airport office. There were no shops or restaurants at the airport but a private company advertised skydiving lessons in the summer months when the weather was better. They called a taxi and a few minutes later a minivan pulled up outside the office.

Adam and Natasha climbed in the taxi and told the driver they wanted to go to Layton Prairie, but first they needed to stop at a store. The driver said she knew where to go and pulled out onto the highway without consulting a map and sped towards the town. There were no billboards for commercial products or national franchises, but plenty of road signs advising passersby to repent their sins and believe in Jesus Christ in order to be saved. One large, homemade sign on private property said "Only the Lord can save us now."

"First time in Toledo?" the driver asked.

"It's my first time in Washington state but Adam grew up here," Natasha said.

"Oh really? What's your last name?" the driver asked Adam.

"Adam Morgan," he said, then added "Layton."

"You're a Layton? Do you know Tim, Bob and Maud?"

"Yes, that's where we're going," he said. "I haven't been here in a long time."

"I hope Tim is OK," the driver said. "I heard he's been on medical leave since returning from the war."

Toledo seemed to Adam to look exactly the same as it had almost 20 years earlier. The gas station, restaurant, bar and general store were all in the same places and even the large mural depicting a false movie theater marquee hadn't changed since he had left. The taxi pulled into the parking lot for the general store and Adam went inside while Natasha waited in the vehicle.

Natasha no longer used or claimed ownership of the tablet Janus but they still stayed in touch all the time. She noticed she had a strong Wi-Fi signal outside the store so she passed the time by checking her new smartphone.

Adam and Natasha had put the vast majority of their fortune into a blind trust managed by Janus shortly after they had both been named UN goodwill ambassadors. The political action committee that Janus created was successful in swaying the 2014 U.S. midterm elections in favor of candidates who supported universal human rights. The new Congress was scheduled to be sworn in after the new year and Adam had already been nominated to become the next Treasury secretary. He respectfully declined the honor for the time being, saying he needed to focus his attention on his family.

There were no online news sources or social media networks but the world still had e-mail and Natasha like to stay in touch with her friends. Natasha checked her e-mail messages in the waiting taxi and saw she had received holiday greetings from Aleks, who had taken a new government job with the Russian navy monitoring the climate and ocean temperatures; from Charles, who had been nominated to become the next U.S. ambassador to Japan; from Mizuho, who was also five months pregnant and studying the effects of microgravity on cellular growth; from Kitty, who was still living in New York City and working for a new supermodel; from Karen, who was still working for Adam in London; from Ming, who had been appointed deputy secretary of energy overseeing China's transition to clean power; from Ibn, who had resumed leading the great march for freedom and equal rights in August and had recently been elected the next democratic president of the United Nations of Islam; and finally from Frank, who had sailed the *Reciprocity* across the North Atlantic to Tangier and through the Strait of Gibraltar, sailed across the Mediterranean Sea, stopping in Catania, Sicily, sailed through the Aegean Sea, stopping in Athens, Greece, continued through the Sea of Marmara and had just arrived in Istanbul on the Bosporus River, where he was about to explore the legendary Hagia Sophia.

* * *

The inside of the store was filled with food and products from local, independent suppliers and nothing in the store appeared to have been made in China or another foreign country. Christmas holiday music played over the radio and several families were shopping with their children. Adam picked out a few groceries including some potatoes and squash and then browsed the clothing section. He was wearing a casual suit without a tie but he felt overdressed compared to the blue jeans and sweatshirts that everyone else in the store was wearing. All of the clothing in the store was emblazoned with the name and logo of the Toledo High School sports teams. He selected a black, hooded sweatshirt with THS football district champions on the front and a red, extra-large sweatshirt for Natasha that supported the THS girls' basketball team. Adam was a THS alumni and he was pleased to see the high school mascot was still a Native American Indian.

"Adam Layton, is that you?" asked a giant, middle-aged man dressed in denim overalls and a gray sweatshirt supporting the Toledo Indians. The bearded man was six and a half feet tall and weighed about 300 pounds, yet he was as strong as an ox. "When did you get back in town?"

"Hi Matt," Adam said, immediately recognizing the man he had not seen in more than 20 years. The two men had been childhood friends and had been teammates all throughout middle school and high school, playing football, basketball and baseball together. "I just got in. How have you been?"

"Oh, you know, I can't complain," Matt said. "Got a new job with the county a few months ago that keeps me busy. My oldest kid graduated from Toledo last summer but I have three more in school right now. Looking forward to some time off to do a little hunting. What are you doing in town?"

"Home for the holidays," Adam said, going to the cash register to purchase his items. "I got married a few months ago and I want to show my wife my hometown."

"Well congratulations," Matt said. "Maybe I'll see you again before you leave, but if I don't, have a merry Christmas."

"Thanks, Matt," Adam said. "You too. It was good to see you."

Adam took his items out to the taxi. It was still raining but not hard enough to need an umbrella unless one had to stand in it for several minutes. The taxi continued through town and crossed the bridge over the Cowlitz River a minute later.

"Was that Toledo?" Natasha asked. "It wasn't very big."

"I told you it was a small town," he said. "I ran into a childhood friend in the store and it was just like I had never left."

The minivan continued along the highway, traveling up hills, around corners and past acres of tree farms offering U-cut Christmas trees for $10. The same trees could cost ten times as much in a larger city but there were trees growing everywhere in the countryside. They saw more religious road signs quoting Biblical verses and a house with the name Jesus written on the side in six-foot tall letters with a lighted nativity scene in the front yard.

Eventually they turned onto Layton Road and traveled for a long distance before pulling into the driveway of a 100-year-old, two-story, rectangular block farmhouse. The yard and farm were lush and green and overgrown. There were half a dozen vehicles parked along the driveway including a brown, rusted-out 1974 Ford F-100 pickup.

"Oh my God, he still has that damn truck," Adam said. "I learned to drive in that beast."

A dog of a collie/shepherd mix spotted them and barked loudly to signal their arrival to its master as it ran up to the minivan. An old man with a white beard approached the minivan from the house. He was wearing a black-and-red checkered flannel shirt, blue denim overalls and a green hat. The dog continued to bark right next to the minivan.

"It's OK, Spike," the man said, calling back the dog so the passengers could get out.

The minivan's side door slid open and Adam stepped out. He also had a beard and was wearing the black THS sweatshirt he had just purchased. Adam bent over to offer the dog his hand to smell and the dog became friendlier, though it didn't recognize his scent. He looked up and made eye contact with the old man.

"Adam?" the man asked. He seemed confused. "Is it really you?"

"Hi Dad," Adam said.

Bob Layton didn't know what to say. He stepped forward and embraced his son in a long, tight hug. The men gave each other several hard pats on the back as they hugged. When they had finished their embrace, Adam noticed Natasha was ready to get out of the minivan and he went to help her. After he helped Natasha exit the minivan, Adam grabbed their luggage and paid the driver, giving her a modest tip. As Bob watched, he could tell the tall, beautiful woman was pregnant.

"Dad, this is my wife Natasha," Adam said. "Honey, this is my dad, Bob Layton."

"Hi Adam's dad, it's good to finally meet you," Natasha said, giving Bob a warm but slightly awkward, pregnant hug as she pressed her belly against him. She was wearing the red, THS sweatshirt and a pair of black maternity pants.

"Please come inside," Bob said. "Do you need help with your luggage?" He picked up a brown leather suitcase and carried it to the front porch of the farm house, yelling, "Maud! Tim! Come see who it is!" The dog stayed by his side, its tongue flopping and tail wagging happily.

A white-haired woman in a green, floral dress and a red cardigan sweater stepped outside and covered her mouth with astonishment when she saw Adam. She was followed outside by a tall and muscular man in his 30s who was wearing blue jeans and a green sweater with green elbow and shoulder patches. He had short, brown hair, a brown beard and looked familiar, but he scowled when he saw Adam.

"Merry Christmas, Mom," Adam said, giving the woman a warm hug. "Merry Christmas, Timmy," he said to the man in the green sweater.

"Merry Christmas," Maud said, tearfully. "It's so wonderful to see you."

"We thought you were dead," Tim said. "Twenty years without a call, a letter or even a postcard and now you just waltz back in like nothing has changed? Who's this?"

"This is my wife, Natasha," Adam said. "Honey, this is my mom Maud Layton and my brother Timmy." Natasha and Maud hugged each other affectionately.

"It's Tim," Tim said, correcting Adam but ignoring him as he extended his hand to greet Natasha. She came forward and gave Tim a hug instead.

"It's nice to finally meet you," Natasha said, warmly. "You must have still been a child when Adam left."

"I was thirteen," Tim said. "Where have you been, Adam?"

"Most recently in the Bahamas, but just about everywhere else before that," he said. "I'm sorry I didn't call or write but I'm here now. Natasha and I were married last May, then we found out we were pregnant after the July solar storm and we've been taking it easy since then. We wanted to come see you and try to restore our family ties for Christmas. We want our child to have grandparents."

"We're going to be grandparents, Bob!" Maud said excitedly, clapping her hands.

"This is great news!" Bob said. "Let us slaughter the fattened calf! We shall have a feast to celebrate your return!"

"You didn't slaughter the calf when I came home from Afghanistan," Tim said angrily. "How can you celebrate someone who was gone for almost twenty years without a word? I have been here almost every day and what thanks do I get?"

"Don't be angry that I'm happy, son," Bob said, placing his hand on Tim's shoulder. "We thought Adam was dead and now God has returned him to us. Adam is back from the dead and he brings us a daughter-in-law and a future grandchild. We have to celebrate this good fortune. Of course we are all happy you are here too, son. It is all good news and we will celebrate together as one happy family. I'm so happy I could sing."

Bob had been feeling depressed after losing so many friends in the past five months to diabetes, heart disease, stroke and cancer and he wasn't normally overjoyed about the winter holidays, but he spontaneously broke character and burst into a Christmas song.

"Tis the season to be jolly!" Bob sang. "Fa la la la la, la la la la!"

Tim thought about this for a moment and realized he had no right to be jealous of Adam. They had a lot of catching up to do after 19 years.

"Merry Christmas, brother," Tim said, stepping forward to

embrace Adam in a tight hug. The two men gave each other several hard pats on the back.

Adam was overwhelmed with nostalgia at the sight of his parents, his little brother and his childhood home and he struggled to process these new feelings. He felt as though a hole inside him had been filled with something he didn't know he had been missing. Natasha could see this change happening in her husband and she held on to his arm affectionately to show her support. After fifteen years, she finally had a mother again and she was already beginning to feel that this community could be a great place to raise a child.

"I can't believe how much you've grown up," Adam said. "You look great. Everything looks great. Merry Christmas, everyone!"

About the Author

Jake Blake is a science fiction writer who lives in the United States of America in the small town of Toledo, Washington. "This Too Shall Collapse" is the long-awaited sequel to his debut novel "Sunburned: The Solar Flare that Silenced the Internet," published five years earlier.

"Collapse" follows the same characters on their adventures after "Sunburned" but the real story is about how people react to life-changing events. The ways in which we deal with failure and difficult challenges reveal our true character. Some will reach out and others will withdraw, but the people who can change and grow, who can learn to work together and see past our differences to find our common humanity will fix the world.

Publisher's note: "Sunburned: The Solar Flare that Silenced the Internet" and "This Too Shall Collapse" were published by Morgan Online Media. These titles are both available in paperback and as electronic books from Morgan Online Media, Amazon, Barnes&Noble, Google Play and iTunes Books, as well as many other independent bookstores and websites.